The
Dutchman

The
Dutchman

MAAN MEYERS

Annette Meyers   Martin Meyers

A Perfect Crime Book
DOUBLEDAY
NEW YORK   LONDON   TORONTO   SYDNEY   AUCKLAND

A PERFECT CRIME BOOK
PUBLISHED BY DOUBLEDAY
a division of Bantam Doubleday Dell Publishing Group, Inc.
666 Fifth Avenue, New York, New York, 10103

DOUBLEDAY is a trademark of Doubleday,
a division of Bantam Doubleday Dell
Publishing Group, Inc.

Book design by Tasha Hall

Library of Congress Cataloging-in-Publication Data

Meyers, Maan.
The Dutchman / by Maan Meyers.
p. cm.
"A perfect crime book."
1. New York (State)—History—Colonial period, ca. 1600–1775—
Fiction. I. Title.
PS3563.E889D87   1992
813'.54—dc20   92-8728
CIP

ISBN 0-385-42603-8
Copyright © 1992 by Annette Brafman Meyers and Martin Meyers
All Rights Reserved
Printed in the United States of America
November 1992
First Edition

For Chris Tomasino

Grateful thanks to Bowne House in Flushing, N.Y., the Tea Council of the U.S.A., the Brooklyn Botanic Garden, the New York Public Library, the wonderful staff of the library of the New-York Historical Society, and to Kevin Jennings. And special thanks to Kate Miciak, who made it all possible.

PAVONIA ↑

NORTH RIVER

Christian
Cemetery

Windmill

The Fort

DeSille
Estate

The
Stone
Church

Market
Field

Gallows

Stuyvesant's
Office

Nutten
Island

TWILLER'S ROAD

The Ditch

PEARL ST.

Stuyvesant's
Great House

Jews
Alley

The
Wooden
Horse

The
Hill

City
Hall

PEARL S

Tonneman's
Home

Coenties
Slip

The
Pear Tree

Tonneman's
Willow Tree

EAST RIVER

North

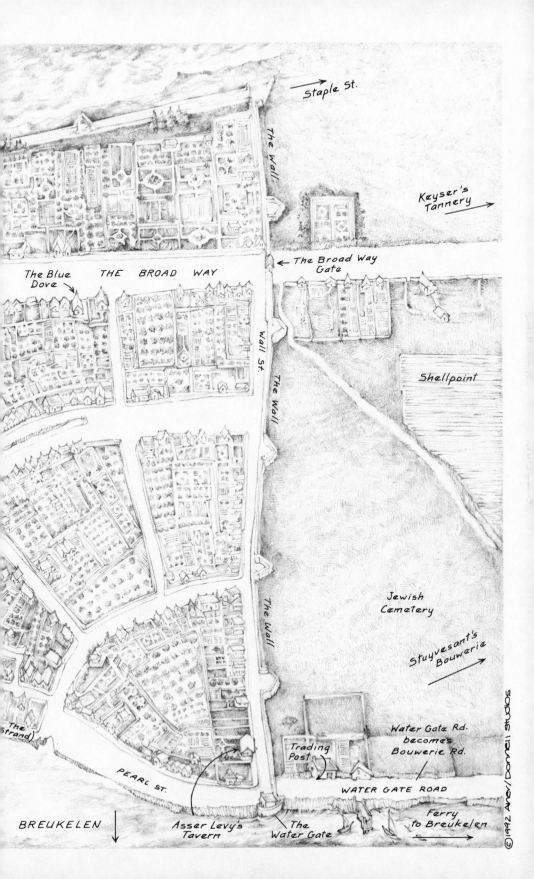

Staple St.

The Wall

Keyser's Tannery

← The Broad Way Gate

The Blue Dove   THE BROAD WAY

Wall St.

The Wall

Shellpoint

Jewish Cemetery

The Wall

Stuyvesant's Bouwerie

The (Strand)

Trading Post

Water Gate Rd. becomes Bouwerie Rd.

PEARL ST.

WATER GATE ROAD

BREUKELEN

Asser Levy's Tavern

The Water Gate

Ferry to Breukelen

©1992 Andy/Donnell Studios

The
Dutchman

BOOK I

The Dutch

Prologue

MONDAY, 30 DECEMBER. *Night.*
Smitt pulled the collar of his beaver coat closer about his neck to ward off the falling snow. The icy wind sweeping off the East River burned his eyes. There was only moonlight, and little enough of that, to go by, but he could find the way drunk, as he had before and was doing now. The cold crept up on him, stiffening his fingers. He'd lost his gloves. Silently, the yellow dog ran ahead, rolled in the snow, and ran back. The animal made a pass at the brace of rabbits Smitt had hanging over his shoulder.

He jerked the rabbits from the dog's reach and with numb fingers fumbling, pulled a flask of aqua vitae from his coat pocket. Behind him, the snow filled in his footprints, almost as if he'd never passed. After draining the flat bottle in one long swallow, Smitt held it down to the dog; the four-footer shoved his tongue into it. Smitt flung the flask away. The yellow dog chased after it.

About to call the hound back, Smitt stopped. There was a movement ahead of him in the moonlight, near the river. Two figures. They came together, separated, then clung to each other in a dance at water's edge. One broke free. The other pursued, clawing, capturing only his victim's long coat. Enraged, the hunter cast the coat aside.

A silver-gray seabird foraging on the icy river's edge screeched angrily, flapped its wings, and fled from the disturbance, settling on one of the snow-covered pilings a short distance away.

Smitt wiped the snow from his face. He thought of moving closer, but if he did he might be seen.

The bird took flight again in a fury of feathers. A wing tip caught the hat of one of the figures and gave it a mighty spin over the river, flipping it away somewhere into the blackness.

In the moonlight, smeared by the falling snow, Smitt saw a hand holding a stick rise, hold a moment, then fall. And rise. And fall.

A cry, so faint that only the striker, Smitt, the yellow hound, and the watching seabird heard, whispered across the frozen harbor. Then came the sound of something cumbersome being dragged onto the wooden timbers of the pier directly toward the place the seabird had chosen for sanctuary.

Indignantly strident, the bird swooped at the man again. Cursing the creature with a shake of his stick, the standing figure pushed the encumbrance to the pier's edge. He paused for a moment as if in thought, then kicked the object off. There came a quiet splash; he hefted the stick in his hand and threw it after the body into the frigid water.

The yellow dog barked and returned to Smitt, who seized the animal by the muzzle and dropped to the ground.

Startled by the sound, the standing figure looked about into the dark night, the icy white puffs of his breath mingling with the snowflakes in the moonlight. He knelt and peered into the water. Then he dusted off his hands, rubbed them together against the piercing cold, and picked something up from the ground.

The falling snow thickened and the figure abruptly disappeared into the darkness, relinquishing the winter night once more to the seabirds, the yellow dog and Hendrik Jansen Smitt.

WEDNESDAY, 16 JULY. *Morning.*
Early on this summer morning, when the dew was as wet as rain and the village was streaked with the waking sounds of its inhabitants, a dog began to howl. The howl continued unabated, the sound so pathetic and eerie that people began to stream sleep-dazed from their homes in search of the animal.

They found the yellow hound, its ears limp, its tail sagging, in front of the Pear Tree Tavern, beside the tree that gave the drinking place its name.

Hanging from a low branch, a loop of rope around his neck, was the animal's master and part owner of the tavern, Hendrik Jansen Smitt. On the ground beneath the corpse was an upturned log. The official verdict of the Town Council was suicide.

That winter Smitt had been charged with violating the Sunday laws by selling liquor. In April he was charged once more with the same crime. A month later he was called up again before the Council. This time for selling after hours, inciting boisterous singing and creating a disturbance.

He was fined twenty florins and reprimanded.

The City Schout, Tonneman, was drunk when Joost Zoelan, Smitt's partner in the Pear Tree, told him of Smitt's death that July morning. The Schout and Smitt had been close friends. After hearing the news, Tonneman ran from his house, which was next door to the

Pear Tree, and forced his way through the small crowd about the tree. "You witless dolt," he raged at the dead man.

Standing on the upturned log, Tonneman demanded that Smitt be drawn on the wooden horse as a fearful lesson to others. "Then he should be brought back to this cursed pear tree and crammed into the ground, without ceremony, and I personally will put a post here to mark his vile act of cowardice."

"That's a little harsh," Joost Zoelan said when he put Tonneman to bed to sleep it off. "Besides, it wouldn't be good for business."

Tonneman had lost his wife the past winter and was still grieving for her. Joost Zoelan knew Tonneman was taking Smitt's death hard, too.

The City officials and many of Smitt's friends took a more tolerant view of the suicide. It was decreed that the tavern keeper be given a decent burial in the City cemetery on the west side of the Broad Way, just north of the Fort.

Everybody assumed Smitt had killed himself over his troubles with the law.

I

Monday, 25 August–Tuesday, 26 August. *Night—Early Morning.*
It was well after the nine o'clock curfew, a hot, airless night. Only the top portion of the horizontally divided door to the Pear Tree was open. Tonneman kneed the lower part and the candles on the bar flickered from the breeze he made as he staggered in. The dim chamber was hazy with smoke forced down by the low ceiling, the air as damp within as without. The Schout crossed to the scarred, wax-spattered bar and rested his two-foot oak cudgel on it.

The yellow hound dog that had once belonged to Hendrik Smitt was stretched out asleep next to the sandbox between the barrels that supported the bar. The animal opened its eyes, accepted Tonneman, and closed them again.

Tonneman gave scant attention to the tanner, Jan Keyser, at one of the long wooden tables, passed out as usual, with his tongue hanging out. The Schout did, however, notice the Jew Mendoza, in his black silk cap, who stood talking to the Englishman Woods, at the far end of the bar. An unlikely couple to do business together, Tonneman thought fleetingly.

Joost Zoelan, the tall, sinewy man with reddish-blond hair behind the bar, rinsed a large glass in the bucket of stale water on the dirt floor and in silence poured Tonneman an ample measure of brandywine. In the eight months since he had been a widower, Tonneman had become a regular late-night customer.

The candlelight glinted on the blue facets of the brandy glass; against his will Tonneman thought of Maria's blue eyes. He shrugged and slouched on the bar. The wooden slab top groaned, and he pulled back; his sword, hanging in its scabbard from the plain brown baldric, flapped against his thigh.

"No!" Mendoza said, his voice harsh with choler.

Joost's lip curled in disdain. "Jews," the tavern owner said.

Tonneman wiped the sweat from his brow with his sleeve. "Christ, Joost, this heat is . . . hot," he finished lamely. He was a thick, powerful man of forty-two years with long arms and heavy shoulders. And he was weary, weary of so many things.

"Miserable night," Joost agreed. "But there are other places where the heat is worse." The tapster drew a beer from a keg on the bar.

Tonneman removed his black hat and set it next to his cudgel. "And when I get there, I'll save you a seat by the fire."

Joost raised his tankard. "To hell with you and to hell with me. And God bless absent friends." He quaffed his beer with one long swallow and belched.

"God bless absent friends," Tonneman said grudgingly. "Hendrik Smitt." Tonneman was still angry at his friend for killing himself. He drained his glass of the sharp-tasting burnt wine and shoved it at Joost for a refill.

In the far corner of the chamber sat a man with heavily pomaded, sleek black hair. He had canny eyes and was deceptively craven looking. This was Councillor Nicasius De Sille, another old friend of Tonneman's and the man Tonneman had replaced as Schout only four years earlier. De Sille licked his fingers and pinched the wick of the candle on his table, putting himself and his companions in darkness.

"What are you doing?" one asked too loudly.

"Damn it, Bridge, quiet," Nick De Sille said, rapping Bridge's arm.

"Don't call me Bridge," Bridge snapped in the impure Dutch of a foreigner. "My name is van Brugge."

The third man, Thomas Atkins, too overdressed in satin and lace for these parts, adjusted his octagonal spectacles but did not comment.

"Why the secrecy?" van Brugge demanded in a harsh whisper.

"Our friend here in his fancy duds sticks out like an Indian in church. It's better that Tonneman doesn't see us."

"What harm can that drunkard do . . . ?"

"Or hear us."

De Sille needn't have worried, for at this time of night Tonneman was past caring about anything except what was in his glass.

"How is the work of the fortifications going?" Joost poured Tonneman another brandywine.

"You have the nerve to ask? The drum beat loud and clear today at five. Since you did not appear to push your shovel with the others, you are hereby fined six florins."

Joost calmly laid out six guilders on the bar in front of Tonneman and jerked his chin up in a silent repeat of the question.

"Slowly," said Tonneman. "Even with all those slaves that arrived on the *Gideon* helping. Close to three hundred, but what with no rain the soil is like stone, hard to dig and hard to pack." He gestured with his glass. "You've heard the order, I suppose. Because of the grain shortage the brewers can't make malt for the next eight— well, one day's gone—seven days."

Joost grinned. "One old salt to another, I might be able to get some extra from the Johnnies. For a price. And if that doesn't work, I'll just have to learn to like that rotgut you drink."

Tonneman took a deep swallow of the burnt wine. He was not a happy man. He worked for the Company as Joost had once, and he chafed at the restrictions. He could not trade for himself; he could not take part in the riches the traders were making. He could not even farm without the Company taking pieces out of him.

"You did right to set yourself free," he told Joost. He clapped his friend's shoulder with a callused hand. "I'm yoked to the Company."

"It's a hard life. A man has to make choices." Joost topped off Tonneman's brandywine and refilled his own tankard.

Tonneman drank his brandy and nodded. He was feeling mellow now. He could sleep, but it was coming dawn. He tamped the tobacco in his long clay pipe with his forefinger and lit the pipe with one of the candles on the bar, spilling tallow in the bowl and on his hand. "Sweet Jesus," he said.

"Too hardheaded to use a taper?" Joost Zoelan laughed, gesturing to the small stack of dried and waxed, hollow-stemmed rush grass on the bar, placed there specifically for that purpose.

"I'm an old dog," Tonneman muttered through drawing breaths.

They turned at the thud. A lean man stumbled in out of the darkness. It was the Algonquin, Cutnose, so called because of the ugly gash he'd received during Governor William Kieft's raid against his people across the North River in Pavonia, back in February of '43. Almost every man, woman, and child in his tribe had been massacred by the Governor's men, and Cutnose had been left for dead.

The settlers saw Cutnose as a ferocious, savage, violent warrior; the Indians knew him as a pretend warrior.

He was nothing more than a drunk, and the scar made him seem fiercer than he was. He used it effectively to scare women and children and as a license to talk loudly in taverns and cadge drinks. Easily

as tall as Zoelan, he was half-naked, wearing only an old, dusty black
Dutch hat, grimy elkskin breeches, and tattered elkskin moccasins.
On his belt he carried a beaver-tooth knife and an Iroquois tomahawk, carved from a single two-foot piece of hardwood with a ball at
one end. A sharp piece of stone projected from the ball.

"Stand me a drink, Tonneman." Cutnose's mutilated face no
longer seemed strange to Tonneman as it had when he had first seen
the Algonquin twenty years earlier, the year Tonneman had brought
his young wife to this New World.

Now Cutnose and the men of his tribe, their heads plucked clean
of hair except for a high-standing center strip that went from forehead to nape of neck, mingled almost freely among the villagers.

The women complained, of course, but for the most part the
savages were peaceful, except if they had hard drink in their bellies.
The Company and the Boss had ruled that no beer or spirits was to be
sold to them, but it was a difficult law to enforce.

"I told you not to come in here, boy," Tonneman said to the
Indian. His voice was low and his tone even, though the burnt wine
had made his tongue thick.

"One drink and I go."

"*No* drink and you go."

The Algonquin's blackened teeth showed in a malicious sneer.
Already soused and unsteady on his feet, he grabbed for Tonneman's
throat.

The Schout backhanded Cutnose easily, knocking him to the
floor. Without opening its eyes, the hound sniffed the Indian's pun-
gent moccasins, inches from its nose, and shifted its head to rest in the
sandbox.

Tonneman said to Joost, "I thought I told you not to serve him
any more."

But Joost's eyes were on Cutnose. The tavern keeper reached
behind the bar for his bungstarter, useful for just such occasions.
When the Algonquin sprang to his feet, tomahawk in hand, Joost
cracked Cutnose over the head with the heavy length of wood, knocking him senseless. The hound dog grumbled in its sleep, annoyed at
the disturbance. Joost tapped Tonneman's cudgel on the bar with his
bungstarter. "This does you no good unless you use it."

Tonneman studied the body of the Indian briefly, then turned
back to Joost. He spat into the sandbox. Offended, the dog got up,
walked to the front door, and lay across the threshold. "Thank you,
my friend," Tonneman said formally, bowing slightly.

"I owed him that," said Joost. "Last time he was here the rascal
passed sham wampum to me."

"You nearly killed him. I'd hate to have to hang you, but that gallows at the Fort is just aching to be used."

"You wouldn't hang me for a frolicking Indian, Tonneman."

"Why not? Pity the poor gallows. A virgin all this time. It's waiting for you or someone like you."

Joost laughed. "Not me. I'm too pretty to hang."

"Yes, you are," Tonneman said, leaning across the bar to pinch Joost's cheek. Then he looked at his hand and shook his head mournfully. "Growing weak as a baby. Time was men stayed down when I hit them." He drained his brandy and put his pipe in his mouth. "Get rid of the heathen sot and don't serve him again."

Joost didn't respond. He would serve anyone with the coin to pay, and Tonneman knew it.

"I'm in dead earnest, Joost. I can keep you out of trouble only if you're careful." Tonneman relit his pipe. "When the Boss came back today, he acted as if I were responsible for all his problems. It's not my fault he got sick at Fort Orange. I didn't send for the English. But he acts as if it's all my fault. If he hears about any trouble in this place, I'll have to close you down." The Schout clapped his black hat on his head.

"The Boss has no time for small things, Tonneman." Joost's mouth twisted. "He's too worried about the English."

"Do as I say," Tonneman warned. He swept the six florins into his buckskin purse, tossed some stuivers on the bar, and picked up his cudgel.

"I understand," Joost replied hastily, coming around to the front of the bar. Tonneman's anger could be dangerous. Joost laid the tomahawk on the Indian's chest, grabbed the lock of hair growing from the middle strip on Cutnose's head, and towed the Algonquin past the dark table where three men sat, very still. He pulled open the back door and heaved the Indian's inert body out into the darkness, tossing his weapon after him.

"And keep the noise down," Tonneman called over his shoulder as he stepped none too steadily over the yellow dog and out the front door. "I'm trying to sleep."

2

TUESDAY, 26 AUGUST. *Night—Early Morning.*
Had he slept? Tonneman couldn't say for certain. Unable to sleep now, he put his feet on the floor and unwound his large frame slowly and carefully so as not to hit his head on the low ceiling. This thin corn shuck mattress was not as comfortable as the perfectly good goosedown bed he and his Maria had shared for so many years, but he wasn't able to sleep in it alone. He had given it to his daughter and her husband.

A pitcher and bowl stood on the chest of drawers near the bed. Tonneman took a long draught of water from the pitcher. The water was brackish and warm. He filled his pipe, tapping the coarse, rough-cut tobacco firmly.

He was sweating profusely. The river was only yards away, but the meager breeze from it did him no good. He ran his fingers through his short-cropped, sand-colored hair and put on his brown duffel breeches, securing them with a wide leather belt, automatically checking that his steel knife was in its sheath. The knife had a carved whalebone handle and was part of another time before his marriage, when he'd lived the life of a sailor.

Tonneman's feet were too swollen from the heat to squeeze into his leather boots, so he put on his clogs, took his pipe and Better lamp, and went outside. He would have preferred staying barefoot, but the shards of oyster shells that abounded on Pearl Street were too daunting. Oysters were plentiful everywhere on the shore, as were clams, just waiting to be picked up. The slight river breeze felt good on his naked chest.

The Pear Tree next door was passable quiet. A blessing.

Another blessing: the Rattle Watch weren't making their usual racket on the steps of City Hall next door, where Pearl Street and Coenties Alley met. Tonneman shook his head. They were a mindless lot; like drinking men the world over, they pissed when they had to. And they often had to when they were on the City Hall steps.

Some nights, between Joost and his customers and the Rattle Watch, Tonneman barely got any sleep at all.

The moonlight cast long shadows on the dark street, and the incessant buzz of the cicadas dominated the night. A dog barked and another responded.

Hot August days when even the children's shrill voices seemed hushed, melted into hot August nights leaving everyone with leaden limbs.

Tonneman's clogs crackled on the oyster-shell paving as he teetered. He felt the liquor in his veins numbing him, but he was awake.

"Two o'clock and all is well." The voice of one of the Rattle Watch drifted on the dead air from somewhere in the village as he made his rounds.

As of today the one hundred and fifty soldiers serving at Fort Amsterdam would be divided into three groups, one group guarding the Wall and the gates and patrolling the City along with the Rattle Watch at night. The second group would do the same during the day. The third would be in garrison at the Fort undergoing a strict training schedule in preparation for meeting the enemy. When they were sufficiently trained, Tonneman knew, they would change places with one of the other groups. The Boss was taking no chances with the English.

On Pearl Street three sailors, entwined one on the other as vines, hailed him boisterously in a flail of drunken arms and legs. Fifty soldiers, God save us, and where was one of them now? And where was the Watch, whose job it was to keep this trash off the streets at night?

Tonneman thrust his Better lamp at them. "You sotheads. You're lucky it's me and not a soldier. One of *them* sees you, he'll put a halberd up your arse. Get off the streets. You'll wake the town and put them all in a panic. You know my rules. Any more noise and I'll put you in irons and pitch you in the bay."

The sailors slobbered at him, making obscene salutes. "*No comprendo, no comprendo,*" one said through his slobber, even though he was obviously a Netherlander.

"Enough." Tonneman made a fist. "In case you don't know, I'm Tonneman, the Schout here. Get back to your ship, or it's jail for you, and your captain will have to pay a heavy fine to get you out. You wouldn't like my jail; it has bugs as big as rats. And their favorite food is sailors."

He laughed as his words took effect on the seamen, and they fled across town in the direction of the other waterfront on the North

River. They must have come from the Dutch merchant ship *St. Joseph,* which had just arrived with goods from the Fatherland.

"*No comprendo?*" he muttered. "Christ save us." He was wide-awake now. He walked through the shadows to the back of his house, remembering how he and Maria and their friends had labored over it, saw again Maria's fine yellow hair under the white cap, skin like alabaster, bent over the drawing she had based upon her childhood house back home in Beverwijk.

There would be an extra chamber, she'd told him, entirely separate from the children, so they could have times alone. She had won the extra chamber, but only their first child, Anna, had lived past infancy. Four other girls and one beautiful boy were buried in the cemetery on the Broad Way. And now their mother lay with them.

His grief was sullen and fierce. When he came around the back of his house, a sound stirred him. Her laughter, like a small tinkling bell, cut through him. He slumped against the side of the house to catch his breath. Listening. No more.

In the shed, Anna's bay and Johan's chestnut stood sleeping. Tonneman's horse, Venus, wide-awake, stared at him stoically. He patted the dun mare. Disinterested, she nuzzled the oat bag hanging on a nail. "I know, old girl. Hot." He forked her some salt hay from the loft overhead. "Now, can you tell me where my rod is?"

Receiving no answer, he went back outside and found his fishing rod where he'd left it earlier in the week, leaning against the back-door. He spent as little time as possible in the house; it was more Anna's and Johan Bikker's house now. In the morning, though, his daughter and son-in-law would be moving beyond the City to the farm in New Haarlem near Johan's people, and then Tonneman would be virtually alone.

As he stopped to light his pipe from his lamp he was hailed by Paulus Cuyter, one of the town's Rattlemen. Cuyter's bowed legs and bent stature gave him the appearance of one of those trolls the Swedish sailors were always talking about. "Any word about the English, Tonneman? Are they coming?"

"It appears they are."

"We're ready for them," the troll said, brandishing the halberd that all members of the Night Rattle carried as part of their office.

"God save us," Tonneman replied, thinking how swiftly the English would destroy them. Two or three ships with heavy guns would be enough. The Dutch fleet was busy elsewhere; it had no time for this little backwater. The men of the Rattle Watch and their rusty pikes would be of little or no help.

"God save us," Paulus Cuyter agreed, taking his leave. "And

God damn the English." He looked at the sandglass he carried, shook the last few grains down, turned it over, and shouted, "Half two and all is well!"

Securing his rod under his arm and his pipe in the waist of his breeches, Tonneman stepped off the road and plucked a pear from the tree in front of the tavern. He had made his peace with the tree after Smitt's death the previous month. A light showed inside the tavern and he could hear some noise, but Joost and his clients were behaving themselves. As long as Joost's after-hours custom didn't disturb anyone, namely Tonneman, and as long as the Boss didn't find out, Tonneman was content to leave Joost be.

He bit into the sweet fruit and spat the small pits out through his teeth as he crossed the Strand, as Pearl Street was often called, toward the water. Thankfully, the wall that was supposed to enclose the town had never been extended to this part of Pearl Street, so he had a clear path and a clear view and access to the East River.

Tonneman followed the slight grade down to the beginning of Coenties Alley, which led to Coenties Slip. Coenties was a diminutive of the first names of Tonneman's friends, the Ten Eycks, Conraet and Antje, who lived there along the water with their young son, nine-year-old Conraet.

He threw back his arm and spun the pear core out into the darkness. The unremitting slap of the East River against the pier and the rocks drowned out the sound of the core's contact with the water, but could not mute the steady groaning of ropes and creaking of wood from the two merchant ships at anchor in the harbor. Here and there a pale light glimmered on the vessels, a voice cried out in sleep.

Tonneman could see a shadow of the watch on the ship nearest him, the barque *Donna Isabella*. Soon the Strand would be busy with traders and merchants and the day would begin again.

He veered left, away from the harbor, to a place where the land came up and teased the bank, where he could sit on the grassy overhang and cast his line below.

A willow tree bent its graceful bough over the bank. Through the years he had claimed the tree as his. He now sat at the base, where, over time, his arse had flattened a spot for him. His thinking place, she had called it.

A frog croaked and crickets stirred. Tonneman could hear the lap, pause, lap, of the tide. A slight breeze came up from the river, ruffling the tall grasses, caressing him. There was a peace here he found nowhere else.

He dug up the earth until he found a night crawler, then loosening the string from the fishing rod, he attached the worm to the hook and cast the line into the moving water below. He was surprised by an immediate pull on the line, but when he hauled it up, it was empty and so was his hook. The fish had outsmarted him again.

He moved a stone the size of a human head from where it was crammed in the bank and withdrew the rawhide packet of rotted meat he kept there. Drawing his knife, he cut the meat, baited the hook with it, and plunged his knife into the earth. Now, he dropped the line back into the water and pulled on a second line nearby.

This line was not empty. Tied to it was a bottle of Rhenish. He drew his knife from the dry grassy ground and swiftly gouged out the cork, unmindful of the pieces that were pushed into the bottle. Tilting his head back, he drank a hefty draught of the light dry wine. He relit his pipe from the Better lamp and had another drink, contemplating the silvery moon hanging high amid the stars in the dark velvet sky.

His eyes grew heavy, his knife slipped from his hands and lay on the flattened grass beside him. He drained the bottle and put it aside. The frogs croaked peacefully.

Tonneman could never say what woke him, perhaps an odd sound, or perhaps the lack of sound. He awoke in a ghostly stillness, not knowing where he was.

Swinging from a limb above him, he saw the dark outline of a hanged man, swaying, swaying. Tonneman jumped to his feet and reached for the shadow, which broke up into so many willow leaves. He brushed his hands across his eyes and remembered.

As was usual they'd both been drunk. He and Smitt had stood on the water's edge, their backs to the East River, tilting toward it, away from the setting sun.

"There's something I have to tell you," Smitt said.

"So. Tell me."

Smitt upside-downed his bottle. It was empty. "I need a drink first."

"The Pear Tree calls us, then." Tonneman shifted his weight. "Stop with me at City Hall for—"

"Nay." Smitt shook his head, almost losing his balance. "Not the Pear Tree. The Wooden Horse."

"Nay," Tonneman said, with a drunkard's stubbornness. "I'm already walking this way."

He never saw Smitt alive again.

• • •

The moon had gone behind a cloud and the breeze had blown his lamp out. The very blackness suddenly seemed unearthly. Tonneman sat down heavily and leaned against the willow tree. He closed his eyes.

"You sold it to the Jew," a familiar voice whispered.

Smitt? Tonneman was overjoyed. Smitt wasn't dead. Tonneman started to rise, but a second voice spoke. "You're mad!"

"It's mine and I want it back." Sounds of scuffling, then: "Where'd you get this gold?"

"I'll share—"

"Tell me."

Tonneman couldn't hear the answer. Cautiously he crept toward the voices. He heard someone laugh, then the laugh became a cough. The brush crackled closer and closer and a man stumbled into Tonneman's view.

Tonneman reached instinctively for his knife. The sheath was empty. He raised his bare hands. There was no need. The intruder reached out to Tonneman, spun, and fell on his back.

The moon burst forth from behind the cloud, bathing the riverbank with sickly light.

Barely able to stand, Tonneman bent over the fallen man. Blood bubbled over the man's lips as he attempted to speak. Tonneman leaned closer and put his ear to the man's bloody mouth.

The man's mouth moved against his ear, but Tonneman heard nothing. "What? What?"

"Pape," the man said through more bubbles of blood.

Tonneman put up his hands and drew back as a large gout of blood escaped the man's mouth, followed by a rattle of dying breath. He would speak no more in this world.

3

Tuesday, 26 August. *Early Morning.*

"Holy Jesus," Tonneman whispered hoarsely. His hands were sticky with blood.

The one wound, a stab to the chest, must have punctured a lung. Whether the wound was from a sword or knife Tonneman couldn't tell. The dead man was small and slight, younger than he, dressed in the fancy blue, red, and gold satin clothes of a continental gentleman, white lace at his wrists and collar and ribbon bows at his knees and on his shoes. On the ground was a red velvet hat with a blue feather in it. A Spaniard perhaps. No. French, that was it. There was a cloying odor of lavender perfume. Only a Frenchy would have such a stink. Well, that was better than what he'd smell like after a few hours in this heat.

The man was wearing octagonal spectacles and the sword at his side, hanging from a richly ornamented gold baldric, was an elaborate rapier with ornamental scrollwork etched on the guard. Tonneman tugged at the weapon. The three-foot, double-edged, finely pointed blade came out easily from its scabbard, making a sound that was almost musical.

Why hadn't the dead man drawn it? Apparently because he believed his killer was a friend. At that moment the moon disappeared behind a cloud, leaving Tonneman in complete darkness. The killer might still be out there. Extending the dead man's sword, he squinted into the dark.

On his knees, Tonneman groped for the lamp with his free hand. The candle had burned out. His bloody hand found the wine bottle and he lifted it to his lips. Empty. An army of mosquitoes attacked his face and his naked arms and chest. He ignored them and listened.

A small sound, the snap of a twig, broke the silence.

The blow hit Tonneman across the back with tremendous force, knocking the wind out of him. He hunched over, gasping for breath, struggling to thrust the sword into the darkness, but it fell from his weakened grip.

Another blow across his back sent him flying into the river below.

He was going to die, of that he was sure. Good. Without Maria why not die?

He thought of Anna. She would miss him, but she had her own family now. The water was surprisingly cold.

His thoughts drifted, first to when he was young, at university with Dinck, then to when he was at sea, when life was truly free.

Maria. Coming with her to the New World. Building the house. How wonderful life was going to be.

Anna being born.

The others. Each being born. Each dying. So young. Just babies.

Memory after memory. Regret after regret.

He never should have gone to the Pear Tree tonight. Perhaps if he hadn't, he'd be home safe in bed and none of this would be happening to him.

But he had gone to the Pear Tree.

So, he thought, this was the way life ended. Tonneman comes to an ignominious end, the death of a drunkard who topples into the river and drowns. Not with a memory of Maria but with a memory of a silly to-do with a dirty Indian in a tavern.

The sheer surprise of the plunge into the chill water had rendered Tonneman's limbs useless, and he felt himself pulled by the mighty tide current of the East River. The terrible noise of the water pounded in his ears. Captive of the drag, he struggled, fighting the sodden weight of his breeches.

No. He would not die. Not now. Not this way.

He came up cursing loudly and got a mouthful of salt water for his trouble. But the cold water sharpened his wits. "No," he cried, feeling himself being sucked into a black vortex, swirling, sinking. As he fought to surface again a death's-head on a human body leered at him from the deepest recesses of the whirling water.

Tonneman flailed against the powerful current until his body crashed into an upright timber and curled around it; gasping, he held on. The timber was part of the pier at Coenties Slip. This time when he surfaced, he howled like a wolf into the night sky.

A ghostly misshapen form lumbered down the road, slowly, painstakingly, silently. Finally it stopped. And separated. The figure got off the horse, lifted the object that lay across the animal's withers, and carried it to the small outbuilding. A scratch of flint on steel and soon a fire was going.

Antje Ten Eyck, a plain blond woman, and fatter than she liked, was eight months pregnant and, as usual, had been unable to sleep because of the heat. The first loaves were already in the oven and she was busy kneading more bread dough when she heard the bellowing from the river. She hurried to shake her husband awake with floury hands.

"Only another drunken sailor," he grumbled sleepily. "Let me be, woman."

The sound came clearly even through the glass windows that, in spite of the heat, were secured against the poison of the night air. The flame on Antje's candle burned feebly. "And what if it's the English, husband?"

Conraet Ten Eyck came quickly awake, his sharp eyes cleared instantly of sleep. He was big and broad and as good-looking as Antje was plain. And he loved his wife very much.

"On the other hand, if it's the English, why would he be calling your name?" asked his wife, immensely pleased with her wit.

Ten Eyck dropped back on the bed, drew his blue nightcap over his eyes, and hid his ruddy face under the large feather pillow.

His wife persisted. "Are you a man, Ten Eyck?" He moaned and pulled the pillow tighter. "Do something before he wakes the boy." Ten Eyck heard the door open and, for the first time, the voice of a man, clearly calling his name. The door closed.

"Tonneman," Ten Eyck said suddenly, coming out from under the pillow. His wife was gone. Still in his nightshirt and cap, he pulled on his breeches and boots and ran the short distance to the jetty where Antje was leaning awkwardly over the planks, her black cotton skirt billowing in the breeze around her.

Two gulls cawed, participating in the clamor and activity. Lights appeared on the ships. Someone called out.

"Tonneman, you drunken booby," Antje said. "Maria, bless her soul, is weeping in heaven over you."

"Quiet, woman," her husband said, coming up behind her. "Help me here."

Together they hauled an exhausted and angry Tonneman to the platform. He lay there on his back like a giant fish, panting, half-drowned. Conraet Ten Eyck turned him over and pressed on his back. Tonneman coughed and spat up mouthful after mouthful of salt water.

"If I'm not a dead man, it's no thanks to him." Tonneman sat up, slapping rivulets of water from his sodden breeches. He was barefoot, having lost his clogs in the cursed river. "He wanted me dead."

"Who?" Ten Eyck asked. "What are you talking about?"

Antje Ten Eyck wiped her hands on her apron. "Come, enough. I'll have bread soon. And tea." She shuffled back to the small house, her back set in disapproval.

Tonneman shook the water from his hair and gaped after her. "What's wrong with the woman?"

"Tonneman, you drink too much and nearly get yourself drowned and you ask a question like that?"

"I was clubbed and thrown into the river. I'm not drunk. For all we know, he could have been an English soldier."

"Who?" Ten Eyck asked skeptically.

"The man who murdered the stranger." Tonneman rose to his

feet. He was almost recovered from his ordeal, but his back was growing stiff and painful.

Ten Eyck shook his head. "You make no sense. Come. You can have my old boots."

"A fancy fellow lies dead under *my* tree," Tonneman said. "Murdered right under my nose."

"I see no English, I hear no English. A brandywine dream, my friend."

"Nay. I saw him. His blood covered my hands."

"There's no blood on your hands, you clod."

"The water washed . . . someone clubbed me and knocked me into the river."

"Come," said Ten Eyck, turning away.

When they trudged into her scullery, Antje held a candle to Tonneman's sturdy back. Across it was a huge double bruise, already turning color.

"Well?" Tonneman felt belligerent.

"What can I say?" asked Ten Eyck. "It's a bad bruise. You've had worse in your life, and you'll have worse again. It's the lot of a drinking man. If you drink, you fall; if you fall, you bruise."

Tonneman snorted his disgust.

Antje shook her head sadly and went back to scrubbing off the pine-topped oak table that she'd used for bread making and would also serve breakfast on. Her husband started toward their sleeping chamber. "Will you eat with us? I have ham and some pigeon eggs."

"No time," said Tonneman, going past Ten Eyck into the sleeping chamber.

Ten Eyck paused. "I'm going to see the murdered man that Tonneman found." Then a twinkle appeared in his eye. "Come with us."

"Ha!" Antje bustled about. "You both intend to drink yourselves into a stupor and you expect me to go along." She put her kettle on the fire. "Go. Go find your dead body. If there is one."

"Boots?" Tonneman asked.

Ten Eyck gave him a worn but serviceable pair, then dressed quickly, all the time shaking his head.

Young Conraet was in the great chamber when they came out, rubbing his eyes, yawning and drinking buttermilk. "You woke me up," he said. He was a sturdy boy of nine years whose features were pleasing though they most resembled his mother.

"I owe you a day of fishing," Tonneman said, tousling the boy's bright yellow hair.

"Tell me when," the boy called after him.

"Antje's a hard creature," Tonneman said as they made their way to the bank where Tonneman's willow tree stood, its drooping branches billowing over the ground like an Indian's wigwam.

To Tonneman's eyes, the moon-glazed river looked almost peaceful, perhaps pleased with itself for having made a fool of him.

"Where's your dead man?" Ten Eyck demanded, holding his lantern high.

"Here." Tonneman swept away the hanging silver-leafed willow branches.

The dead man was gone.

4

TUESDAY, 26 AUGUST. *Before Dawn.*

In a wood close on Jews Alley, Nick De Sille stood with the man known both as Charles Bridge and Carel van Brugge. Except for moonlight and the flicker of a small fire in the vicinity of Mill Street, the night was dark.

Dry grass rustled, a twig snapped, their partner appeared.

Van Brugge scratched his head nervously. "You have the letter?"

"No, but I know where it is." The partner produced a flask of brandywine from his coat pocket, took a quick drink without offering any, then brought his smoldering pipe out from another pocket.

"They'll see," van Brugge objected nervously.

"Let them." The partner puffed at the long pipe. Smoke floated up from the white clay bowl in the moonlight.

"Atkins?" De Sille asked.

A swallow of brandy and one word. "Done."

"Next," said De Sille, "we deal with the Jew."

"I don't think more killing is necessary," van Brugge objected.

"I do," said their partner, "and that's the end of it."

"Agreed," said De Sille, patting his lustrous black hair.

Their partner took a long thoughtful pull on his pipe. The night air was strong with the smell of lavender.

. . .

"So where's your dead man?" Ten Eyck demanded again, this time with a snort and then a chuckle. He raised the lantern higher and swung it grandly back and forth in an exaggerated motion, lighting the area. The glow picked out Tonneman's empty wine bottle. Ten Eyck pointed to the bottle and howled. "Dead body, Mary Magdalene's whorish ass!"

"I don't believe it . . . there was a body here . . . a man, in foppish clothes, wearing spectacles . . . and a fancy sword. . . ." Tonneman's halting explanation and Ten Eyck's laughter were interrupted by a high-pitched shout that seemed to come from the village, but surrounded as they were by water one could never trust the direction of sounds.

Tonneman and Ten Eyck, both now fully alert, pushed aside the leaf-and-branch curtains of the hanging willow tree and moved quickly along to Pearl Street as the shouting continued and grew louder.

No illumination came from the Pear Tree, but candlelight darted this way and that in windows around City Hall, to the accompaniment of an uneven chorus of gabble from men, women, children, and animals.

"Hallo," Tonneman shouted as he and Ten Eyck rounded City Hall. "What's going on?"

"Who's that?" The voice with the candle was that of Carl Visscher, one of the Rattle Watch.

"Jesus save us," said Ten Eyck, his lantern wavering. "It's the English. They're here. Maybe you were right after all, Tonneman."

"No." Tonneman looked beyond the foot of the island, lit by the full moon, to the bay, where the waters of the East and the North Rivers merged on their way to and from the sea. "I was right about that body. But the English don't seem to be out there. Not yet."

Visscher's high-pitched voice was even higher now. "Fire! Alert!"

Answering cries arose as people forced themselves awake. Fire! One small blaze could destroy everything.

As Tonneman crested the small hill with Ten Eyck at his heels he saw the glare of light coming from the west portion of the village, near Mill Street.

Visscher leveled his flickering candle at Tonneman. "Come, quick, Schout. Fire in Jews Alley. We need a ladder and more buckets."

"God's blessed name," shouted Tonneman. "I can see it."

The three threw the doors to City Hall open and rapidly gathered the needed equipment. On the run Tonneman yelled, "Ahoy, in the tavern! Come and help put out this fire. Joost, you drunkard, come out and do some work!"

Ten Eyck and Visscher added their voices, but no answer came from the tavern.

"Fire!" Carl Visscher squeaked again. "Alert!"

Tonneman gestured to the others to go. Visscher, struggling with his candle and five buckets, took the lead. Tonneman and Ten Eyck followed close behind, balancing the lantern, a ladder and two hooks, and eight buckets more.

They quick-timed the short distance over the Broad Canal bridge to Jew's Alley in a few minutes. The Broad Canal was a ten-foot-wide inlet from the East River. Commonly called the Ditch, it went more than halfway to the Wall. Jews Alley, a section of Mill Street, was just below it.

Women's voices shrilled, children ran back and forth along the footbridges spanning the Ditch. "Aelbert," one woman called, over and over. "Aelbert."

Amidst the fearful panic that the blaze would spread to all their homes, there was a macabre festive feeling. A child squealed, "Mama, I want to carry water." A line of neighbors, Christians and Jews alike, had already formed at the Ditch, and buckets were being filled and passed along the line to Jews Alley.

The crackling flames spewed and rolled, casting the world in an eerie light. Every physical feature was peculiarly enhanced by the fire glow: noses enlarged, jowls swelled, eyes bulged. Under the other voices, "Aelbert. Aelbert," could still be heard.

"Louisa, where are you?" a boy called.

Directing the work at the Ditch was the leader of the Rattle Watch, Captain Lodowyck Pos, a short, broad-chested man who was as strong as an ox and whose pleasing face was adorned by a fine jet-black beard. All ten men of the Watch, including those not on duty, worked alongside soldiers and hastily wakened citizens. Once they'd scooped water from the Ditch, they passed it along to the Fire Wardens and Chief Warden, Claes van Der Werff, who stood ready at the blazing building where Abraham Mendoza and his son and daughter-in-law lived.

"Please, please," an anxious woman called, "bring water over here or the fire will spread to our home."

The village lived in constant fear of fire. With reed-and-clapboard roofs and wooden chimneys, everything could go up at any time like a tinderbox. Every householder paid a tax for the numbered leather buckets, each marked with the City seal of a wreath encircling a beaver, and the ladders and hooks that were placed at stations about the town to face such an emergency. So why had Visscher been forced to go to the Hall for more gear? Tonneman was sure some rascal had stolen the leather buckets from their assigned places.

"If those embers blow over here, they'll start a new fire."

"Aelbert. Aelbert."

Tonneman knew the Jews used the Mendoza house as a place for worship. As he watched the diminishing blaze he wondered if they'd been performing one of their secret rites, some pagan fire ceremony. Had that caused the fire?

"Where's my mama. I want my mama."

An errant ember struck Tonneman's bare shoulder. He brushed away the mild pain and he thought of Beverwijk. Maria and he should have stayed in Holland. They'd have a fine brick house by now with all their children. Life would be a lot simpler and safer with a brick house. There were some in New Amsterdam, but his was not one of them. In New England the smart Johnnies were building with stone.

Chief van Der Werff, a big shaggy man with a wide forehead and a mighty voice, shouted orders as the line of water carriers wavered. "Carry on," he bellowed.

"Carry on," Captain Pos echoed. "Don't stop now." Pos watched Visscher and Ten Eyck handing off the equipment they'd brought to the Fire Wardens. When they hurried to the bucket line, his eyes shifted to take in Tonneman. He came and stood beside the Schout.

"Report," Tonneman said, surveying the area.

Before Poz could do so, an excited grizzled giant of a man rushed up to him. The old man cloaked himself in pure goodness and rectitude; whether it was deemed the truth or not depended on the beholder: Johannes Megapolensis, minister of the Collegiate Reformed Protestant Dutch Church in New Amsterdam, St. Nicholas Church, the Stone Church in the Fort. "I only just heard," he boomed. "Whose house is burning?"

"The Jew Mendoza."

"Well, they're God's creatures, too," Megapolensis said, even though he had been staunchly opposed to the Jews' permanent settlement since their arrival ten years before, when he'd referred to them as "godless rascals." "Is anyone hurt? What can I do to help?"

"Everything is under control. You can go back to your bed now."

"We missed you at church Sunday, Captain. There were special prayers asking the Lord to grant us a sufficiency of rain."

"Not now, preacher."

The minister took a breath. "I'd like to help."

Pos nodded wearily.

"Then get on a line and help pass the buckets," said Chief van Der Werff as he ran past.

"Thank you, thank you." The predicant, rushing to serve, bumped into Tonneman. "Good morning, Heer Schout." He looked toward heaven, asked God's blessing, and joined the line.

Pos shook his head, then turned back to Tonneman. "The fire started in the shed behind the house, then it jumped to the fence and into Mendoza's house. Luckily, the wind's died down."

"Everybody out?"

"So I've been told."

"Where's the Boss?" Tonneman frowned. From the outward damage, Mendoza would have to rebuild entirely.

"Not here yet," said the Rattle Watch captain.

"He will be."

"Don't I know it."

"Tonneman," a deep voice boomed.

"Speak of the devil," said Pos, not without a small smile on his blackened face.

"Sir?" Tonneman responded.

The man with the silver-ornamented oak leg stomped toward them. He was very robust for all his fifty-four years, and losing his right leg twenty years earlier in a battle against the Spanish had never stopped him, let alone slowed him down.

The young African torchbearer, Ditmar, followed quickly, keeping his master always in light, which flickered across a falcon beak of a nose.

His brown hair was shoulder length, but under his black hat the dome was bald. He was a foul-tempered Calvinist moralist of sour disposition and vile nature. With a choleric scowl, he now considered Tonneman's bare chest. "I don't deem it seemly for a man of your high office to go around not fully attired."

"Yes, sir."

"If that fire spreads to my house, I'll see you tied to the wooden horse and leave you there till winter comes and goes. Understood?"

"Yes, sir."

"There's no danger of that," Pos said hastily. "The Great House is safe. Van Der Werff says it's far enough away."

"Indeed, Captain." The man pivoted on his oak leg. "I can see my house from here, just the other side of Stone Street. Can *you* see it?"

Pos looked at the two-story building with the whitewashed stone front and its two small staircases up to the door. "Yes, sir."

"Tonneman?"

Dutifully the Schout looked, too. The Director-General's house always seemed to him as if it had been plucked from the old country and transported to New Amsterdam as if by magic. "Yes, sir."

"If we can see it, the wind can certainly find it. And if one spark from this wretched Jew's house is carried on that wind to my house, Pos, and singes one timber, you and the Chief Warden will join Schout Tonneman on that wooden horse. Understood?"

Pos turned his eyes straight ahead. "Yes, sir. Understood."

"Your doing?" De Sille whispered, crouching with his partner behind a stand of chestnut trees just west of the busy fire site.

"Yes," said his partner. "Everything according to plan."

Nick De Sille smiled. "And if our plan prospers, we can live here like kings and forget Patria."

His partner nodded.

"Nice touch," said De Sille. "The fire, I mean."

Van Der Werff and his men seemed to have contained the blaze. Others were getting water from the well behind the house, which was accessible now that the flames had lessened.

The noise of falling timber and the loud lowing of a cow made it difficult to continue talking. A Jewish woman coming from near the fire site was singing softly to the suffering creature, its udders distended, coaxing it to move. They waited until she had the four-footer past them.

Tonneman felt the slight ripple of a breeze across the hairs on his chest. His gaze was drawn back to the fire.

The harsh voice continued. "Is it truly under control?"

"Yes, sir," Pos said.

"Good." The rough tone softened, but only moderately. "I would hate for those wretched souls in the Poor House on Beaver Street to be burned out. . . ." His voice grew harsh again. "But it wouldn't distress me at all if the Jews and their house of Beelzebub burned clear to the ground. God curse them, if the soulless English are out there waiting to attack, this blaze would certainly give them a clear target."

"Captain." Chief Fire Warden Claes van Der Werff was running toward them. "The wind from the river is picking up and spreading the flames."

Tonneman watched the Mendoza house for a moment. The building was burning actively anew. He felt a surge of hunger in his belly. When had he eaten last?

The babble of the people on the water line grew louder as they echoed the Chief Warden's fears. "It's going to spread, it's going to spread." Some ran to their own homes with slopping buckets. "My house. Don't let it spread to my house."

"The Mendozas are still inside," a woman wailed.

"We thought everyone was out," van Der Werff sputtered. At once Tonneman and Captain Pos ran toward the building. The man with the silver-banded oak leg glowered.

5

TUESDAY, 26 AUGUST. *Dawn.*
Caleb's sharp bark woke Racqel Mendoza from a sound sleep. She was gasping for air and soaked with perspiration. She could hear voices outside the house . . . but it was still night. What was wrong? Was it the English?

Coughing violently, she swung her feet to the floor and felt in the darkness for the tinderbox. At last she found it. She scraped flint on steel, tinder burned with a weak blue flame, the fatty wick of the candle sizzled and then lit.

Bathsheba, her collar bell tinkling, jumped on Racqel's lap and clawed her arm. The cat's pale yellow eyes glowed in the flickering light, but beyond the bed it was darker than dark. Racqel couldn't breathe.

The roaring sound was like the dreadful storm at sea she'd known as a child. Through the roar she could hear yelling.

"Racqel! Fire! Fire! Help!"

The candle went out. Racqel scooped Bathsheba up and ran to her door. Her throat was raw as if the fire were inside her. Gasping and coughing, she kicked at the door with her bare feet. It wouldn't move.

Suddenly there was a thunderous clap and she was driven backward by a burning wind, but she didn't fall. To fall would be to die, she thought.

Beyond the black-gray mist she could sense rather than see that the door was no longer there. The staircase was obliterated by smoke. Her eyes stung and she clasped the writhing cat to her as she plunged down the narrow staircase through the smoke.

"Racqel!" It was her father-in-law. But where was he? His voice seemed to come from outside the house. "Daughter!" There it was again. Now it seemed to come from behind her. She could hear the snapping of flames; her throat tightened. Just a short way to go, she knew, to the door.

Another blast of hot air knocked her to the floor as she reached the open door. She struggled to rise. If she stayed there, she would surely die. Scorching heat blistered her arms, her bare feet. The frightened cat clung to her shoulders, stabbing her skin with its claws. And then Bathsheba tore from her grasp with a fearful shriek. Racqel put her hands to her face in prayer. God save me, she thought. I am dead.

Arms lifted her, carrying her into the night. She began to breathe again with rough scraping gulps. The voices of the villagers, first a great mumble, began to come to her clearly. Farther down on Mill Street she could hear John Woods's frightened horses neighing in panic.

Caleb's bark had awakened her, she remembered. "Father Abraham, David, Caleb, Bathsheba."

"What? Are there others inside?"

"Only the two men and the woman," someone said. "The old man is her father-in-law, Abraham Mendoza, the other is his son David. They are accounted for. She must be talking scripture."

Racqel forced her eyes open. The air, already heavy with heat from the hot spell, was now crushing with the added heat from the fire. Her eyes burned and teared. "Father. Brother," she croaked, finding no clear voice.

"They're alive."

"And Caleb? Bathsheba?"

"Were there others?"

The flare of candles and torches made it even more difficult for her to see. "My dog. My cat."

A hearty laugh burst from the man who held her. A Dutchman's laugh, for they always seemed to be amused by life. It was then she recognized the Schout, Tonneman. She turned her head to him. His chest was bare, a broad expanse of skin and muscle, covered with crinkly white-blond hair, which smelled faintly like a singed chicken.

Tonneman laughed again and set her on her feet. "The pitiable mongrel sits with old Mendoza. As for the cat, the crazed creature raced out of the house when I came through the door. She'll return when she knows there's nothing to harm her. Mark my word."

Racqel became aware, then, of the shouting, the activity, men running back and forth with buckets dousing the fire. The lightening sky was filled with flying cinders and smoke.

"Thank you for saving me," she said to the big Dutchman, who stood with his thumbs in the waist of his breeches, observing the fire scene.

"An honor and a pleasure," Tonneman said.

The words seemed mocking, but when she looked up at him closely, all she saw was a broad, kind smile.

"You have burned us to the ground and now you stand uncovered for all the world to see." The whiny, accusing voice belonged to David Mendoza, Racqel's brother-in-law. "For decency's sake, cover up." He cast a blanket over her, covering her head.

Racqel threw it from her face and draped it around her like a shawl. The blanket was hot and stank of smoke. Depend on David to be ridiculous and worry about her modesty and reputation at a time such as this. Would he rather she perish than appear in her night-dress?

"You are the husband?" Tonneman asked.

"He is my brother-in-law. I have no husband anymore," Racqel said, unable to keep the bitterness from her voice.

She felt Tonneman's eyes on her and regretted her rancor. "We Jews do not air our dirty linen to the gentiles," her father-in-law had said, after Benjamin left her.

"Racqel, the blanket," David prodded.

"Leave her be, son," Tonneman said mildly. "She came near being roasted alive."

Racqel raised her eyes and saw the Schout studying her brother-in-law with more attention than he deserved. She tried to imagine what he was thinking by staring at David with such intensity. And then, by the early light of dawn on the East River, she saw that David was fully dressed, his clothing clean and not disheveled. He had not been to bed this night.

6

Tuesday, 26 August. *Dawn.*

A great cry of pain rose over the area. Racqel turned her gaze from her brother-in-law. She recognized the voice of Abraham Mendoza. He was lying prone some small distance from her, haphazardly dressed, but wearing his prayer shawl and silk cap, beating his fists on the ground, in anguish and grief. "The Torah," he cried. "The Torah."

Without hesitation David Mendoza darted back into the smoldering building, past Chief van Der Werff and his wardens, who were poking at the structure with their hooks in an effort to bring down any beams that were still smoking or glowing to end the danger of the conflagration spreading. "Wait! No," a woman on the bucket line shrieked, and then other voices rose, joining hers.

"Stop," Captain Pos cried, chasing after David. "Stop, you fool."

"You stop, Captain," Tonneman ordered, catching Pos by the arm. "No sense you both getting killed."

Pos halted and, nodding at the wisdom of Tonneman's words, called and motioned to the bucket line, "Keep the water coming, neighbors."

Then, after only a short time, David Mendoza reappeared, his dark beard and hair and black silk cap singed and smoking. In his blackened hands, high above his head, he carried the Ark. The ornately carved wooden box was still smoldering. Racqel could see bits of red and yellow sparks in the wood. Overcome with joy, Abraham struggled to his feet. "Blessed be the name of the Lord," he shouted.

"Amen," said David.

"Amen," said others.

Gently as he could, considering the circumstances, David set the Ark on the ground. He slapped at the sparks, heedless of being burned. Abraham did the same.

Curious, Tonneman and Pos watched as other Jews crowded around the box.

Abraham opened the box.

"It's the Ark that contains our covenant with God," Racqel murmured. She stood at Tonneman's elbow, outside the circle.

Praying volubly, Abraham lifted the three scrolls in their now scorched blue velvet mantles and kissed the mantles fervently. He examined each scroll with care, running his hands along the poles to which the parchment was attached and over the small silver crowns adorning them. "God is good to us," Abraham said, rubbing at the soot on one crown till the rampant lion perched on it was clean and shiny.

The Jewish families shouted hallelujah and clapped David Mendoza on the back, and a young man sprinkled water on his head and beard.

Racqel understood her father-in-law's fervor. Torah was the holiest thing in their life. If these scrolls had been damaged by the fire, they would have been buried with all the sanctity of a funeral. Over generations, the Mendozas had carried the sacred scrolls in their carved box into exile from Spain to Portugal to Holland and thence to New Amsterdam. Abraham had often said that without the Torah, without the word of God, Jews were nothing.

"I'm sorry, Father," David said, his short stocky body sagging in defeat. "I had to leave the Sabbath lamps."

Abraham sighed deeply, then caressed his son's face, wiping the soot from his beard. That they were father and son was obvious from the same swarthy skin, the same high-bridged noses, dark eyes and squat solid bodies. "We will survive. You did what was most important. You consecrated God. You saved the Torah." He kissed the holy scrolls and nodded with bowed head. "Thank God."

"Amen," said David.

"Crazy people, these Jews," Captain Pos whispered to Tonneman. "I wager that when they finally accept Jesus, they'll be better Christians than most Christians."

"They are a devout people," Tonneman said, watching the Mendoza woman. He liked the way her chin came to a delicately defiant point over the blanket she held about her. Had she been recently widowed the same as he? Tonneman remembered the bitter sound of her voice when she said her husband was gone. It was a bitterness Tonneman could understand.

A dirty, singed black cat appeared from nowhere and rubbed itself against Racqel's blanket, making its little bell ring. Racqel looked down, and her face, for all its grime, glowed. "Bathsheba." She knelt to the cat and stroked it lovingly, pressing her face into the beast's unkempt fur.

Tonneman watched, enthralled. The thick black braid of her

hair, though marked by the flames, had a life to it that made him want to touch it. He curled his fingers into his palms.

Racqel looked up, meeting Tonneman's eyes for an instant. What a nice man, she thought. So gentle for a man, so kind. Such a pity he's a Christian. Her body felt burned and bruised. She was sure she had blisters. No matter, she would heal. They were alive, and the Torah was saved. And what was burned could be rebuilt. Then she heard the unmistakable, booming voice of the Director-General.

"The wind has risen, Chief van Der Werff. Take care for the safety of my house."

Everyone turned in his direction, including the people on the bucket line.

"Hear me, Israelites," Pieter Stuyvesant shouted. "If my house or my family suffers any harm because of this fire caused by your blasphemous religion, it will be on your heads. By all that's holy, heaven will curse the damn Jews." He spat on the ground.

"Shame," someone cried. "For shame."

"Curse the English," someone else cried. "They are our enemies."

Racqel's face became a mask. The Jews clustered closer, as if defensively. It was happening again. Racqel stood up, holding the cat in her arms.

"Tonneman." Stuyvesant spoke in contained fury.

"Yes, sir."

"Tomorrow morning. At the Fort."

"Yes, sir."

"Pos, van Der Werff, and the minister, too."

"Yes, sir."

Suddenly a gust of hot wind blew from the north, sending a flurry of sparks into the air and toward his house. "Look, damn you! Burn in hell, you godless vermin," Stuyvesant ranted. "You Antichrists." He shook his fist at the Jews and strode away in his swaying gait toward his Great House.

7

Tuesday, 26 August. *Dawn.*
The wind reversed itself and whipped in from the East River, scattering red-hot cinders in a treacherous whirlwind over the area. The leather buckets were filled faster.

The low rumble of thunder came like the lazy growl of a dog, slowly rolling across the dove-gray sky. Ten Eyck and Joost, who'd been working the bucket line, heard the warning and looked up just as jagged white lightning flashed; in a moment the heavens opened up and rain, first in sharp, probing droplets, then heavy and swollen, then great sheets, sweeping and swooping, drenched everyone, everything; the fire and the danger were over.

"Praise God," said Minister Johannes Megapolensis.

"Praise God," said Abraham Mendoza, a hundred feet away.

From people around, Christian and Jew alike, came a hearty amen.

"A little late," said Pos caustically.

Tonneman smiled. Pos was a witty fellow.

Delighted with the rain for finishing off the fire, they felt cheered now that they could return to their homes and begin their day with only the English to worry about.

Tonneman tilted his head back and let the sweet-smelling rain wash the grime of the fire from his face.

Pos inspected the fire site with Chief van Der Werff and returned to pronounce the fire out.

In the rain, the men, women, and children of New Amsterdam began to straggle homeward. Chief Warden van Der Werff called after them. "The buckets must be returned to their designated places. No buckets go home with anyone." The weary people paid no attention. It was chore enough to deal with Mill Street, which was a swamp of ashes and mud.

"Thank you. Thank you for your help." The elder Mendoza, oblivious of the rain, went from man to man. His grizzled beard was wet and matted, and his face drawn, but his eyes burned like hot coals, giving him the appearance of a madman.

The rain blurred Tonneman's sight, but it tasted fresh and sweet on his lips and was cooling on his bare skin. The Mendoza woman. Where was she? Through the torrent he searched for her among the remaining townspeople. Not seeing her, he felt a curious pang of disappointment. Suddenly his heart lightened. There she was behind Abraham.

"Do you have a place to sleep for the night?" Tonneman asked the old man.

"Yes, thank you for asking, Schout." He called out, "David, cover the Torah well. We must keep a good vigil tonight."

"What about food?" Tonneman asked, knowing the question was unnecessary, but wanting to stay perhaps to talk again to the dark-haired woman.

Abraham offered a grim smile. "Again, thank you for asking. We will take no food or drink. We have been witness to a desecration of the Torah and must fast in penitence. In the morning we will take the Torah to Asser Levy's house at the Wall and hold services there." The old Jew bowed to Tonneman and backed away. The dark-haired woman went with him. She did not look at Tonneman.

Tonneman suddenly longed to be home. To sleep, perhaps. He began to walk. When he saw Ten Eyck and Joost, wet and dirty, on the road ahead, he fell in step with them. Pos caught up, his face grimy with soot and streaked with rain. "A beer, my friends." Pos clapped Tonneman on his bare back. "The Pear Tree? I'm sure Joost would open for us."

"I could be persuaded," said Joost, eyeing Tonneman.

The rain swept across Pearl Street with a crackling sound, making hardly a mark on the dry shell surface.

"Not me," said Ten Eyck. "Silversmithing doesn't take care of itself. And I've got an angry wife waiting."

"Horse piss," said the captain. Water poured over the brim of his big hat in a stream, adding more wet to wet clothing. "That woman's never been angry a day in her life. You're a lucky man. Tonneman?"

"Home for me. My daughter and her husband leave for New Haarlem this morning. They'll farm near his family."

"And what about the English?"

"What about them? They can't worry about the English. I know I don't. When the English come, we'll deal with them. Till then life goes on."

"So you'll be alone?"

Tonneman shrugged. "Maybe I'll sell the house and live in City Hall."

In spite of the rain Joost stopped in his tracks. "You're not serious."

"Too many memories," Tonneman said, not stopping. "I have to start a new life."

Joost shook his body like a dog and resumed walking.

"Marry again," said Pos, his face a mass of streaks between flesh and soot. "That's the answer. There are young girls here, eager to marry. Some with rich fathers." As the rain continued, their path along Pearl Street turned slippery.

"Young girls?" Tonneman exclaimed as they came upon a litter of leather water buckets near the Ditch, where people had left them. "What would I say to a young girl?"

"It's not what you say, man, it's what you *do*." Pos's laugh was a high whinny. Two seabirds, hearing Pos's peculiar sound, answered him and flew in sweeping arcs along their route.

Now Tonneman laughed, again raising his face to the rain.

"A man is a man," Pos continued. "Of course, if a young innocent girl doesn't tempt you, there are always the widows. Rich widows. Van Tienhoven's old woman, for instance. She's got that big house near you on the pier."

Tonneman frowned. The fat and sharp-tongued Widow Van Tienhoven held no appeal for him.

The rain slacked off into a fine drizzle. The air hung damp and humid, smelling of the sea beyond the bay, but it didn't wipe away the biting stink of smoke that clung to their clothing and filled their nostrils. Reddish light streaked the sky, and the breeze from the East River was cool.

And then, magically, the sun appeared and somewhere a rooster crowed and a dog barked. Another rooster answered as he, too, welcomed the new day.

"The sun," Ten Eyck exclaimed needlessly.

Tonneman thought of the dark-haired Jewess again. "Yes," he said with a half smile. They were standing in front of his house. "There are always the widows."

8

Later, when the rain had stopped, Racqel stood with her brother-in-law, staring at the wet ruin of their home as the dog Caleb dug furiously in the rain-softened earth. Racqel and David had suffered slight burns, she on her feet and he on his hands and face. From her father's teachings Racqel knew what to do. She prepared a decoction of chickweed to bathe the burns and draw the pain and an unguent made from the elder shrub to further soothe and heal them.

They had refreshed and cleaned themselves and were wearing borrowed clothes from Jewish friends who lived nearby. Their Christian neighbors had offered the same, generously, for unlike the Director-General, most bore no malice toward the children of Israel. In fact, the Dutch thought of themselves as the new children of Israel, and that they, too, were chosen.

"The fire must have started in the shed," Racqel said, pulling at her ill-fitting borrowed skirts. She pointed to the fireplace area, which was still intact. The open hearth that was right up against the wall showed no sign of being the source of the blaze that had destroyed their house; the heavy cast-iron fireback was undamaged. "See, my cooking place is untouched." The sight relieved her of the guilt she had felt but not of her anger. David's accusation that she had been careless with the fire had wounded her deeply. She took pride in the care she displayed running her home.

Bathsheba had found a pine cone somewhere and was friskily pushing it under Racqel's feet. Racqel smiled at the cat's antics, glad for the momentary distraction.

The Mendozas leased their late dwelling from Asser Levy. It was one and a half stories high in the front and one story in the back, all timber frame and clapboard, the backdoor leading to a garden. The shed beyond was separate from the main building.

The second floor had been a garret where David and Benjamin had slept on straw pallets. After Racqel and Benjamin married, Benjamin had divided the garret into two enclosures and built a bedstead into the side wall.

Below, running the thirty-foot length of the house, was the great chamber, with Abraham's wooden bedstead set into a corner space.

The large fireplace served for cooking and heat, and Racqel's ironware pots and pans were stored in a small nearby pantry.

She sighed. The cow was lost. Wandered off. And all the chickens were gone. Burned to death or scattered. They would need a new cow and more chickens. She shook her head. They would have to rebuild. And Asser Levy and Abraham would have a long talk about who would pay and how much. The entire great chamber, though least touched by the fire, smelled too much of smoke to ever be sweet again. Even herbs wouldn't help. She sighed again and continued her walk through the scorched remains of what had been her home for these last six years. God had brought the rainstorm just in time.

Although the transom windows in the front had burst from the heat, most of the damage seemed to be in the back of the house. She came out and said as much to David, who did not appear to feel either sadness or affection for their former home.

She didn't have to raise the skirts of Rebecca Da Costa's dress as she stepped over the sill; the dress was too big for her but also too short, Rebecca being heavier by more than a stone and smaller by a hand. Because of this, the hem of the borrowed dress revealed more ankle than normal.

"You're becoming more Dutch than the Dutch, sister," David snapped, pointing angrily at her ankles.

"What would you have me do, run naked?" Her response was tart, and regretting it instantly, she fell silent.

David shook his head and clucked his tongue. "My brother allowed you too much independence."

"He had no choice. I may be his wife, but I am my father's daughter."

"Your father is dead. And so is my brother."

"We don't know that about Benjamin."

"One day we will. And on that day you will marry me. It's the law."

"I will never marry you, David Mendoza. And as long as there is no proof of Benjamin's death, I am not free to marry anyone." She said the last triumphantly as she stalked back into the ruined house, although she didn't feel at all triumphant.

She thought of life as it used to be, when she was young.

Jewish teaching required that a Jew could not live in a town that had no physician. Since there was none among the Jews in New Amsterdam, the tiny community had sent a request to the Netherlands. Racqel's father, Moses Pereira, accepted, and he and his pregnant wife and their daughter, Racqel, set out for the New World.

Abraham Mendoza, a trader and a lifelong friend of Moses Pereira, decided that New Amsterdam would be the place where he could make his fortune, thus he and his two sons Benjamin and David made the voyage with them.

This was in 1655, a year after the original twenty-three men, women, and children had come to New Amsterdam, not by their own choosing.

Nine months before that, the Dutch surrendered Brazil to Portuguese soldiers led by General Francisco Berreto. Berreto had assured the more than six hundred Jews in Brazil that there would be no repetition of the Inquisition. He said they could stay if they pledged allegiance to Portugal, or they could leave, and in that instance they would be given three months' grace.

Disregarding the huge losses that resulted because of quick, lower-than-market-value sales of property, many of the Dutch who had settled in Brazil, Jew and Christian alike, chose to return to the Netherlands.

General Berreto provided transport: sixteen Dutch and Portuguese ships. Fifteen arrived safely in Holland. One ship, the one the Twenty-three were on, was blown off course. They were still in the South Atlantic when they were captured by Spanish pirates who intended to sell them as slaves. They were rescued by the small, five-gun French frigate *St. Charles,* commanded by Jacques de la Motthe, a privateer who knew a good business deal when he saw it.

De la Motthe promptly contracted to take the Dutch to New Amsterdam, where he was bound anyway. It was not known what he charged the Christians; the twenty-three Jews were charged twenty-five hundred florins. Since they had only nine hundred and thirty-three florins in cash, the captain made them all responsible for the debt.

In the first week of September 1654, directly after landing in New Amsterdam, de la Motthe sued for the balance of fifteen hundred and sixty-seven florins. The Jews had no money and the captain and the City officials were in no mood to give them time to get it from friends and relatives in Amsterdam. Whatever property they had was held as security, and they were given four days to raise the money or their goods were to be auctioned off, starting with those of Abraham Israel and Judicq de Mereda, who had the most.

Four days later the auction was held and every scrap was sold, and at the end the Twenty-three still owed four hundred and ninety-five florins to the French captain. De la Motthe went to court again and asked that David Israel and Moses Ambroisius be held under civil arrest for the balance.

Meanwhile, the Director-General for the Dutch West India Company settlement in New Amsterdam, Pieter Stuyvesant, was working to deport the twenty-three members of "the deceitful race."

The Twenty-three prevailed with help from friends in Holland, some of whom were stockholders in the West India Company, which owned the town of New Amsterdam. These friends sought help from the important Amsterdam Chamber, whose members more or less ran the powerful West India Company.

The Chamber told the Director-General that it had granted the Jews permission to journey to and trade in New Netherland and to live there, provided the poor among them should not become a burden to the Company or the community. The Chamber said it had no other choice considering the considerable loss sustained by the Jews when the Portuguese took Brazil and also because of the large amount of money the Jews had invested in the West India Company.

The Twenty-three lived in rented quarters, for despite their important friends they were not allowed to own property. It was only in recent years that that ban had been lifted.

More Jews came early in 1655, among them Racqel and her family and Benjamin and his. Racqel's mother lost the child she was carrying when the birth came, too soon, during a furious ocean storm; mother and child died and were buried at sea.

After Racqel's father died of mortification of the bowels in 1658, the community sent to the Netherlands for another physician and once more requested a rabbi. The physician, Luis da Silva, arrived on the next ship. But again no rabbi. And until this day there was no rabbi in New Amsterdam. Racqel, having studied carefully her father's methods of healing, had always hoped in her secret heart that she could be the new physician. But the world in which she lived did not offer this possibility.

Brushing aside the memories and disappointments she turned once again to the gutted house. She heard David stamping around in the back near the shed. Carefully, she looked about the chamber, taking a mental inventory of what was salvageable.

Her wedding contract, the *Ketubah,* that had been presented to Racqel at her marriage, had miraculously survived the blaze. It was in a beautiful carved wooden frame of intricate design, including a raised carving of a rampant lion at the top. The frame, once highlighted in brilliant red and blue, was now blackened and scorched. "Lion of Judah," Racqel said softly, fingering the carved animal. She eased the frame from the wall, where it left a clean mark, and hugged it to her.

The trunk of majolica china her mother used for Passover and had hoped to use in New Amsterdam was grimy but whole.

The rear of the house and the garret where her bed had been were totally destroyed, which meant she was bereft of personal mementos of two prior lives—her childhood and her six years as the wife of Benjamin Mendoza, less the almost eight months since his strange and abrupt disappearance.

They had argued viciously. She still heard the echoes of their angry words. Yet, in spite of his anger, her husband couldn't have just left her. How could she think that? He had a life here. Family.

There had been another argument earlier that day. Not between her and Benjamin but between Benjamin and David. Although she hadn't heard the words, the anger in their voices had been frightening. But they were brothers, and brothers have argued since Cain and Abel. A cold chill touched her heart. Where were her thoughts leading her?

There was always the hope that Benjamin had gone to meet the trappers to bring back beaver pelts from up the North River and had been captured by Indians.

If he was not dead, he would have returned. She knew that. Benjamin Mendoza was a complicated man, but he loved her. All at once, here in the hot sun, Racqel felt chilled by the shocking realization that she did not love him, that she had never loved him.

It had been her father's dying wish that Racqel marry his friend Abraham Mendoza's first son, and she had done so. She had quickly assumed the duties of wife of the eldest son and housekeeper, for there was no woman in the Mendoza house, Sara Mendoza having perished from consumption in Amsterdam long before the voyage to the New World.

The sun streaming through the open struts of the house found something on the floor. Racqel touched the hard object with her foot, then bent and retrieved Sara Mendoza's silver candlesticks, where they lay covered by seared pieces of wood from Racqel's trunk, which must have fallen through the ceiling when the floor in her chamber burned.

She shuddered. She could have been burned to the same wretched condition. She ran her fingertips over the bruised candlesticks. They would be almost as before with polishing and some straightening.

A ship from the Netherlands had arrived the day before with the cloth and china that Abraham Mendoza received in trade for beaver pelts. She would have new clothing made and they would rebuild the house. . . .

David brushed by her carrying a canvas bag and began filling it with refuse. "Why do you stand there? Pack up what is worth saving and bring it outside."

She took two of the majolica plates, her marriage contract, and the silver candlesticks outside to the women who were waiting for her.

The neighbor women had buckets of water. Esther Diaz took the objects from Racqel's hands, murmuring words of reassurance.

Racqel smiled at her gratefully and went back toward the house. David appeared holding a nine-branched lamp, grimy and dented but intact. He was in better humor. She told him about the china.

He shook his head. "You call that good news. Miracle of miracles, I found my phylacteries, some prayer books, and the Hanukkah lamp. That's good news. Women! No sense of what's important."

"Where is Father?" she asked, seeking to change the subject.

"Watching over the Ark at Da Costa's house and praying. He is fasting today, as will I. You are not wont to heed my suggestions, but since it has to do with Torah . . ."

"I will fast, too."

"We're going to take the Ark to Asser Levy. Two Africans will deliver building timber. I hired them this morning. If all is clean and ready, we will begin rebuilding this afternoon."

Racqel held up the ravaged handle of a broom and laughed. "Nothing left here."

"Go see if the rake is in the shed," David ordered, taking the broom handle from her and throwing it at the blackened skeleton of the staircase.

"There will be nothing intact. The fire started . . ." She peered out at the shed through a gaping hole in the rear wall of the house.

"Go and see."

She went outside. The women at the table had made progress. Racqel's dishes, drying in the morning sun on the linen tablecloth, shone like new.

Caleb preceded her, barking joyfully. David followed, carrying a full bag of refuse. Mariana Da Costa stood at her mother's side, dipping dishes into a bucket. Racqel saw Mariana smile and blush, and noted with a start that the child had turned into a woman. And the woman, all of fifteen, had her eyes on David. Pleased, Racqel hummed to herself as she made her way to the back of the property. Ashes and soot were thick over the ground, which gave gently under her feet in their borrowed buskins.

The shed was a blackened hulk, but still standing. The door fell away when she touched it, a mass of soft, airy charcoal. A peculiar smell hung over the area. Caleb put his nose in and then backed out, whimpering. "Caleb, what's wrong?" Racqel peered through the tangle of dark burnt wood, alerted by the dog, sensing something herself, afraid to go further. A burnt object, standing straight, pierced the rubble.

"Stop mooning like a child," David cried behind her, irritated. "There's work to be done. Why do you stand there?"

He pushed past Racqel into the shed. Staring, he reached for the object sticking out of a burnt mound. It was a knife. A foul stink filled the air around them. David shuddered and screamed as if in pain. He had pulled the blade partway out. Abruptly, he released his hold. "Blessed art Thou, the true Judge," he cried as he backed away and stumbled from what was once their shed.

"Amen," Racqel responded spontaneously, then asked, "What is it? Is it still hot?" She edged forward.

"No!" David shouted. "The dead are unclean. Merely being in the same place with that body makes us unclean." He tugged at her, dragging her back. "He was killed with that knife."

"Who? Let me see."

"No."

"Are you sure he's dead?"

David glared at her.

"Shouldn't we . . . ? Don't we have a responsibility . . . ?"

"Don't try to teach me the law," David snapped. "Ours or the gentiles'. If I pray over the man as if he were a Jew and he is really a Christian, that wouldn't be fitting."

"You cannot abandon him without so much as a word."

He nodded abruptly and mumbled to the dead body, "Dust you are and to dust you shall return." To Racqel he said, "It is not enough, but it will do no harm."

Racqel's head spun. The dead man might be more than a Jew. He might be her husband. "Benjamin," she cried. "It's Benjamin."

"It can't be." David stared at her in horror. Still, he moved toward the body even while it was obvious that his instincts were telling him to keep away.

"Look. You must look."

There was one sure way to determine if the man were Jewish or not, but David could not bring himself to touch the unclean lump. "I cannot. All my being demands that I keep away." With an urgent swing of his arm, he waved Racqel off. "Blessed art Thou, God," he said firmly, moving away.

She entered the shed.

The sight so transfixed Racqel that she didn't hear David's footfall or feel his hand grip her arm.

On the ground lay the burnt body of a man, his face undone to the skull.

9

Tuesday, 26 August. *Morning.*

Tonneman patted his daughter's solemn face. "Don't worry. I'm a grown man. I know how to care for myself." He laughed at her concern and helped her into the cart.

Carrying broad and low, Anna had lost some of her spring. Her pregnancy was more tiring than she liked to admit. "Yes, Father." She sat, blinking rapidly to keep tears from falling.

Johan Bikker finished tying up the provisions, cloth, china, pots and pans, and the brightly painted blue-and-yellow floral kas that had belonged to Maria. He, too, looked solemn.

The horses were restless, eager to go. Anna's bay was fine by himself, but he was having difficulty working with Johan's chestnut mare.

Tonneman clapped Johan on the shoulder. He was a strong, steady young man of good Friesland stock, sturdy as the cattle they raised there. "Take good care of my daughter," Tonneman said. "And my grandson."

"She might be a girl, Father," Anna said, laughing. Good. That's the way she should always be. Laughing.

The men shook hands. "I'll take care of them," Johan promised.

"And yourself," Tonneman added.

"Katrina Root will come every day to clean and make your evening meal," Anna said.

"You told me."

"She'll do your wash, too. Four stuivers a day."

"I know."

"You'll come to see us."

"In the autumn, I promise."

"And if the English come?"

"They will come, be sure of that. Don't worry, we're a crusty lot, but we're not fools. We'll negotiate with them, and if the Boss keeps his wits about him, we'll be fine."

Johan's eyes met Tonneman's. They both knew the Director-General was a hothead. The New Haarlem settlers, mostly farmers, had little use for the Great Muscovy Duke, as they called the Director-General. Or for the West India Company, although New Haarlem, like New Amsterdam, was a Company town.

"What will be, will be," Anna said. "God's will."

Tonneman watched the heavy-laden wagon trundle off up Pearl Street and go through the Water Gate. Truth to tell, he was relieved to see them leave. If there was going to be fighting with the English, it would be in New Amsterdam first.

The Schout shrugged and took a deep breath. The air was still smoky from the Mendoza fire. He went into his house. It was so still, he felt the loneliness like a weight on his shoulders. If Maria had lived . . . He pushed aside the bread, cheese, and buttermilk Anna had left for him and poured the remnants from the pitcher of beer. It was flat but savory. He drank, thinking back through his adventures during the night. He was certain the dead man in his fine clothes had not been a dream made of brandy and wine. After the meeting with Stuyvesant at the Fort, he would go back to the willow and search the site for some proof of the killing.

In his chamber he found more of his daughter's handiwork. She had left the pitcher with fresh water. He filled the bowl, removed his garments, and washed the smoke and soot from his body.

He changed into clean, fresh clothes and saddled Venus. It wasn't that far to the Fort, but he liked to let the dun mare out every day if he could. Not relishing the meeting, which he knew would be tedious and suspected would bring more bad news, he mounted the mare and slowly rode along Pearl Street, past Twiller's pier and several warehouses.

At Stuyvesant's Great House, which stood white-faced in the morning sun, Tonneman turned toward the Broad Way, slowed to a walk, and cast his eyes to Mill Street, hoping to see the Mendoza widow across the short distance. Her dark eyes had quickened his blood and made him feel vital for the first time since Maria had died.

There were women moving back and forth in front of the burnt-out house. One of them could have been she. Ride over and say good morning, you fool, he told himself. Almost angrily, he kicked Venus with both heels. The mare jerked forward. He stroked her crest. "Sorry, old girl."

The road ahead of him was empty except for some of van

Etting's hogs, sullen pink beasts that refused to stay in their yard where they belonged. It was all right when they went after bugs or field mice, but they weren't satisfied with that. Like the other wandering hogs that plagued the town, they were always getting into other people's garbage and making a stinking mess. He'd have to talk to van Etting about keeping his animals penned up. Not that it would do any good.

Tomorrow, in spite of the English, the Market Field would be crowded with farmers from Breukelen, Amersfoort, Staten Island, Esopus, Rensselaerswyck, and Jonkheer's Land. New Haarlem, too, of course. And with Indians and sailors, all anxious to buy and trade. Maria used to love Market Field days.

"Heads up, Tonneman," two patrolling soldiers, their blue uniforms streaked with dust, cried as a team of grays towing a wagon with a load of wood went rushing by him.

"What?" Tonneman wheeled his horse and raced after the wagon. Two Africans, free ones by his memory, were in the wagon. The one driving reined in the two old gray nags, which were panting and puffing noisily, spraying wet steam through their nostrils. "Damnation. What do you think you're doing?"

"Carting wood, Heer Schout," the driver said.

"You know the law. Nobody rides wagons except on the Broad Way, and even there, slowly. Everywhere else in town you walk and lead your horses. Is that understood?"

"Yes, Heer Schout," said the driver.

"Yes, Heer Schout," the other echoed.

The wagon was so laden with newly cut logs its wheels had dug up patches of the dry earth of Twiller's Road. There was no sign here of the flooding storm of the night before.

"You're lucky I'm in a hurry, else I'd take you in and fine you. And look how you're treating those two old dobbins. Water them right away and then walk, do you hear me, *walk*, and lead them to where you're going. Understood?"

"What about the horses' hats?" called one of the soldiers.

"Yes," the other one yelled. "Isn't that the law? Don't the horses have to wear hats to keep the sun from their sweet, pretty little faces?"

The two black men looked puzzled and concerned.

"Never mind them." Tonneman gestured the Africans off. "Be gone."

The pair got out of the wagon and led the horses away. Tonneman shook his head and resumed his journey.

As he drew abreast of the soldiers again one said, "Can't ride with your eyes closed, Tonneman," and he and his partner laughed boisterously.

With good nature Tonneman smiled and waved.

Fort Amsterdam lay straight ahead. A rectangle with a triangular bastion at each corner, the garrison was faced with stone. Inside, it was largely unfinished. Flying over the Director-General's building were two flags of various stripes and colors.

The flag of the Netherlands was red, white, and blue horizontal stripes; the top stripe of the West India Company's flag was orange instead of red and, in the white middle, contained the Company's monogram.

A third flag, cleaner than the others by virtue of the minister's zeal, flew from the church steeple: a plain orange field, and on it, emerging from heavenly clouds, a sword-wielding arm, sheathed in mail. Like the Director-General, Predicant Megapolensis took the view that this was the vengeful arm of God eager to destroy the unholy enemies of the Dutch.

The Fort was never expected to hold off an attack by a professional army. Its ramparts were only eight to ten feet high and three to four feet thick. It was moderately fortified with twenty-four cannons, one cannon for the point of each triangle, and the rest placed at equal intervals along the walls. The powder magazine held less than two thousand pounds of powder. Undefended by an outer ditch or palisade, Fort Amsterdam was hardly an imposing statement to invaders.

It was ringed by private homes, higher than the walls in many places. Cellars, which could be invaded and used to gain entrance, ran from these structures to within five yards of the Fort.

In front of the Fort was the gallows. Tonneman always thought of it as a joke, nothing more than a symbol of punishment. The citizens of New Amsterdam were a mischievous lot and liked their drink and their quarrels, but real crime was rare and murder was even rarer. Until now.

10

Past the gallows outside the Fort, a ten-man squad stood in square formation, halberds at the ready, the ax blade of each honed and shiny in the morning sun. A drummer boy beat out a tattoo, and a sergeant looked on as a corporal put the men through their paces.

Other soldiers lolled against the Fort wall in small clusters, some smoking, talking. Off in a corner Tonneman could see several kneeling while one shielded what they were doing from the sergeant. Tonneman grinned. He was sure they were playing double stones. What a fighting force.

He rode through the open gates unchallenged and dismounted in front of the Director-General's building, tethering Venus at the rail next to other horses. Damn, there were pigs running loose in here, too. And dogs. He heard a sound and got a whiff. Goats, too. "Noah's frolicking ark," he said. As if in response to his thoughts, two cows scrambled through a gaping hole in the Fort wall. "Heaven help us."

Fort Amsterdam was like a small village. Over the animal tumult was the usual hum of human activity. A knife sharpener's grinding wheel cut through the barnyard din, accompanied by the blacksmith's constant clang.

Fully one quarter of the Fort's space was dominated by the huge Stone Church in the northwestern corner. Above the massive door, carved into the stone, was the true name of the church, St. Nicholas. To the left of the door was a leaded window, with a sailing vessel enclosed in a circle at head height. The leaded window to the right, which was commissioned in the Fatherland and much prized by the congregation, depicted the banishing of Adam and Eve from the Garden of Eden.

The first thing ships coming into New Amsterdam's harbor saw, high above the Fort walls, were the church's shingled steeple, the orange flag, and representing the Apostle Peter's denial of Christ thrice before the cock crew, the copper weathercock. A magnificent sight.

The only problem was that the church had been placed so that it blocked the Company gristmill, just beyond the northeastern corner of the Fort, from its needed wind.

Over at Ernestus Beels's shop there were freshly bloodied clothes draped about the constantly whitewashed pole that stood in front. The barber-surgeon probably had just bled someone who might or might not have had a fever, some soldier, perhaps, who'd made the mistake of malingering and experienced Beels's knife for his mistake. The barber loved to wield his blade, and only the uninformed or witless gave him a chance to use it on them, except for a shave.

Well, if this foolish fight was really going to be fought, Beels would have more demanding knife work to perform soon enough, Tonneman thought. And his victims would have no choice. He'd be giving them a lead bullet to bite on or smashing them in the face with his fist to knock them out, and if that didn't work, he'd be pouring brandywine into screaming mouths. If one were fortunate, it would be laudanum, and the whole while Beels would be cutting flesh and muscle with a knife and sawing away at the bone. In a minute or less, gunpowder-ruined arms and legs would be severed and would fall into blood-sodden boxes of sawdust. The wounds would be cauterized with boiling oil or hot irons, for all the good it would do. Not many had the luck of Pieter Stuyvesant, who had survived cannon shot and the surgeon's knife. The minister would be working just as hard preparing all those souls to go with those severed bodies. Most would be dead soon enough. But some would linger, their wounds stinking, putrefying into necrotic pus sores of gangrene, and finally, pale, fighting for air, almost corpses already, they would die by infection or by bleeding to death. And those that lived would be in agony for a long time.

A chuckle formed in Tonneman's throat, surprising him. After all his black thoughts, perhaps the bloody towel was only the result of the barber cutting someone while he shaved him.

The various other structures in the Fort included the Director-General's quarters, which he used as an office, and the barracks that housed between sixty and seventy men at any one time. Now, however, with the threat of English invasion, the Company force had swollen to one hundred and fifty, a mix of pikemen, musketeers, and very few mounted cavaliers. The overflow was lodged in the Fort jailhouse and the Stone Church.

There was no well. The only water came from the twenty or so casks that were stored in the Fort and replenished when necessary.

The West India Company, which owned Fort Amsterdam lock, stock, and barrel, and most of New Amsterdam as well, employed private soldiers, carpenters, coopers, bakers, millers, brewers, shopkeepers, and the blacksmith, the knife sharpener, and the barber-surgeon. These, like Tonneman himself, had been lured to Manhattan Island by promises of wealth and a new life.

The Company also employed Hilletjie Wilbruch, a fat good-natured widow, a midwife, who also ran the soldiers' hospital. Since the fortress was already overcrowded, the hospital had been built close by.

The Netherlands flag that was mounted in a bracket just outside the Director-General's open door flapped indolently as Tonneman hastened into the office. "And a good morning to all," he said cheerfully.

"You're late," the Director-General roared, pacing, body thrust forward on his wooden leg.

"How are you feeling today, Boss?"

"Bilious, if you must know." Stuyvesant picked up a glass of cloudy brown liquid from a long oak table. "If I wasn't guzzling barley water, I'd be on the jakes all day." He made a face and drank.

Tonneman nodded to Captain Pos. Seated at the long table and standing about the smoky chamber were the Vice-Director-General, the other eight members of the Council, including Nick De Sille, the two Burgomasters, the five Schepens, and Chief Fire Warden van Der Werff.

Also in attendance were Oloff Stevensen van Cortlandt, a former Burgomaster, married to Goovert Lookermans's daughter, and one of the richest and most respected men in town, Reverend Megapolensis, Captain Stephanaus Van Dillen, leader of the Civilian Militia, and Colonel Caspar van de Steen, commander of the regular soldiers. The colonel was in battle dress, a metal breastplate and helmet.

Stuyvesant, his Vice-Director-General, and the Council represented the government of the Dutch West India Company, not the States General of the Netherlands. The Burgomasters, Schepens, and Tonneman, Pos, and the Fire Warden represented the City government of New Amsterdam. The two factions were constantly at odds, the rights of the Company versus the rights of the people.

Everyone was smoking the rosemary-sauced tobacco P.S. favored, which he always put out in a silver box at these meetings.

Tonneman hated the rosemary tobacco. Still, he needed a smoke, and he didn't have his pipe with him. He cast about for the guest pipes the Boss always provided. None was visible. Tonneman decided now was not the right time to ask.

He took a seat by a mullioned window of rippled glass, fixed in circles of lead, and watched a horsefly buzz around P.S.'s head. The Director-General blew smoke at the insect, and it flew off, only to return.

"First, to review," Stuyvesant said, waving the fly away again. "We have fifteen hundred citizens, about five hundred of whom are men. They're to be divided into three work parties so that every day approximately one hundred and sixty-five men are at work shoring up the walls. A pound and a half of lead is allotted to each member of the citizens' guard."

Colonel van de Steen barked a short laugh. He was tall and broad, with short-cropped blond hair and a neat sword scar on his right cheek, from cheekbone to jawbone, which he was fond of stroking.

He looked every inch the professional soldier. "They'll have to throw it at the enemy. We're down to six hundred pounds of powder and my men need it all."

"I'll have something to say about that." Captain Van Dillen was as broad and powerful a man as the colonel but not as tall. His black hair was stringy, and while he had no scar, he did have a bristling black mustache that he was fond of twisting.

Stuyvesant went on as if neither man had spoken. "The two hundred and ninety blackamoor slaves that were on the *Gideon* are to help with the work on the fortifications."

"Less food for the rest of us," Nick De Sille said.

Tonneman raised an eyebrow at De Sille. De Sille raised an eyebrow in response.

Stuyvesant frowned and continued. "The brewers are to make no malt for eight days starting yesterday."

"Ridiculous," said van Cortlandt. "Work is standing still in my brewery. When the Amsterdam Chamber asks me what happened to profits this month, I'll tell them to ask you."

Stuyvesant's face reddened. "Don't threaten me with the Chamber. If they don't care about black powder or cannon for us, why should I care about profits for them? No malt for eight days."

"Now, that's what I call bad news," said Pos. "The malt part, I mean." Tonneman put his fingers to his lips.

Again Stuyvesant continued, this time more belligerently. "One third of our force, fifty men, is to guard the gates and patrol the City at night. The four Rattle Watch are to continue their rounds, too. A second third of the soldiers is to perform the same duty during the day. The rest are to commence vigorous training. Has all this been done?"

There was a murmur of assent from the other men in the chamber.

"Good. I'm doing my best to get us more cannon." The men around the oak table hammered it lightly with their fists to show their endorsement. "Have I left anything out?"

Willem Beekman cleared his throat. He and the Director-General had come over together on the same ship, the *Great Crow,* back in '47. Beekman had started as a clerk for the Company, had become a rich man, and like van Cortlandt had served previously as a Burgomaster. "Yes, Petrus," Beekman said, using the Latin form of the Director-General's first name as relatives and close friends did. "Tomorrow is Market Field day. Do we cancel it?"

"It wouldn't do any good, Willi. They'd still all come. Colonel, patrol the market diligently and tell your men to be vigilant. It makes sense for the illustrious governor of Connecticut, that English snake John Winthrop, to put spies among us. Keep your eyes open for strangers."

The dead man under the willow had been a stranger. Tonneman wondered if perhaps he was an English spy but elected not to mention it until he and Stuyvesant were alone.

"It's what I would do," said van de Steen.

"If they're not here already," Tonneman observed dryly.

"True," said Stuyvesant. "You keep an eye open at the market, too. Anything else?"

"Curfew," said Pos.

"Drinking, the same. Nothing served after nine. And as long as this emergency lasts, no one on the streets after ten without good reason, and all fires put out or covered. Tell the Watch to call it out. Anything else?"

"Fire buckets," said Chief van Der Werff. "Everybody keeps stealing them."

The Director-General looked at Tonneman.

The Schout nodded. "I'll get after it."

"The mosquitoes," said the minister.

"Yes, of course." Stuyvesant rolled his eyes at Tonneman. "Anything else?" He didn't wait for a response. "To work, then. I'm putting you each in charge of a section of the City."

Tonneman wondered how he was supposed to find lost fire buckets, watch the market and his section, whichever it was, and take care of his normal duties, too. He needed a deputy, that's what.

"What about the mosquitoes?" asked the minister.

"I think you're the best person to take care of that," Stuyvesant told him. "I suggest you offer a special prayer to God to protect us from the English *and* the mosquitoes. A special church service might be appropriate." He turned to the others. "For years I've been trying to get this community to come back to the bosom of Jesus Christ. Perhaps now the people will listen. Through prayer we can overcome all obstacles. I cannot signify too strongly how important that is. The citizens must be ready to fight to the death for New Amsterdam."

"But the Company. What about the reinforcements? Aren't they coming?"

"And lead and more powder."

"And more cannon."

Stuyvesant stomped the floor with his wooden leg, his mouth a hard line. "I've told you, I'll do my best to get more cannon and ammunition, but we can expect no further help from the Company."

Pos and Tonneman exchanged looks. It was much as each had speculated.

"Why not?" Schepen Timotheus Gabrie, a small man with a thin, tight face, demanded.

"Have some sense, man," Stuyvesant sputtered. "Any message we send would be like pissing in the wind. This time of year it takes seven to nine weeks to make the voyage from here to Amsterdam. Do you honestly think any request or demand I make now will matter?"

"Shit," said Captain Van Dillen.

"Amen," said the minister, then he flushed with embarrassment.

"However," continued the Director-General, disregarding them, "I have sent word to Flatbush and Rensselaerswyck and our people on Long Island that we need men and powder. I suggested they send one third of all their men."

"Good luck," said the colonel sardonically.

"The New Amsterdamers won't fight—" Pos began.

"On behalf of the Militia I resent that," said Van Dillen.

"What do you mean?" Stuyvesant bellowed. "Not fight? That's traitor's talk."

"No, it's not," said the colonel. "He's right. Why should they fight? They've no good reason. There's no honor or patriotism involved here. This is just a Company town. My soldiers will fight; that's what they're paid to do. But how long can one hundred and fifty stand up to a larger force, and we don't even know how large."

"Who says it's a larger force?" Stuyvesant blustered.

"I do, Boss, and so do you," Tonneman ventured. "The people have no loyalty to the Company. Many own their land outright from the Indians. Some are not even from the Fatherland."

"They are good, God-fearing people. They want peace without

bloodshed and without loss of property," offered Reverend Megapolensis.

Stuyvesant's eyes blazed. "I don't want to hear fart-and-dung explanations. You are paid by the Company. You will roust the citizens." The horsefly had returned once more and was circling over Stuyvesant's head, buzzing loudly.

Tonneman's mouth was parched. He longed for a beer. "It'll do no good. They talk, talk, talk and do naught."

"You must tell them to be strong, and quit themselves like men," Stuyvesant pronounced.

"Amen," said the predicant.

"Is there anything else?" Stuyvesant demanded.

Tonneman cleared his throat. He was considering asking if anyone knew anything about the man with the octagonal spectacles, or if they had seen Cutnose. No, not until he had discussed the situation with the Boss. And it didn't seem as if that was going to be today. It was the wrong time to talk about the missing dead man. He let the moment pass.

"How close are the English?" the Vice-Director-General asked.

Stuyvesant lashed at the fly with his hat, squashing it on the table. He smiled all around at his victory and placed his hand on his sword. His smile became cheerless. "Four English men-of-war have been sighted in full sail off the coast of Connecticut. The wind is behind them."

II

TUESDAY, 26 AUGUST. *Late Morning.*

"What do you think?" Pos's normally merry face was worried. The two, along with van Der Werff, had left the Fort together afoot, Tonneman leading Venus between him and Pos and the Chief trailing. Pos stepped ahead of the four-footer to get a clear view of Tonneman. "He's going to force blood, the stubborn old bastard."

Tonneman grunted and rubbed the mare's soft nose. She turned, showing her great teeth, snorted, and butted his hat in a loving gesture.

Pos aimed a kick at the fat pink rump of a van Etting porker, which had just deposited a giant pile of stinking shit in their path. They circled, giving the steaming pile wide berth.

Shrugging, Tonneman said, "We'll not let him have his head on this. We're Dutchmen, by God. Not a bunch of rag-tailed peasants, jumping to do the bidding of the lace-collar aristocracy." He turned sharply to Pos as if he had just thought of the question. "Would you die for the sheep-tupping Company?"

Pos was quick to respond. "Not I. Would you?"

"I came here twenty years ago, newly married, to build a life, and I did. The Fatherland is a dim memory, and the Company is naught but a lily-livered group of soft, greedy men who sit on their fat arses in luxury, collecting their profits on our hard work." He stopped suddenly, surprised at his own vehemence, to look at Pos, who was nodding enthusiastically.

"Yes, yes, you're right. What do you think, van Der Werff?"

"Don't ask me," said the Chief Warden. "I'm not political."

"But you have an opinion," Tonneman insisted.

They went a few more paces. "I sew my canvas," said van Der Werff, who was also a sail maker. "I live my life. I just want to be left alone."

"That's it?" asked Pos.

"That's it."

Pos shrugged and grinned. Van der Werff shrugged and grinned back at him.

The puzzle of the dead man nagged at Tonneman anew. "Have either of you seen Cutnose?" he asked.

Each shook his head.

"What about a foppish fellow with octagonal spectacles?"

"I can't help you," said van Der Werff.

Pos scratched his head. "Sounds familiar, but I can't quite place him."

Van Der Werff laughed. "If you saw him, it was in a tavern and one or both of you were drunk."

"How can you say that?" said Pos, pretending to be wounded. "I don't drink anymore."

"But you don't drink any less," said Tonneman.

All three laughed.

They paused at Mill Street, where Pos and van Der Werff took their leave to examine the fire site again. "You never know when sparks are sleeping beneath a pile of burnt wood, just waiting for a chance to flare," said van Der Werff.

"And after that," said Pos, clapping him on the shoulder as they moved off, "we'll have a beer."

"*You'll* have a beer," said the Chief Warden. "I've got a whole loft of work to do."

"One beer."

"Well, maybe one."

When Tonneman reached home, he stabled the mare, plucked two apples from the tree near the barn door, and patted her flank as he fed one to her.

In the yard he stumbled over his cudgel where he'd probably dropped it the night before. He picked up the two-foot piece of wood and tucked it under his left arm. Biting into the second apple, he let the sweet tartness fill his mouth and went out on the Strand, intent for the waterfront.

Next door, the Pear Tree was open for business, thriving, in fact. Men were hanging over the bottom half of the double door. Just above the entranceway was the simple rendering of a pear tree, which Maria had painted. There were so many things to remind him of Maria, but at least he could think about her now without the terrible grinding pain.

Tonneman entered the smoke-filled tavern. The air was clamorous with complaining and bickering voices; he was at once hailed by several townsmen. He squeezed his way to the bar. The yellow hound under the bar, awakened by his entrance, barked excitedly, and its wagging tail softly struck the surrounding men on the legs.

"What news, Tonneman?"

"What are you all doing here? It's the middle of the day."

"We might ask the same of you, Schout."

He smiled broadly. The meat of the apple was still sweet in his mouth. "Why, don't you know, it's my job to be in here."

There was a loud mouth-fart, then someone asked what they all wanted to know. "What about the English?"

"The sun is shining brightly. You should all be working."

"Tell us about the English."

"Did someone call a holiday?"

"The English."

"All right. Four English frigates have been sighted off the Connecticut coast, moving quickly."

"Kiss my arse!" A tankard slammed on a table.

The chamber was in immediate uproar. The agitated dog barked at a higher pitch.

Tonneman spoke firmly, raising his voice over the din. "This is no surprise."

"Stuyvesant is itching for a fight."

"Tall Matthew, are you ready to go to war?"

The free African, who lived in Breukelen but worked in Manhattan as a cargo handler for Asser Levy on the docks of the North River, sipped his beer, undisturbed. Tall Matthew was a man of great strength, taller and leaner than anyone had ever seen. Perhaps twenty hands and perhaps fifteen stone. Taller still than Sweet Lips, the woman with the traveling whores. Even in his homeland he had been taller and leaner than most.

"What does he know about fighting? He's just a black heathen. Isn't that right, boy?"

Tall Matthew smiled. In Accra when he *was* a boy, before the slavers took him, there had been warriors: here there were just talkers. He touched the sides of his head lightly, first the left, then the right. The tribal scars there and on his chest were all he had left of his homeland. And his memories. The good memories of home and the warm smell of the sea. The bad memories of the searing metal burning the mark of the Dutch West India Company into his right arm and then of being forced deep into the foul-smelling ship that carried him to this land, sitting between another man's legs like a woman and having another sitting on him, each being soiled by the other's stinking piss and shit for how long? He never knew. And the bad memories that followed. Of being in this strange, mean and cold land. Had he been left alone in his home country, he could have been a great warrior, even a great chief, for he was descendant of priests. This could have been had the fates been friendly. But they hadn't been, and he was here and thinking wouldn't change any of that. Tall Matthew drank his beer and let them talk.

"We've barely enough powder to defend ourselves if a dozen Indians attack. Four frigates. Christ Almighty."

"Do you think there will be actual fighting?" John Woods, the Englishman who had lived with his family in New Amsterdam for some years, sounded worried. Woods, a miller, spoke with scarcely an English accent. He was solidly built, bald, with a straight nose and a no-nonsense manner, and though he had a stiff left arm that hung uselessly at his side, he was still formidable. The miller's sleeves were rolled up today, and his left arm looked normal enough, but it was just as useless as it had been since the day he had fallen out of his loft years before.

"What do you care?" the tanner, Jan Keyser, demanded in his puling voice. "Damned Englishman. I'll wager you're not having trouble getting grain for your mill. We all know about your brother on English Long Island. For years you've been cheating me for grinding my bark. Bad enough I have to do business with you and bad enough I have to live in the same town with you. But I don't have to drink with you. Get out." Keyser poked the Englishman in the chest with stubby, brown-stained fingers. His thick jagged nails were gummy with muck.

"I will not," said the burly miller, easily brushing the smaller man's hand aside with his good right hand.

Keyser poked him again. "Out," he screamed.

Woods took a despairing breath and slapped Keyser across the face, rocking the little man.

The hound yelped repeatedly and snapped at the two men.

"Then I'll make you," Keyser said, drawing the well-honed tanner's knife from the sheath at his belt.

"Do your damnedest," said Woods, balling the fist of his good hand.

The crowded chamber fell into deadly silence. Even the hound ceased its noise, dropped its tail, and found a reason to go to the back of the tavern.

Slowly, Tonneman put the remains of his apple on the bar. His cudgel was still under his left arm. Sweet Jesus, he thought. Help me. Give me the strength not to knock this little simpleton's head off. "Put it away, Keyser," he said, standing stock-still and making no move for his cudgel. "We're not in the old country. Twelve guilders or six weeks. Draw a sticker in this town and it's a hundred florins' fine or six months at hard labor on bread and water."

"Where are you going to get the bread?" the now frightened tanner shouted. "We're running out of grain."

There was one loud snort of laughter.

Tonneman kept talking steadily as he eased closer to Keyser. "If you cut him, it's three hundred guilders or eighteen months. You can't afford either. Put the blade away and I'll forget it ever happened."

The tanner, ignoring the Schout, advanced on Woods. The big miller readied himself.

"Keyser!" Tonneman commanded.

With stubborn fury Keyser stabbed the knife into the bar, and then, as if he had suddenly gone mad, he did a stamping dance step in front of Woods. Keyser's wooden clogs sounded heavily on the rough floor. Bewildered, Woods looked down at the tanner's feet. Keyser hit him in the jaw. It was no more than a fly bite to Woods.

Keyser, unnerved, punched Woods in the stomach. Again to no avail. Woods, who had stood there with a bizarre patience, finally hammered Keyser on the head with his good fist, and the little man crumpled to the floor. The hound moved forward and licked his face.

"This never was." Tonneman's eyes darted around the chamber.

"Agreed," said Joost Zoelan. "Everyone have a drink."

"Your treat?" someone asked.

"And everyone pay the score," said the tavern keeper, laughing.

"I thought so. Tonneman, what about the English?"

"Nothing has happened yet. We have the soldiers. The Boss has sent notice to Flatbush and Rensselaerswyck and our people on Long Island for support."

"And who'd look out for their families? They'd be fools to come."

Tonneman nodded in agreement. "We'll see. In the meantime, pass on the news. We must be ready." He placed his cudgel on the bar and took the tankard of beer from Zoelan. "For all the good it will do us," he said, under his breath so only Joost could hear. The smell of flowers that always came with drinking good beer filled his nose. It was part of the pleasure. He sniffed and drank deeply.

"If this goes on too long," Joost said out of the corner of his mouth as he came around to pick up Keyser, "my reserves will run out."

"I shouldn't worry," the Schout said in a normal voice.

"Ah, but *I* do."

Tonneman spat in the sandbox and grinned wryly. "You are a selfish pig."

"Not for me, for the people. They were banging on my door at the crack of dawn, Tonneman. At times like these, people get parched easily."

The Schout laughed, for he had a raging thirst himself.

Joost worked Keyser's knife from the bar and held it up to the light. "This is a fine blade, tanner, I'll give you five beers for it."

Tonneman made a face. "It's just a knife."

"Ah, but you know how I love a trade. Tanner?"

"How about one beer for nothing," the little man grumbled, grabbing the knife and returning it to its sheath.

"As you say," said Joost. And he gave Keyser and Woods fresh beers. "Here you go, men. And no score to pay." The yellow hound stood under the beer keg, tongue out, waiting for drops of beer to fall from the spout.

Tonneman beckoned the tavern keeper back to him. "Did you happen to see a fancy, gaudy fop of a fellow in here last night? Octagon spectacles. Gold baldric. Flashy sword. Might have been a Frenchy."

Joost scratched his head; he answered slowly and deliberately. "No, can't say that I did."

"After I left last night, did anything happen in here?"

"Same as any other night."

"What about Cutnose? Did he come back?"

"No."

"Keep this quiet, but I found a body near my willow, last night."

Joost's eyes widened. "Who was it?"

"The fancy fellow with the spectacles. He'd been stabbed."

"You reckon Cutnose did it?"

"It's possible. There's something else."

"What?"

"Somebody stole the body."

"Somebody stole the . . . You mean *you* lost it, you old piss pot." Joost burst out laughing so loud all the men in the chamber turned to look at him. The yellow dog barked.

"Is that the way you keep something quiet?" Tonneman said in a harsh whisper.

"Sorry," Joost whispered back. "I never thought I'd say it about you, but I guess you really did have too much to drink this time. We all get old, old friend."

Tonneman didn't respond, merely gave him a sour look.

"Well, with the body gone, you don't have a problem." Zoelan had a hard time muffling another burst of laughter.

"No, I have two problems. The dead man and the killer. Where can I find Cutnose?"

"How would I know what that heathen does? Probably sleeping off a thick head in the woods somewhere."

"You've been a great help to me, Joost."

"Always glad to be of service."

Tonneman saw his half-eaten apple lying on the bar and finished it. Then he emptied the tankard, pulled his purse from his jacket pocket, and slapped two stuivers down.

"You don't have to do that," said Joost.

"Yes, I do."

"In that case, you owe me another three stuivers. The price has gone up."

Tonneman tossed three more coins on the bar. "Gouger."

"I need the money. You know it costs me twenty-four florins a year just for my license."

"I weep for you. You get that back when you sell one drink to an Indian for one beaver pelt."

"Is beaver that high now? My, my, that's what inflation will do. I'm in the wrong business. Have another beer. This time my treat."

The Schout dropped his apple core into the sandbox and thought about another beer. The first hadn't been nearly enough.

After sniffing at the apple core, the yellow hound drank from Joost's rinse bucket, circled once, lay down on his spot beneath the bar, and went to sleep.

"What will one beer more hurt?" Joost goaded.

Tonneman was tempted. "No," he said, cramming his purse in his pocket. He picked up his cudgel and went out the door. The yellow hound followed, playfully snapping at Tonneman's heels. When he paid him no mind, the dog started sniffing the ground under the pear tree, scratching at it. Suddenly the hound yapped once and set off toward the Broad Way as if it had an urgent appointment.

Tonneman smiled at the animal's antics and headed toward the waterfront.

12

TUESDAY, 26 AUGUST. *Mid Morning.*

Racqel pounded David's arms, which held her in a viselike grip as he pulled her from the awful shed into the bright sunlight. "It's Benjamin. I know it's Benjamin."

"It's not Benjamin," he said, finally releasing her.

She looked at her brother-in-law. His mouth was set in a rigid line. "How can you be so certain?"

David turned away, and Racqel had the sudden, startled feeling that he was hiding something. "We will not alarm our neighbors," he said, still not meeting her gaze. "Not a word to those women about this. Understand?"

"I understand." She could hear the murmuring voices of the women and their low laughter as they shared secrets.

"Father and I will take the Ark to Asser Levy. First I must wash my hands."

"But the dead man . . ."

"Our first obligation is to the Torah; however, someone must tell the Schout." He closed his eyes for a moment, then opened them. "When the first wagonload of wood arrives, you will tell the workers not to touch the shed. They are to bring wood and cut boards. Leave them to their work and go to City Hall for the Schout. Frederick Philipse will come with some men to start the rebuilding of our house."

After he left, Racqel went back into the shed and stared at the body. David's admonitions about the dead being unclean and tainted had no meaning for her; she had seen dead men before. Racqel had assisted her father from the time she was a young girl. She felt nothing now except sorrow that the fire on their land had killed someone.

But it hadn't. The man had been stabbed to death. Or had he? She moved closer to the body. It seemed that the knife had been thrust in and out several times, but because the body was partially burnt, she couldn't tell if the wounds had bled. If they hadn't, that would mean the knife was thrust in after the man had died.

She wondered at the unmistakable anger of the thrusts, and the thought came quickly that if the man was indeed already dead before the fire, then perhaps the fire had been started to hide the fact of the killing.

Hearing Caleb's barks and the rattle of an approaching wagon, she turned and left the shed. Two strapping Africans had already begun unloading the wood. She walked toward them. "Quiet, Caleb." Playfully, the dog danced away. "My brother said just bring the logs and cut boards; he'll return as soon as he can. There's no need to go into the house or the shed."

"All right," the larger one said.

"We are not slaves, Vrouw Mendoza," said the other proudly. "We are freemen." They continued working.

"What are your names?"

"They call me Goliath," said the big one.

"And you?"

"I am David," said the other.

Racqel smiled and returned to the small group of women who had halted their cleaning to talk intently. Esther Diaz and Miriam Isaacs had joined Rebecca and her daughter.

"Is anything wrong?" Mariana Da Costa asked.

"No, just the men with the wood."

"I meant before that. We couldn't help but hear you and your brother-in-law."

"Oh, it was nothing. I was upset again about the fire. Don't go in the shed. It's . . . filthy."

"I won't," the young woman answered, looking at Racqel curiously. "Thank God, no one was hurt." Then, with great enthusiasm: "Have you heard? Captain Pos just told us there are four English warships coming." She looked excited, but she was young, younger than the other women, who were uneasy.

"There'll be fighting," Esther Diaz said. She had reason to be worried; she had four grown sons who would be expected to fight. Now, to her husband's great joy, in her old age, like the ninety-year-old biblical Sarah, she was pregnant again. "We have a great deal to lose."

Racqel looked at Esther's full belly with envy. Why her and not me? she thought.

"You don't have to worry," Rebecca Da Costa said tartly. "Jews are exempted from militia service."

Esther Diaz was grim. "When the English land, I think Captain Van Dillen and his militia will relax the ban against Jews in their ranks. There will be enough fighting, and perhaps dying, for all. Even the Director-General will welcome Jews to the fray then."

Rebecca agreed and Miriam Isaacs nodded. After a moment Mariana Da Costa nodded, too. Miriam, whose new pregnancy was just beginning to show, was rocking her son Micah's cradle with her foot. Racqel tried not to stare at her. Bathsheba, who had no such compunction, was alternately staring at Micah and licking her fur.

All the women wondered if they would have to move again. What country would they have to journey to this time? Again outcasts.

"My father-in-law says the English will let the Jews be," Racqel said, giving voice to their main concern. "That our people are not persecuted in Rhode Island."

"I wouldn't depend on the English," said Esther Diaz harshly. "Better the Dutch devil we know than the English devil we don't."

The women, having finished the cleaning, seemed reluctant to leave. But they had their own homes to care for, so they bade Racqel farewell, leaving her among the small pieces of her life that had been salvaged and scrubbed: her china, her silver, and the small duffel-cloth bags of herbs that were all that remained of her lovely garden. She unfolded a clean cloth and draped it over the china and silver. The hot sun was beating down and the soaked earth was drying. Soon the dust would be on everything.

Her foot brushed against something under the table. Her father's medical chest. Tears welled in her eyes; she missed her father so much. Since his death . . . Suppressing the tears, Racqel placed the carved treen case back under the table.

She had learned to trust her intuition, and her intuition was telling her now that David was right. The dead man was not her missing husband.

She could delay no longer. It was time to find the Schout and tell him of the body in the shed.

13

TUESDAY, 26 AUGUST. *Late Morning.*
A breeze stirred the oak and chestnut trees along Pearl Street, making them rustle like taffeta. The whitewashed fences around each house that kept dogs and livestock penned appeared yellow in the sunlight.

Overhead the sky was a sharp, deep blue. The Peyser twins, pretty little girls, were jumping a rope with the Van Nordens's three young daughters, their voices raised in excitement, yellow braids bouncing. Racqel watched them for a moment wondering what it would be like if one of the children were hers.

On the City Hall steps two soldiers, supposedly on duty, stood huddled in a corner, matching stuivers on the backs of their hands, each cackling loudly when he won and complaining loudly when he lost. They reeked of beer.

Four more soldiers and four African slaves came out the door and down the steps, past Racqel. They moved along Pearl Street toward Stuyvesant's Great House. By their speech these four soldiers were not Dutch. Norwegian perhaps.

"I'm looking for Schout Tonneman," Racqel said to them.

"Captain Pos!" one of the soldiers called, his young voice cracking.

Pos came and stood in the shadowed entrance to the City Hall.

Racqel moved toward him and smiled. "Thank you for your help last night."

"Only my duty."

"Then thank you for doing your duty so well."

Pos almost smiled. He shifted his feet and raised his hand to his hat in salute, embarrassed.

The door to the Hall opened and Hugo Evertsen, clerk to the Burgomasters, stuck out his bald and freckled head. "Pos, have you seen Burgomaster van Cortlandt?"

"I think he's still at the Fort with the Boss, Hugo."

"Oh," Evertsen said, looking distressed. He nodded to Racqel. "Vrouw Mendoza."

"Heer Evertsen," she answered politely.

Evertsen backed in and closed the door.

"Is Heer Tonneman inside?" Racqel asked.

Pos shook his head. "Excuse me." He turned to the gambling soldiers. "You two, shouldn't you be walking your rounds?"

"We're not under your orders," one grumbled softly. "We're soldiers."

Unfortunately, Pos heard him. "One of two things can happen. You can walk your rounds, or I can break your heads. Understood?"

"Yes, sir."

His face stiffened, but his voice did not get louder. "Then walk."

The pair scuttled down the stairs and hurried along the street that bordered the near side of the Ditch. Their footsteps made an odd sound, going alternately from the dirt street to the stone-paved paths that led to the sturdy three-story houses.

The Captain of the Rattle Watch turned back to Racqel. "Now, is there something I can do for you?"

"No. I need to talk to Schout Tonneman right away."

"I don't know where he is. You could try the tavern." When she frowned, he raised his hand and crossed to the Pear Tree, where some men were leaning out over the lower door. "Tonneman? You in there?"

"No," many voices within shouted. "He was here earlier," said one of the men leaning on the half door.

Pos came back to her. "It appears not." He grinned. "Try his resting place."

"Thank you." Racqel started for Tonneman's house; she hadn't gone but a few paces before the captain called after her.

"Not there." He rubbed his bleary eyes. "Under the biggest willow tree. Over there." He pointed across the Strand. "On the waterfront. Straight across from here. Don't go in the alley. Keep left. It's a good thirty yards."

Buskins crunching on the oyster shells, Racqel hurried down to the waterfront, aware that Pos's eyes were on her.

Soldiers seemed to be everywhere now. Strangely, there were no sailors. The ever-present odor of tar permeated the air. Resting place? In the middle of the day? She shook her head. These gentiles. It was a chore to understand them. Would the Schout be in a drunken stupor in the privacy of his willow tree? The Dutch liked their beer and carried drinking to an extreme. But he seemed such a nice man. She surprised herself by hoping he would be different.

The path along the river narrowed and became grassy. Seabirds dived for fish and called to each other in triumph. The cooler breeze from the river made her feel as if a weight was being lifted from her shoulders, as if it were another time, when she still had a husband and was looking forward to being a mother. In the sudden sweet solitude of the moment Racqel pulled her white ruffled cap from her head and in pure abandon unpinned her dark hair, letting the wind whip it around her face.

It was wonderful. She felt so free. A small boat pulled away from one of the ships in the near distance. They couldn't see her, but immediately aware of the impropriety, she swiftly pinned her hair up, replaced the cap, tucking dark strands up carefully, and resumed her journey to Tonneman's willow tree.

_14_

TUESDAY, 26 AUGUST. _Late Morning._

After leaving the Pear Tree, Tonneman ambled down to Coenties Slip and stopped at the Ten Eycks' step-gabled brick house. He opened the front door and called, "Hallo."

Six fresh loaves of bread stood on the pine tabletop, a knife beside them. Tonneman cut a loaf in half and held one of the halves to his nose. He loved the smell of fresh bread. Maria used to . . .

Antje Ten Eyck answered him from the back of the house. Bringing the bread with him, he went through the great chamber to the yard.

Sitting proudly in the immaculate white chamber was a huge painted birchwood kas. Dutch majolica, brass candlesticks, and chafing dishes were lovingly displayed. A small looking-glass framed in tortoiseshell hung on the wall beside an oil-on-wood painting: Daniel in the lion's den. Nearby were two other paintings, Jesus turning water to wine and a sea battle, which was Tonneman's favorite. Two oak drawbar tables, one covered with a bright Turkish rug, and eight maple chairs with red velvet seats and backs were placed about.

By far the most striking things in the chamber, however, were the silver pieces, most of them Ten Eyck's handiwork. He turned them out in the workshed next to the house. On the covered table was an etched silver beaker. One of Conraet's newest pieces, no doubt. A beautiful piece, delicately curved and balanced. The man was a true artist.

Tonneman pushed open the door to the yard, which faced the river, where Antje was hanging bed linen on the fence to bleach in the midday sun.

She stopped, hands on her hips, smiling as Tonneman took a bite of the fresh bread. "Eat, eat. Soon we'll have no grain at all, and the English will take New Amsterdam. Our people can't live without bread and beer." She laughed. "Beer in particular. We may have to drink Spanish sherry wine, heaven forbid."

"I drink wine."

"You drink anything."

"So, you've heard about the English?" He took another bite of bread.

"Yes. Ten Eyck was here. He went out to talk with the ships' captains."

Tonneman nodded. "Where's little Conraet?"

"With his father. And happy as a lark about it."

"I'll be on my way, then."

"Come back and eat with us later. There's plenty. Cold prune soup. Hutsepot stew and a nice fat duck. And I've baked olykoek. This may be your last chance for a good meal. When the English come, we'll all have to eat crumpetcake."

"I might like crumpetcake."

"You would. Will you come?"

"Maybe." He started toward the water, then stopped. "By the way, Antje, do you know the Mendoza widow?"

"Nay. Why?"

"No reason. Merely asking."

There was silence between them.

"Tonneman, you're killing yourself with drink."

He wiped the crumbs from his mouth and said, "I prefer it to the rope. To tell the truth, I never thought Hendrik would choose the rope either."

"Nor I."

"I dreamed of him last night. Just before I saw the dead man."

"Maybe you dreamed it all."

"Nay, the dead man was real. I had his blood on my hands."

Tonneman looked at his hands, then at Antje. "I have Hendrik's blood on my hands, too."

"What are you prattling about? Hendrik Smitt is long dead."

"God save me, I remembered last night that he wanted to talk to me. Something was eating at him. I was too drunk. We were both too drunk, falling down in the road. I walked away from him. Then he was dead." Tonneman rubbed his eyes and saw the vision of Smitt's body again.

"If he was that drunk, how could he tie himself a noose and put it over a tree?"

Tonneman's eyes snapped open. "What? What are you saying? Are you saying he had help?"

Antje snorted a laugh. "Maybe some friend was kind enough to put the rope around his neck, tie it to the tree, and give Hendrik a friendly kick into hell."

Not suicide, Tonneman thought, grasping at the concept. Not suicide. Murder. He felt as if he was choking. "Jesus Christ in heaven," he roared, his big hands clenched. "Hendrik was murdered and I cursed him for a suicide."

Antje left her wash and went to him. "Shh, dear friend, shh." She stroked his fist until he opened his hand to her. "Come inside." She led him to the kitchen and poured him a cup of buttermilk.

Tonneman stared into the cup, enraged. "Why would anyone want to kill Hendrik? He was trying to tell me something, Antje, but I wouldn't listen. What a stupid fool I am."

"Enough," Antje said. "Drink."

He made a face at her and drank the buttermilk, wishing for brandy.

Rage burned in his belly as he headed for his willow tree along the edge of the river. Then crushing remorse. Smitt had something to tell him. Was that why he'd been killed? Had Smitt come back last night to tell him? All these years and no murders in New Amsterdam. Now perhaps two? Smitt and Spectacles last night. Did the two deaths have anything to do with each other?

The sky was the clearest blue, with only a few white smudges of clouds. The air was hot and dry. The river on his right was a deep rushing green, full of swift currents. Had the body been thrown after him into the river last night?

When he parted the hanging leafy branches of the willow and entered under its protection, he dropped his cudgel on the ground, got down on his hands and knees, fingering the grass where the body had lain. He moved slowly outward, nose to the ground, hands spread. He saw from this vantage point a slight dark patch and, touching the spot, found it stiff. He smelled it. Blood. Without looking up, he knew the patch had been sheltered by the dense willow branches and leaves, else all would have been washed away by the heavy morning rain.

Well, if to no other, he had proven to himself that there had been blood spilled here the night before.

Toward the outer edges of the space that the branches shaded, he found another such spot, slightly larger and irregular. Was that from the body again? Someone had dragged it before carrying it off. When he was finished here, he would look around for wheel marks, although with the rain he didn't expect to find any.

Shade or not, Tonneman was sweating heavily. He took off his black hat and buckskin jacket and mopped his face with his sleeve. Then again, arse high, nose to the earth, fingers searching, he moved backward, outward.

His fingers closed on a small metallic object.

15

Tuesday, 26 August. *Midday.*

For Racqel, who had half expected to find Tonneman in a drunken sleep under the tree, it was a curious position, nose to the ground like Caleb on the scent. She resisted an urge to laugh. "Schout?"

Tonneman's fingers closed around the metal object quickly when he saw the Widow Mendoza's comely face and figure in the hazy sunlight as she parted the branches of the willow tree.

"Madam." He struggled to his feet, vaguely embarrassed at the arse-high view he had presented. He picked up his jacket and put it on, pocketing the metallic object in the process.

"Have you lost something?" she asked, letting the leafy curtain fall behind her.

"Would you please hold back the branches again that I might get a better light?"

She pleased him by not asking questions, stepping back at once and doing exactly as he had requested. Whereupon he dropped to his knees and went over the same ground again.

"What's that over there, shining?" Racqel pointed to something glinting, just as his hand found the item in the low grass. It was a shard of glass, the size of his thumbnail and, much to his annoyance, very sharp. "Merciful God," he cried, and then, "I beg your pardon." He stared at the small shard, which was almost shrouded by the grass. A red bubble oozed from his palm. He thought of the bubbles of blood from the mouth of the dead man last night.

She released the branches and, producing a linen handkerchief from her sleeve, knelt beside him and took his hand in hers.

With his other hand Tonneman picked up the jagged shard and placed it in his pocket with the piece of metal.

Racqel, meanwhile, removed a tiny sliver of glass from his palm with a neat delicacy that surprised him and blotted the blood into the nosecloth. When she was done, she drew his hand closer to her face to inspect the damage. "There are more splinters still in there, but I can't get them with my fingers. They should come out."

He laughed. In his years as a sailor, a farmer, and even as a Schout he'd had a lot worse. All he'd ever done was use some spit and a wipe. He would do that now, but he enjoyed her attention and so left his hand in hers.

Carefully, like a good little mother, she wrapped his hand with her handkerchief. Their faces were very close, and he could study the delicate curve of her ear, the fullness of her lips. He wanted to put his fingers, his lips, to them. She raised her luminous dark eyes. Suddenly conscious that they were breathing the same air, she rose.

He sighed softly, lay full out on the riverbank, and lowered his cut hand into the cold river water to wash away the blood. "Just a nick," he said, standing, squeezing the cloth and waving his hand dry. When he looked back at the widow, she was gone. Surprised, he moved the branches aside and stepped out into the sunlight. She was waiting for him.

"Heer Schout," she said abruptly, "there's a dead man in the shed in back of our house."

Another body? What was going on in quiet, peaceful New Amsterdam? Well, that was what he was paid to find out.

He took up his hat and cudgel, and they began walking along the path to Pearl Street. "Do you know who this dead man is?"

"No. My brother-in-law and I discovered him. The face is badly burned."

Just off the pier at Coenties Slip three soldiers watched while two black slaves rolled a heavy keg into a shallow trench.

The Lookermans boys were standing behind the soldiers and slaves pretending to be soldiers, too. Nine-year-old Christoffel was pointing his stick at the horizon and yelling something about the English. Gerrit, two years younger, repeated the orders of the soldiers to the Africans in a high-pitched pipe, all the while holding a hoop over his head and spinning about.

Tonneman strode purposefully down the Strand, leaving Racqel Mendoza struggling to keep up.

There were still a few stragglers in front of the Pear Tree, but it seemed as if most had gone back to their work, at least until sundown.

At City Hall Tonneman called out to a soldier who was idling on the steps. "Hallo. Where's Captain Pos?"

"Sleeping."

Tonneman nodded. He'd wanted Pos with him. He was curious about why Pos hadn't discovered the body when he had inspected the fire site. Probably hadn't looked inside the shed. Not him and not van Der Werff.

A horse and cart passed them to the left, clattering on the road. "Walk your horse," Tonneman called. At that moment the hoop came rolling into the street, followed by the two little boys. Tonneman tossed his cudgel aside, grabbed the children by the scruffs of their necks just as the horse stepped on the hoop, crushing it.

"Don't play in the street," Tonneman said gently, lightly smacking the two on their bottoms.

Gerrit wailed, "My hoop. I want my hoop."

"Be quiet. Your father will get you another one." As always, the Lookermans boys' faces were blotched with cherry juice; their father had a large cherry orchard the other side of the Wall.

The cart driver, Crispijn Peyser, had pulled over to the side of the road. "Are they all right?" His voice was anxious. He didn't need any trouble from a rich man like Lookermans.

"Fine," said Tonneman. "Not even frightened. No thanks to you. But it might have been worse. Obey the law, Peyser. That's what it's there for."

"Sorry, Tonneman, I won't do it again." Peyser climbed down, led his horse to his house on the far side of the Pear Tree, and tied up at the rail post.

Racqel stood talking to the children. She sent them on their way, then picking up his cudgel, walked to Tonneman. "They could have been killed. I offered to see them home but they said no. They're trying to be little men."

Something, a catch in her voice, made him study her flushed face. Her dark hair peeped out from under the white frilled cap. He wondered how it would look uncovered. Spread across a pillow.

Tonneman gestured to the road and they started walking again. "You have no children?"

She dropped her eyes for a long moment, then raised them to his. "No." The word came out sharply, perhaps with more force than she had intended.

"I'm sorry," he said gently, taking the cudgel from her. "It's sad to be widowed without children. I have a married daughter, and soon a grandchild." They were almost to the Mendoza house. The woman appeared agitated. She was twisting her hands in an odd motion. "What is it? What have I said?"

Her response was so low that he had to bend his head to hear her. "I am not a widow. My husband, Benjamin, went away almost eight months ago. Something terrible must have happened. He's dead, else he would come back."

This last was said with such great pain that even he, clod that he knew he was, felt her grief. "Eight months. He must be dead. No man would leave someone like you alone for that long unless he was dead." He touched her arm lightly, feeling the softness under her cotton dress. "You'll marry again and have children."

She looked up at him with a half smile. "You don't understand. The law, our law, says that he is deemed alive and my husband, no matter how long he is missing. I am barred forever from remarrying until my husband's body is found, as long as it takes, even till the Day of Judgment. What does it matter?" she added bitterly. "I am barren. That's why he left me." Oh dear God, she thought, why am I telling this stranger, this gentile stranger, my innermost fears? "Please forget what I've just told you." Her eyes begged him.

"Forgotten," he said briskly, and turned his attention to the business at hand, but what she had said, and her anguish, gnawed at him.

"Did you ever know my husband?" she asked in a whisper.

"No." Now his response was more abrupt than he had intended.

The ground in front of the remains of the Mendoza house was covered with sawdust. To one side a pile of logs, to the other a large number of freshly cut boards, neatly stacked. The scent of fresh timber had reclaimed the air from the stench of smoke. The work was being done with speed and precision by David and Goliath.

The Mendozas, father and son, were nowhere to be seen. It being a day like any other day, Tonneman assumed they would be on Staple Street taking care of their profitable business as traders. He moved toward the shed.

"Wait, please." Racqel Mendoza placed her hand on his arm. She stopped at a long table on which a cloth covered bulky objects, crouched, and pulled a worn wooden box with a fine patina from under the table and opened it. From the box she took tweezers and a small flask, then rose and cleared a space on the table. "My father was a physician. May I see your hand?"

"It's not important." He waved her off and started for the shed, which stood a dark skeleton against the bright summer sky.

"Please. Before you touch the dead."

Something in her voice, perhaps a knowledge she had that he had not, made him stop. He walked back and gave her his hand.

She uncovered the flask. "This will hurt."

"Do your worst," he said, keeping a serious face to match hers. Racqel felt he was making sport of her, but she didn't stop.

The liquid had a mild sting. He smelled the flask. "Waste of good brandywine, if you ask me."

She took a glass disk framed in wood from the medical case and held it over his palm. It made the cut seem bigger. Looking through the disk, he could see tiny pieces of glass. With the tweezers she plucked a chip of glass from the cut, then another. "There, I told you," she said triumphantly.

Tonneman laughed out loud, an open, unconstrained laugh. There was no stopping this one when she decided to do something. And when she was proven right, she was not afraid to say it. Maria had been the same. He smiled. "I am in your debt."

"No. You saved my life. It is I who am in your debt." Realizing she was still holding his hand, she released it.

After a moment he said gruffly, "The instrument you used. It's a magnifying glass, yes?"

"Yes."

"I know about this. It's the same principle as the telescope." He took it from her. "May I?" He tucked his cudgel under his arm, brought out the shard from his pocket, placed it on the table, and looked at it through the glass as she watched.

He was disappointed; all he saw was a piece of glass. On an impulse he held the shard to his eye and found himself looking at Racqel's face, larger than life. Then the magnifier. Again Racqel seemed larger. Again the shard. The same effect once more. The shard was as the magnifying glass.

He was about to take the metal object from his pocket to examine it under the magnifying glass when Pos came running toward them.

16

Tuesday, 26 August. *Midday.*

"If I may borrow this?" Tonneman asked, gesturing with the magnifying glass.

"Please, of course."

They both watched as Pos with his loping walk approached, breathing heavily. "A soldier told me you were looking for me."

"I was. You think the fire started in the shed?" Tonneman asked solemnly. "I mean when you and van Der Werff inspected the shed. You did inspect the shed, didn't you?"

"Of course."

"What was in there?"

"A shed. A burnt-out shed."

"Look in there now."

Wary, Pos advanced on the scorched outbuilding. He let his hand rest on the scorched door frame and stepped inside. Tonneman saw Pos's knuckles go white as he gripped the door frame tighter. After a moment Pos backed out. Above his beard his face was crimson. He rubbed the crusts of sleep from the corners of his eyes. "Don't blame van Der Werff for this. He inspected the house. The shed was my job. I didn't do it."

"Come, forget it, man." Tonneman slapped Pos on the back. "No harm done. But I couldn't resist a little jollity at your expense."

Racqel, who had packed up her father's medical box and returned it to its temporary place beneath the table, followed the two men to the shed.

All around were the thumping and whining sounds of axes and saws on wood. The sweet smell of fresh-cut timber was not strong enough to cover the smell at the shed or the aura of something sinister that hung over the smoky blistered framework.

"I don't think you want to go in there," Pos told her. Racqel smiled as she brushed past him.

"Madam," Pos said, with formal certainty in his voice. "This is no place for a woman."

"She's a physician's daughter," Tonneman said, his expression serious. "She is not squeamish."

Racqel gave Tonneman a doubtful look. Was he making sport of her again? She stepped to the side.

"Holy Jesus." Tonneman, stunned, gaped at the body. Most of the clothing had been reduced to ash; the man lay there, an obscene burnt thing, with Tonneman's whalebone knife stuck in its chest, like a challenge. But a challenge from whom?

Muttering behind him, Pos said, "It's not seemly for the woman to be here."

Tonneman paid Pos no heed. The fury within him was monumental. Someone was bent on rubbing his nose in it. But he'd best save his rage for another time. He had to keep his anger in check and force himself to think clearly.

He handed Racqel his cudgel and squatted near the remains. The body was scorched enough not to be too stinking, but it was in remarkably fine condition considering the fire.

The sun filtering through the blackened walls made strange patterns on all their faces, each intent on the remains of the unknown man. Shadows blocked sight when a head moved, a position changed.

Wordlessly, Tonneman got to his feet and pulled the knife from the body. Pos pushed his hat back on his forehead, considered Tonneman, then the knife, and scratched his head.

Tonneman was about to stab the sharp steel blade into the ground to clean it when Racqel touched his arm. "Let me see the knife, if you please." She turned it in her hand once. "Ah, yes." Then relinquished it.

Tonneman cleaned the weapon and shoved it in his belt. He picked up several scorched boards and handed one to Pos. "Let's turn him."

Pos took the lower part, Tonneman the upper. The body, stiff as the boards they had used to turn it, fell over with an eerie slapping sound. Horribly, the head had not turned with the rest of the body. It was still the way it had been, face up.

"Pretty, eh?" said Tonneman.

"Prettiest I've ever seen," said Pos. "Wait." The Rattle Captain drew his knife and knelt at the gruesome head.

"What?" asked Tonneman.

"A thought," said Pos. He turned to Racqel. "I'll say it again, madam, this is no place for you."

"Believe me, sir, I am, I was, my father's apprentice. Had he lived, I would be a physician beside him today."

Tonneman grinned at Pos's discomfort. Tonneman had by this

time quite gotten used to the strange widow. No, not widow. Not yet. Not until proven. He would have to do something about that. But at least now he could be sure she would not be marrying one of her own people. "What thought?" he said to Pos.

Pos probed delicately with his knife at what was left of the man's face. "Aha."

"What?"

In answer Pos pointed with the tip of his knife at the body's singed hairline. "This poor bastard was scalped. Excuse me, madam."

"Before or after he died?" asked Racqel.

Pos looked surprised. "I don't know."

"So," Tonneman said. "An Indian did this. Or someone would have us believe it was an Indian." He gave the head a light push with his board and it rolled, still connected to the body, but barely, exposing the back of an unburnt and gory head, grisly proof that Pos was correct about the scalping. A thin piece of metal wire lay bent on the earth where the butchered head had been.

Tonneman picked up the metal wire, holding it between thumb and forefinger. As bent and twisted as the object was, it required no great feat of thought to realize that it had once been a pair of spectacles. A jagged piece of glass was still attached to one of the octagonal-shaped eyeholes. Tonneman's suspicion was now confirmed. This body was the same body he had discovered last night on the river edge, but for a few significant differences, aside from the toasting. That man had not been scalped, his sword had not been in its scabbard, and Tonneman's knife had not been stuck in his chest.

"What do you have there?" Pos asked, looking at the curious object in Tonneman's hand.

Tonneman handed it to Pos over the body.

"Spectacles, I would think," said Pos, handing them back. "Of course. The man you were ask—"

Tonneman shook his head slightly. Pos stopped.

Racqel noticed the interplay but did not comment. She had an observation of her own to make. "See the ground where the poor man's head lay?"

Both men looked first to her, then to where she pointed.

"Scarcely any blood at all," she said in her triumphant way, which Tonneman now recognized. "And there was scarcely any blood on that knife, which proves he was killed, or at least scalped, someplace else. I would even say that that knife did not kill him."

"Maybe," said Pos grudgingly. The captain stared at Tonneman, waiting for an explanation of what the Schout's whalebone knife was doing in the dead man.

But Tonneman kept his own counsel. He placed his hand on Racqel's arm, moving her out of the shed with some purpose, and pitched his voice low enough for Pos not to hear. "Did your husband wear spectacles?"

In the bright sunlight she stopped and faced him. "This man is not my husband."

"I don't think so either, but how can you be so sure?"

She answered without hesitation. "My husband was taller and broader in the shoulder. And while most of this man's hair is gone, one way or another, what little that is left is light. My husband had black hair and dark skin, like mine, like all the Sephardim. This man's skin was light . . . his hands . . ." She paused. "One of our men can examine—"

"That won't be necessary. Stay here, please. Don't come in the shed." He added, "I must have your word."

She noted the stubborn set of his jaw and accepted her defeat. "You have my word."

He returned to the shed where Pos and the body waited. Now that he looked carefully he saw that the body was clad in the powdery remnants of the costly blue breeches, further confirming that this was the man of the night before. Quickly, Tonneman knelt, drew the whalebone knife, and cut the blue breeches away. The dead man was not circumcised. He was not a Jew. Tonneman covered the man and got to his feet. "I'll have to let the Boss know. As of now, besides being Captain of the Watch, you're my deputy, Pos, until I find out who did this. The clink of a few more guilders in your purse ought to bring a smile to your ugly face."

Pos beamed, then tugged at his beard. "Who is he and what in Christ's name was your knife doing in his chest?"

"Those are only two of the questions we need to ask. Why the body was burned is another."

"Simple. To hide the man's identity."

"I agree. But who was he? A thief who fell out with his comrades? An English spy? Why was his body burned in the Jews' shed? Any place would have done as well."

"Maybe someone doesn't like the Mendozas? Someone who did business with them?"

"Or was it done to make trouble for all the Jews?"

"Or," said the captain, "the Jews are involved."

Tonneman suddenly remembered what he'd overheard on the river's edge before this man died. *You sold it to the Jew?* the voice had said. Which Jew? The Jews could very well be involved. He shrugged.

"What do we do now?" Pos asked.

"I go to the Fort to tell the Boss. You go see Jan Keyser. Have him get this lump out of here before the rot sets in and stinks us out all the way to New Haarlem." He kicked at a burnt beam and inspected the cindered earth beneath it. "Tell him to wrap it in canvas and deliver it to the cemetery. But stop first to tell Frederick Philipse I want a cheap coffin at the cemetery and to put it on the City's score. I'll tell Megapolensis and have him do the burying. After you see Keyser, ask around in the taverns if anyone's seen Cutnose. Let everyone know I want to talk to that Indian. And take that fancy sword and scabbard. Ask if anyone recognizes the sword, or if they've noticed a man with octagonal glasses wearing it."

A devilish gleam came into Pos's eye. "And your knife?"

Tonneman didn't answer. He went out into the sunshine. Pos followed. Racqel was waiting where Tonneman had left her. He reclaimed his cudgel. "The dead man is not a Jew."

In spite of herself, Racqel blushed.

Tonneman approved of the blush. He liked a woman to be strong, but he also liked a women to have a woman's feelings. "When did you last see your husband?"

Her face showed concern, shame, a moment of fear. She glanced at Pos, who discreetly walked toward the road. "He had business with a man just across the river in Breukelen."

"What man? What day? What month?" Tonneman was suddenly impatient with her. It seemed as if she was holding back, while he was overly determined to prove the husband dead. He was hot and angry. Someone was making a fool of him with his knife in the dead man. And that, by Jesus, he could not allow.

All these years with no murders. And now, only a month after Smitt's death in July, another.

If Antje was right and Smitt had not died by his own hand, then Tonneman had not only failed his friend, but he'd failed in his job as Schout.

He would not fail again.

Tonneman turned his anger on the woman. "Speak."

Her dark eyes flared at him. "It was last December. A cold snowy night. The man Benjamin was going to see is Abner Simon, the Ashkenazi."

"The what?" He was listening with only half his mind because there was something she wasn't telling him, and he was trying to hear what she wasn't saying.

"A Jew, but not one of us, not of the Sephardim. He's from Saxony, I think, a German."

Abruptly Tonneman lifted his hat to her and walked to the road to join Pos, who stood waiting. He was puzzled. What was it she'd said that bothered him? Silently he repeated her words. December. Cold. Snowy. Night, she had said. A man had left a beautiful wife and a warm house on a cold winter night? For what reason? The whole story stank worse than that body in the shed would in a few more hours.

17

TUESDAY, 26 AUGUST. *Early Afternoon.*
Cudgel in hand, Tonneman stood at the junction of Jews Alley and Twiller's Road, sweating as Pos headed to the other end of town. His rage over the contemptuous misuse of his knife gnawed at him.

Before he went any further, however, Tonneman wanted to have a good look at that piece of metal. He took it and Racqel's magnifying glass from his jacket pocket and placed the metal object under the glass. It was a piece of tarnished silver no bigger than a florin. On one side there was nothing; on the other was engraved the rearing figure of a lion.

Tonneman had seen that lion before, recently. But where? He returned the silver disk and the glass to his pocket, nodding his head even though he knew no more than he had known before.

Sending Pos to see the tanner Keyser had reminded Tonneman of John Woods, the man Keyser threatened to stab earlier in the day. Tonneman took off his hat, mopped his brow with his sleeve, and decided he could delay seeing the Boss while he had a little talk with Woods. Woods's mill was only a short way farther along on Mill Street.

In a town as small as New Amsterdam it would be best to talk with everyone. Someone had to know who Spectacles was. Perhaps Spectacles would lead to answers about Hendrik's death. Tonneman knew he had to do it right away, for he'd found that people involved in everyday life tended to forget quickly, or the reverse—to enlarge upon the ordinary.

Another, and more important reason for him not to take too long was that it wouldn't do for P.S. to hear gossip about the dead body before his own Schout told him.

The Englishman Woods's establishment, known as the Old Mill, was actually two mills side by side under one roof, one for grain, the other for bark, with a solid wall in between to keep the dust of one from mixing with the dust of the other. The wall didn't always help. On certain days the bread made from John Woods's flour had the slight flavor of wood. "And now you know why they call it Woods's flour," the local wags liked to say.

The building on Mill Lane was a two-story structure, with two big batten doors like a barn. Above was the loft, where back in '26, the first church services had been held. It wasn't until '42 that the present church in the Fort was established.

Under the loft two horses, a large bay gelding for the grain and a large black gelding for the bark, usually walked in separate circles, each moving a huge millstone that ground against another millstone and crushed grain or bark.

The mill doors were open wide. Woods was out front, smoking his pipe, keeping a watch on his apprentice. An enormous, spotted cat sat nearby, lazily cleaning her paws. The ground beneath them was paved with discarded millstones. Contrary to Jan Keyser's accusation, the grain mill was idle. The horses now took turns sharing the bark work. An apprentice was busy putting coarse bark in and taking fine bark out. The bay, whose turn it was, worked by himself. He knew what to do and he did it without supervision.

Fine dust flew continuously. The pure sweet voice of the apprentice, singing a hymn in praise of Jesus to keep himself company, rose and fell over the steady groan and clamor of the mill.

"What news of the English?" asked Woods.

You tell me, Tonneman thought, allowing Keyser's accusation to prejudice him. Out loud he said, in English, "Nothing. I'm on my way to see P.S. now." Tonneman, who had first picked up some English as a sailor, was always seeking to sharpen his skill by talking to English settlers in New Amsterdam.

"Please," said the usually mild Woods, loudly and forcefully in Dutch, "not in English. Not these days."

"Makes nothing," Tonneman said, lapsing back to Dutch. "Maybe the Boss will have more to say about your people."

The miller glared at Tonneman. "Do you doubt my loyalty? Does the Director-General?" The miller's bare pate was russet and densely freckled from constant exposure to the sun.

"Don't be foolish, Woods. We're all in this boat together. About the fire last night—"

"Yes?" Woods asked, hostile and full of suspicion.

"Did you notice or hear anything?"

"No. After I calmed my horses, I went over to help with the buckets. Didn't you see me?"

Tonneman hadn't, but he let it pass. 'We found a body in the Mendoza shed. A stranger from the look of him, but I can't be sure. Do you know where all your people are?"

Woods gestured with his pipe. "My wife, two boys, my little girl, the apprentice. They're all here, all safe, thank you."

"Have you seen a stranger around? Fancy type. Pretty clothes. Pretty sword. Might be French."

"That ilk are usually down at the docks, mostly on the North River, Staple Street. I don't bother with them, they don't bother with me."

"Much obliged." Tonneman, preparing to take his leave, turned back. "Oh, by the way. You know the Indian Cutnose?"

"Yes. I've seen him in the Pear Tree."

"Have you seen him today?"

"No."

A cart drawn by a pretty white mare came toward them down the lane. The driver was a small, gnarled black woman dressed as Dutch women dressed in brown duffel and a white cap. Next to her beneath a dark red silk parasol sat Madame Geertruyd De Sille, her pug dog in her lap. The elaborate European dress she wore was the same vivid color as her parasol and showed much more bosom than the dresses worn by the other women in New Amsterdam.

Tonneman grunted, irritated. Nobody ever paid attention to the law against riding vehicles in town, and he was getting tired of trying to enforce it.

"This stupid terrible weather," Geertruyd De Sille said by way of greeting as the gnarled old woman reined in the horse. She had a high voice and spoke with a faint lisp, like a child.

Most of the people in New Amsterdam were content with brown or black clothing made of rough and inexpensive duffel cloth shipped in bulk from the Netherlands. No woman but Madame De Sille, or the whores, would dream of wearing the red she was wearing today. On her right cheek was a *mouche,* a black beauty patch. There was another on her right breast. At her side was a fan, also the same red. "So hot." She raised the fan to her face, peering over it as she fanned herself and the pug with small rapid movements.

Woods's cat stood, stretched, sniffed, and went into a defensive spitting arch; a high whine came from its open jaws. The ugly, silver and fawn pug yawned noisily, wriggled, and finally resettled in Madame De Sille's lap, making muttering noises as it slept. The ribbon around its neck matched its mistress's.

The white mare dropped a load, then pawed the ground. Flies and bees gathered around the steaming mound. The horse flicked its tail to chase away the insects and pranced in place, eyeing Tonneman. Like the pug, the African woman was dozing.

"Good day, Geertruyd," Tonneman said pleasantly. "You are well, I trust?"

She glowered at him, resenting his use of her first name. "How am I supposed to be? This weather. The English. This unspeakable place." She had a clear unblemished complexion, translucent skin marred only by patterns of blue veins running close to the surface. Her golden hair was tightly bound under her lace-covered red bonnet. Her hand was fretting over the dog, so much so that the animal opened its eyes and yipped at her. "I'm so sorry, lambkin," she lisped. The miller's cat went on alert again.

"What brings you this way?" asked Tonneman.

"Flour, of course. There isn't a speck to be had. Miller?"

"Naught here either," Woods said, eyeing Tonneman warily. He kicked at the hissing cat, who retreated into the mill house. "I've been all bought out, and there's no more grain to make more."

"La," she said, fanning, "I'm sure you could find just a little something for me."

"Please, you wouldn't want to get me in trouble with the Schout or the Director-General."

"Goodness sake, nay, but I had to ask."

Was the man contrabanding grain? Tonneman wondered. And had Geertruyd come here to buy the illegal goods? Ordinarily, he would be amused, but these last two days everything that happened seemed to be unbalanced. A climate of suspicion and fear was starting to creep onto the island. Was it worry about invasion, or had the village suddenly become more infested with sellers of contraband, spies, and murderers?

Woods scratched his freckled pate with the stem of his pipe and waited for someone to speak.

"What I really came for was bark," Geertruyd De Sille finally said. "I need it for garden mulch. My poor violets are simply swooning from this terrible drought." She turned to Tonneman and smiled.

"How much?" John Woods asked.

"Enough for my garden," Geertruyd De Sille answered impatiently, pulling nervously on the dog's neck ribbon.

"Frans," the miller called to the apprentice. "Two bags of chipped bark for Madame De Sille."

"And how is Nick?" Tonneman asked, referring to Nicasius De Sille, Geertruyd's husband.

In 1660, when the Burgomasters had finally persuaded Stuyvesant and the Amsterdam Chamber that the City government should be separate from the Company, Tonneman became the first City Schout, depriving De Sille of his post as the Company's Schout Fiscal.

"La, Nick." She lifted her fan higher and lowered her eyes, avoiding his.

"I haven't seen him lately." As he said the words Tonneman realized how strange they sounded. In New Amsterdam everyone saw everyone else almost daily.

"He's been busy."

"Tell him I was asking. Have you seen a stranger in town? French, maybe. Small man, all dressed up in blue, red, and gold satin. Lace and ribbons all over the place. Red velvet hat with a blue feather."

"No, but la, I would enjoy such a rare and pleasant sight."

The apprentice Frans loaded two canvas bags in the back of the cart, causing it to slip forward. The white horse snorted and tossed its head.

Madame De Sille closed her fan with a snap. "Put it on my score, miller. Annabella," she shrilled. The black woman awoke. "Home."

Without a word the African snapped the reins and turned the cart.

"Return the bags," Woods shouted after them. "She won't," he confided to Tonneman. "That kind never do. Rich people don't care about other people. Put it on her score. A paltry ten stuivers. Not to me, to her. More trouble than it's worth. I'll never see those bags again, or the ten stuivers. Frans," he yelled. "Where's my ledger?"

It would have served dear Geertruyd right, Tonneman thought, if he fined her for not walking the horse. A likely thing, Geertruyd De Sille walking the dusty roads like ordinary folk. The picture made him smile.

Why had she been so nervous? Had she come to see the miller about something other than bark mulch for her garden? What if it were not illicit flour she'd come for? Perhaps Keyser was right about Woods. Perhaps he was an English spy. And perhaps Geertruyd De Sille was one, too. Tonneman frowned. He had to control himself. This agitation in the air was starting to affect him. He was seeing English spies behind every bush and under every rock.

18

TUESDAY, 26 AUGUST. *Early Afternoon.*

Racqel's eyes followed Tonneman as he walked away from her. He did not look back and her heart sank. She found herself filled with an inexplicable sorrow. She had wanted to say to him, *Find my husband, quick or dead, and I will owe you my life once again.*

But she had not. She had been unable to speak the truth, that she and Benjamin had quarreled that night, about her being barren. He had called her a witch and accused her of mixing herbal potions to prevent herself from bearing a child.

Benjamin was wrong, of course. She had begun mixing her herbs only after she understood that there were to be no children unless she had help. She'd hoped the herbs would provide that help.

The arrival of the carpenter Frederick Philipse and his mixed crew of white men, free blacks, and slaves interrupted Racqel's disturbing memories. Philipse had brought a keg of beer. The men who'd come to rebuild the house had tapped it immediately and were drinking freely while they worked. Vexed, Racqel couldn't find a place for herself. She chafed over the decaying body in the shed, which was starting to give off a foul stink. There was no work for her to do until the house was done, and she didn't feel like visiting her neighbors to hear the endless terrifying stories about the English.

She felt uncomfortable with them, as if they blamed her for Benjamin's disappearance, or did she feel so much guilt that it was she who imagined blame and put it on herself? Whatever it was kept her from revealing her fears to the other women.

Racqel wandered from Jews Alley, taking an idle promenade, like a duchess, she thought, who had many servants to do for her. Bathsheba, her little collar bell ringing, kept throwing herself at Racqel's ankles while Caleb pawed at her feet and clung to her skirts, but her mind was elsewhere, and she ignored them.

She strolled slowly to Pearl Street, and then east, passing soldiers, some armed with halberds and some with wheel lock muskets. The sun blazed down on her, and she blotted the perspiration from her face with her linen handkerchief. The black cat followed her step for step, but Caleb ranged back and forth, inspecting the soldiers and lifting his leg on various fences, sniffing, barking, and looking back for her.

"It's late. Where are you going?" she had cried that night as Benjamin rushed down the stairs. She'd followed him in her night-dress, oblivious of the cold. Had David heard them arguing again?

Benjamin reached for his ancient belt, the heirloom of eldest sons that had been in his family for generations. The belt was made of many pieces of silver, each with the image of a lion on it. Unlike his father and brother, Benjamin was tall and slender. With his small, silky black beard, he looked like an ancient king of Judea or Israel.

"Where are you going?" she had repeated when he didn't an-swer. The old man, Abraham, had not even stirred in his bed.

Then he had done that horrible thing. He spat at her, as if she were dirt at his feet, and said, "As far away from you as possible, woman." He took his beaver hat and long blue coat from the hook near the door and rummaged for a moment in the deep pockets of the coat as if looking for something. Assured, he stepped out into the winter night. She never saw him again.

An involuntary moan escaped Racqel's lips. She wiped her eyes as the ruffling breezes of the waterfront cooled her. Negro slaves were unloading large barrels from a newly arrived ship. Beneath the ordi-nary, day-to-day work, the area had a mood of excitement, an air of expectation.

The river's pure blue green was cut by choppy little waves. Gray gulls cawed, swooping down on a bit of refuse or something alive, but not for long, in the water. Bathsheba's eyes twitched and shone. Her head tilted up and shifted back and forth as she watched the birds.

Where had Caleb gone? "Caleb!" Racqel passed City Hall and thought fleetingly of Tonneman. Down Coenties Alley she heard the animal's bark and the high laugh of a child and a woman's scolding voice. She went into the alley that led to the rear of a house on the river.

The backdoor opened and Caleb tumbled out in a black-and-white flurry, followed by a sturdy boy of eight or nine, with a shock of yellow hair. Behind the boy, a large, ruddy-faced, enormously pregnant woman of at least thirty years smiled and beckoned to Racqel. "Forgive my Conraet. He's full of mischief, I'm afraid."

"Caleb loves to play. He loves children."

"I am Antje Ten Eyck."

A garden grew at the far end of the yard; this side of it was a pile of white sand. In the center of the pile of sand rose a tall, beautifully molded sand castle. Caleb ran to the pile and lifted his leg on the castle.

"Oh," said the little boy.

"Oh," said Racqel, feeling flustered but wanting to giggle.

"Makes nothing," said the jolly woman, laughing. "A little piss never hurt anyone."

The boy covered the destroyed part of his castle with fresh sand. As he rebuilt it Racqel spoke to him. "That's very good."

"Yes," he said. "When I grow up, I'm going to be a silversmith like my father."

"And are you studying your letters, too?"

"Yes, at the Collegiate School with Heer Wouter Groenveld."

"Conraet has a good eye and good hands," Racqel said to Antje wistfully.

Antje Ten Eyck was in the midst of folding linen and putting it in a basket that sat awkwardly on a white wooden bench. More linen flapped on the yard fence. "I'm going to have a mug of beer. Will you have some?"

The boy was now running in circles around his mother, Caleb chasing him, barking. The women watched, smiling. Bathsheba was slithering behind Racqel along her legs, stalking something. "I'm Racqel Mendoza. Thank you, but I must return to see how the carpenters are building our home."

"Oh, yes, of course." Antje Ten Eyck went into the house but continued talking. "I'm sorry about the fire. Tonneman spoke of you." She reappeared with a glass of beer, pushed the basket aside, carefully eased her thick body down, and drank. "Ah, that's good. And now we have the English on our doorsteps." She smiled.

Racqel smiled back. She did not quite understand this amiable woman, except it was obvious she was a friend of Tonneman's.

"Are you sure about the beer?"

"Yes, thank you."

Antje studied Racqel, openly curious. So this was the woman Tonneman had asked about. She saw a tall, dark, too slim woman dressed in ill-fitting clothes, whose black hair was hidden under a cap more delicate than the one Antje wore. Her black eyes returned Antje's frank gaze.

There was nothing about Racqel Mendoza that spoke of Maria, but Antje Ten Eyck understood Tonneman's interest in the woman. Being an Israelite, she was different, even mysterious. A woman like that could make a man feel young again. Antje wanted to talk to Racqel about Tonneman, but she barely knew the woman, and perhaps it was not yet the time. Instead, she called to the boy who had gone outside the yard and was running along the waterfront, dodging the cargo handlers. Caleb was close at his heels, barking excitedly. "Come Conraet, you little imp. We must let Vrouw Mendoza take her dog and go home now." The boy came hurrying back, the dog close behind.

Racqel gathered Caleb to her. He licked her face. Suddenly, for some unknown reason, she felt very happy. "Thank you," she said to Antje.

"Whatever for?" Antje Ten Eyck asked as she gave her son a sip of her beer.

A snarl of victory and Bathsheba pounced. She had caught her mouse.

19

TUESDAY, 26 AUGUST. *Early Afternoon.*
The atmosphere at the Fort was tense. A sergeant barked orders; several squads of soldiers in blue uniforms and burnished helmets and breastplates practiced loading, aiming, and dry-firing their wheel lock muskets.

The extreme shortage of gunpowder allowed for no real firing, which was unfortunate since many had rarely fired a musket and had no real idea what sort of recoil the weapon had. Watching them, Tonneman smiled but his eyes were grave. Several of the men were even using matchlocks, and those weapons were so old and rusty they could easily explode and kill the musketeers firing them.

Another squad was at ease, accepting water from two boys who wore scraps of uniforms—a hat on one, vests that hung to the knees. The walls of the Fort had been hastily and poorly repaired, and the animals that usually wandered freely had been banished; still the Fort had a bleak, spare look rather than one of readiness.

Call this an army, Tonneman thought. And, the New Amsterdamers were tradesmen, craftsmen, workers, not soldiers.

In a short time he was repeating his thoughts to the Director-General. Stuyvesant, behind his desk, his right leg stretched out as he scratched just below the knee, where the oak limb was attached, agreed. "But they'll do. They have to. There's no help for it. Our people in Jonkheer's Land and elsewhere have as good as turned their backs on us." He was dressed for combat, breast armor and all, and was sweating profusely in the August heat.

"What did you expect?" The clang of the blacksmith's hammer on his anvil came through the open window.

"You too? You're like everyone else, Tonneman. Full of defeat before the first battle is even fought."

"The first battle will be the last battle."

"God have mercy on us, then. We live in a selfish time. Every man for himself, eh? That English devil Nicolls will be here any day now." He picked up the dagger that was lying among his papers and held it before him like a crusader's sword, a cross. "We must all be ready. I am. For the Company, for the Fatherland. But is anyone but Petrus Stuyvesant thinking of the community? Nay. Just self."

"You can't blame them. They all have families to consider."

"The Company is our family first. I know what they want to hear, the craven *mobile vulgus*. If I say what they want to hear, that we will surrender to the English without a fight, they would crown me with laurel and carry me on their shoulders. But I have a duty to do and not everyone is going to like me for it."

"Boss." Tonneman seized the moment. "I hate to give you this news, but as you speak of your duty, I have my duty. . . ."

"Get on with it." Stuyvesant pushed back his chair, stood up, and began pacing the chamber, the dull thump of his peg leg alternating with the shuffle of his boot on his good left foot. "Can't you handle it?" he bellowed. "I have too much on my mind now."

Tonneman heaved himself out of his chair. He was in a mood to take his cudgel and smash it over the Director-General's head. "I can handle it, but you should know about it. I found a dead man in the shed behind the Mendoza house. It looks like murder. A Frenchy most likely, by his clothes."

The Director-General stopped pacing. "Where did he come from?"

"I don't know."

"All these years nothing like this. Now two in two months. Last month that friend of yours Smitt hanging himself, now this."

"I am no longer so certain that Hendrik killed himself. . . ."

"Bah."

"I believe he was far too drunk to manage it."

"You stand there and tell me we've had two killings in my city, under my guardianship? And no one has been punished? This is your trust, Tonneman. And one that you have failed. You have failed me and the Company."

Tonneman glared at Stuyvesant and slammed his cudgel on the floor.

The Director-General glared back; neither man wavered. Then Stuyvesant said, "It must have something to do with the Hebrews. One of their unholy business dealings. This dead man of yours did not spring whole out of Zeus's head."

"He's probably from one of the ships. There's no chance I have of finding out which if they don't want to tell me. As for Hendrik, his murderer has been living among us."

Stuyvesant began pacing again, punctuating his comments with angry gestures. "*If* he was murdered. And that remains to be seen. I can't be bothered with him or the death of some Frenchy. I've got the damned English to worry about."

What, Tonneman wondered but didn't say, if the Frenchy was working for the damned English? And what if, somehow, Hendrik had seen or overheard something while serving drinks at the Pear Tree? Men always spoke freely with a belly full of beer. "It's a heavy burden, sir."

Once more Stuyvesant glared at Tonneman, this time studying the man to see if he was mocking him. The Director-General planted himself in front his Schout. "I don't need this new muddle you've gotten us into. You handle it. I've got enough on my plate. Sooner or later the English will be blockading the port, and then where will we be? What will we do for supplies? Leave it to those cursed Israelites to make trouble at a time like this. I—"

An urgent knock at the door interrupted his tirade.

"What?" Stuyvesant roared.

"A messenger from Colonel van de Steen," Willem Avercamp, the Director-General's clerk, called through the door.

"Send him in." Stuyvesant smoothed his white collar and wiped the sweat from his face with a linen nosecloth. He returned to his desk and sat down.

A soldier knocked, entered, and saluted. In his left hand was a fold of paper.

Stuyvesant returned the salute impatiently and put out his hand. "Give it here, son, it won't fly to me." He cut the red wax seal with his dagger and read the message quickly. A look of triumph spread over his face. This time he held the dagger as it was meant to be held, point out. "Have at you now, you English swine. We're ready for you." Then he turned to his Schout, eyes gleaming. "God is truly with us, my boy. We have not been forgotten by the Company. Colonel van de Steen informs us that a shipment of black powder arrived this morning on the *Gustav*. Our soldiers are unloading it now." He dis-

missed the messenger with an imperious wave. "Let the English do
their worst."

"Outstanding news, Boss." Tonneman was aching to move on.
"I've made Pos my deputy."

"When will he sleep?"

"He doesn't need a great deal."

"All right, he's your deputy. *You* pay him."

"No, I will not . . . sir."

"You're like all the rest. You worship money. Ye cannot serve
God and Mammon."

"He's a good man."

"All right, but only for the duration of this emergency. He will
not be allowed to slack on his night patrol, and I'd better not catch
him lying abed, sleeping. Fourteen stuivers a day."

"Counting Sunday?"

"No. No work on Sunday, no pay on Sunday. Three guilders a
week. That's final."

"Four."

"Three and a half. You take care of this carcass problem. Get it
settled before we have the English on our necks. You're the third-
ranking officer in New Amsterdam, Tonneman. Act it." The Director-
General was shouting with so much force his face was red and a thick
vein in his forehead was pulsing. "Now get out."

"Yes, sir, Boss," Tonneman shouted back, but he was smiling.

20

TUESDAY, 26 AUGUST. *Early Afternoon.*
Before leaving the Fort, Tonneman stopped in at the Stone Church to
tell Johannes Megapolensis about the dead man. The minister looked
harried, but said that he would tell his sexton Kruseman Wolters to
see that the unknown man had a decent Christian burial.

Tonneman paused in front of the church to mop the sweat from
his face. The day was stifling and this was the first chance he'd had to
catch his breath. The words of the night before came back to him.
First: *You sold it to the Jew.* Then: *It's mine and I want it back.* And

finally from the dead man: *Pape.* The first two were simply if not readily explainable. But what about the last one? Pape? Papist? Was Spectacles a Catholic, then? Well, they would be giving him a solid Dutch Protestant burial.

He had a smile on his face when Dirk Baalde, the blacksmith, called out to him. Tonneman walked the few steps from the church to the forge. The smith was a red-haired man with arms and legs like tree trunks. His beard shone greasy in the hot sun as he shod a sorrel stallion.

The spirited animal tossed its head back and forth as a honeybee flitted about its face. The blacksmith shook his hammer at the horse. When that didn't work, he twisted the animal's foot. The stallion gave a sharp neigh, then quieted.

"One day, Baalde, I think I'll twist your foot like that."

"Always the jester, eh, Tonneman?"

"Don't be so sure."

The smith went on with his shoeing. "I hear we've had a shipment of gunpowder."

"News travels fast."

Baalde's laugh was a roar. "It'll be over before it starts," the smith said, looking around and lowering his voice so that only Tonneman could hear.

Now, what did that mean? Tonneman asked himself as he left the Fort and walked east on the Broad Way.

To his left was the cemetery. It wasn't a ritual, but today he felt like going in. He went through the roofed lich gate.

The sun was hot and pure on the neat, well-kept plots. All the stones were erect. He liked that; there was a sense of order to it.

When Tonneman knelt at Maria's marker, he didn't pray and he didn't talk to her. He merely ran his right hand over the smooth warm stone and thought about what was past. After a few moments he rose and ran his hand over the five stones of his son and daughters. He thought about visiting Hendrik Smitt's grave but he couldn't bring himself to it. He owed Hendrik a great debt for not listening to him. "I swear, old friend," he said aloud, "I will repay that debt by finding your murderer."

Past the cemetery was the De Sille estate, surrounded by fruit trees. The air along this part of the Broad Way was saturated with the sweet perfume of ripe peaches. When he had built his house on that piece of land, Nick De Sille had had great plans for the future: in this New World he would become rich. It had happened just as he'd planned.

It could have been me, Tonneman thought ruefully.

Though the Broad Way was the widest street in New Amsterdam, it was always crowded, people riding and walking in every direction, all going somewhere, doing business, shopping or trading. So many, you'd think all fifteen hundred citizens and the soldiers and the Africans and the Indians and the traders and sailors from the ships were all here at once, talking at the top of their voices. Not only people. On the road there were the horses, cows, and goats. Cats, dogs, and pigs moved freely, underfoot everywhere.

"Good day, Heer Schout," townspeople called as they passed, and Tonneman tipped his hat to them absently.

He could have chosen another life, other than with the Company, become a trader perhaps. There were opportunities in this New World. And he had never taken advantage of them.

Beyond the De Sille property and over the unfinished new wall, Tonneman could see across the North River. The land there was hilly and green. The same was true further north on both sides of the river: hills and deep ravines, and forests, especially oak, from which the Company was making a great deal of money. Some smart independent traders were also getting wealthy on lumber.

"Again?" he rebuked himself as he caught himself once again thinking about money and his lack of it. He liked a florin as much as the next man, but he knew he wasn't born to be rich. What did all that wealth buy? Possessions. But all the money in the world wouldn't bring Maria back.

Tonneman ran his tongue around the inside of his mouth and spat. The early-morning rain not withstanding, the road was dry and dusty, as was common in the summer; the rest of the year it was muddy. His throat was parched and he had a yearning for beer and a taste for salt cod. Then another beer, and a pipe. The Jew Asser Levy served a nice piece of salt cod in his tavern over on the Wall.

"Ho, Tonneman."

"Good afternoon to you, Tall Matthew. Have you seen Cut-nose?"

"No, sir."

The dust rose in the air, choking everyone around as a drove of some twenty hogs approached from the east. People cursed and got out of the way. The dust swirled into Tonneman's nose and lungs as the hogs passed by. Peering through the dust cloud, he saw Philip van Etting almost even with him on an aging dapple-gray gelding. "Pull up, you flea-bitten arsehole," Tonneman shouted through his coughing and the squealing hogs.

"Skooee," the rider called. He was a fat man with pink skin stretched tight as a sausage. The hogs milled about, oinking, grunting, and digging up the road with their snouts as van Etting reined in his horse and rode around them, herding the animals in a tight circle. He pulled a large red nosecloth from his sleeve and blew his florid snout, then waved at the air with the soiled cloth to dispel the dust. "What's the problem?" he asked, pursing his pink lips. "Have the English landed?"

By God, Tonneman thought, the man was looking more like his hogs every day. "I'm tired of your porkers running loose shitting up the roads."

"I'm not the only one who keeps hogs."

"I counted more than five this morning nigh Twiller's Road. Pen those swine up or I'll fine you."

Van Etting shoved his nosecloth into his sleeve and jerked at the reins. The gelding reeled toward Tonneman. "Good day to you, Schout."

"Hold that nag, you blockhead." Tonneman stepped out of the way. "What the hell are you doing, driving pigs on horseback?"

"It's too hot and I'm too fat to go afoot." As he spoke the gelding bumped into Tonneman a second time.

"That's the last straw. I'm fining you right now. A guilder for each loose hog I saw this morning. Five florins. Pay up."

"Five florins?" Van Etting's little eyes disappeared into his puffy cheeks. No longer pretending deference to Tonneman's authority, he pulled off his hat and shook it at the Schout. The gelding shifted uneasily under his weight. "You can't do that," he shouted over hog squealing.

"Make that *two* guilders a hog, and if they're still there on my way back, it will be three. They're a hazard to everyone and you've been warned."

Van Etting looked this way and that. "There's a hog running loose, and there's another, and they're not mine. They're black. I don't have black hogs. I don't see you fining anyone else. I won't pay. I'll appeal to the Council. Skooee," he yelled, clamping his hat on his head and kneeing the gelding. The alarmed animal stumbled headlong into the hogs, who scattered and ran squealing down the Broad Way, creating another enormous cloud of dust as they continued their trek south.

"And get some rings in their noses!" Tonneman called after van Etting. When the dust settled, Tonneman smiled, pleased that he'd had a small revenge. The fat booby had been fit to be tied. Tonneman brought his attention back to Tall Matthew in order to ask the African if he'd come across the man wearing the octagonal spectacles. But Tall Matthew was nowhere to be seen.

"Good afternoon, Schout." The greeting came from the little schoolmaster, Wouter Groenveld.

"No school today, teacher?" he asked the badger-legged man.

"Finished for the day." Groenveld's teeth hung over his lips when he spoke. He patted his clean-shaven cheek with a delicate hand. "Hot, isn't it?"

"It'll do. Have you seen Cutnose?"

"Who?"

"The Indian . . ." There was a blank stare in Groenveld's eyes. "Thank you," said Tonneman as the teacher moved away, dragging his longer right leg. The Schout shook his head, pondering how a man could live in their small world and not know every man or, at the very least, not be aware of the dangerous ones.

Tonneman wove in and out of the sweating, jostling people, bawling children, and squalling animals, first near the shops, then to make more progress, along the wide dirt road. Then, because it was to talk to people that he was making this tour, he pushed back to the walk, going past houses and into warehouses and shops: the boatwright and the sail maker above in the loft, and the goathouse and other shops and food stalls and taverns and taprooms, each spewing out its own particular stink.

There were more drinking houses than anything else in this town. He stopped into all of them on the Broad Way to ask if anyone knew of the dead man with the octagonal glasses or had seen Cutnose. It was hard to refuse the offer of a beer at each one, but after the second tankard he did. He would take some ease at Asser Levy's place.

He waved a buzzing bee away from his face and admired a pretty yellow-and-brown butterfly as it darted and skimmed in the air. Among the bad odors he caught an occasional fragrant whiff of sage that came from the gardens behind most of these structures.

All had fruit trees, bearing peaches, pears, apples in season. Some planted carrots and beets and other such vegetables; some grew herbs like sage to purify the household of bad odors, and many others, for food seasoning or medicine. Almost everyone planted flowers to be reminded of home. Most planted grain to make spirits or beer.

Maria had had such a garden, and his daughter, Anna, had left it in good repair, but he had given no thought to it. Like "dear Geertruyd," others were mulching their gardens with bark to retain what little water the earth still had and to keep roots as cool as possible.

Unless there would be heavy rains—and with the bright sun and clear sky it didn't seem likely—he would have to do the same. If he ever found the time.

Plenty of gardens, he thought, but not many real farms, and with so few farmers here there was a chronic lack of milk, cheese, and eggs. The citizens of New Amsterdam had to depend on farmers from across the North River or Long Island. Most of whom were English. Considering the Boss's news, the town was in for a lot of trouble.

Theirs was a trading economy: New Amsterdam sent furs and lumber to Europe and received in return shoes, stockings, canvas, linen, traces, lines, halters, chinaware, furniture, and home food.

This part of New Amsterdam was bustling with activity. The entire town was noisy, smoky, hard drinking, brawling, rude, disorderly, insolent, and crowded, everyone yelling and pushing and shoving, vying for attention, trying to buy or sell something. Were they concerned about the English? It didn't seem so. New Amsterdam was becoming a very important mercantile center.

He'd heard some of the officers from off the sailing ships who'd been everywhere say it was the most sophisticated town in the New World.

"Yes, of course," Tonneman said as he stepped over a dead dog, scattering the flies that buzzed around it. There was always litter of all sorts on the Broad Way, dead animals, dead birds, especially pigeons, garbage, ashes. That and dog shit and horse shit and pig shit and cow shit and goat shit and the human shit from the privies and the sun beating down was enough to make a grown man cry. But usually Tonneman barely noticed the stench. He loved the energy and the confident hopefulness. He loved New Amsterdam. For all its dirt and tumult, it was his home.

Though lately he had caught himself thinking how nice it would be to live in the country. Make a new life for himself somewhere. The face of the dark-eyed Jewess came to his mind. Maybe the best thing for him to do was just to keep walking up this road and over the small stone bridge spanning the stream that crossed the Broad Way not too far from here, circle round the Boss's farm, and walk until he got to New Haarlem. Then he could spend the rest of his days with his daughter and her family, drinking beer, smoking his pipe, and bouncing grandchildren on his knee.

"Do you want the entire walk for yourself?"

The words were perfect scholar's Dutch, the voice that of an orator. The speaker was a large man of close to fifty years, with a huge overhanging beer gorbelly and enormous drooping jowls. Everything about him seemed obscenely swollen. Lubbertus van Dincklagen, the only lawyer in New Amsterdam, and one time Vice-Director-General under Stuyvesant, was an old comrade of Tonneman's. They'd been schoolmates at Leiden University in '37.

The next year the bottom had dropped out of the tulip market, and Tonneman's father, a speculator, had lost all his money. Tonneman, barely sixteen, had been forced to leave school and go to sea.

"How have you been, Dinck?"

"Not well. This heat vexes me. And there's the dropsy, you know." His jowls wobbled when he spoke. "It's a hard life."

"I know. Still getting free medicine from the Company?"

"One does what one can."

"You've done all right."

"I try," Dinck said modestly. "I don't see enough of you since Maria died. Come to my house tonight. I have a fresh shipment of Leiden cheese. That and some beer would sit nicely, wouldn't it? We can talk about our schooldays, when we were young and . . . slender." He gestured at his bloated body. Under his arm he carried a coil of pork sausage. A passing dog snapped at it. Dinck whipped at the mangy gray animal with the sausage, sending the dog scurrying off howling, and held the meat higher out of harm's way.

"A tempting invitation, Dinck, but what with the English and all . . ."

"Pish the English, but I understand. It must be quite a trial working for our great Muscovy Duke at a time like this. You're welcome anytime. Why don't I send around a wheel of cheese to your house? Do you prefer caraway or cinnamon?"

"Caraway would be fine, but it's not necessary."

"Consider it done. Don't let that odious old wolf Stuyvesant bite you and don't be a stranger." He kicked away a large brown dog that was now after the sausage. "By God, it's hot. I think I'll go home, get a bucket of water, and pour it over my head."

Tonneman laughed. "You do that. By the way, Dinck, speaking of strangers, we've got a dead man on our hands. He died in the fire last night and was so badly burned it's hard to say what he looked like, but by his dress he might have been an aristocrat or a rich merchant, French maybe. He wore octagonal spectacles. Does that mean anything to you?" The crowd pressed in, jostling them.

"I'm afraid not."

"Do you know the Indian Cutnose?"

"I'm afraid yes. That's a bad Indian."

"Have you seen him?"

"No, not recently." Van Dincklagen blinked watery eyes under his tall hat.

"Well, if something comes to mind . . ."

"Say no more. Is there any other way I can be of service?"

"Yes, did you know the Jew Benjamin Mendoza?"

"Jew? Are there Jews in New Amsterdam?" Dinck laughed heartily. "I thought the Archangel Stuyvesant kept out all but the Lord's favorites."

Despite Stuyvesant's feelings that Calvinism was the only true way to salvation, the Fatherland had steadfastly maintained a policy of religious freedom in the Netherlands and in the New World. New Amsterdam was home to more than a few Catholics, Mennonites, and Lutherans, not to mention the odd Quaker and the two dozen or more Jews.

And despite Stuyvesant's religious fervor, very few Calvinists were the churchgoing kind. "I understand that God's messenger on earth has proposed that wheat will be used only for the host, and if you want bread, you'll have to go to church for it."

"Dinck, please. What about Benjamin Mendoza?"

"Yes. Honest man, good trader. Crafty but not greedy. You said, *did* I know? Has anything happened to him?"

"I'm not certain. No one's seen Mendoza since December."

"Can't help you on that either, but I'll keep my ears up and ask about." He smiled broadly. "The cheese will be at your house tonight." Dinck turned his large body and moved away with painful steps. In moments he was swallowed up by the crowd. The talk of food and drink had worked its influence on Tonneman's belly, which groused loudly as he continued on his way. He stepped inside Lichtman's bakeshop and bought a stuiver roll. "Why so small?" he demanded.

"Ask your friend the Director-General," Jan Lichtman answered, pointing to his meager selection on the wooden rack beside the oven.

Tonneman bit into the roll. "Tastes different."

"There's no wheat. I made it from Indian meal. I'm getting too old for this sort of foolishness. If things get any worse than they are, I'll have to move from this place. What do you think? Is the maize ground fine enough?"

Tonneman shrugged and left, the rest of the Indian corn roll in his mouth. This wasn't up to Lichtman's usual, but what could he do without wheat? Even so, Maria was a better baker. In the morning she would serve him warm rolls and beer. . . . He shook the thought away and chewed voraciously; the bread had helped to stem his hunger, but he still had that taste for fish and beer.

Three soldiers staggered past him, talking and laughing. Two were swilling beer from tankards. When they saw Tonneman, they straightened up and tried to walk in a more military fashion. Tonneman thought about seizing the bastards, washing the dry Indianmeal roll down with their beer, and turning them over to their colonel, but what good would that do? The colonel wouldn't put them in that scummy jail of his, not with the damned English breathing down their necks.

All around he could hear complaints about the high cost of everything. One man's voice rose above the others. "High prices will get us before the English do."

Tonneman turned to see who had spoken and noticed the Indian, Man Who Walks Like a Fox, coming toward him. The whites had shortened the Indian's name to Foxman. Foxman was a shrewd, mean Mohawk Iroquois, a cannibal. It was hard to say how old the man was. All Tonneman knew was that the Foxman had been there when he'd arrived, twenty years before, and he had looked the same age then as he did now.

The Dutch traders used the Iroquois as middlemen to deal with the Algonquins. Iroquois bought furs from the Algonquins for produce or wampum and sold them to the New Amsterdamers for guns. Man Who Walks Like a Fox was one of the best of these middlemen. But for the moccasins on his feet, he dressed like a white man in town, wearing duffel breeches and a cotton shirt. At his waist hung a European-made iron tomahawk, with an ax at one end and a pipe at the other.

His bare head was shaved smooth as an egg, except for a scalp lock at the top; there was no center strip in the manner Cutnose wore. His dark eyes, which turned up at the corners, never showed what the Indian was thinking. Tonneman respected the man as a formidable enemy, neither liking nor trusting him, but then, Tonneman didn't like or trust any red man, no matter how friendly.

The Schout had never been able to prove it, but he was certain Foxman controlled the counterfeit wampum that came in from Long Island and Johnnyland up north.

Cutnose was just a farmer-hunter with dreams of warrior greatness. Where Cutnose was a pretend warrior, Man Who Walks Like a Fox was the real thing. Which made them both mean Indians, but in different ways.

"Foxman."

"Tonneman." The Indian walked by, his straight lean body assured in white man's clothing.

"Have you seen anything of that rascal Cutnose?" Tonneman called after him.

There was no response from the Mohawk, who continued through the crowd, probably on his way to Staple Street and the waterfront, where the fur traders gathered.

"Hey, Indian," Tonneman called. "I'm talking to you."

Man Who Walks Like a Fox didn't stop. He made a loud noise in his throat, spat in the road, and kept walking.

2 1

TUESDAY, 26 AUGUST. *Early Afternoon.*

A thin woman, taller than Tonneman by half a hand, came sailing along the Broad Way from the direction Foxman had gone. Although only nine and a half stone at most, she'd been known to knock a healthy, sober man to the ground with one punch. Her free-flowing hair was hay yellow and unkempt. She was wearing a gold gown cut low over her bony bosom. Her long gaunt frame was like that of a man's in a dress; there was nothing alluring about it. On her feet, red boots. In her right hand she carried a gold mesh purse and from her right wrist hung a pink ostrich feather fan with an ivory handle; the other hand held a long gold boa, which dragged in the dirt.

As she came near, Tonneman smelled the familiar scent of rosewater. She drenched herself in the stuff. Her right cheek had one lone large smallpox mark, and her back, Tonneman knew, was flog marked. On her right arm was a scar where she had overburned a branding she'd been given for whoring.

If the bawd was here, her husband and protector, the Polish Jew fiddler Isadore Korbonski, would not be far behind. Neither would her congregation of traveling whores.

She peered down at him. "Ain't it Tonneman? I'm right charmed to see you again, Schout." Her voice was harsh and she spoke in short choppy phrases.

He knew the Englishwoman, not by her real name, only her nekename. "Good afternoon, Sweet Lips. I thought you were south."

"We were, but goddamn, I missed you, love."

"I should have known this talk of fighting would bring you here."

"Of course. Think of all those bloody needy men and boys who crave a frolic." She swung her spare hips and winked at a group of sailors who had appeared in her wake.

"Wherever the money is."

"Correct."

"No matter which. English or Dutch."

"Makes no difference. English or Dutch, when the poor sod pisses it's water, when he pays it's money. Of course, anything you want is free to you, love. That's me or any of my girls and drink, and maybe even a few florins could find their way into your purse."

The sailors had moved in. Like bees sniffing out honey. "You're beginning to annoy me, boys," Tonneman proclaimed. "Don't you have something better to do than cluster around here?" The sailors, reluctant to leave, mumbled, each in his own language, and backed off only a few steps. "Move along. *Heraus. Portare. Allez.*"

One eye still on the dispersing sailors, Tonneman said, "Maybe you can answer a few questions. Have you seen a pretty fellow among your frolickers, wearing octagonal spectacles and maybe smelling of lavender?"

"No," she said, stepping close and fluttering her eyes at him. Her breath had the stink of burnt garlic. "But if I do, I'll keep him for myself."

"Do you know the Jew Benjamin Mendoza?"

"What's he look like?"

"Tall. Wide in the shoulder, black hair. Dark skin. What we have around here. What they call Sephardim. Like a Portagee."

"No, but I'll ask Izz."

"What about Cutnose? Have you seen him?"

"The Indian with the big pecker? No. But we've only just got here. I'll see him by and by." Sweet Lips smirked at him. "I see you all by and by."

"Let me know if you do. Or if you hear anything about the Jew or the man with the spectacles."

"Anything you want, love. We're setting up a pleasure tent the other side of Staple Street, behind the warehouses on the dock. A red one."

"That's valuable space to give away."

"Give away nothing. We're paying a sweet stuiver for it. And wait till you meet my new flock. Three pieces of the best-laced mutton you ever hope to see. One black, one white, and one Indian." She had raised her voice and was really speaking to the community at large, advertising her wares. The sailors stood enthralled. "The white one is special, just arrived from Europe. She's got teats so big I'm surprised she doesn't fall down. A little thing except for that, hair as yellow as sunshine. You'll be missing something if you don't try her." Sweet Lips let loose a shrill giggle. "If she ever hit you over the head with those udders, she'd knock you into the ground up to your knees. Ask for Frederika. Frederika Van der Leun, if you please. Of course, if you prefer a more savage frolic, there are the other two. The Indian, Sparrow, is what they call a Hackensack; and Black Suzie, she has a gold tooth in front."

"Sounds like quite a group."

"I like to cater to many fancies. Don't forget what I said about that drink." She stepped even closer and, with the boa shielding her movement, grabbed Tonneman's crotch. "Or anything else your heart desires, love."

Tonneman put his hand over hers to loosen her fingers. He smiled tightly and backed away till he was out of her grasp. "You can buy me a drink. Just don't make a commotion. If the Boss gets wind of you, I'll have to shut you down."

"Ha!" It was a laugh without mirth. "So, I'll move."

"Careful I don't arrest you for being a spy."

"Your arse. What would I spy on, the size of Dutch peckers? Everyone knows you bog buggers have tiny little frog things. Ain't it the truth? Except you, of course, love," she said, reaching for him again.

"That will do."

"Yes, Heer Schout. Next time you be blissom for a woman and covet a frolic be sure and come to see my chickens, they're more than—"

A woman shrieked, there was a crash. Tonneman turned swiftly. A hog intent on eating garbage had knocked over a privy.

"Damn those hogs."

"God be with ye, love."

Tonneman kicked at the hog and poked it with his cudgel. The animal kept rooting in the garbage, not about to give up a meal. People walked obliviously around Tonneman and the hog and the overturned privy. They were used to it, as they were used to the stink of the garbage and the privy.

"Go get him, Schout, it's probably an English hog."

Laughter came from all directions.

Tonneman ignored the hecklers, and after several more kicks and pokes, he gave it up as a lost cause. "I've too much work to waste my time on this shit," he muttered, wiping his sweaty brow with his sleeve and resuming his walk.

But the hog and the privy weren't the end of it. Up ahead a

cluster of citizens were having a yelling match to see who could be the loudest.

"That's cow dung and you know it! We've beat them damned English before, we can do it again!"

"You're so brave, sign up for the army!"

"The trick is being ready!"

"Things will probably be better under the English."

"Yes, no more pious Duke Stuyvesant to bother us."

"Maybe the goddamn English will bring more farmers, and we'll have some milk and eggs around here."

"If there are any more farmers, they should be Dutch. I might want to do some farming, you know."

"You've been here twenty years. The only plowing you've ever done is when the whores come to town."

"Don't shove me." This was a new voice and it was speaking German.

"I'll shove you anytime I want." Another new voice, also speaking German. The two were just to the right of the first group.

Tonneman forced his way to where two men were facing each other. They weren't townsmen. Sailors, again. One, a big man with wide-set black eyes and a thick black mustache, held a dagger low.

His opponent was somewhat smaller, with runty features. His little bead eyes were set in a round moon face perched on a fat neck. In his hand, a cutlass, extended, pointing at the other man.

Tonneman searched the crowd to see if any soldiers were about to give him a hand. No. Never there when you needed them, drunk or sober. He'd have to handle this job by himself.

The man with the black mustache grinned, displaying a gap where his two front teeth should have been. "You've got the master blade," he said to his foe. "Use it before I shove it up your arse."

"We'll see whose arse grows steel," said the second man, advancing on the first.

"Enough, boys," Tonneman said in German, hefting his cudgel. His plan was to eliminate the swordsman first. "It's over."

Both men promptly turned their weapons on Tonneman. "Who says so?" the moon-faced man snarled.

"I do."

Pos, his bearded face, dripping with sweat, had sneaked up behind the two men. He held the dead man's sword in his left hand and his own in his right, and both were digging into the backsides of the two belligerents. "Drop your weapons or you'll *both* have blades up your arses."

22

TUESDAY, 26 AUGUST. *Afternoon.*
The hammers and saws and the builders' rough talk were unceasing. By the middle of the afternoon the carpenters had the new floors laid and the first floor temporarily fit for living. The two Africans helped Racqel move the Mendoza possessions back inside. It would be uncomfortable living amidst sawdust in an unfinished house without window glass, but thankfully it was still summer.

She would need new Turkish carpets and storage chests. Tiles and wall hangings. And mirrors. She had to have mirrors. All would come from the Mendoza warehouse. Then she would have a home again. A home, she thought resentfully, for a barren woman with no husband.

This had to be resolved. She could not live forever neither a widow nor a wife, in dead space where she would become an old woman, a housekeeper, a caretaker for other people's children. The prospect shriveled her soul.

Philipse's sweaty laborers stopped work, drank beer, and listened as Racqel told him she was going to Staple Street to see her brother-in-law.

She paused only long enough to strew fresh herbs in her new house to banish that awful smell from the shed and keep insects away. Her four-footers kept clinging to her, and she decided she could not leave them in the yard with the dead man so near. Caleb was already slinking and whining, his tail between his legs, and the new fence wasn't even up. She would ask Rebecca Da Costa to keep the animals in her yard.

Rebecca was on her knees, cleaning her scullery. They talked of the English again, but not about Benjamin. She saw pity in the woman's kindly eyes. Children ran in and out for food or with cuts and bruises; each time Rebecca would stop, admonish, and then kiss with love and pride. How Racqel envied her.

Leaving the Da Costa yard, Racqel walked toward the Broad

Way. The appearance of Tonneman was a tiny bright spark in her otherwise empty existence, and she was almost happy for the fire that had brought him. He had saved her life. She felt in her soul he would find Benjamin. And if he did discover her husband alive, perhaps a prisoner of the Indians, and brought him back, she would devote herself to bearing Benjamin a child. But Abraham and David had both explored the possibility that Benjamin was a prisoner of Indians and had found naught.

If Tonneman discovered proof that her husband was dead, she would be free to marry again. But who would have her? What dowry could she bring? The dowry she had brought when she had married Benjamin belonged to the Mendozas now.

And who was there to marry in this community? Boys too young, men too old. Certainly not Abraham. And certainly not David, no matter what he said. Yet despite urging from Abraham, David had not chosen a bride from among the eager younger girls. Only that morning he had threatened her with marriage; she would never marry David. One Mendoza was enough.

Tonneman was a widower. He had a child who was grown and married. Racqel stopped herself. Beads of perspiration formed on her upper lip. She was thinking forbidden thoughts. No. She must not allow herself to think of *any* other man than Benjamin, and certainly not a Christian.

The afternoon sun had lost some of its heat, but the air was damp and oppressive. Or was that only because she feared the meeting with David? What she planned to do was not fitting. Yet she had to confront him. What she was living now was not a life. More determined than ever, she straightened her shoulders, lengthened her stride, and made her way through the crowd on the Broad Way.

A hog was rooting at a pile of garbage, fouling the walk. People passed blithely by, scarcely noticing. Racqel took a small ball of lavender from the embroidered drawstring bag hanging at her waist and held it to her nose. The filthy unholy creature disgusted her.

The Dutch were supposed to be so clean. It had often been suggested that the vile swine be barred from the city, but naught had ever come of it. If the townspeople picked up after themselves or used any of the five places set aside for garbage and didn't allow their privy waste to flow into the streets, perhaps there wouldn't be such a problem with the pigs.

Her palms were wet and her hands trembled. Why had David and Abraham not alerted the authorities when Benjamin first disappeared? What were they hiding? Calling it a personal matter and not wanting to involve the gentiles was not enough of an answer.

She went through the Broad Way Gate and on to the North River and Staple Street. All the ships of Europe landed here at one time or another to buy or sell or cheat or steal. And now to invade?

The Tower of Babel wasn't gone with time, her father-in-law had said often, it was here in New Amsterdam, the New World's center of confusion. Indian and African sounds mixed with Europe's cacophony. French, Italian, Danish, Swedish, Norwegian, Slavonic, Spanish, Portuguese, even the English. Especially the English. They'd be here soon again. For good? She thought yes.

According to West India Company mandate, ships had to pay a duty on their cargo in New Netherlands or offer their goods for sale. Thus Staple Street became a singular marketplace. Today, as on most other days, all along Staple Street people were looking for bargains among the many wares that were on display.

The one-level wood-frame building owned by the Mendozas was a warehouse office. Here they stored the furs received from the trappers and Indians as well as the goods that arrived from Europe.

She paused at the entrance, arranging words in her mind, dreading the meeting. The door opened and she found herself face-to-face with the Indian who wore white man's clothing, Foxman. He bowed in a voluptuous motion like a French courtier, giving her a full view of his almost smooth head. He wore a wolf-claw necklace that clicked softly when he moved. When his head came up again, his stare was insolent. The man had an evil eye. Her mother would have said his soul was owned by a demon, an evil spirit. Her father would have laughed.

"What are you doing here, Racqel?" David's voice broke the moment. He stood at the door, the square black silk cap he always wore to the warehouse standing high and haughty on his head like a crown, his gaze following the departing Indian. When Foxman was out of sight, David walked swiftly to the rear of the warehouse and Racqel followed.

The heat inside was suffocating, and the reek of the skins worse than that of the decaying body in the shed. The chamber stank of dried blood and wild animals. She was grateful for her bag of lavender. The hot air buzzed with flies. Worse, Racqel knew the skins were alive with fleas. Caleb had once become so infested that he nearly went mad. She had gotten the barber-surgeon at the Fort to shave him clean. "Where is your father?"

"On the pier. The *Gustav* came in this morning with a very important shipment: black powder."

"Black powder?"

"For guns. Months ago, when Father learned about the possible

English invasion, he talked to our friends in Amsterdam in the Company. They arranged for a shipment of gunpowder, which has now arrived. Father is with Colonel van de Steen at this very moment. The colonel said it was a very important contribution to the defense of our community." David turned from her and walked further into the large chamber, past bundles of furs waiting for shipment.

At the furthest section of the chamber, partitioned from the rest of the area, was a long desk with two chairs, one at each end. A huge ledger lay open, a gray goose-quill pen beside it. David sat in front of the ledger.

"I'm sorry to intrude into your business, David, but I must see your father."

Her brother-in-law was impatient. "Did you deal with the dead man? Did the carpenter come?" He picked up the quill and after a search found a small knife under the ledger.

"Frederick Philipse is working now. The Schout came and inspected the dead man. Someone will come and take him away." She watched David's bent head. "It is not Benjamin."

"I knew that." His tone was patronizing, as if she were a simpleton. She hated him, suddenly, and Benjamin, all the Mendozas. She was angry for all the years . . . but especially for the last eight months. She buried her anger, putting on the cloak of subservience she normally wore.

Painstakingly, David trimmed several strips away from each side of the quill's point, then dipped the pen into the small pot of pale ink on the standish next to the abacus.

"He is also not a Jew." When her brother-in-law did not respond to this, Racqel lost her patience. "David, where is Benjamin?"

"I do not know." He began writing in the ledger. The pale ink would dry black.

"He was doing some business with the Ashkenazi in Breukelen."

"Abner?" David stared at her. He lay down the quill.

She couldn't discern if he was surprised or guilty. "You know about it?"

"Nay." He placed his palms on the desk and stood.

"You're hiding something. You have to know what Benjamin was doing, where he was going, yet you don't even look for him. I have to know if he is alive or dead. I am tired of waiting for answers that do not come."

David sprinkled the page he had written on with fine sand from the dredger next to the standish, then shook the sand from the book out on the floor. "If I knew for certain he was dead, you would already be my wife."

Bitter bile threatened to choke her. Marry him? She hated him. She started to reply that this would never be but held her tongue. "Then let us go to Breukelen and talk with this Abner."

"No," he responded angrily. "He knows naught of Benjamin."

"How do you know? Have you talked with him?"

"I have."

"When?"

David's black eyes blazed at her. "Do not interfere." With a sudden movement he came from behind the table and grabbed her arms, shaking her.

Racqel's eyes blazed back at him. She attempted to shake him off, but his grip was unyielding. "I will go to Breukelen myself and talk to this Abner. Then I'll know what I am." She broke away and ran through the warehouse, hearing his deliberate footsteps behind her and her name shouted over and over again.

23

Tuesday, 26 August. *Middle Afternoon.*

"Ho, Tonneman," Pos said, after the two sailors were disarmed and squatting on the ground, hands behind their heads.

"We've had a delivery of gunpowder," Tonneman said, by way of greeting.

"So we fight." Pos made a rude noise. "Witless fools."

"Looks like it. Have you seen Keyser?"

"Yes. He'll take care of the body. Better still." Pos's eyes gleamed. "He said Cutnose was in Breukelen."

"How does he know that?"

Pos wrinkled up his face. "I didn't ask."

"Makes no difference. Lock these two in the jail, then go to all the taverns from here to the Wall and check on whether anyone has seen Cutnose, on the chance Keyser is wrong."

A broad smile flooded Pos's ruddy face. "I like that sort of work, my friend."

"Remember, you're on duty, deputy. Don't drink too much."

"There's never enough beer in the world for me to drink too much."

"I believe you. By the way, you're now getting three and a half florins a week."

"I like that, too."

"You might as well tell everyone about the powder. Good for their spirits. That is, if they don't already know. Also, you should get to the ships on both sides of the island and ask if they have a man missing that fits Spectacles' description."

"Do you want me to do that before or after I make the sun stop moving in the sky?"

Tonneman smiled. Pos was right. It was an impossible task for two men. Perhaps he could ask Ten Eyck to help. "Have some respect. And thank you for your timely rescue."

Pos saluted with the two swords and dagger he held in his hands. "That's why I get the kingly sum of three florins and fourteen stuivers a week. Beer money, if I'm lucky, the way prices keep rising. That's twenty beers if the tapster will trust me two stuivers."

Tonneman laughed. "On your way."

"Of course, there's always the generous twenty-four stuivers I get a night for being captain of the Rattle Watch."

"Away."

"Not to mention money for candles and firewood."

"Away. And don't let the Boss catch you sleeping. There'll be more to pay than the usual ten-stuiver fine."

Pos winked broadly. "I never sleep. All right, you two pissants, move. Up and out."

Tonneman continued to the end of the Broad Way in town and stopped at the Wall. As usual, the women had hung their day's wash to dry along the Wall, which always gave the Director-General a fit. Tonneman hoped fervently that wash on the Wall would be the most of their troubles; the capricious structure, five feet here, lower in some places, higher in others, was fairly solid, but could it withstand English cannon? He doubted it.

Four years earlier, in 1660, the Wall had been strengthened. Additional walls were built along the North and East River shores. Six bastions, on which brass cannons were mounted, had been placed at regular intervals on the eastern wall. So except for the western end of the City, which was commanded by the Fort Amsterdam's cannons, most of New Amsterdam was walled, resembling a fortified European city. But could they stop the English infantry? Tonneman doubted that, too.

There were only two gates built into the Wall, one at the East River, called the Water Gate, and one here at the Broad Way. The river walls were for the most part an extension of the wooden palisades built after the Indian raids a few years back, and it was doubtful they could withstand even an Indian attack, let alone the English. These partial new walls were in terrible condition. They had never been completed and were falling into constant disrepair, showing more gaps than wall. It was a good thing this wasn't winter. Everyone knew the Indians stole pieces of the Wall for firewood.

Asser Levy's tavern stood next to the Water Gate. Just the place where Tonneman could sit in a cool spot, eat his fish, drink his beer, and consider the events of the last two days. But first he would make a stop at Jan Keyser's tannery.

At the Broad Way Gate a soldier waved him through.

Less than a quarter of a mile past the Wall was the van Cortlandt estate, spreading from the Broad Way to the North River. To the right of the Broad Way was the path called Maiden Lane, named for the young girls of the town who did their daily wash in the freshwater brook that flowed here.

The van Cortlandt house was set in deep from the road. On the front lawn where the elder van Cortlandt liked to bowl on Saturday, young boys were throwing a beef bone at a collection of other beef bones, playing loggats. The scene made Tonneman think of his daughter, Anna, again, and her yet unborn child.

Van Cortlandt had built outside the Wall to get away from the noise and stink of city life. He hadn't reckoned on the Boss banishing Keyser to the country. Even at this distance the putrid stink of the tannery floated toward Tonneman on the hot breeze.

The Broad Way was the high ground that extended from the Fort all the way to the northern end of the island. The Boss had a farm a few miles out. This side of the farm was a towering hill, commanding a view of the whole island and falling off gradually to Shellpoint, a deep, clear freshwater lake with an island in the middle. It was one of the many basins that collected the waters of the hills that surrounded them. Shellpoint was also where some of the freed Africans had been given land to build homes.

The quiet was immediate. After the din and bustle of town it was good to be where it was still. A mosquito buzzed in his ear and settled on his cheek. Tonneman slapped at it and took off his jacket.

One of Shellpoint's feeders was a brook that came from beyond Staple Street from a big stretch of marshland, low and wet, with no trees, and dense with grasses, sedges, rushes, and tall, reedy cattails, home to mosquitoes, frogs, and water snakes. Just like the old country. If a Dutchman was going to find a home in the New World, this was where it had to be. Holland, after all, meant bog land.

This beautiful island was dotted with marshy spots, but as van

Cortlandt's land and Lookermans's cherry orchard and other pros-
perous farms proved, most of New Amsterdam was fertile, bounteous
in wild fruits and nuts and flowers, except for this year with its damnable drought. Still, it was a paradise for hunters and fishermen.

Up north, where the trappers sought the beaver, was very different: all rocks and thick forest of ancient oak, hickory, and maple
trees.

As Tonneman passed the end of Shellpoint the full force of the
tannery's smell hit him. "The stink of hell" was what the Boss had
called it. That was why he had banished Keyser out here where it
wouldn't bother anyone. A mighty stink indeed, considering what
smells the townspeople tolerated without complaining.

Keyser's tannery was on a knoll. It was a rough, one-story building, open to the front. Most of the work was done outside, making it
noisy as well as reeking, what with all that digging and woodcutting
and pot banging and the carts rolling back and forth and those cursed
cats, breaking the countryside's peace. In the back of the property
was a one-and-a-half-story structure where Keyser, his wife, his son,
Adolphus, and the apprentices lived, heaven help them.

Adding to the tannery stench were the many smoky fires, kept
going day and night to keep the mosquitoes away. Somewhere underneath that, when the wind was just right, was the good smell of
leather.

The mosquitoes didn't seem to mind the fires at all.

There were four apprentices, all young boys. They and Adolphus
were rushing about as they did every day, six days a week, sunrise to
sunset, and longer.

Each day was devoted to driving heavily laden tumbrels, carrying
water, two buckets at a time on shoulder yokes, chopping wood,
scraping decomposing meat from reeking hides, salting the hides, wetting them, removing the hair, and curing them.

Time left was spent burying hides, digging them up, tending fires,
shoveling and percolating the ashes, leaching them for the lye, making
caustic dyes, boiling bones, making soap, and making candles. It was
a hard life and very dangerous work. They could be burned,
poisoned, even killed.

But it was a way out of poverty, a way to start with nothing and
end up with a trade, a future. The Chamber in Amsterdam had been
sending boys and girls from almshouses and orphanages to New Amsterdam as apprentices for ten years now. They were fed and clothed
and sheltered and committed to serve four years. At the end of which,
they could serve in the same employment for better terms, or they
could go out on their own and be granted up to fifty acres of land. It

was a fair and noble opportunity. Would the English honor those terms?

"So, are the English here yet?" Keyser, having caught sight of the Schout, did not look up from his supervision of an apprentice, who was pouring caustic lye into a trough.

"No, but we have more gunpowder. A shipment just arrived."

"Good." The creases in his brown face ran wet with sweat in the heat of the afternoon. "I suppose."

"Damn," said Tonneman, slapping ineffectually at a mosquito.

"Stay here for a while." The tanner smiled evilly. "You get used to them. Or they get used to you."

"*You* get used to them. P.S. has sent for reinforcements."

Keyser snorted loudly, an obscene sound, like that frolicking hog at the privy. "Hold your breath."

"If I put my hands around your neck, you won't have any breath to hold."

The tanner looked carefully at Tonneman, uncertain if the Schout was jesting. Steam rose from a nearby cauldron being stirred by a fat apprentice. Keyser snapped, "Don't stop, thunderhead, that's soap, not soup."

Wiping his hands on his canvas apron, the tanner took an earthenware jug from a shelf and came out of the open building, toward Tonneman, clumping across the muddy ground in his wooden shoes. He took a long pull from the jug. "Good milk," he said as some of the burnt wine dribbled down his grimy elkskin shirt.

Tonneman spat in the dirt. He wanted a drink but not from this man's jug. A cat scrambled over his feet.

"What more do you want from me, Schout?" Keyser complained. "You didn't come here just to bring me the news. I told Pos everything I know."

"I notice your dirty water is running down the grade on the front side. It's going right into Shellpoint. I thought you were told to channel it down the back side to avoid fouling the pond."

The tanner's face twisted belligerently. "What's a little dirty water?"

"I, for one, don't like to drink lye. Fix it. If it's not made right by the next time I'm here, I'll close you down. Do you understand?"

Keyser sent a surly glance at Tonneman, but apparently decided not to argue. "Yes, Schout."

A large chunk of meat lay in a foul decaying state on the ground, its flesh teeming with writhing white maggots. Three cats pounced on it.

"Have you seen to the body?"

"I'll come to it," said Keyser, kicking at the cats and picking up the rotting piece of meat. He flung it into the woods. The cats sped after it and were joined by others, screaming, spitting, and snarling. "There's other work that has to be done around here. I'm just one man." He groaned. "And I've got a fearful misery in my head." He drank again from his jug.

Tonneman backed away from the rank odor of the meat and the man. "Get a move on. It must be awful high by now, and it's too close to the Boss's house. Give it a good look. Let me know if you've seen the man before. I found octagonal spectacles under his body."

"By rights I should have them," the tanner said. Greed glinted in his eyes. "It's the custom for the one who prepares the body. It's my due; I should glean my lawful harvest."

"Horse piss. Anything else, show me. You can have it, but I need to know what it is. Don't let me find out you held back on me. Do you hear me, you little toad?"

"The Jew cemetery?"

"No. He was a Christian. Didn't Pos tell you where?"

"Who listened?" said Keyser. He shouted into the building, "Adolphus, bring the horse and wagon around!"

"One more thing," Tonneman said. "You told Pos that Cutnose was in Breukelen."

"That's right."

"Who told you that?"

"Nobody. I saw him in a canoe paddling toward Breukelen this morning on my way from that bastard Woods's mill."

Tonneman sighed. That was it. A wasted walk on a hot day. He had delayed his beer and fish for naught.

As he turned to go the sun dazzled his eyes. And he saw Hendrik Smitt swinging slowly back and forth. God, what he needed was a drink. "Keyser, who took Smitt's body to the cemetery?"

"I did. Why?"

"What did he have on his person?"

"Nothing," the tanner said, immediately on the defensive.

"Damn your eyes, Keyser. Talk straight to me."

"Not much. Just a guilder and a couple of stuivers. Which was mine by right."

"I don't give a bear's piss about your rights. Anything else?"

"No."

"I'll be off then." Tonneman wiped his brow with his sleeve. "What about the rope? The noose?"

"What about it?"

"What happened to it?"

"How would I know?"

"You mean you didn't claim it as was your right?"

"I meant to. It was there on the ground. All I had to do was take apart the knot. . . . It wasn't really a noose . . . more a bowline . . . and it would have been as good as new. But when I looked for the rope after putting Smitt in canvas, it was gone. You know that goddamned Englishman had the nerve to raise the price of ground bark?"

"We all have our problems." Tonneman looked at his jacket in his hand, draped it over his arm, started his trudge to town, then stopped. He turned back to Keyser. "Are you sure it was Cutnose you saw?"

The tanner scowled. "Well, I wouldn't swear to it. All Indians look alike to me. And he was quite a way out when I saw him. It looked like Cutnose, I'll say that."

Tonneman nodded. "Did you see him land his canoe?"

Adolphus, a small lad with a large head, the image of Keyser, brought a horse and cart around from behind the tannery.

"No. Saw him on the water, that's all."

"So you can't say for sure he went to Breukelen?"

"If you put it that way, no. The best I can tell you is I saw him in a canoe in the East River. Can I go back to work now?"

The same cat or another was on Tonneman's feet again; he struck at it with his jacket. Dozens of fat cats continually prowled the tannery site and the woods around, feeding on whatever rotten meat they could filch and stalking the mice and rats the putrefying flesh attracted.

"Don't forget to take care of that dirty water."

"I heard you the first time," Keyser shouted.

"And the body."

"It can stink till the crack of doom for all I care."

Tonneman laughed as he went down the hill to Shellpoint. He knew that Keyser would see to the body. He wasn't so sure what the tanner would do about his dirty water. The little bastard hadn't even offered him a drink of clean water, and he had another three-quarters of a mile to go before he had his beer.

He swung his cudgel violently, made a fist of his left hand, and pummeled his thigh. His anger wasn't directed at Keyser, or even Smitt, for that matter. Drink had obliterated his wits that July morn, or he would have seen at once that it was impossible for Smitt to have hanged himself, let alone tie a fancy knot on the noose. He wondered what had happened to that rope.

Quiet again. Now the sound of wind whispering through

needles. Tall pine trees grew here around Shellpoint. Underfoot was a supple, perfumed carpet of needles. Tonneman dropped his jacket and lay flat on the bank. The water had an amber-green glow to it from the pine needles that dropped from the surrounding trees. Tonneman wet his face and drank.

He sat up quickly. What with the English, he couldn't afford the luxury of drinking in that manner again. He'd have to think as they used to when the Indians were on the prod. His now wary eyes scanned the woods as he took a final drink in one cupped hand. The cool water, which smelled and tasted of pine, was a tonic. Not beer, but it would do for the nonce. Refreshed, he resumed his walk, pointing for the Water Gate. His boots made soft snapping noises on the needles.

Among the pines, white-rayed daisies and glossy yellow buttercups grew along the path, and blackberries that smelled so sweet ran wild. Large black butterflies darted among them. Maria had taught Anna to follow the black butterflies to find parsley.

The woods on either side were lively with game. A turtle basking on a rock in the pond to his right stared at him with small, glittering eyes. Tonneman hadn't eaten turtle for quite a spell.

All he had to do was flip it over, hit it with his cudgel, and cut its head off, and he would have a fine meal. As if reading his mind, the turtle slipped into the water with a plop. Ah, well, it made no difference, this land was abounding. There would be another time and another turtle.

He was sorry he hadn't ridden and brought his wheel lock. Wild turkey or partridge or a rabbit would have made a nice supper. Then again, Antje had invited him to eat with them. Cold prune soup and hutsepot stew and duck. That would be all right, too. But for the moment he had a craving for salt fish and beer.

When he turned onto the Water Gate Road, which was an extension of Pearl Street, he was almost to the Wall. Tonneman liked the woods, but he thought how much better it would be for all of them if this was farmland. Then they wouldn't have to depend on Europe or the Johnnies on Long Island and in New England for their grain and produce. And if there were farms along the borders, they would be a first line of defense against the enemy.

Tonneman stopped outside the Wall. Off to the left, resting on pilings above the water of the East River, was Asser Levy's slaughterhouse. It stank almost as much as Keyser's tannery. Levy's butcher shop and tavern were just inside the Wall.

Opposite the outside Wall under an abundant juniper tree was an

Indian trading post set up by the Company. Sybout Huygens, who ran the post, sat outside on a log, whittling a branch. He was a quiet man with patches of dry brown hair and shiny skin on his head because of the fire he'd been in when he was young.

Not an Indian in sight, which was highly unusual. Did they know something Tonneman didn't know? Were they staying as far away as possible from the white man's war? Huygens was a member of the Civilian Militia. His musket leaned against the trading-post, barrel down in the dirt. "Ho, Huygens. Slow day?"

Sybout Huygens shrugged and kept whittling.

"Your gun's getting dirty," Tonneman called, passing through the Water Gate onto Pearl Street. "You fixing to shoot worms?"

If Huygens made a response, Tonneman didn't hear it.

At this spot, only about five hundred yards from the tip of the island, where the Fort lay, the Wall was a low wooden fence joining the main Wall. The fence obscured his view of the water, but that was about all it did. A lazy river breeze felt good on his face. He put his jacket on and quickened his pace.

On his right was Asser Levy's tavern, which had no name, merely a sign out front of the standing figure of a lion.

24

TUESDAY, 26 AUGUST. *Middle Afternoon.*

Tonneman fingered the silver disk in his right-hand jacket pocket as he stepped up to the bar and asked for his beer and salt cod. The tapster was Asser Levy's son-in-law, a scraggy-bearded young man Tonneman knew only as Zedekiah.

Zedekiah sneezed. "Right away." He sneezed again, this time so hard his black silk cap shot off his frizzled brown hair. Quickly he picked the cap up and, sniffling, set it back on his head.

"Good health," said Tonneman, smiling.

The only other customer was a bony, powerful-looking man. The skin fit his forbidding face tightly, like one of the tanner's pelts left to dry. At his feet was a fiddle case. He drank his beer, wiped his mouth with a surprisingly delicate gesture, and shook something in his hand.

He rolled the double stones out on the bar and exhaled wistfully. "Fellow came in here and taught me this game. If you cast a trey with the stones, you win. I can never seem to do it." He spoke a vulgar German-accented Dutch. "Want to try?" He offered the dice to Tonneman without looking up.

The man appeared awkward with the stones, when in truth he was most adroit and dexterous, as Tonneman well knew. A good man in a fight, a bad man to have as an enemy.

"How have you been, Korbonski?" Tonneman asked Sweet Lips's husband. "Still playing the old treytrip game? I would have thought you'd have given up on that and resigned yourself to playing the fiddle and living off your wife's talents."

"Tonneman. Didn't know it was you. Never look at faces. Mostly I look at hands. I can tell what people are going to do that way."

"Like pull a knife."

"You know I'm a peaceful man. I meant, take out their purse and put some money on the fiddler's plate."

"Oh, yes."

"Oh, yes, indeed."

"You seem to know a great many things, Korbonski."

"This and that."

"That sign out front. The lion. Is it a coat of arms? Is it Jewish? What does it mean?"

"That's one thing I don't know, Schout. Why?"

"Merely curious. The way I'm curious about you. Where are you from, Korbonski?"

"New England. Virginia. From wherever I've just been."

Another sneeze exploded from Zedekiah as he set a plate of fish and a tankard of beer before Tonneman. "Good health," said Tonneman. He drained the tankard. "Zedekiah?"

"Heer Schout?" the tapster said, rubbing his nose, attempting to forestall the next sneeze.

"What does that lion on the sign out front represent?"

"The Lion of Judah."

"A graven image," said Korbonski.

Zedekiah looked at the Pole sourly.

"It's a Jewish emblem, then," said Tonneman.

"Yes, I would say so," Zedekiah answered, searching the Schout's face for the hidden insult that usually came with such questions. Zedekiah had strange pale eyes for a Jew, almost green, now watery from sneezing.

"Another beer," said Tonneman. Zedekiah hurried back to the bar. Tonneman ate his fish quickly; the salt coated his tongue. He was impatient for more beer. "I mean, where are you from in Europe?" he said to Korbonski through a full mouth.

"Saxony."

"I thought you were a Polack."

"We move around a great deal." Korbonski rolled the stones in his hands. His fingers were long and slim, almost womanly.

"You're what they call an Ashkenazi."

The fiddler grinned. "Schout, you're pretty smart for a gentile."

Zedekiah was sneezing again. "Good health," Tonneman called out. "Don't sneeze in my beer." Then to the fiddler: "You know a Jew named Abner Simon, in Breukelen?"

"Never heard of him."

"He's an Ashkenazi. From Saxony."

"So? One thing I will tell you, though."

"What?"

"Remember that I helped you when you needed it."

"Let me hear it first to see if it helps me."

"That fire last night."

"Yes?"

Korbonski knew about the fire, though he'd just arrived in town. Well, why not? You could still smell it in the air and New Amsterdamers loved to gossip. Korbonski looked to be sure that Zedekiah was out of hearing. "It was set to spite our host."

"How would burning the Mendozas out spite Asser Levy?"

"He wants the property. Mendoza won't move out." The fiddler fell silent as Zedekiah set down Tonneman's beer.

Tonneman waited until Zedekiah had gone back to his place behind the bar. Then he said, "That makes no sense. The fire hasn't changed a thing. Work on the new house is starting today." He took a long swallow of beer to wash the salt away.

Korbonski's fingers closed around the die. He looked as if he were in pain. "All right. Maybe I was wrong. Think of this, then, Schout. The fire was set to spite David Mendoza."

"That sounds more like it. Who would do such a thing?"

"A competitor maybe. Maybe an Indian or a trader Mendoza cheated. All these Sephardim care about is profit. Take it from me." The fiddler drank his beer and looked hopefully at Tonneman.

The Schout shook his head. "New Amsterdam is too small for me not to have heard rumors if either the Indians or traders were unhappy with anyone."

"I have it," said Korbonski. "Maybe it had to do with the missing brother." He leaned closer to Tonneman. "This is something you *wouldn't* hear. Those Sephardim don't talk. They were fighting over the woman. The older brother's wife."

2 5

TUESDAY, 26 AUGUST. *Late Afternoon.*

Fury enveloped Racqel as she ran from the Mendoza warehouse, ignoring David's sharp calling of her name. He would not follow her, she was sure; the gentiles' opinion of him was foremost in his mind. How would it look for the Jew Mendoza to run shouting in the open air after his sister-in-law, even out here on Staple Street away from the more traveled public roads?

Racqel laughed at the thought, and her laugh dissipated the blind anger. She slowed her pace, thinking she would go to the ferryman, Dircksen, and have him take her to Breukelen. Racqel had been there once before with her father when they were searching out herbs for medicines.

She stopped and considered her route. Dircksen's farm was almost directly south as the crow flew, but she didn't want to be seen trudging through open fields alone and have her private affairs become a source of gossip. She took the path back to the Wall. Two soldiers stood leaning against the weather-scarred and damaged barrier near the Broad Way Gate. The Wall was so poor a structure she did not see how it could keep anyone out.

If it were a proper wall, Racqel and her people could travel freely within the town on the Sabbath. By Jewish law a walled city could be considered a private estate and therefore a devout Jew could journey anywhere within it on the Sabbath and carry things. But there could be no break in the wall. And, sad to say, in New Amsterdam there were many breaks in the Wall.

"Good afternoon, gracious vrouw," one of the soldiers called as she approached. He elbowed his partner and they both laughed. The way he looked at her made her uncomfortable, but she smiled politely and went through the gate.

A horse and cart advanced on her in a billow of grit, traveling much too fast, forcing her to the side of the road. In spite of the rain the dust on the road was so thick from the long dry summer that she could not even catch a glimpse of whoever was driving the cart. The dust settled over her, a blanket of dirt. She coughed, choking.

Perhaps there had been further news about the English, and the cart driver was in a rush to get home. Racqel hurried her steps along Wall Street, passing the soldiers manning the gleaming brass cannons, oblivious of the slow sinking sun in the western sky and the women removing their dried wash from the Wall.

Racqel walked past Asser Levy's butcher shop and his tavern very quickly, lest she be recognized. She went through the Water Gate without comment from the soldiers sitting in the grass, cleaning their weapons, or the one on duty at the gate.

Immediately, the fetid smell of the slaughterhouse filled her nostrils, making her gag. Stepping over a lump of greasy white animal fat, she spied Sybout Huygens across the way at the trading post. He was standing in his door, eyeing her, a bottle in his hand. She paused to catch her breath.

"Are you looking for someone?" he asked.

"No, thank you. I'm on my way to Dircksen's farm."

"It's not wise for a lone woman to be outside the Wall these days."

"I'm all right. There's someone meeting me."

Huygens leaned against the door frame, took a noisy gulp from his bottle, and emitted a series of loud belches.

The breeze from the river was a relief from the heat and dust of the road, even though flies and mosquitoes abounded. She scrambled over the grassy bank to the sand below and dipped her handkerchief in the cool water. Removing her ruffled cap, she wiped the dirt from her face.

It was silent except for the birds and the faint buzz of the insects, but she felt the hair on the back of her neck tremble. Intuition told her she was not alone. Turning slowly, she found she was looking directly into the flat dark eyes of Foxman. The Indian had discarded his white man's clothing; all he wore was a loincloth and moccasins. He had even removed his wolf-claw necklace. At his waist was the tomahawk she had seen on him before. And tied to his right calf with a leather thong was a knife.

Racqel slipped backward and lost her balance, falling to her knees into the river. The Indian made no move to help her. She climbed back on land awkwardly. Her leather buskins and stockings were drenched, as were the bottom of her borrowed dress and her pettiskirts.

The Iroquois's lips pulled into a thin line. "You think you can follow me, spy on me?"

She averted her eyes from his nakedness. "I'm not following you. I'm on my way to the ferryman."

"You are going to Breukelen?"

She nodded. "To Abner Simon." Fear had made her tell more than she wanted. In the hope that it might stay his murderous hand, she added, "He's expecting me."

Foxman's hooded eyes were glinted slits. "I will take you to Simon. Pay me, not the ferryman. And *I* will take you faster." He bared his teeth in what she prayed was a smile.

She stepped back, unthinking, into the water again. The man frightened her. Was he trying to be friendly? "No, that's not necessary, thank you." Her wet, sandy garments clung uncomfortably to her, but she didn't move.

"The ferryman is on his way to the Fort. Wooden Leg has called a meeting about the English." Foxman turned his naked back to her and strode along the riverbank away from her.

Racqel stepped out of the water and, gathering her wet skirts up, followed him to a small inlet where he pulled his canoe from its hiding place in the marsh grasses. "What about the English? Have they come?"

The Indian didn't respond. She watched him put the canoe into the water, entranced by his grace as he got into the small boat and started paddling. "Wait," she cried, waving at him. "Take me. I'll pay you." Unwittingly, she patted the small drawstring bag at her waist.

Foxman's paddle motion changed almost imperceptibly. Suddenly he'd pointed the canoe back toward the beach. He was showing his teeth again.

26

Tuesday, 26 August. *Late Afternoon.*

Tonneman finished his fish and beer and left Asser Levy's tavern. It had been a long day, one of his longest since he'd been City Schout, and he was tempted to go to the Pear Tree and drink burnt wine and talk to Joost until he fell down. But there was no getting away from it, he would have to go to Breukelen.

The orange ball of hot August sun was sinking in the west as he left the village through the Water Gate. Less than a mile beyond the Wall he came to the Dircksen farm.

Dircksen didn't own the land; he leased it from the Company. And a hard piece of barren rock it was, he complained to anyone who'd listen.

Taking the battered oxhorn hanging by a worn leather thong from a chestnut tree near the water's edge, Tonneman put his lips to the yellowed mouthpiece and blew. The lowing sound rose and floated north over the rolling hills, echoing back at him.

He sat on a flat gray slab of rock next to the tree and waited. Was he going to Breukelen to find Cutnose and get more information about what had happened the night the stranger was killed or was it to talk to Abner, the Jew?

And buzzing around his head like a nasty bumblebee was the passing comment the tanner Keyser had made about the fancy knot in the noose that had killed Smitt. Tonneman moved his hands about to clear away the imaginary insect and set his thoughts on Maria, then Anna and how she would look with the new baby. His grandson. He should be going to New Haarlem. But no, he had to go to Breukelen to find Cutnose.

Ha! He was going to Breukelen to talk to Abner the Jew and discover what had happened to Benjamin Mendoza.

Tonneman blew the horn a second time and hammered on the flat rock with his cudgel. Again, the sounds hovered briefly, then expanded. When the echo came back over the Dircksen farm, it went out over the river and into Breukelen.

"I'm coming, I'm coming." A squat man with feet like beaver tails crashed through the brush. "I've got a farm to take care of, too, you know." Cornelis Dircksen, the younger, who like his father before him ran the ferry to Breukelen, grumbled and complained unceasingly about the interruptions, but enjoyed the extra money the ferry service brought him.

"Take me across, Dircksen, this is official business."

Dircksen rubbed his pockmarked face with a fat, callused hand and pushed one of the three rowboats into the water. "Let's go. What of the English?"

"Tow a second boat so I don't have to wait on you later."

"There's no need for that. I'm not deaf."

"Horse piss. If the wind's wrong, I could blow all day and you'd never hear me across the river."

"How's that?" Dircksen cupped his ear, smirking, pretending deafness. His teeth were tobacco-stained stubs. He tied a second boat to the first and handed a second set of oars to Tonneman before he got into the boat. "Where are you going?" he asked, holding the boat steady as Tonneman stepped in.

"Across." The river had a blue-black sheen in the late-afternoon light. He could see the craggy hills of Breukelen clearly as the day's heat finally lifted.

"Where?" The ferryman, dipping his oars for the first bite, was certain that Tonneman had information about the English and their coming; he was determined to wheedle it out of him. He had a wife and children and a profitable farm to think about. The English could confiscate his three cows and his horse and then where would he be?

"Just across," said Tonneman, adding his power against the strong current.

"You don't give much away, do you?"

"I'm looking for a Jew, name of Abner Simon."

"Why didn't you say so? He has a place on the water opposite where Crispijn Peyser lives."

After a hard forty minutes they beached on the Breukelen side. Cornelis Dircksen jumped out and dragged the boats to shore, pulling them between two large boulders. "All I need, to get my boats staved in by these rocks," he crabbed under his breath.

The ferryman ran to a stand of sickly birch trees, picked an old brass horn from a pile of dry leaves, shook it out, and blew into it. He frowned at the ugly noise the horn made and hung it on a branch of one of the trees by its frayed rope. On his way back to Tonneman he considered the sky. "Looks like rain." He turned the second boat over and pushed the oars underneath.

"That wasn't necessary," Tonneman complained.

"It's my boat," Dircksen replied, digging at his ear with his little finger. "Say, Tonneman? If you're going to row back yourself, why did I have to row you in the first place?" He kicked away the stinking remains of a dead bass.

"Have a smoke and wait for me."

"Didn't bring my pipe," the ferryman mumbled. Louder he said, "I've got a farm to tend. Give me my four stuivers, and I'll go."

"Just so," said Tonneman, smiling. "That's why I wanted the second boat."

"Could have rowed yourself," Dircksen mumbled again, holding out his grubby palm. He was not a man who understood a joke.

Because of this, Tonneman could not resist having a little amusement. "Company business," he said solemnly. "Apply for it."

"Don't be a stone breaker, Tonneman. Four stuivers."

"I'll get you on the trip back."

"Four stuivers."

A tern lighted where the dead fish lay and looked it over.

Tonneman gave the ferryman the coins and watched him push off. The tern made an angry noise and flew out over the river. Tonneman walked west to Abner Simon's place.

Breukelen was more sparsely settled than Manhattan, rocky, with jagged hillocks. Tonneman felt an immediate change in atmosphere, a pastoral ease, a soothing balm against the intense activity of New Amsterdam.

Up ahead near the riverbank was something draped with a dirty, weather-beaten piece of canvas. Tonneman walked to it and lifted the canvas. A rowboat.

He looked inland and up. Standing somewhat precariously on a small incline, just about where Cornelis Dircksen said it would be, was a cottage. He climbed a path of broken rocks and flattened sand grass to get to it.

The closer Tonneman got, the more he saw how poorly put together the wooden hut was. It looked as if a strong wind could knock it over. A gray-haired man of uncertain age was seated on the ground near a large boulder, in front of the house, weaving a chair seat. The black patch over his left eye did little to hide a deep white scar that crept from under it down his otherwise brown cheek into a dirty, gray-streaked black beard. The man's good eye, black, beneath a bushy gray eyebrow, watched Tonneman suspiciously as his hands worked the chair.

A powerful, short-haired mastiff with black spots on his gray coat stood behind the man and peered over his shoulder. Its appearance gave truth to the idea that many people and their dogs looked alike. The dog's drooping ears flattened at Tonneman's approach. Like his master, his black eyes also watched Tonneman suspiciously.

Long strips of hickory bark were all about the man. A bottle, a wooden bowl with water, and a sharp knife lay on the ground, within easy reach. A sparrow pecked away at scattered bread crumbs. When Tonneman came close, the dog began to growl menacingly, and the bird fluttered off. "You're Tonneman, aren't you?" the man said in perfect Dutch, the kind his friend Lubbertus van Dincklagen spoke, which otherwise Tonneman hadn't heard since university days.

"Yes." He sat on the boulder. Only then did the dog quiet down and relax. "You're Abner Simon?"

"Yes. What can I do for you?"

"I'm looking for a bad Indian."

Abner's nose twitched. "They're all bad. And mean." The two-inch strip of hickory bark he was weaving came to an end. He cut a tongue in it and tied it to another piece with a taut knot.

As Tonneman watched the man work, it struck him that the two Ashkenazic Jews, Korbonski and Abner, should both have such good hands. "Name of Cutnose. Algonquin." A breeze came from the river, rustling scrub grass and bushes.

"I know him. I gave him something to eat this morning. He talked about going up-country."

"Shit," said Tonneman. "I should have come after him sooner. Where up-country? Manhattan or Breukelen?"

"From here. Shank's mare. Why do you want him?" The question was asked seemingly without curiosity.

"A stranger has turned up dead, scalped, in the Mendozas' shed."

Because he was watching Abner's deft hands, Tonneman caught the momentary pause and recovery. "I think he has a canoe hidden someplace," Abner Simon said.

"How long ago was he here?"

"Sunup."

Tonneman rose from the rock, grunting. The mastiff went on guard. Tonneman looked up at the late-afternoon sky. Cutnose was too far ahead of him. Besides, the Company didn't pay him to track that damnable Indian; it paid him to look after the people of New Amsterdam.

Tonneman slapped at a gnat. The air was thick with them. Abner didn't seem to notice. The dog did not take his eyes off Tonneman.

"Of course," said Abner, "just because he said it, doesn't mean he did it."

"You think he didn't go?"

"He may have told me that because he knew you would come looking for him and that I would tell you. He has never told me his secrets before. No Indian has. It's not their way."

"Will you get word to me if you see him again?"

"You know what they say?" The old man dipped his hands into the bowl of water and continued working. "One hand washes the other."

On impulse Tonneman pulled from his jacket pocket the piece of silver he'd found under the willow tree earlier. "Do you know what this is?"

Abner's good eye flicked over the silver object, but he didn't answer. His hands kept weaving the hickory strips on the bottom of the chair, two over, two under. Then the next line, one over, two under, two over, two under.

Tonneman tried again. "What does the lion represent?"

The Jew nodded at the bottle on the ground. "That's rum. You like rum?"

"Rum's all right."

"Have some."

Tonneman took a swallow. It was sweet but good. He moved closer to Abner to hand him the bottle. The dog growled, showing vicious teeth.

"Still, Schatzie." The one-eyed man drank and settled the bottle in his lap. "As I said, Schout, you help me and I'll help you."

"Go on."

The Jew gestured with his bottle. "Let's drink a bit more."

"How can we help each other?" asked Tonneman, searching his pockets for his pipe.

"I don't trust a man who won't drink with me."

Over the next two hours they finished that bottle of rum and most of a second one. They talked of hunting and fishing things but not of Abner's problem. Finally, Abner said, "Not long ago I paid a man a hundred florins for . . . something."

"Something? That's a nice piece of change for . . . something."

Abner waved his hand. "I don't care about the money."

"Keep talking, I'm impressed by a man who doesn't care about a hundred florins. Especially when the Company pays me only sixty florins a month. What was the . . . something you bought?"

"Insignificant."

"If you won't tell me that, how do I know I can believe anything you tell me?"

"Just a piece of paper. Important to me, but to no one else. There is someone in your jurisdiction who would as soon have me dead. You're the Schout. . . ." Abner stopped to take another drink.

A piece of paper . . . paper . . . *pape*. Spectacles' last word had been *pape*. Was it paper, then, the dying man spoke of and not some Roman Catholic plot? Was this paper the item the man in the dark had said was sold to a Jew? If so, Abner Simon was that Jew.

"Who wants you dead?"

Abner shrugged. "A business transaction that went sour, nothing to speak of, but there is much enmity."

"What do you expect of me?"

"Talk to him. Tell him it's in his best interest. . . . You know what I mean. Will you help me?"

"When I know who he is."

"I can pay you well."

"Curse it, man, who is he?"

The dog cocked its head as if listening to something. Abner watched the animal for a moment, then appeared to lose all interest in talking to the Schout. He became busy with his weaving again.

Tonneman had one more card to play. A card from a different game perhaps, but it was the only one he had. "Is Benjamin Mendoza alive or dead?"

A blast of the ferryman's horn interrupted all intercourse, but not before Tonneman again saw Abner's hands pause and recover. This time his good eye twitched. The horn blew again. He'd get no more from Abner Simon this day.

Reluctantly, Tonneman walked halfway down the rocky path, peering across the river. Cornelis Dircksen was rowing toward them like a madman. "Ho, Tonneman!" he shouted.

"What's this about, Dircksen?" Tonneman called as the ferry-man brought the boat in.

"The Boss wants you. Now."

Tonneman turned back to Abner. "Our business is not done."

"We'll speak again," said Abner, "when we each have something to say."

27

TUESDAY, 26 AUGUST. *Dusk.*

The narrow, elm-bark canoe smelled sickeningly of bear grease. Racqel sat hunched behind Foxman on a bundle of dry twigs. There was no room to spread her skirts to dry. Soon enough her wet buskins would blister her feet, already tender from the fire.

Over her shoulder she saw Manhattan growing smaller as the sun sank behind the island. Her father would have said the bright orange sunset augured another hot day for the morrow. The section of Long Island known as Breukelen was only a short way across the river, but she felt as if she were embarking on a great journey.

She stared at Foxman's naked back and was at once overcome by the danger she had invited by her rashness. No one had seen her go with the Indian. She could disappear just as Benjamin had. How did she know he was taking her to Abner? And even if Foxman was true to his word, would Abner be able to help her? She had no assurance of anything, but for all that, she wasn't sitting at home, helpless, wondering.

She had to believe Foxman wouldn't harm her. After all, he did business with the Mendozas. Why would he jeopard that? Ninny, she thought, the savages don't have our values. Trust no one but yourself from now forward.

The soft air and the smooth movement of the canoe lulled her. She let her fingers drift in the cool dark water. Overhead, gulls circled, as if watching their passage. Tendrils of hair fell into her eyes; she realized with horror that she'd lost her cap, probably in that instant of surprise when Foxman had first appeared behind her.

How wicked she was to have uncovered her head. Jewish law said that the constant wife does not show her hair, only wantons do; a woman's hair is nakedness that only her husband may see. But the Christian women were modest about their hair, too.

With the wind in her hair, Racqel felt as if she'd slipped her bonds and was suddenly free of everything that troubled her, from David and his imperious harping about what was correct. She'd had so little sleep. Her eyelids were getting heavier and heavier.

She shuddered back to awareness. But at first in the deep dusk she didn't realize where she was, had no memory of how she'd gotten there. As her head cleared and her eyes became accustomed to the darkness she saw they were in a rocky cove and that Foxman was knee-deep in the water, guiding the canoe past thrusting rocks.

It was quiet as the grave. "Where are we?" she whispered as he beached the boat. "Is Abner Simon near?"

The Indian motioned for her to get out of the canoe. She tried, but without his help it was awkward. In the dim twilight she could see him kneeling, perfectly still, his ear to the ground.

She stumbled, twisting her ankle painfully on a rock, and cried out. Foxman was on her in an instant, clamping his hand over her mouth so that she could scarcely breathe. His rough hands had the same greasy smell as the canoe. He dragged her across the stony beach and up into the undergrowth, then dropped her and faded into the woods.

Stunned, she lay flat, her body pressed to the ground. Prickly thorns scratched at her face. The earth was pulsing beneath her, a soundless steady trembling.

Foxman came out of the shadows, gliding like a great cat as Bathsheba did when she was stalking a bird. He squatted beside her.

His sharp odor was also like that of an animal. "Soldiers. Horses. Many. They are coming this way."

She sat up. "The English?"

His hand darted out. She shrank back. He tore the drawstring bag from her waist. She could see his teeth in the shadows. He rose, moving away from her, back toward the beach. Racqel went after him. "I don't care about the money . . . don't leave me here. Where is Abner's house?"

He stopped and pointed down the beach. "Walk until you find the path up to the house," he said softly, and he continued to the beach and his canoe.

"How far?"

"Walk." He stepped silently into the water, pulling the canoe after him.

She looked across the river and saw darkness except for a faint flickering a long way off to the left. "I have no light," she cried. Her voice, faint and frightened, came back at her, but Foxman was no longer there.

28

TUESDAY, 26 AUGUST. *Dusk.*

Cornelis Dircksen rowed Tonneman directly to Coenties Slip.

"Ho, Tonneman. Dircksen." Conraet Ten Eyck was working on one of the pier pilings, daubing it with pine tar. Tonneman waved to his friend as he jumped out of the boat.

Head down, Ten Eyck muttered, "Soon as I've finished with this rotten . . ." He looked up and saw Tonneman running. "Why the rush? What's amiss? Is it the English?"

"Nay," Tonneman called as he raced through the alley. "No time to talk." He ran to his stable with Cornelis Dircksen in hot pursuit.

"Four stuivers, Tonneman," Dircksen badgered, breathing hard.

"I don't have it," the Schout said as he saddled Venus. He was thirsty from the salt fish. What he wouldn't give for a tall tankard of beer before he had to face the Boss.

"That's all I ever hear," the ferryman complained. "I want my four stuivers. It should really be eight."

"Go into the Pear Tree and tell Joost I sent you. He'll give it to you." Tonneman mounted the mare and reined her toward the Fort.

"What if he doesn't?" Cornelis Dircksen shouted after him. "And what about my other boat? The one you left in Breukelen. That's four guilders at least."

Tonneman's mind was on Stuyvesant and what the news would be. Had the English made their appearance? But where? There were no strange ships in the bay. Could the English be at the Wall, then?

A pity for the interruption. His question about Benjamin Mendoza had aroused a response in Abner Simon as nothing else had during their meeting.

Would he be so interested in the whereabouts of Benjamin Mendoza if he were not so interested in the woman? Of course he would, he assured himself. Mendoza was a citizen of New Amsterdam. Venus whinnied and he patted her flank. But what of the woman? He had no answer.

Outside the Fort two ten-man squads were lined up in two ranks, the front rank kneeling. They were practicing firing their wheel locks at targets hung in the trees. The front rank fired while the rear rank loaded and vice versa. In spite of the heat all were wearing leather jack coats, breastplates, and helmets.

Some of the men had old matchlocks, so they first had to place their weapons on aiming forks that they carried with them. In each of these soldiers' right hand was a coil of wick called the match, which previously had been lit to a glow. This match was needed to ignite the gunpowder. In the newer wheel lock, the spark to ignite the powder was produced by the friction of a steel wheel against a piece of iron pyrites.

When time came to fire the matchlocks, the match was attached to the serpentine, which held it in place, and which, when the trigger was pulled, would move the hot match to the powder and ignite it. Many of the coils were no longer glowing and were dragging on the ground. It was a muddled and disorderly exhibition.

From the ranks came the cry, "Light some lamps, Sergeant, so we can hit the targets."

The sergeant's laughter was like the boom of a cannon. "We'll light the lamps, all right, but you still won't hit the targets."

Responding cackles erupted from the troops.

Lamps were lit and the shooting drill continued.

"By the numbers," the sergeant shouted, exasperation in his voice. "One. Pour measure of gunpowder from charger into barrel. Two. Place wad in barrel. Three. Force wad home with ramrod. Four. Drop bullet in and place second wad. Five. Force wad and bullet home. If you have any problem with the second wad, spit in the barrel. If you've got any spit. In the middle of battle spit is a hard thing to come by."

"If we don't have spit, can we piss in the barrel, Sergeant?" a soldier jeered; his speech was muffled because of the four bullets in his mouth, carried there by all musketeers for quicker loading.

"No talking in ranks," the sergeant roared. "But you'll find that piss is even harder to come by; you'll have wet your breeches by that time." He squared his helmet and bellowed, "Six. Replace ramrod in pipe."

"Isn't spit six?" someone else called.

The sergeant scowled. "Let's see how humorous you are with the enemy crawling up your arse. Remember, matchlocks, on aim you blow on your match so that it's hot enough to ignite the powder in your pan, then you clip your match to the serpentine. All of you, now: ready? Aim. Fire. And reload. Now let's do it *in veritas*."

To Tonneman's surprise many got it right, even one or two armed with matchlocks. The explosive sound and puffs of smoke coming from the locks of the weapons were comforting. Not so comforting were the targets hanging from the trees, unscathed.

"We'll do it again. By the numbers. One . . ."

Stuyvesant and Captain Stephanaus Van Dillen, leader of the Civilian Militia, and Colonel Caspar van de Steen, commander of the regular soldiers, were watching the performance. This time all three men were dressed for combat.

Shaking their heads in dismay, the three adjourned to Stuyvesant's office within the Fort.

Tonneman followed.

As he entered the office the others were lighting their pipes. The chamber reeked of Stuyvesant's rosemary tobacco.

The Director-General stamped to his desk. "Have a pipe, Tonneman."

As much as he hated Stuyvesant's cloying tobacco, the Schout took the clay pipe the Director-General offered. It was a real short-stemmed nose warmer, the normally long clay stem having been cut down too often after each guest had used it. Perhaps it was a hint from Stuyvesant to state his business quickly and get out, which would suit Tonneman just fine. He needed to get home and get some sleep.

He sat, and reached for the silver tobacco box. The noise of musket shots repeated randomly. "Good sound, that," he said, filling the pipe.

Van Dillen and van de Steen came away from the window and

took chairs facing Stuyvesant. "We can thank Abraham Mendoza for it," said Colonel van de Steen, stroking his scar.

Van Dillen twisted his mustache. "It was he who had the Company ship the black powder."

"They'll make money," Stuyvesant snarled. "We'd be better thanking God."

"But that's not why you sent for me." Tonneman hoped the crazy old man hadn't brought him back for some kind of prayer meeting.

"No," said Stuyvesant, leaving it at that.

Captain Van Dillen cleared his throat. "The English—"

"I'll tell him," the Director-General roared, getting to his feet. "The soulless English have landed four hundred and fifty men about two leagues from here at Gravesend on Long Island, and they are force-marching toward us at this very moment."

"That puts them six miles away from sitting in our lap," said the colonel.

Tonneman sighed. "It was bound to happen. It won't be long before they're facing us across the East River, so close I'll be able to spit at them."

"You see what Nicolls is doing, God rot his soul." Stuyvesant clenched his fists and paced fitfully, thudding and thumping across the chamber. "He's in Gravesend Bay now. He'll bring his ships straight up the Narrows and have us between Scylla and Charybdis. Those troops in Breukelen will come at us from one side by land, and he'll attack from another by water. The devil take Nicolls to perdition. He means to encircle us completely. I—"

Tentative scratching noises at the door interrupted his invective. The door swung open. Willem Avercamp, Stuyvesant's ginger-haired young clerk stood there, his full red lips trembling.

"Yes? What is it?"

"A message from Captain Van Vliet."

"My artillery officer," offered Colonel van de Steen.

"Go on, man," Stuyvesant said truculently.

Avercamp took a deep breath and rushed into his message. "He says the new powder is no good. It won't fire."

"Hogwash," roared Stuyvesant. "Listen to them out there, blasting away." There came another ragged volley of musket fire, as if to prove his words.

Colonel van de Steen stroked his scar and shook his head. "God help us, that's the old powder."

Van Dillen twisted his mustache.

Stuyvesant sank slowly back into his chair. He puffed up his cheeks, let the air out, then puffed them up again. "Those cursed Israelites. In the pay of the English, that's what, every one of them. Godless traitors. They betrayed Christ, why shouldn't they betray us?"

"Calm yourself," said the colonel. "We must contain our inner passions and fancies in pursuit of proper purposes."

Stuyvesant's face grew fiery. "You dare to preach to me, you woman-chasing tosspot?"

"It does our cause damage to argue among ourselves," the colonel said smoothly, over the sound of another volley from the muskets. He stroked his scar. "What do you propose?"

Van Dillen twisted his mustache.

"The first thing," the Director-General shouted, "is to tell those witless arseholes to cease firing. They're wasting precious powder."

29

Tuesday, 26 August. *Dusk.*

Racqel sat down on a piece of driftwood and let the hot tears flow unheeded. Her cheeks stung where the thorns had scratched her. She had only a vague idea of where she was, but it was nearly dark and she had no light. The beach was a mass of boulders, rocks, stones, and pebbles.

She wiped her eyes and stood, wincing from the pain in her ankle. Almost in response to her fears, the moon came into sight from behind a dark cloud, beckoning her forward. Above her from the woods she heard a hum, like that of a swarm of bees. Flares of light punctuated the darkness. Quickly, she hid herself behind a large boulder.

Men and horses, the men in scarlet uniforms, were streaming out of the woods into the clearing. There seemed to be hundreds of them. They started to make fires and set up camp. What language were they speaking? Their voices were muffled. They had to be soldiers. Then she heard the sweet tenor voice of a young boy wafting to her on the air. *"It was a lover and a lass with a hey and a ho and a hey nonny nonny. . . ."* The wind shifted and she heard no more singing. Such an innocent voice but it was certain who he was and what he was here for.

Soon, she thought with a jolt, they would be down here at the river's edge. Their objective, after all, was New Amsterdam. They would want to look at it.

Racqel began to tremble. If they found her . . . They would treat her as a spy. No, as a whore. She had to flee this place. She scrambled to her feet and ran limping along the shoulder of the river, sometimes slipping on the slimy stones, falling, getting wet, rising, going forward.

Behind her the voices faded slowly, but the fires glinted from the clearing and beside the river, where she had hidden.

Smoke floated toward her, rich with the scent of roasted meat. Though it was most assuredly unfit meat, she craved it. The sun had set; her time to fast was over. Hunger and exhaustion tugged at Racqel. She felt chilled to the bone in her wet clothing.

Staggering, she tripped on a jagged rock and fell heavily. She didn't have the strength to rise.

30

Tuesday, 26 August–Wednesday, 27 August. *Night—After Midnight.*
The dark figure stepped out of the shadows and pushed the boat into the river. The only sound was the ripple of the water. With strong, even strokes he rowed across. Once on the other side, he pulled the boat out of sight into the scrub and climbed the small incline to the cottage. He had no light. He didn't need one; he'd been there before.

Tonneman was hungry as a bear when he got home, but it was too late to drop in on the Ten Eycks. However, Katrina Root had left him his evening meal. It was salt cod.

But all was not lost. Dinck had been as good as his word. Just inside Tonneman's backdoor was a wheel of Leiden caraway cheese. He cut himself a piece, and that, with the beans that had come with the fish, made a serviceable meal. He consumed most of a bottle of brandywine, which deadened his limbs but, for once, not his brain.

The windows were opened. Unlike most people Tonneman didn't believe that the night air was poisonous and had to be closed out; he had spent too many nights on an open deck. This night was cool, the first in some time. Autumn would soon be here. And so would the English.

It was still dark when he thought he heard tapping at his door. The Rattle Watch had called the hour only minutes before, but Tonneman couldn't remember what it had been. He lay on his corn shuck mattress, clad only in his breeches.

His thoughts would not let him sleep. Maria. Smitt. The body in the shed. The English. Anna and Johan and the unborn baby. Would they be safe? He shifted his bulk on the mattress. Racqel Mendoza. This was the first time he had thought of her by name, not as the widow or the Jewess. The memory of her soft, slim body made him even more restless.

This time he heard the tapping clearly and sat up. His candle was still lit, about half-gone, the flame circled by moths. He looked out the window at the sky. It was a good three hours till dawn. He crossed to the front door and opened it. The African Tall Matthew stood on the stoop. Tonneman's candle sputtered and died.

"I have a message for you, Heer Schout. From Abner Simon." Tonneman stared into the darkness, trying to read the man's face by the light of the moon, but Tall Matthew's color made that impossible. "He says you must come."

"It'll wait till morning." Tonneman backed away, ready to close the door.

"No, it must be now. He says tomorrow will be too late."

Tonneman scratched his head. What was so important it couldn't wait for daylight? The whereabouts of Cutnose or Benjamin Mendoza? Whichever, he was interested. "Don't stand there. Come in." He found his flint and tinder and relit the candle. "This is madness. Do you know the English are in Breukelen right now?"

"Yes, sir, but it has little to do with me. I'm in the white man's country. Are you coming?"

"All right." Tonneman wet his face with the remaining water in the pitcher on the table and drank some.

"I have a skiff."

"Good. Dircksen would be unfriendly at this hour, and I wouldn't have liked swimming." He pulled on his boots and took his shirt from the back of the chair where he'd left it. "How do you come to know Abner?"

"He used to own me. A few years back he set me free. Now I stop by sometimes to see if he needs anything."

Tonneman secured his baldric with knife and sword. While he was lighting the Better lamp from his candle he noticed the silver disk and the magnifying glass he had set on the table next to the pitcher when he'd come home. He put them in his jacket pocket. "You're a good man."

"It moves up the road and down the road."

Tonneman put on his jacket, took up his cudgel, handing the Better lamp to Tall Matthew. "Let's go."

The skiff, a clean, trim little craft, was lying in Coenties Slip, and Tonneman had half a mind to raid Antje Ten Eyck's larder, for events these days seemed to conspire to keep him from a good meal. But it was far too early, even for Antje.

Tall Matthew rowed out a few yards into the blackness, past three anchored merchant ships, till he caught the wind, then the sail took them across in only one tack. The boat grated and scraped alarmingly when they came up on the stony shore. Tonneman took the lamp and his cudgel and got out. He turned to steady the boat for Tall Matthew, but the black man was rowing back into the river. Surprised, Tonneman called after him. "Aren't you coming with me?"

"No, sir, I'm late as it is. I've got work to do for Heer Levy."

Tonneman, shaking his head in puzzlement, made his way up the uneven path he'd climbed the day before. Here the mosquitoes were legion. Fireflies flickered like little torches. An owl hooted and somewhere off a loon sounded its crazy mournful laugh.

Abner Simon's cottage was dark and silent; the door was closed. Tonneman had half expected to see the man still sitting in front with his dog, waiting for him.

The light cast by Tonneman's Better lamp showed the chair Abner had been making, on the grass, on its side. A creature's eyes flashed like two beacons as the light of the lamp caught them. The creature, frightened, scampered away into the scrub. Was it the dog? No, the dog would have barked or growled. And it was much larger. Where was the dog?

A faint scent of lavender settled over Tonneman like spring dew. His mind snapped awake. He held the lamp away from his body and raised his cudgel in readiness as he walked forward.

When he reached the house, he set the lamp down and opened the door with his left hand. "Simon, are you there?" His voice sounded flat and low to his ears. He picked up the lamp. Its wavering glow scarcely lit the chamber.

He hadn't seen so many books since he was at university. Regrettably, they were all piled on the dirt floor and many were torn asunder.

Abner Simon was past response.

He lay, a crumpled heap, on the blood-boltered, book-strewn floor of his cottage, the back of his head split open. Sticking out of the wound was a European-made iron tomahawk with an ax at one end and a pipe at the other, just like the one Tonneman had seen at Foxman's waist.

As he bent over the corpse Tonneman heard a whisper of sound, a catch of breath. He turned, raising the lamp and the cudgel. Again he caught the scent of lavender.

A powerful blow struck him on the side of his head.

Blindly, battling the numbness, he found the door and tumbled forward.

31

WEDNESDAY, 27 AUGUST. *Middle of the Night.*
When Racqel opened her eyes, she saw directly across the river the flickering lights of Manhattan. A few yards away was a boat, but it was upside down.

While her desire to know the truth about Benjamin remained acute, foremost on her mind was the need to alert the people of New Amsterdam that the English were close by.

She was cold and stiff and hungry, and her head and body ached more than she could believe was possible. How long had she slept? She stood on shaky legs, limped to the boat, and tried to right-side it, but could not even raise it from the ground. She looked for a piece of wood with which to prise the boat.

Up ahead and high, a light. Her eye on the light, she abandoned the boat and resumed her walk.

One minute there was the light, the next none. Only the moon.

Apprehensive, she crept to where the light had been. Here, she found under a sheet of canvas another boat. To her right, a narrow path went up a steep hill.

Relief swept over her. This had to be Abner's boat, and she would find Abner's house at the top of the path.

With new determination, she climbed the rocky path and in the moonlight saw the dark shape of a cottage ahead. No friendly light shimmered from a window. No lamp or torch lit the outside. Only silence and the rustling of the trees.

Then a loon's sorrowful laugh came over and over, mocking her. She stood at the top of the hill staring at Abner's cottage. A loud moan cut through the stillness.

32

WEDNESDAY, 27 AUGUST. *Approaching Morning.*
"Tonneman." The voice contained an urgency that scattered the dust from his brain. He had a wakening sense that his name had been intoned more than once.

His immediate sensation was pain. He groaned. A gentle hand touched the side of his head, identifying the source of his pain, and he groaned again.

When he forced his eyes open, the first thing he saw was the silver-white full moon, clear and sharp in a star-strewn sky. It all came back to him swiftly. Abner Simon was dead.

Tonneman lay there, amid curled strips of hickory bark, angry with himself. He'd arrived too late to save Abner, too late to get Abner's information, and just in time to get clubbed by Abner's killer. But why hadn't the killer killed him, too?

An owl in the woods hooted. He sat up. Flickering fireflies danced in front of his face. Red fireflies. He felt as if he had guzzled a full bottle of bad booze and had none of the enjoyment and all of the misery. His head throbbed. The night bred strange shadows; the wind moved through the bushes and trees in an uneven rustle.

He looked for his hat, then remembered the voice. Only when he turned did he see the small dark figure crouched behind him. He stared, amazed. He knew this face, this fine, delicate face.

Her dark hair fell oddly unobstructed, voluptuously to her shoulders and past. She was as bedraggled as a wet cat, this woman who had been calling his name over and over. Racqel Mendoza. "Are you all right?" she asked.

Warm blood trickled from the wound at his hairline down the

left side of his face. He stopped its course with his hand. Carefully he reached higher, to the tenderness, and found a raw bump. It was sore as the devil, but it didn't seem to be mortal. He was fortunate to have so hard a head. "Where's the dog?" he said, struggling to his feet.

She rose, too. "I didn't see a dog. Are you all right?" she asked again, hugging her arms.

"I think so." His head was hammering like the clapper in a bell. "What are you doing here at this time of night?"

"I came to see Abner Simon, but that's no longer important. I just saw English soldiers. Hundreds of them."

"Where?"

"Back there. Less than a mile."

"What kind? Foot soldiers?"

"They had horses."

"Any cannon?"

"I didn't see. The camp is not far from here. We must get Abner and warn the people."

Her news was no surprise to him. Ever since Colonel Nicolls landed men at Gravesend, he'd been anticipating it.

"Did you see anyone else?"

"No. Except . . ."

"Except what?"

"Foxman. He brought me over here."

"You came here alone with that Indian?" He was as enraged with her as if she were his woman. But she wasn't, and he had no right to be so angry.

"Yes." She spoke with little emotion. "I hired him to take me to Abner Simon. He took my purse."

"Where is he?" Anger blazed. "You fool. No white woman puts herself in the hands of an Indian, certainly not one so savage as Foxman."

She seemed to shrivel in front of his eyes. He felt remorse for his words; he wanted to open his arms to her, take her in and hold her, comfort her, snatch the words back, and wipe out the sting of them.

"He left me in the wrong place when he saw the soldiers."

Tonneman, confounded, eyed her and reflected on it. The facts fit. The tomahawk in Abner's head, the missing dog. It all pointed to an Indian. Only the answer was not the one he'd expected. Not Cutnose. Foxman. After leaving her, Foxman could have doubled back like his namesake the fox and killed Abner. But why? And what of the man in the shed? An Indian might well have slain him. And what urgency was there that she had to ask the savage to take her to see

Simon? He wished his head would stop pounding. He needed some answers. "Help me find my lamp and we'll go."

"What about Abner?"

Tonneman looked back at the cottage and then at her. "He won't be coming."

"What do you mean?" Her great dark eyes stared at him.

"He sent Tall Matthew, the African, to get me, but I was too late. He's dead."

"Dead?" She sounded confused.

"Murdered. Most likely by the same hand that put a dent in my head. After what you've told me, my feeling is that it could have been Foxman and probably was."

"But he was paddling away in his canoe when I last saw him."

"That makes nothing. I never met an Indian yet who didn't go one way and then double back to go another. Foxman carries a European-made tomahawk."

"Yes. He had it when I was with him. Many of the Indians do."

"Abner was killed with just such a weapon."

Racqel's eyes went wide; she opened her mouth but no words came.

He gave her a hard look. "Is there anything else you want to tell me?"

"Yes. I'm wet and I'm cold."

She'd gotten a bit of her tartness back; he smiled under the shield of darkness as he searched for his lamp in front of the cottage. He found it and his hat both all but hidden by Abner's half-finished chair. Tonneman felt in his jacket pockets. Purse in one pocket, magnifying glass, piece of silver in the other. No tinderbox. "Pig shit," he said, dusting his hat across his breeches. "Sorry." He put his hat on. It didn't fit right and it hurt. "I'm going into the house to find flint and tinder."

"We mustn't delay," she said insistently. "They'll be on us soon, and we have to warn our people." Her speech was breathless as if she'd been running.

"We're going. But with the English here I may never get another chance to look about Abner's house."

The interior of the cottage was black as pitch and he stumbled in the doorway. He'd never find anything in this cursed place. Then he caught a whiff of tobacco. He followed his nose. His hand touched a jar, a pipe, some tapers, and a tinderbox.

He lit his lamp, being careful to cover it from the one glassless window. "That's better," he said under his breath, bending to one knee beside the dead man.

"I can hold the light if you like." Racqel was at his side. Tonneman squinted up at her and handed her the lamp without a word. He had learned not to argue with Racqel Mendoza about anything, and he was in a hurry now.

Abner's body was cool but not cold and not yet rigid. It had to have been the killer whom he'd surprised when he came into the house.

Without his asking, Racqel moved the lamp to light Abner's broken pate. She made a small sound when she saw the bloody ax pointing up from Abner's head, but otherwise said nothing, and the light did not waver. Tonneman pulled the gory weapon from Abner's skull and drew the blade back and forth across the dirt floor, cleaning it of blood, bone fragments, and brains.

When he held the weapon to the light to examine it, he heard a small gasp from above him.

Tonneman was surprised at her reaction. She, the physician's daughter, had been so calm about the body in the shed. She murmured something and shook her head. Tonneman frowned. In the back of his mind something teased him. "Your father-in-law and brother-in-law trade these, don't they?"

"Yes," she answered straightforwardly. "To the Indians. That might very well be one." The lamp shook violently with her shivering. Tonneman stood, took off his coat, and placed it around her shoulders. Then he took the lamp from her and held it high to survey the rest of the chamber.

The books. In Latin and Greek, Hebrew and English, other languages he couldn't identify. Whatever the searcher had been looking for was that which could be concealed in a book. And whatever he was, Abner Simon was a reader, but not of Dutch literature. So many English books. Had he been an English spy?

There was no profit in it for Tonneman to search the bookish muddle. He turned the body over. Abner's arm, which had been folded under him, was at an odd angle, probably broken in his struggle with his killer. The fingers of his left hand seemed to be clutching something tightly.

Tonneman set the lamp on the floor and pried at Abner's fingers. Resistant in death, they would not open, would not release their hold. With a sharp snap one finger broke. Racqel gasped again but did not speak. The hand was open, revealing nothing. Tonneman lifted the hand closer. The broken, dirt-encrusted nails were gummous with what looked like blood and bits of skin. So, Abner had damaged his killer.

A sudden curiosity struck Tonneman, and he reached down and flipped back Abner's eye patch. Without the patch the Jew's face was grotesque. Some ancient injury had gouged the eye out. Now in its place was a small folded piece of paper. Tonneman plucked the paper from its socket nest.

Was this what Abner had spoken of yesterday, the *pape* Spectacles had referred to? Tonneman unfolded the paper. It seemed to be an official document, in English. The writing was in a small pinched script.

He considered asking Racqel if she could read the document, then chose not to. It was very confusing to feel as he did about this woman yet trust her so little. He refolded the paper. Antje could read English. He would show it to her.

A faint noise outside. Instinctively, Tonneman shielded the lamp with his hat and moved quickly to the window, but he saw and heard nothing more.

The Jewess did not react. Had she not heard? Bah, soon the shadows would become ghosts and send him running home like a frightened child.

He felt like a juggler tossing balls in the air: the document, the burnt body in the shed, the death of Abner, the tomahawk, the disappearance of Benjamin Mendoza. And what of Smitt? Were they all connected?

And now the English were in Breukelen.

The singed smell of his hat being burned by the candle brought Tonneman out of his musing. "Enough," he said, more to himself than to the woman. He took the hat from the Better lamp, sniffed it, and put it on his head.

Returning to Racqel, who still wore his jacket on her shoulders, he shoved the document into the pocket that held the magnifying glass and the piece of silver.

Was that a smart thing to do? Bah, more ghosts from shadows.

He raised the lamp high. The tomahawk was still in his left hand. He gestured toward the door with it. "We must leave here."

Still thinking of the noise he'd heard, Tonneman walked cautiously around the north side of the house looking for his cudgel. Racqel followed.

It was then they saw the body of the dog. Tonneman's cudgel lay beside it. Had the poor creature been killed with his stick? No, the mastiff's throat had been cut. Its dead eyes glinted in the candle glow for a brief moment.

Behind him, Racqel made a faint noise.

Tonneman tried to cram the tomahawk into the waist of his breeches but it fell to the ground, next to his cudgel. Racqel picked up both and handed him the cudgel. "I'll carry the ax."

He grunted his assent. They found the narrow path and hurried down the steep hill, Tonneman leading the way. Abruptly he stopped.

"What?" Racqel asked.

"Shh." Stock-still, he snuffed the candle and listened. The sound was unmistakable. Someone pissing. It was so loud he wasn't sure if it was man or horse.

With little undergrowth the going was fairly easy; they circled round off the path and made their way down the slope, away from the pisser. As they headed for Abner's boat the loud breaking of a branch stopped them. Tonneman pulled Racqel down with him into the shadows.

She was frightened by what might be out there, and then by his closeness. She remembered his bare chest covered with crinkly white-blond hair. And she wanted him to hold her the way a man holds a woman. "What is it?" Her voice trembled.

"Be still." His blood was pumping, preparing him to fight or run. Mixed with that was the awareness of her soft body so close to his, her loose hair, the touch of her, the smell of her, tinged with a faint trace of smoke and lavender. Lavender?

They waited, breathing together. Twigs snapped as clumsy feet trod on them. "Wait here," Tonneman whispered. Staying low, he moved off in the direction of the sound.

Several moments later Racqel heard the unmistakable sound of blows falling and groans, followed by the cracking of twigs and branches. Then a sudden ceasing of night creature sounds. More groans and a voice she recognized. She rushed toward them. "David Mendoza," she cried, brandishing the tomahawk. The men, who had been rolling on the ground, stopped, sat up, and looked at each other. Tonneman stood and dusted himself off.

"What in blazes are you doing here, Mendoza?"

"You could have broken my arm with that stick of yours." Mendoza was scrambling on the ground, searching in the dirt and twigs. He retrieved his black silk cap and his black hat and put them on. When he stood up, he was flexing his right hand.

"You're lucky I didn't hit you squarely, and that I didn't break your head."

Mendoza rubbed his right arm. "Not because you didn't try."

"What the devil are you doing here?"

"That's no business of yours."

"That's where you're wrong," Tonneman whispered hoarsely. "Another man has been murdered and I want an explanation."

"He fol—"

"Keep your voice down," said Tonneman. He had not missed the look exchanged between Racqel and her brother-in-law, and suddenly he was extremely weary. "We are not in the Market Field."

"He followed me," Racqel said softly.

"That's of some interest, but it still doesn't answer my question. What are you doing here?" The Schout felt anger again burning in his gut. "Don't trifle with me, Mendoza. I've had enough."

"You mustn't blame him," said Racqel. "I thought Abner Simon—"

"Be still." Mendoza's whisper was a command. "This is not for *them* to know."

"*Them?*"

"A private matter, Tonneman."

"Nothing is private when murder is involved. What does your brother, Benjamin, have to do with Abner Simon?"

The Jews were silent. The woman looked down at her feet, and David Mendoza stared at him sullenly.

"Do you hear me?" Tonneman said softly but intensely. "I want answers. Now."

"So do I," a strange voice said loudly, coming from the woods behind them.

The three spun around.

The moon reappeared in full glory as if drawn by the helmets and metal corselets of soldiers in scarlet uniforms who suddenly were all around them.

The voice spoke again. "All of you, raise your hands. You are my prisoners."

"By what right?" David Mendoza demanded. "By whose authority?"

"By the right and authority of Charles the Second, King of England, Ireland, Scotland, and Wales."

BOOK II

The English

33

WEDNESDAY, 27 AUGUST. *Just Before Dawn.*
Torchlight flared and the bright scarlet uniforms that surrounded them seemed to bleed into the subtle brightening of the eastern sky.

"I am Subaltern John Brick-Hill of the King's Musketeers. Identify yourselves." The young officer was lean and while not as tall as Tonneman, more threatening, with his blue-gloved hand resting lightly on his undrawn sword.

"You have no authority. . . ." David began in the heat of the moment, then let his words trail off.

"Shut up, Mendoza," Tonneman said under his breath, wondering at the Jew's proficiency in English.

"Yes, shut up. Mendoza." Brick-Hill's Dutch was as fair as Mendoza's English. "Relieve them of their weapons and then to the high ground with them, Nesbitt."

A sergeant shouted orders. The tomahawk that was hanging loosely in Racqel's grip was taken, as were Tonneman's weapons. And while Racqel stared at her brother-in-law in mute disbelief, a small knife he had hidden at the back of his breeches, amidst his religious fringe, was discovered and taken, too. They were then herded back up the incline, so they stood once more in the clearing near Abner's hut.

Tonneman watched the soldiers warily as they spread around the clearing. Ten of them, by his count, probably an advance scouting party for the larger force still to come. Soon one of the soldiers would enter the hut and find the body.

"Subaltern Brick-Hill, I am Tonneman, Sheriff of New Amsterdam," Tonneman said in English. "This is David Mendoza, a trader, and his sister-in-law, Racqel Mendoza."

Racqel, whose knowledge of English was part of her father's legacy, was struck by Tonneman's stiff formality.

"Your business here?" Brick-Hill's eyes fell on Racqel and her dishevelment.

Tonneman watched a musketeer enter the dark cabin. "I'm investigating a crime."

"God's tortured body. Kiss my arse if we haven't got a poor
poop-noddying bastard here." The words spewed from inside the cottage and two more musketeers crowded into it.

"Mind the billingsgate," Nesbitt reproved. "Lady present."

Tonneman continued, "There's a dead man in the hut. He sent
for me but was dead when I arrived."

Brick-Hill's eyes went to Racqel again. He frowned. The sergeant
approached him and cleared his throat.

"Our boat sprang a leak last night," Mendoza said, indicating
himself and Racqel. "We barely made it ashore, and then we were
stranded until morning."

Brick-Hill did not react, and for a moment Tonneman thought he
had not heard him. "The list, Nesbitt?" he said to the sergeant at his
elbow.

Nesbitt brought forth a paper from inside his tunic and snapped
his fingers at an enlisted man behind him. The man, bearing a torch,
moved smartly forward. He and the sergeant and the other musketeers were dressed in grimy white shirts with wide unadorned collars.
Their tunics, breeches, and their stockings were all scarlet. The but-
tons that ran down the sides of their breeches were black, as were
their shoes.

Every man was armed with a musket and a short sword; all wore
helmets and corselets, sleeveless jackets of light metal that reached to
the thigh. Slung from each shoulder to hip were leather straps. Half a
dozen chargers, metal flasks of powder, hung from each strap. At the
bottom of one strap was a leather wallet; at the bottom of the other
was the sword. What, thought Tonneman ruefully, would the rabble
at the Fort do against disciplined soldiers such as these?

The sergeant handed Brick-Hill the paper and spoke softly.

Brick-Hill was *not* dressed in scarlet, but rather a bright blue
satin that he and his mistress had spent an hour in choosing one
charming afternoon in London. He wore a breastplate, but this and
his scarlet baldric, which was embellished with clusters of small daz-
zling diamonds, were his sole concessions to the military. Otherwise,
he was dressed in the fashion of the dead man with the octagonal
spectacles. He had lace at his wrists and on his wide white linen
collar, and bows at his knees and on his shoes. On his head was a
broad, blue velvet hat with a glorious white plume.

"Quite so," Brick-Hill said, running his finger down the
paper.

Three soldiers burst from the hut and rushed at the double to Sergeant Nesbitt.

"There's a dead man, sir. In the hut."

Brick-Hill looked up from the paper. "Tonneman . . . Mendoza . . ." He bowed his head to Racqel. "You are my prisoners. Nesbitt. Two men."

"Carlyle. Jones." The two soldiers behind Johnson stepped forward in precise moves. "These three are in your care." As the two men went to either side of the prisoners the sergeant said, "Sir, the hut."

"Please excuse me." Brick-Hill moved off and spoke quietly with the sergeant, after which they disappeared inside the dead man's cabin.

Mendoza shifted his feet and swung his arms.

Carlyle whistled sharply to Jones and tilted his head at Mendoza.

"Here," Jones said. "Quit that."

Mendoza immediately turned on Racqel and began berating her in Portuguese, which Tonneman understood, it being the language of the sea. "See what damage your wilfulness has done." He drew a large silk handkerchief from his coat and thrust it at her. "Cover your brazenness."

Racqel bowed her head. Wordlessly, she took the cloth and tied it around her head, covering her hair. Tonneman stared, fascinated by the small sensuous moment. Desire for her almost made him lightheaded. Her eyes came up and met his. It was as if she'd read his thoughts.

Brick-Hill came striding back to them, his sergeant at his side. "Dutchman," the subaltern said, reinserting himself into the group. "You're bloody right about the man in the hut. What crime are you investigating?"

"Another man, a stranger, was murdered in New Amsterdam only yesterday. Scalped," Tonneman added grimly. The musketeers stirred uneasily.

"The Jew in the hut had a hole in his head," said Brick-Hill. "Evidently killed by the ax we took from the woman."

"Tomahawk. We have Indian problems from time to time," Tonneman said. There'd been peace with the Indians for some time, but anything to make the enemy uneasy.

"*She* didn't do it, did she?" Brick-Hill asked with a foppish wink. "Affair of the heart and all that."

"Not hardly," said Tonneman.

"What is the inclination of your people? Are they determined to fight? Do you expect help from the other settlements?"

"Our people are inclined to good food and good drink. They love a good fight but are not averse to a good talk. And some of us believe if we need help, the Lord will provide."

"Pulling my leg, aren't you, old boy? That's all right, a man needs a sense of humor. How many soldiers are garrisoned at Fort Amsterdam?"

"You do not really expect me to answer?"

"No. But I already know. You have one hundred and fifty and are low on black powder."

"How could you know that?" Mendoza blurted out, astonished.

"Quiet, Mendoza," Tonneman barked.

The subaltern smiled. "Yes, quiet, Mendoza. Until you're spoken to." He studied the blue-and-white fringes of the prayer shawl that hung from under Mendoza's shirt and then turned back to Tonneman. "So, Dutchman, it appears that you now have two killings to investigate."

"Yes."

"And how do I know that *you* didn't chop the Jew's head with the tomahawk?"

"You do not. Just as I do not know it was not you."

"Quite so. How amusing. Very well, then. We won't interfere with your work. On your way. All of you. Nesbitt, their weapons."

"What?" Tonneman was incredulous.

"Would you spit on good fortune?" Mendoza's voice was high with tension, his body taut. "He said on our way. Let's leave."

"Jones," Nesbitt bellowed. "The prisoners' arms."

Jones returned their weapons, including the tomahawk, which he presented to Racqel, all the time leering at her with his crooked mouth gaping.

"It's no trick, I assure you," Brick-Hill said graciously. "I have no further business with you. You are free to go." He looked directly at Racqel, who was holding the tomahawk in one hand and clutching Tonnemen's coat about her with the other. He removed his white plumed hat and executed the grandest of courtier's bows with a deep bend of his right knee and an elaborate flurry of his right hand. "Madam. I hope I haven't inconvenienced you too much. A safe journey home."

Tonneman nodded to the subaltern and motioned Racqel and Mendoza to go before him.

"Till we meet again, Dutchman," Brick-Hill called after them.

34

Pale yellow marked the deep gray sky, and a dry, cool wind from behind gave an extra hand to Tonneman as he rowed Abner's boat across the river to Manhattan. The heat spell had broken at last, and soon they would be sliding into autumn and lonely winter. An English autumn and winter. "Oh no," he said aloud to shake off the melancholy he'd begun to feel when Brick-Hill had recognized the Mendoza name on his list.

Racqel, in the bow of the boat, huddled under Tonneman's duffel jacket, looked up eagerly at his sudden utterance, but he paid her no heed. Disheartened, she returned to her own thoughts. She was exhausted and knew only a deep misery from the events of this past day and night. Her future was just as wretched; she was trapped until death, condemned to a netherlife.

It was clear, thought Tonneman. There they were, prisoners of the English. Then the list, and they were no longer prisoners. Set free, just like that. It made no sense, unless the Jews were traitors. Spies for the English.

No, perhaps not all. Not his lovely Jewess, not his Racqel. How could she be a spy? What was that? *His* Racqel? Not yet. First he had to prove the missing husband dead. The Mendozas, father and sons, on the other hand, and Abner Simon, too, might well be English spies. That could explain Benjamin's disappearance. He could be with the English colonel, or waiting in Connecticut. Or he could be dead.

Racqel watched their island come clear as a fine painting in the lightening sky. Anything Abner Simon knew about Benjamin's disappearance had died with him. She was lost unless the Schout found a way to help her.

Tonneman ran the boat up on the shore not far from Coenties Slip, jumped out, and gave his hand to Racqel without thinking. Mendoza pushed his hand away rudely and took Racqel's arm, pulling her from the boat with such unnecessary vigor that she cried out in pain.

"Go easy," Tonneman said softly, holding his temper.

Four soldiers slept curled up on the dew-soaked grass and two leaned against a powder barrel, snoring. Their wheel locks lay useless on the ground beside them.

"On your feet!" Tonneman bellowed. The six men leaped up, stumbling and off balance. One reached for his weapon but desisted when Tonneman tickled his throat with his sword. "What if I told you the English were just across the river? Heaven help us when they come. You fribblers certainly won't. Get to your places. Look sharp." Tonneman shook his head. "Bah," he exclaimed, sheathing his sword, as the six men scrambled away to their posts along the shore.

He had one more thing to do and then he could sleep. His job was to deliver his intelligence about the English to the Director-General. After that, it would be P.S.'s problem. He didn't know how many more men would follow Brick-Hill, but it was clear that the sorry force at Fort Amsterdam was no match for them.

"I'm sorry," Racqel was able to murmur before Mendoza pulled her off down Pearl Street.

Tonneman followed more slowly, rapt in thought. He liked being Schout. It was too bad but now he would have to find another line of work. He would leave New Amsterdam to the English and buy some land in New Haarlem. Start a new life. All he needed was the land and a wife. God help him, he hadn't meant to think that. But there it was. *A wife.*

He caught up with the Mendozas in front of Stuyvesant's Great House, which looked out into the bay with a clear view of Breukelen. And soon enough it would have a clear view of the English fleet.

"Do you want me to go in with you and tell what I saw?" Racqel asked, shaking off Mendoza's arm but not his glare.

"Are you addled?" Mendoza demanded. "Why should you go in there? So old Timber-foot can spit on you?"

"I am witness to—"

"No," snarled Mendoza. "I am witness. To your foolishness. Do you think that man inside will thank you? Nay, he'll blame you and all of us for bringing the English down on them."

She touched Tonneman's arm with the tips of her fingers, then pulled back. He stared at the spot she had touched as if expecting to see scorch marks. "You must tell the Director-General that there are more soldiers than the few we met. The large group with horses I saw earlier." She took a breath, not daring to meet his eyes. "Hundreds, I think . . ."

"Racqel. I *insist* you come home now."

"It's all right," said Tonneman. "I'll tell him, Vrouw Mendoza. Good day to you both."

Mendoza clutched her arm, attempting to tow her along. "Come. We have much to do. I have still to say my morning prayers. I have to put a mezuzah on the doorpost of the new house and there's work awaiting me at the warehouse."

Sadly, she turned away and allowed her brother-in-law to lead her off.

Tonneman rubbed his bleary eyes and climbed the white stoop to the right of the front door of the Great House. He knocked one loud clap on the heart-and-crown wrought-iron knocker and studied the P.S. monogram cut out on the back plate below the heart. At last he heard a stirring within.

His breeches were filthy. He brushed himself off and straightened his shirt, which was torn in several places. The Director-General was sure to have something to say about the way he looked.

The door was opened by Eva Runkel, the bent old woman who took care of the Great House. "He's gone to the Fort." She closed the door in Tonneman's face.

"Good morning, Tonneman," he muttered, going down the left-hand white stoop. "And how are you this fine day? Wouldn't you like a taste of beer to quench your thirst or a piece of sausage to break your fast?" He could see Racqel and Mendoza ahead of him on the way to Jews Alley. Tired to his bones, he plodded toward the Fort.

35

WEDNESDAY, 27 AUGUST. *Early Morning.*
The Fort fairly rattled with energy. Preparation for war, at least within these walls, had become a fever. Sergeants bellowed orders and soldiers hastened to carry them out, chasing around, accomplishing nothing.

Tonneman ignored Dirk Baalde's urgent beckoning and went directly to the Director-General's office. The blacksmith would have to wait to hear the war news when everyone else did.

Avercamp informed him that Stuyvesant was with the barber.

Sapped to his limit, Tonneman turned around and dragged himself to Ernestus Beels's shop, again ignoring the blacksmith's frantic gestures and shouts to come and talk. The pole in front of the barbershop had been newly whitened and no fresh bloody cloths adorned it as yet, but the day was early.

Inside the small chamber, lit only by the sun coming through one large gleaming window and the blaze from the fireplace, Tonneman found Stuyvesant being shaved by Beels. The barber, a stumpy man with a thick mustache and long blond hair tied back with a leather thong, had to poise, tiptoed, often on a bench, to do his work. A large black kettle of water was bubbling over the fire, and Beels was scraping at Stuyvesant's face with a glinting sharp steel razor.

While the Director-General was being shaved, his eldest son, seventeen-year-old Balthazar, and Colonel van de Steen stood by. Stuyvesant was in midspeech about the need to shore up the Wall to protect the town from land invasion.

". . . know what Nicolls is thinking. Along the East River would be the best place."

Beels laid his razor down and picked up a steaming towel.

Stuyvesant interrupted himself. "Tonneman, there you are. What news?"

"There are English soldiers in Breukelen. On horseback."

The barber attempted to place the towel on the Director-General's face. Stuyvesant snatched it from him and pushed himself out of his chair. "Cavalry?"

"So it would seem."

P.S. wiped his face with the hot towel. "There, the encirclement I predicted. Scylla and Charybdis. That snake Nicolls is advancing by sea, and his soldiers will descend upon us from Breukelen. Misfortune and more misfortune. The Company sends no reinforcements, only orders me to defend their property. And our people, a cowardly lot, would rather become English than damage a roof pantile."

He halted his thumping parade in front of the window and raised his arms to the heavens. "It's all on me. It would be better that a millstone were tied around my neck and I were cast into the sea." Lowering his arms, he glared at the three men. "Believe me, Winthrop had a hand in this. May he and his Colonel Nicolls burn in hell." Flushed garnet red, P.S. resumed his angry pace about the chamber. With stubby fingers, he probed his upper lip to assess the state of his thin mustache, then cheeks and jaw for any traces of errant beard. He nodded approval at the barber, who smiled and turned away shyly. Stuyvesant tossed his head like a horse, smoothed his brown shoulder-length hair, and patted his bald pate. "Van de Steen, assemble the men and march them to the shore of the East River."

"That's exactly what Nicolls wants." The colonel stroked his scar and looked from Tonneman to the Director-General. "He's not trying to encircle you at all. It's a feint at your flank, forcing you to commit your troops and leaving your front exposed. You're falling right into his trap."

P.S. stopped pacing to consider van de Steen's words; he nodded. "The serpent is more subtle than any beast of the field. What do you suggest?"

"Surrendering might be a good tactic at this point," Tonneman suggested. His eyes were heavy. He leaned against the doorjamb.

"Never!" roared Pieter Stuyvesant.

Young Balthazar cleared his throat. He, too, had a beak of a nose over full lips, duplicating his father's stern image. "Why not, Father?"

Beels wiped up soap from the floor with a rag, then stropped his razor on the leather band attached to the chair, taking in every word of the conversation around him.

The Director-General stared at his son as if he'd been stabbed. "You too?" He took a deep breath. "No matter. Let everyone be against me, even the fruit of my own loins. The answer is still never. *Never.*" His hand rested on his breastplate over his heart. "The soul of New Amsterdam is in my keeping. I am a servant of the people. And as that servant I will not violate the faith the people have in me. Look to yourself, Tonneman. Your dress is not fit for your office. Give him a shave, Beels. Open your eyes, man. You're falling asleep on your feet."

The barber held the chair for Tonneman. Tonneman shook his head. "I've been up all night, Boss. About that business with the man in—"

"How many soldiers did you sight?" van de Steen interrupted.

"Twelve. Ten musketeers, a sergeant, and an officer."

"Ha!" Stuyvesant roared.

"There were more. Hundreds."

"How do you know that if you only sighted the twelve?"

"They were seen and described by a local." Tonneman was too tired and unwilling to go into the whys and whats of the Mendozas at this point.

"Get some sleep." P.S. turned his back abruptly. "And be back here by noon."

"Yes, sir." Tonneman left gladly. The old man seemed somewhat less sanguine than before. Behind him Tonneman could still hear Stuyvesant haranguing his son.

Tonneman yawned. "Plenty of time to sleep when I'm dead." Avoiding the blacksmith again, he left the Fort. He would find Tall Matthew on the shore of the North River. Except for the murderer, the African was probably the last person to see Abner Simon alive.

36

WEDNESDAY, 27 AUGUST. *Early Morning.*
"Will you please stop shouting at me?" Racqel was close to tears. She was exhausted and melancholy but she would not cry.

"I am not shouting," said David. His voice was low and velveted but filled with anger. "I am not what we are talking about. It is you. You who shame us. You who are a wilful creature who does not know her place."

Abraham shook his head sadly. That in his later years he should be surrounded by bitter discord within his family baffled him. He walked to the rear of what would be the great chamber of their partially finished house, touching the bare uprights lightly, murmuring prayers. On the other side of the house Frederick Philipse and his men were still working noisily. The old man sighed and then shuffled back to the entranceway where his son continued to berate Racqel.

"And your behavior with that drunken lout of a Schout is not that of a good Jewish woman, either." David plucked furiously at the sleeve of Tonneman's jacket, which was still about her shoulders. "Look how you flaunt yourself like a Jezebel, his clothes draped about you as if you were his chattel. It is more than unseemly. It is lewd and loathsome. And get rid of that heathen weapon. Not only is it vile, it is unholy, tainted with the blood of a dead man. A dead Jew, Ashkenazi or no."

In her deep exhaustion Racqel had forgotten she still clutched the tomahawk. She now lifted it ever so slightly so that she could get a better look at it. "You're the one who sells them. Are they holy things then, when you sell them, and only become weapons when the savages use them?"

"Quiet, Racqel," the old man said. "Come, my son, let her be.

She knows she's done wrong." To Racqel he said, "It darkens my heart to hear all the things David has told me. I thank God your father, may he rest in peace, is not alive to—"

Racqel started to speak.

"Silence when my father is talking to you," David commanded.

"Enough bitterness," the old man said to him. "Let us leave her to wash herself. She's covered with filth. It is not proper that she appear thus." Abraham walked slowly outside, head bowed.

"Take off that gentile's jacket," David ordered before following his father.

Racqel tore David's silk handkerchief from her head. Her snarled hair was still damp. She went to the backdoor, Caleb at her heels.

Who *was* the man in the shed? she wondered as she pulled up the wooden bucket at the well. The bucket was cracked and little rivers of water streamed from it. She set it down, almost too tired to care. Caleb licked greedily at the water on the ground.

She heard the voices of the Africans David and Goliath as they picked up pieces of scrap wood and put them in a wagon. They spoke a patois to each other that she could not understand. The two gray horses hitched to the wagon were nibbling lazily at the few clumps of grass that had not been destroyed by the fire. One wore a red velvet hat with a blue plume and looked so foolish that she laughed out loud. The laughter felt good; it warmed her cold aching heart. The Africans stopped work and bobbed their heads. "Good morning, vrouw," they said together.

"Good morning." There was a new bucket at the side of the house. Almost spent, she trudged to where she had last seen it.

". . . my everlasting shame," she heard Abraham say.

Oh no, they were still going on about her. She pressed herself against the side of the house.

"No, Father, not your shame. Benjamin's."

"The Mendoza name has been dishonored. How could he let that spawn of the devil, that Ashkenazi maggot Abner Simon involve us in his terrible intrigue?"

"If he were here, I would throttle him for doing this to us."

"Don't speak of your brother that way. He did what he thought was right, for the safety of the family."

"No, Father. He did what he thought was profitable."

"Enough," said Abraham. "I cannot bear the pain."

"Accept it, Father. Benjamin's lust for profit led him to treason."

She heard hand meet flesh with a sharp report. "Don't speak ill of the dead."

The dead? Racqel bit her knuckle to keep from crying out. She looked back at the Africans. They were picking up wood and putting it in the cart, unconcerned with her.

"Are you so sure he's dead?" asked David.

"One cannot make a pact with the devil and go back on it," the old man said. "He brought shame to our house. Better for us that he be dead. I have said Kaddish for him in my heart ever since that terrible day in December."

Racqel allowed herself a small breath. Not dead, not for certain. Only a religious metaphor.

"You are too harsh, Father. He saw he was wrong and was going to put it right. And he's not dead. Life would be so much simpler if he were. We could forget about his shameful act, I could marry Racqel, and we could go on with our lives. I love her. She needs a strong man, a man who will give her children. Her father allowed her to learn too much of man's affairs. She asks too many questions. She will destroy us if she uncovers Benjamin's intrigue with the English."

"You are a devout man, my son. In your mind. But in your heart . . . Benjamin would have had children if the woman could conceive, but alas she could not. Look elsewhere for a wife."

The conversation ceased. Racqel closed her eyes to clear her thoughts. Benjamin was not dead.

Caleb danced about her feet playfully. She bent and hugged the wriggling animal.

What had they been talking about? What pact with the devil? The words sank into her tired brain. Benjamin had been in some kind of questionable transaction with the English. Benjamin was a traitor.

37

WEDNESDAY, 27 AUGUST. *Morning.*

The rough seam on his hat where crown met brim pressed painfully against Tonneman's head, reminding him that since Tuesday night he'd been pushed, thumped, pounded, and bashed like some poor dumb animal. He lifted his hat and gingerly touched the left side of his head. A knob the size of a goose egg and some broken skin. It would heal soon enough. What wouldn't heal was a head cracked open with a tomahawk. Gently, he set the hat in place.

People had begun to arrive for Market Field. The settlers and local tradesmen walked or drove in on wagons, the Indians afoot or horseback, dragging their wares on hides stretched over two poles and pulled by their horses or their women.

Straightaway, the smell of roasting pig tantalized him. Tired though he was, Tonneman followed the scent around behind the Fort, past the windmill. The early birds had already set up. And here on Market Field day, all nations mixed without hostility. The German Brafman had set up his chickens in wooden cages and his splint basket of eggs next to the Frenchman de Blanche and his butter and cheeses. It amazed Tonneman how commerce just carried on, business as usual, in spite of the threat of invasion.

The wagons became stalls, and fronting them were lengths of wood, pegged across two poles, for leather thongs from which to hang game and crafts. The Indians had poles leaning against trees that served the same purpose.

Near one pole an Indian sat chewing a twig while his woman, her dark brown hair in two long braids, wove a basket from sea grass. Two young boys arm-wrestled behind her, and an infant, wrapped in a colorful cloth-and-hide bundle, slept at her feet.

They were Iroquois. Mohawk, by the look of them. The same as Foxman.

"When were these killed?" A townsman pointed to the rabbit and turkey displayed on the Indian's pole.

"This morning," said the Indian woman, not looking up.

The townsman sniffed the meat. "More like yesterday morning."

Throughout the Market Field Tonneman was greeted from all sides. Out of the corner of his eye, he saw his daughter's in-laws, Margrieta and Willem Bikker, and their young daughter, Clara, with baskets of red apples, peaches, and pears from their orchard in New Haarlem. Bees buzzed lazily around the ripe produce.

"How goes my daughter, Vrouw Bikker?"

"It won't be long before we are fat old grandparents." Margrieta Bikker laughed heartily; her eyes crinkled in her smooth, round face. She was a good-looking woman still.

Willem Bikker pumped his hand. A man of few words, he wisely let his wife do the talking.

"You must come and visit," she said. "The farm is splendid. Such a fine house. Not as big, but as fine as the Muscovy Duke's house on his Great Bouwerie."

"Now, Margrieta—"

"What are you hearing about the English? Any sign of them in New Haarlem?" Tonneman interrupted.

"Well, you see none of the English farmers here today," Willem Bikker said.

Tonneman looked around. Bikker was right. Not one English farmer was in evidence. Odd that he hadn't noticed till now.

"Broadsides have been posted everywhere. The English farmers have been warned they will be burned out if they provide us with either food or service." Margrieta hefted a basket of apples into a cart for a customer while Willem took the coins in payment. "Not only that. They've been beating the drums on Long Island to raise volunteers for the expedition against New Amsterdam."

"We nearly didn't come today," said Willem. "But we couldn't afford not to. We've heard the English have landed a force in Breukelen. Is this true?"

"So I've heard," was all Tonneman would say.

"Ah, it is bad enough they menace us from land and sea, but what will the hothead who sits in the Fort do? Will he compel a bloody fight?"

"I don't know," Tonneman said, trying to move on. "Give my daughter loving greetings."

"Take care of yourself, Tonneman," Margrieta called to him.

"My wondrous salve will cure warts, bee stings and animal bites, and scabious sores of any kind! And only five stuivers a pot!" This chant came from a rotund man with long, grizzled hair standing on a wagon. The wagon's carved and painted sign proclaimed him to be Teunis De Vries, Médecin Extraordinaire.

"De Vries, you old quacksalver, still selling your mixture of shit and grease?"

"Mock all you want, Tonneman. My salve has been known to cure the French pox and on occasion even the smallpox."

"In a pig's arse."

"Is that a little bump there, peeking out from under your hat? I'll give you some of my wondrous salve, gratis."

"Nay, thank you." Tonneman pulled the hat snugger to his head, wincing.

"Are the English nigh?"

"Why? Do you want to sell them some salve?"

"Not I. The English bring with them a great evil. They are blasphemers and fornicators."

"Keep talking like that, De Vries, and you could become Director-General."

"You flatter me, Heer Schout."

"I'll do more than that if I find out you're selling that quackshit for more than two stuivers a pot." A small group of customers had formed behind him. Tonneman shook his head as much at the people who would buy the salve as the man who sold it.

He heard the music before he saw the musicians; then he saw Korbonski and his fiddle. With him was a bearded dwarf of swarthy complexion, like a Spaniard. A furry grayish-brown creature about three hands high stood beside the dwarf, its tail wrapped around the diminutive man's leg. On the creature's head was a red felt cap. The hair on its head was like a monk's cowl; the face, a skull. The dwarf, only about nine hands high himself, was playing a flageolet, a small, end-blown wind instrument. To Tonneman's tired ears the sound was sweet as honey. Hanging from a leather thong around the dwarf's neck was a tabor. Korbonski's scruffy black hat lay, brim up, on the ground, waiting for contributions. Tonneman moved closer, not to put any money in the hat, or even for the music, but to have a better look at the little, misshapen man and his companion.

"A good morning to you, honorable Schout." Korbonski grinned crookedly, his chin resting on the fiddle. He looked none too clean, but Tonneman knew he himself at this moment was none too clean either.

"Korbonski."

"Do you like this tune? It's called 'The East Indies Rose Tree.' " He gestured at the dwarf. "This runty fellow is Lizard. Pretty little thing, isn't he?" A group of curious children had gathered around the threesome.

The dwarf stopped playing his flute to beat a rapid pattern on the tabor with his left hand. His voice was deep and melodious. "Good morning, Your Honor. Do you like *my* little friend? I love him because he is so much smaller than I. He is Capuchin, my little friar. Say good morning, Capuchin." The animal lifted the red cap in greeting and chattered at Tonneman.

It was a strange animal, but Tonneman had seen its like a long time ago when he was sailing. More important, it reminded him of something he had seen recently, something that had troubled him . . . but he couldn't remember what. When Tonneman didn't respond, the dwarf shrugged and resumed playing his flageolet.

A man carrying a noisy chicken upside down by the legs came rushing up to Korbonski. "Where?"

Korbonski shook his head.

"Where? I've got this chicken to pay for one of your chickens. The sap is rising in me. I'm as stiff as a tree and lusty as a bull."

The chicken screaked desperately.

"Not now," Korbonski said through gritted teeth, eyes veering toward Tonneman.

The man looked at Tonneman and, with sudden recognition, mumbled something and slinked off.

"Where is Sweet Lips, by the way?" Tonneman asked, smiling. Ever mindful of his original intent to find Tall Matthew, he was moving again.

"This time of morning?" Korbonski called after him. "Deep in the feathers."

"Working or sleeping?"

"Working or sleeping? Very amusing. I have to remember that. A good Dutch joke. For the English. Ha-ha."

"Stop a minute, Tonneman," On Jonas Gutwasser's spit, turning, roasting, was a beautiful pig. Gutwasser, a hearty portly man whose farm was near Stuyvesant's beloved Great Bouwerie, was standing in Tonneman's path with a gobbet of cooked meat in his hand. "Roast pig. Worthy as any you ever ate anywhere. Have a taste."

Tonneman hadn't realized how hungry he was. He tore into the meat.

"Savory, eh?"

"Delicious. Now if I only had a beer, I would think I've died and gone to heaven."

"No beer, alas. No grain, no beer. But . . . How about some apple cider?"

"I don't mind." The farmer passed Tonneman an earthenware jug. Tonneman tilted it and drank greedily. "Good. Tasty." Immediately he had to fight for breath. "Sweet Jesus. I have tasted some poisonous drink in my time, Jonas, but this must be the stuff Jan Keyser uses for tanning hides."

"Strong, eh?"

"Strong enough."

"Tell your friends. Tell them Gutwasser makes good water." He laughed. "The right kind of water, and only twenty-five stuivers a jug."

Music swirled around him. Children were dancing. Thumping, crashing dances. A juggler entertained with wooden balls. A man stood on his hands and walked back and forth.

A gaunt dark man, with a burning torch in a bracket on the side of his wagon, was attempting to swallow a sword. After making two or three attempts and failing, and cutting his fingers with the blade, the man dropped the weapon to the ground, brought out a bottle of brandywine from the wagon, and seized the torch.

A mouthful of brandywine.

And a mighty spit.

Flames flared and died. The brandywine trickled from the man's mouth, and he rubbed his singed lips in obvious pain.

Tonneman would have moved on, but something stopped him. The sword looked familiar. It was an elaborate rapier with ornamental scrollwork etched on the guard. Tonneman picked up the sword.

The double-edged weapon looked very much like the sword belonging to the man with the spectacles.

"Yes?" asked the would-be sword swallower–fire eater. Tonneman had never seen him before. His accent sounded Italian.

"Where did you get that sword?"

"In Palermo," said the man, lightly dabbing his injured lips. "My papa left it to me. Why?"

"No reason." Tonneman saw few coins in the dirty orange hat at the man's feet.

The man tried again to eat the fire from his torch. He was sure to end the day with cuts and burns and pots of De Vries's quacksalve to put over them.

Tonneman walked on. He had counted five soldiers patrolling the Market Field. Good, he thought, especially when the Schout isn't around to do it. And where was Pos? Sleeping most likely. Smart fellow.

He was ready to leave the Market Field when he saw a man watching him nervously. A sentinel, by his manner. When the man's gaze went to a wagon with a small group of people about it, Tonneman walked over. A man stood behind a table on which there were three thimbles; two men were in front of the table. "Find the pellet," the man behind the table cried, "and win ten stuivers. It's easy, even a child can do it."

"I've already won almost two guilders," said one of the two players, smiling broadly. The second man looked unhappy and confounded. Tonneman knew the first man worked with the man behind the table and the sentinel. Like the would-be sword swallower–fire eater, they were strangers to Tonneman.

"Try to find the piece of lead," urged the man with the three thimbles, pushing them around briskly. "All you need is ten stuivers to win ten stuivers."

"I'll hazard a florin," said Tonneman.

The man behind the table took Tonneman's measure. "Let's see the shine of your money."

Tonneman stared at the thimble man with hard eyes. "I'm good for it. Don't you trust me?"

"Of course." The man became wary. "One florin, it is."

Tonneman pulled two of the thimbles toward him and turned them up, revealing nothing. He nodded at the one remaining. "It better be under that one."

"You win," the thimble man said hastily, not turning the thimble up. "Here's your florin."

"Thank you," said Tonneman. He turned to the unhappy player. "How much have you lost?"

"Twenty stuivers." The man looked as if he were going to weep.

"Here's a florin. Now you're ahead eight stuivers. Begone."

"Yes, sir, thank you, sir," said the man, leaving on the run.

Tonneman turned back to the thimble man. "What's your name?"

"Jan van Amsterdam."

"And yours?" Tonneman asked the winning player.

"Johan van . . . Rotterdam."

Tonneman cast his eye on the sentinel, who looked away. "I suppose his name is Carl van Leiden. I'm Schout here, Heer van Amsterdam. You get out of town. And take your friends with you."

"But I gave you your florin. . . ."

"Get, before I charge you with fraud, trying to bribe a City officer and being an English spy. We have two lovely rat-infested jails, one right here in the Fort. You can have your pick."

"I'm leaving, Heer Schout." The thimble man motioned to his cohorts.

"Good. I knew you'd see it my way. Wait. Have any of you seen a man who wears octagonal spectacles and fancy clothes and smells of lavender?"

"No," said the leader, "but for a few florins . . ."

"Get."

Tonneman watched as they packed up and led their wagon away. Just thieves? Or English spies? He didn't know. But he did know there were too many strangers about. Even the man who had been losing was a stranger. He turned and bumped into Lubbertus van Dincklagen. "Good morning, Dinck. Thanks for the cheese last night."

Van Dincklagen was shucking and swallowing oysters. The juice made streaks down his dirty chin onto his copious chest and belly. In the fly-stormed wicker basket he carried were, besides the oysters, a slab of venison and two lengths of sausage. "To feed a friend is a blessing. Try one of these oysters. They're leviathans. So big each one could feed two."

"But not two like you, Dinck," Tonneman said, obliging his friend by cracking open a shell and popping one of the oysters into his mouth. "Walk with me, I'm in a hurry." He gave his friend a hard look. The fat man's face was gouged and scratched, his clothing torn and soiled, and his boots were soaked. "What gets you up this early? What happened to you? You look as if you've been dancing with a bear."

"When I saw the price that heathen woman was asking for oysters," Dinck answered, "I thought I might gather them myself. The best spot is right here, near the Fort. Unfortunately, I stepped in a hole and fell on my face. I thought I was going to die for certain." He wheezed and whispered into Tonneman's ear, "Scared me so much I bepissed my pants." His laugh was somewhere between a wheeze and a cough, and his scratched and dirty face had gone beet purple. He didn't look at all well.

"Those are bad scratches, Dinck."

Van Dincklagen touched his face. "Oyster shells."

"If I didn't know better, I'd swear you'd been to one of Sweet Lips's chickens for a frolic and she played too rough."

"Don't make me laugh, Tonneman. I haven't been up to frolicking for years." He stopped. "A minute. I can't walk fast anymore. What's happening with the English? Are they close?"

"You know what I know, Dinck."

"I doubt that. When? Today? Tomorrow?"

Tonneman clapped van Dincklagen on the shoulder. "I have to be on my way. A good day, Dinck."

"You too. That Indian woman had crabs for sale. Perhaps I should get some."

"Don't eat too much." Tonneman started for the Broad Way, but in spite of his haste he was still concerned about his friend. Tonneman turned around to look at the man again. As the last time they'd met, Dinck was having trouble with his sausages. This time one of van Etting's hogs was trying to steal them.

"Away . . . you pink cannibal."

Tonneman smiled sadly. His friend had changed a great deal over the last years. His illness and his squabble with the Company for his pension had taken its toll, physically and mentally. Dinck had never been one to gather his own oysters when he could pay someone else to do it. His finances had to be dire, and by the look of him, he'd been in a fight.

38

Wednesday, 27 August. *Morning.*
De Sille sat in the corner of the Wooden Horse Tavern with van Brugge. Van Brugge nodded toward the door at their partner coming toward them.

"Do you have the paper?" asked van Brugge.

"I?" asked the newcomer. "I thought you had it."

"This is not a matter for humor," said De Sille. "I'm sure Tonneman has it."

"Then *I'm sure* we'll have it *soon,*" said the newcomer.

Van Brugge put a lit taper to his pipe. "And *soon* the English will be here."

"Yes, what a lovely morning." De Sille looked out the window at the sunny day and smiled.

The scent of sweet, ripe peaches wafting from the De Sille property filled Tonneman's nostrils, wiping out all the smells of the Market Field. Geertruyd De Sille, her little pug dog in her arms, rushed out of her house. "Good morning, Tonneman." Her golden hair was uncovered and bound with a ribbon of the same yellow hue. It was difficult to tell where one ended and the other began. Her face, its paleness given emphasis by the black *mouche* on her right cheek, was framed by long loose curls. Fat gold earrings dangled from her ears, and about her neck hung a locket from a gold chain. Her curls danced as she stopped to catch her breath.

She was truly a beautiful woman, but Tonneman had never found her coquettish ways at all winning and now he was weary. "Good morning, Geertruyd." He raised his hat and continued on his way.

"Why so brusque with me?" She caught up with him, smiled, lowered her eyes partway, and looked up at him, cooing, "It's such a lovely day. Come sit with me in my garden."

"I really don't have the time, Geertruyd."

"I have beer."

She'd said just the right words. He stopped. She placed a soft pale hand on his arm. The pug yipped, showing its sharp little teeth. What was on her mind? Something told him he should find out. It was just a feeling, but he'd never gone wrong following his feelings. "Well, just one." He allowed her to lead him to the formal herb garden at the back of the house.

"Isn't this lovely?" She smiled at him sweetly. "It's the envy of everyone in New Amsterdam."

The fenced-in plot was laid out like a cross and geometrically precise. Hard by the fence were aromatic bayberry shrubs that grew higher than the fence, giving the garden some privacy. Bordering the shrubs were the ornamental tomato plants, heavy with fruit. Not for eating, of course; everyone knew they were poisonous.

In the center of the garden an apple tree shaded a whitewashed slatted pine bench and a long oak stretcher table where a blue majolica jug and an assortment of china indicated that Geertruyd was having her morning refreshment. Off to the side away from the shade of the tree was a sundial.

Geertruyd De Sille arrayed herself and the flat-nosed dog on the bench, plucking at the dog and the dress and her shawl, moving arms and material about until she was satisfied. "Ah," she said with a noisy sigh. She had arranged the carelessly draped shawl in such a way that her white shoulders and plump white breasts were conspicuous in their display against the gold trim of her silver-gray silk dress. The fan in her hand was gold on one side and silver on the other. The shawl over her right arm and across her lap was also gold on one side and silver on the other, and because of its many folds showed many combinations of silver and gold. The silver-and-fawn-coated dog was haughtily enthroned upon it. The sleeves of the dress were cut high. Under them large swaths of white gauze showed.

"Annabella," Geertruyd called, fanning herself impatiently. Her high voice trilled in the morning air.

The gnarled old black woman came to the backdoor. "Yes, madam."

"Posset for me. More wine this time. Not so much milk." Stroking the *mouche* on her right breast, Geertruyd turned to Tonneman. "Would you care for one? They're very refreshing."

Tonneman shook his head. He was unable to take his eyes from her bosom.

She smiled wickedly. "A beer for the Schout, then."

A piece of embroidery on a small hoop rested in front of her on the table. She put down her fan, picked up the hoop, and began to work as he watched. He was uncomfortably aware of her crisp, yellow hair and her large partially exposed breasts and her lavender scent. Again, lavender. Did everyone in Manhattan use lavender?

He was determined not to talk until he had his beer. He closed his eyes. And dozed. When he opened his eyes again, she was staring at him intently. "Where's Nick?" he asked.

"Nick? Oh, out and about. Playing tennis, I think."

Tonneman shrugged and pinched the tip of his nose in a desperate effort to stay awake. He stood and shuffled into the garden proper.

The paths of the garden cross were made of crushed oyster shell like Pearl Street and were bordered with violets. Yellow butterflies and black butterflies and fat yellow-flecked bees floated and buzzed about.

The upper left quadrant formed by the cross had white chrysanthemums, dill, fennel seed, wild licorice, and wild sassafras and lavender. In the upper right quadrant were yellow chrysanthemums, parsley, sage, chamomile, and mint and lavender. The lower left, yellow chrysanthemums, costmary, hyssop, and flax and lavender. The lower right, white chrysanthemums, rue, yarrow and foxglove, and more lavender.

In the dry, warm sunlight, everything seemed so sweet and pleasant.

When Annabella brought the drinks, he sat heavily on the pine bench, draining his beer quickly. With all this great variety of flora about them, there appeared to be only one smell coming from Geertruyd and her garden. Lavender.

"You seem so very, very tired," she lisped.

"I've been up all night. My bones ache and my feet are sore."

"You should have your boots off. Here, let me help." She took his cudgel from his hand and laid it on the bench. In a trice she was at his feet tugging at his boots.

"No, no, no," he protested sluggishly.

"Yes, yes, yes," she lisped, tugging at one boot and then the other.

When she had one off, he took it from her. "Have you seen the Indian Cutnose?"

"Oh, la, Tonneman, what would I know of that savage?"

"What about Abner Simon, the Jew from Breukelen? Do you know him?"

"As a matter of fact, I do. But no more silly questions." She stood, tottering, and giggled. "Now that you've had your beer, you must pay the piper. You must dance with me."

She was so tipsy he reckoned she'd been drinking since dawn. "I've got one boot off and one boot on, Geertie, and I don't dance."

"It's easy. I'll show you." She grabbed his hand and pulled him to his feet. "This is an English dance called Roger of Coverly. If there were more of us, we would be row facing row, each couple taking its turn. Come, back-to-back now. Hook arms. And we go up and down between the rows." One boot on and one boot off, his stocking bunched about his bootless foot, he was dragged up and back at a lively gait. "Now face-to-face," she said, panting, bosom trembling. They were face-to-face and body to body. Her eyes gleamed, perspiration shone on her fair skin, and her lips parted.

Geertruyd's kiss was moist, and he could taste her drink on her tongue. It hadn't been posset. Not by a long shot. Not wine with the milk. Brandy. But what did he care what she drank? He hadn't had a woman in a long time. He put his hands on her soft white shoulders.

She pulled away, oh so regretfully, it seemed. "La, it's gotten chilly. Shall we go inside?" She picked up her fan and the dog, cast Tonneman a sly look over the fan, and went into the house. He stood watching the door through which she'd entered. "You're a fool," he said aloud, then somewhat meekly, one boot on and one boot off, cudgel under his arm, he limped after her.

He followed her into the great chamber, where she sat on a dark green plush couch arranging herself and the pug all over again in another alluring picture.

The couch was opposite the large mullioned window that looked out on the Broad Way. Had she been sitting here like a queen, waiting for him to pass by?

"Annabella," she called.

The African woman was there in an instant. "Yes, madam."

"Another beer for the Schout, more posset for me. And stop drowning it with milk."

A tiny bell tinkled. Tonneman looked around.

"The clock." Geertruyd pointed to the brass lantern clock on the maple sideboard. "It's eight o'clock. Better than a sandglass or a sundial, don't you think? Have you ever seen one before? Such a beautiful thing, a clock."

"God's angels, ma'am. The only clock I ever seed was the church clock, but never in a home."

"Please don't take offense."

"But I do. You must think me a true bumpkin."

"No, I don't. And I'm genuinely glad to see you, dear man. It is so tedious spending one's time alone in this big house." She giggled, then hiccoughed.

On the carved table before the couch was a backgammon game, already in progress. Watching him, she picked up the stones and said, "Will you play with me?" She opened her arms and gave him another fair look at her white bosom. He moved closer. The tip of the pug's pink tongue protruded from between clamped teeth as it growled.

Madame De Sille stroked the animal's smooth coat. She nuzzled and murmured into its floppy black ear. "There, there, darling, don't be upset." She smiled up at Tonneman. "And don't you be upset either, darling. Here, sit next to me."

He made no move toward her, his obligation to duty in battle with his carnal desire.

"Why do you always carry that silly stick? Do you actually strike people with it?"

He placed the cudgel on a large-bottomed chair.

"Sit." She patted the spot next to her on the couch and kicked off her tiny silver shoes.

Spellbound, he obeyed, and in an instant she had her tongue inside his ear, her hands inside his shirt; her left foot was rubbing his right calf. He was lost, he knew. Then she said, "Now, what did you want to ask me about the Jew Simon? Whatever he told you, I promise you, it was not the truth. He was a liar and a thief."

"Was?" Tonneman cried, imprisoning her hands in his. "Why do you say *was?*"

Flustered, she giggled, but this time the giggle had a different quality, more fear and less joy. She took a breath and threw herself at him, kissing his throat and making high mewling cat noises. He released her hands to let them roam where they would. She tugged at his shirt and his breeches. But she wasn't trying to undress him.

"What are you looking for?"

"Your purse," she said, surprising him with the truth.

"I don't even have five stuivers to buy a beer," he protested, remembering that he'd left his jacket on the shoulders of Racqel Mendoza. All at once he felt doltish. He knew he should remove himself before he acted the complete fool.

She slipped to the floor, tugging at his other boot. This view of her breasts dazzled him; he yearned to press his face to them. "Abner Simon had a document. It was mine," she said, groping inside one boot, then the other. "Stolen from me."

"What sort of document is it? Why is it valuable?"

"Oh, darling." She jumped up and threw herself at him again, this time knocking him off balance. "That would be telling. You're a very attractive man. You know that, don't you?"

He was aroused, which embarrassed him. Despite his suspicions,

Nick De Sille was his friend. It was not dignified. "What would you give for that document?"

She pushed him down on the couch. "Anything. Anything you desire." She covered his face with kisses.

"Good morning, Geertruyd, Tonneman." Nick De Sille walked into the great chamber. "Tonneman, I would never have thought it of you. Any other man in New Amsterdam, nay, New Netherland, but you? In flagrante delicto with my wife?"

He was dressed in black silk breeches and jacket and a light green cambric shirt. His hair gleamed with pomade. On a braided leather strap that hung from his shoulder was a finished elkskin wallet.

Geertruyd quickly drew away from Tonneman, sank back to her side of the couch, picked up the fan, and opened it in front of her face. With a small tight smile Tonneman pulled on his boots. He sniffed. "That's a new kind of bear grease you're slicking your hair with, isn't it, Nick? Scented, too? Lavender, I think." Tonneman rose and circled round his old friend, sniffing again. "That's what it is, all right. Lavender. Not like the old days, eh? When you were jumping to a boatswain's bark and pulling cable with the rest of us poor sailors."

How out of place his old friend now was, Tonneman mused, in a rough frontier town like New Amsterdam, with his fine black silk. He would fit right into the court of Charles II, or would have made a fit companion for the fancy fop with the octagonal spectacles. "Where are you coming from, Nick?"

"Business."

"What sort of business?"

"My business."

"Where were you last night? Were you at the Pear Tree?"

"I discover you with my wife, attempting to cornute me, and you have the audacity to play Schout with me. You ought be ashamed. It's I who should be asking you questions." De Sille picked up his wife's glass and licked the rim. "And you should be ashamed, too, dear Geertruyd. Didn't you tell me you were going to stop drinking laudanum until at least after sundown?" He sneered at Tonneman. "Thought 'twas passion, did you? Nay, old friend, 'twas opium and brandywine with some milk to disguise it. And a little avarice."

Tonneman waved his hand, brushing De Sille's words away. "Perhaps," he inquired casually, "you were in Breukelen last night?"

"I was, of course, at home all night with Geertruyd." Removing Tonneman's cudgel from the large-bottomed chair, Nick sat down comfortably and slipped the cudgel under the chair. He crossed his legs, one calf delicately over the other, and lit an already filled pipe lying on the side table. "Wasn't I, my love?" he asked between draws of unscented tobacco smoke.

"Yes, dear," she said, lowering her fan demurely.

"Do you know a man who wears octagonal spectacles?" Tonneman demanded.

"No, can't say that I do."

"What about the disappearance of Benjamin Mendoza?"

"Who?" said Nick De Sille, winking at his wife.

"I think," Tonneman drawled, "that the two of you have been out to make a fool of me."

"Oh, la." Geertruyd laughed, curling up on the couch, unruffled, fanning away. "Nickie, dear, he has the document, I know he has. If you'd waited just a bit longer, I would have found it." She giggled. "I know I would have."

"If I had waited just a bit longer, you two would be the beast with two backs and I would be wearing horns." De Sille's smile to Tonneman was full of pretense. "Tonneman, why don't you return our document to us, and I'll say nothing to the Boss about your un-Christian behavior with my dear Geertruyd."

"Document?" In quick steps Tonneman was standing over Nick De Sille. De Sille, watching Tonneman carefully, came immediately on guard. Tonneman's hand shot out and down. De Sille flinched. "Just getting my club. What document?" Cudgel in hand, Tonneman moved toward the door. The pug showed its teeth and yipped.

De Sille dropped his subterfuge. "The document that the Jew in Breukelen stole from me."

"And you think I have this document?"

"The Jew had it. I understand you went to Breukelen to talk to him."

"And how do you understand that, Nick? Could it be that you were there? Just before me, perchance? Abner told me there was someone who wanted him dead. Could it be that you're the bastard who gave me this lump on my head? Could it be that you killed Abner Simon?"

"Oh, is the Jew dead?"

"Enough games, Nick. And if you're going to act surprised about Abner's death, Geertruyd should do the same. She knew Abner was dead all the time, didn't you, dear Geertruyd?"

"Did she?" Nick glanced at his wife. "How mortifying. I wish she had told me." To Tonneman he said, "Well, if he's dead, Tonneman, perhaps you and I should negotiate, old friend."

"Negotiate?" Tonneman wanted to spit. Instead he strode toward the front door. He was tired, dirty, and misused. His head hurt.

Most of all he was angry at this little game of the De Silles. He'd been a fool. Here, now, and earlier. He'd left the document in his jacket. Racqel Mendoza had it.

"Where are you going," Geertruyd cried, rapping the table with her fan. "Stop him, Nickie."

De Sille took a puff on his pipe and smiled. "He'll be back."

"You're right, Nickie," Tonneman said loudly. "I'll be back."

39

WEDNESDAY, 27 AUGUST. *Morning.*

Thick planks of oak framed the Mendoza's new house, which had been built over the old cellar. When all the work was done, the planks would be painted red. The quarry stones that made the cellar wall were sooty but did not warrant replacement. In time, they would be whitewashed clean.

The leasing agreement between Asser Levy and the Mendozas made the Mendozas responsible for the all costs due to the fire. However, the new house would have certain amenities the expense of which their landlord, Asser Levy, had agreed to absorb, the primary one being a glazed pantile roof.

Racqel's small herb garden would have to be resodded and replanted. The apple tree was somewhat scorched, a limb here and there burned through, but otherwise very much alive. Apples lay scattered on the ground, beginning to rot. Because they stood on the farthest side of the house, the two peach trees were virtually untouched and heavy with fruit.

Racqel had carried the earthenware basin into a corner of her new scullery. Caleb had followed. Bathsheba was nowhere to be seen.

Although the walls outside were in place and the inside walls completed, no plaster had been spread. All one could see were the exposed struts and beams. Once the plastering was done and had hardened, the chamber would be painted with sour milk and brick dust.

There was no fire, much as Racqel wanted one. With its choking smoke, it never warmed her enough, but oh, how she mourned its absence now, to heat her water. The large, straight-back brick wall behind the fireplace wasn't finished yet, nor was the scullery porch, behind the kitchen, which would house most of her beehive oven. Only the large cast-iron fireback that protected the fireplace wall and helped retain and deflect the heat was in place.

When all was done, there would be the open hearth, wide as twelve feet, fire flush against the wall, directly under a manteled hood that would lead to the chimney.

In the winter, when it was bitter cold, the animals would be brought in by the fire, thus giving lie to the saying that the two-piece doors were there to keep the animals out and the children in. Why was it her every thought was of children?

Still, she began to hum. She would have her new oven in which to make proper bread, perhaps as soon as the coming Sabbath. And the little chamber next to the beehive oven would be warm enough in the winter. It would be the perfect place for a newborn babe to sleep. She sighed and gave herself a cold washup. "And we shall have many mirrors," she murmured as she brushed her thick black hair.

She could hear scrambling, tapping, and singing above her as slaves laid yellow pantiles on the roof. Just below them, David and Goliath, having completed the steep and narrow staircase, were now installing the floor of the garret.

As she tied her hair back under a clean cotton cloth she decided that she would have to borrow another dress from Rebecca Da Costa. Normally Racqel, as did most of the women, made her own clothes, but there was a Frenchwoman and her daughter on Beaver Street who did sempstress work. Later she would pick out some fabric from the warehouse.

She placed her towel on the bare floor. Caleb came to sniff at it. Racqel patted the animal on his silky crown and rested her aching body on the towel. The dog turned one circle and lay down next to Racqel's head. Bathsheba appeared at the entrance to the chamber. Feigning indifference, the cat sauntered to Racqel's feet, sat, and cleaned her paws. Soothed by the steady tapping of the hammers and the lilting voices of the Africans, Racqel slept.

It was the middle of the morning when she awoke to a gnawing hunger. Sunlight streaked into the chamber through the two glassless windows, playing on the new brick hearth and the struts and beams. The four-footers were both asleep, Bathsheba in light, Caleb in shadow. Not moving, Racqel watched the pale sand-colored boxes of sunlight on the floor and thought of the big Dutchman with his pale sand-colored hair and his eyes the same blue as the fringe of a prayer shawl.

Such a man should have sons and sons and more sons. He would marry again, she thought, one of the fat Dutch widows. Or one of the slim blond girls. She sat up abruptly, a heretofore unknown swirling of jealousy in her head and belly. She didn't want to think of him with another woman.

His jacket lay crimpled near her on the floor. She took it up and held it to her face. It smelled of him and the salt sea. She threw it down as if it burned hot. Something separated from the garment, rolling and spinning like a coin. Hovering, she caught it in the spin and held it.

It was a piece of tarnished silver engraved with the standing figure of a lion. The Lion of Judah. The last time she had seen this piece of silver was with others like it mounted on the silver belt Benjamin had been wearing the night he left. "Benjamin," she said softly, stunned, turning the piece of silver in her hand.

It must have fallen from one of Tonneman's pockets, she thought as her hands searched feverishly to see what other singular objects she might discover.

What was the Schout doing with a portion of Benjamin's belt? Had he seen Benjamin? Did he know what had happened to him?

In the left-hand pocket she found a buckskin purse with a few coins and her handkerchief, neatly folded, which she had given to Tonneman for his cut hand. It was spotted with blood. His blood. Pausing, she thought: he had kept it meaning to return it to her. But no. She knew better than that. There was something between them. A connection they both felt. A feeling she had to deny. She replaced the handkerchief and purse in the pocket and continued her search.

The right-hand pocket contained her father's magnifying glass and a folded piece of paper. The paper whispered under her hesitant fingers and beckoned her to unfold it and read. She hesitated for a moment. It was the paper that Tonneman had plucked from Abner Simon's eye socket. It might tell something of Benjamin. She unfolded it.

It was an official document, in English, an agreement between the bearer and Governor John Winthrop of Connecticut on behalf of His Royal Majesty, Charles II.

Abner had owned this document, and Benjamin had been doing business with Abner before his disappearance. God help them all if this letter had anything to do with Benjamin. She remembered the conversation she had overheard between Abraham and David. No. She would not think of that.

She looked down at the terrible document in her trembling hand. It stated that: "The bearer shall be loyal and faithful to King Charles II and do whatever is required of him in the service of King Charles II.

The bearer's reward shall be monies and land now belonging to the Dutch West India Company in an amount that will be left to the generosity of a grateful Sovereign."

So absorbed was she in the contents of the letter that she was not aware of David until he was upon her, snatching the document from her hand.

"What are you doing here, idle woman?" he demanded, holding the paper away from her grasping fingers. "Why aren't you seeking clean clothes? Look at you, you're a disgrace."

His scornful tone subdued her. She stepped back from him, her eyes still on the document. "I am not your wife, David Mendoza, no matter what you dream," she replied with less passion than she wished. "Is it necessary for you to burst in on me without even a knock on the wall or a by-your-leave, as if I were some black slave?"

"I have no time for your foolish prattling. Father has gone to the warehouse. I must join him. For good or for bad, this land is our home. We must prepare to meet the English side by side with the Dutch. This war with the English . . . Never mind. That is not for a woman's head." Unexpectedly he moved closer, catching her by her wrist, pulling her to him. "Racqel, Benjamin is dead. Don't you feel it?"

The dog whined in its sleep. The cat stretched, saw it was in shadow, and moved the few inches required to get into the warm light.

He was hurting her. "No," she said, struggling to get free.

"Don't you know how much I love you? How much I want you. You are still young, strong, and healthy. You can give me many sons."

"No." She broke loose. "You don't want a wife, you want a brood cow. And I don't want you. Not even if Benjamin were dead. I don't want you at all."

"You have no choice." The paper fluttered from his hand to the floor. He picked it up, suddenly curious. "What is this? 'Royal Majesty, Charles II . . . monies and land . . . Dutch West India Company . . . grateful Sovereign.' Are you insane? Like Benjamin you want to ruin us. This must be destroyed."

She grabbed the paper from his hand before he could let his actions follow his words. "No. This is Tonneman's property. He needs it to find out who killed Abner. If you dare to destroy it, I'll tell him what it says and what you did."

He retreated from the ferocity in her eyes and voice. "I'll say no more about it. But get rid of it. If it is found in our possession, Stuyvesant will burn us at the stake." He stalked away, then halted and turned, fury strong on his face. "Without a rabbi here to say no, I will declare that Benjamin is dead, and then, as heaven is my witness, you will marry me."

Wild with anger Racqel screamed, "Your father won't allow it!"

His face was taut above his black beard. "My father knows in his heart that Benjamin is dead. He's an old man and this is a New World. He will do as I say."

David stormed out. Racqel slipped to her knees and bent over, her head in her arms. She felt as she had when Benjamin left. A terrible foreboding, a fearful dread.

40

WEDNESDAY, 27 AUGUST. *Late morning.*
Approaching the Mendoza house from the rear, Tonneman saw the scorched fruit trees, the yellow pantiles of the new roof, and the two African workers. But what held his attention most was one of their gray horses. It was wearing a red velvet hat with a blue plume.

"Good morning, heer," the two black men said together as they loaded their wagon with scraps of wood.

"That's a nice hat your horse is wearing," Tonneman said.

"We're going to get a hat for the other one pretty soon," the larger African said. He was not quite as tall as Tall Matthew or even Sweet Lips, but almost.

"That's good, uh . . ."

"I'm Goliath, heer."

"Goliath."

"We're sorry we don't have a head covering for the other one."

"Never mind that," said Tonneman.

"We know we're supposed to have it account of the sun," said David. "We'll get a hat for the other one right away."

"Never mind," Tonneman said again. "Where did you get this one?"

"Found it," said David.

"Where?"

"Oh . . ." Racqel Mendoza stepped out the backdoor, holding a basin of water. The three men turned to the sound of her voice.

"Good morning," said Tonneman. "I've come for my jacket."

"I'll get it," she answered, hurrying back into the house without emptying the basin.

"Where did you find the hat?" he asked again.

"Behind Heer Zoelan's tavern," David answered.

"When?"

"Yesterday."

"Yes, heer. Yesterday."

"It's very dirty," said Racqel, appearing once more, this time without the basin, carrying the jacket. "I'm sorry. I've cleaned it as best I could."

"Thank you." Tonneman took his hat off and turned it in his hands. He was as unsure as a boy.

Racqel stepped closer to him and put her hand to his head. It was like an angel's kiss. He didn't move. "Oh, your head. Let me get my father's case and clean that wound."

"No!" The word came out a shout. She flinched. Softer, he said, "I have work to do."

At that moment Rebecca Da Costa turned the corner of the house. "Forgive me." Her voice was harsh and unpleasant. "I didn't mean to intrude."

"I was just leaving," said Tonneman. He set his hat gently on his head, took his jacket from Racquel, and put it on.

"Not on my account," said Rebecca Da Costa. She turned on her heel and marched away. Racqel's smooth dark cheeks blanched.

"I'm sorry," said Tonneman. "I hope that doesn't cause you any difficulty."

Racqel bit her lip. "I don't understand what's come over Rebecca. I thought she was my friend." She sighed. "Have you discovered what happened to my husband?"

"No." He touched his hat with his forefinger, taking his leave.

Racqel stared at his broad back as he walked away. She yearned to talk to him. Tell him she'd read the document, seen the piece of silver. She knew then he would tell her about Benjamin. Was he alive or dead? She had to know. "The tomahawk," she called out.

He turned to her.

"I'll get it." She ran inside and reappeared with the tomahawk that had killed Abner.

As soon as he was out of sight of the Mendoza house Tonneman shoved the handle of the tomahawk in the top of his breeches and pulled the document, disk, and glass from his jacket pocket. He made an attempt at reading the document but to no avail. He would take it to Antje to translate, but at this moment his prime concern was his thirst.

The Pear Tree was smoky and noisy with grumbling and quarrelsome voices. The yellow hound added to the noise with its anxious yelping bark. Dinck stood at the bar next to Jan Keyser.

"Any news?" Keyser asked.

Tonneman heard but wouldn't be stopped from reaching the bar. He wanted naught to do with anyone until he could still the savage need for a drink.

"Did you find your dead man with the spectacles?" Joost asked, hauling out a bottle of brandywine.

Tonneman made a motion with his hand, and Joost poured him a large glassful. Tonneman drank it quickly and held the blue-faceted brandy glass out for another.

The tapster poured again and drew the Schout a beer. "Well?" Joost prompted. "Did you find him?"

"No. But I found his hat, and outside your backdoor, no less. What do you think of that?"

"Not much." He drew a beer for Dinck, who was listening eagerly to their discussion.

"I've got a new problem. Did you know the Jew Abner Simon, from Breukelen? He's dead now, too."

"Why is that your worry? You're not the Schout of Breukelen. Moreover, one less Jew is always a pleasure. And that Jew was an Indian lover and not worth spit. How did he die?"

Tonneman pulled the tomahawk from his waist and drove it with force into the bar. The tomahawk quivered, the drinks and coins on the bar bounced, Dinck's jowls twitched. "Cracked his head open."

Joost, eyes on the vibrating weapon, stepped back. "What did I tell you? His friends the Indians did him in. Leave it at that and drink up."

Tonneman took alternate swallows of the burnt wine and the beer. "That sounds like excellent advice." The tomahawk rested.

"I say the English will plunder and rape," Keyser shouted.

"You talk too much," someone said, and a fist descended on the tanner's head, dropping him to the floor.

"You can't do that."

"I just did."

More fists descended on more heads. The yellow dog yipped and barked and ran out the backdoor. Tonneman glanced at the tomahawk on the bar. No, that was too serious an instrument. He hefted his cudgel. He hadn't used it to any effect for a long time. The suppressed anger and frustration he'd been feeling of late exploded. He charged into the middle of the brawl swinging his club left and right, picking up rowdy citizens as he found them and flinging them toward the nearest door. For a time chaos reigned.

But it was over very quickly. Only four remained in the tavern. Tonneman, Joost, Dinck, who had positioned himself behind an overturned table, and Keyser, who was still flat out on the floor. "Brandy," Tonneman yelled. "For everyone."

"I'll drink to that," said Keyser, sitting upright.

"As will I," Dinck agreed, getting painfully to his swollen feet.

"Yes, sir, Mijnheer Schout," Joost pronounced grandly, pouring his friend a double draught and singles for himself, Keyser, and Dinck.

They all drank. Dinck drained his glass and wiped his lips with a nosecloth. "Thank you," he said to Tonneman, "for the drink. And for an entertaining afternoon." He tipped his hat and left.

"Did you bury the body?" Tonneman asked Keyser.

"I said I would and I did. He was putrid pudding. Stank something awful."

Zoelan laughed. "That's saying some for you."

"The ground was too hard," the tanner complained.

Tonneman finished his drink and poured himself another. "You never put one word after another without complaining."

"When do I get paid?"

"Give me a note and you'll have your money tomorrow."

"Tomorrow? I need it now. You owe me a drink at least."

Tonneman nodded at Joost and the tapster poured another brandy for Keyser. The little man slurped noisily and said, "That man you asked about . . . ? I didn't remember before because my head was full of drink, but I remember now. The man with the spectacles and fancy clothes was in here Tuesday night. The night of the fire. You remember, Joost. He was back there with De Sille and van Brugge."

Tonneman leaned on the bar. His elbow slipped and he nearly fell. Joost reached out and steadied him. Tonneman brushed his hand away. He shook his head to clear the fog that was setting in. "But Joost, you said you didn't see him."

"That's because he wasn't here."

"Yes, he was," the tanner said angrily, raising his voice.

None of the three looked at each other or spoke further. The yellow dog stuck its nose in the backdoor. The animal hesitated. But when it saw all was calm, it entered, tail wagging, and trotted over to sit at Joost's feet.

Keyser blew his nose in his fingers and flicked the efflux into the sandbox. "I remember, Joost," he said, wiping his still-snotty hand on his dirty leather pants. "I saw you talking to him."

Joost scratched the yellow dog's head. "How would you know what you saw, you were sotted."

"Not so sotted . . ."

"What about it?" Tonneman demanded, impatient. His voice, even to his own ears, sounded blurred with booze. "Was he here or not?"

"Yes," said Keyser.

"No," Joost insisted.

"You're both liars and you can go to the devil," Tonneman shouted. He collected his cudgel and the tomahawk and staggered out the front door into the painfully bright afternoon sunlight.

Joost Zoelan put a rush-grass taper to the candle in front of him on the bar and lit his pipe.

On the Strand Tonneman came to a reeling halt as he got a whiff of lavender tobacco floating through the air. When had Joost started smoking that lavender shit? A noise came from off to the side. "Who's there?" Tonneman mumbled, cudgel and tomahawk at the ready.

"Only I," said Dinck, coming from around a corner, a pipe hanging loosely in his hand. "Merely having a little walk for my health. God be with ye, Tonneman."

"Good night, Dinck," said Tonneman.

"It's only afternoon."

"Whatever you say." Drunk, still angry and confused, Tonneman staggered the few feet to his house. Lubbertus van Dincklagen never took walks for his health in his life. So many things needed thinking about, but all he could manage was his mattress and sleep.

41

WEDNESDAY, 27 AUGUST. *Evening.*
The nap had not helped. Tonneman went around to the shed. His muddled head was hammering. "Sorry, Venus, old girl." The mare took a moment from her oats to nuzzle his ear, then she was back to

feeding. Tonneman splashed his face with water. The shirt hanging on a nail in the shed was cleaner than the one he had on. He changed, smoothed his hair with his hands, and wandered over to the Ten Eycks.

"You look terrible," said Antje. "We're just sitting down. Come and eat with us."

"I was hoping you'd say that. My stomach is empty as a hole."

Old Conraet and young Conraet were playing the hand-slapping game. "I win again," young Conraet screeched happily.

"I reckon you do," said his father, kissing the boy full on the mouth. The boy pulled his face away and ducked his head. His father tickled him under the arms. "Good evening, Tonneman. You look terrible."

"I already told him that," said Antje.

"Good evening, Tonneman," said little Conraet, wriggling and giggling. "You look terrible." His giggle erupted into full, happy laughter.

Everybody laughed, including Tonneman. "Old news, youngster. They already told me."

Ten Eyck lifted a pewter pitcher and poured beer into a large earthen mug. "Do you need this?"

"Does a fish need water?" Tonneman seized the mug and quaffed half of it in one long swallow. He set the mug down, belched, wiped his mouth with the back of his hand, and said, "Now I feel better."

"Then tell me about the whale," said young Conraet.

"Not now," said Ten Eyck.

"Yes, Father."

"What news?" asked Tonneman.

"All of New Amsterdam now knows of the English presence in Breukelen," Ten Eyck told him. "The people have demanded a meeting with Stuyvesant. He refused to see them."

"No news, then," said Tonneman, drinking the rest of his beer and refilling his mug. He told the Ten Eycks about Abner and the document while they ate their pickled fish. Ten Eyck cut a small loaf of bread into thick slices.

"Bread, by God?" said Tonneman. "Where did you get flour? Are you trafficking with the enemy?"

"The only enemy in this house is you," Antje said, setting down platters of jugged hare, green peas, and beans.

"And who am I the enemy of?"

"Yourself, you ninny."

"Sounds like wisdom to me," said Ten Eyck.

"Sounds like wisdom to me, too," echoed his son.

Antje cleared the empty platters and returned, laying a red earthenware dish of marchpane in front of them. "Here, you don't deserve it, but here."

Tonneman and Ten Eyck ate the sweet almond-paste confection, drank more beer, smoked, and talked.

A more mellow Tonneman told Antje and Ten Eyck about the missing body found in the Mendozas' shed, burned to a crisp and with Tonneman's own knife through its chest.

"Your knife?" This was from Ten Eyck. Antje merely raised her eyebrows.

Tonneman laughed harshly. "Yes, when I get whoever did this, he'll pay for that bit of humor." He coolly described how he'd found Abner Simon, the sudden appearance of the Mendozas, and the arrival of the English.

Ten Eyck said, "And you think these deaths have to do with the English?"

"Of course. It makes the most sense. And then there's the matter of Hendrik Smitt."

Ten Eyck's eyes went to his wife. She was nodding, encouraging Tonneman. "Yes . . . yes."

"You are not going on about that again, woman?" The usually lighthearted Ten Eyck was angry.

"You don't agree with Antje, then?"

"Agree? Agree with what? The man killed himself. What more is there?" Ten Eyck bumped the table impatiently, raising a chorus of rattling platters.

"Could a man as falling-down drunk as Smitt have negotiated such a suicide? I think not. I was in a similar drunken stupor that night. I couldn't make water without wetting my boots. God save me from being a worse fool than I've been. I'm to blame for not recognizing murder when it was staring me right in the face."

Antje made a derisive sound and patted his arm.

"Let it be, Tonneman," Ten Eyck said. "Let dead dogs lie. It's done with. The man took his own life. There's no bringing him back."

"Nay, he keeps coming back as a hanging man in my dreams. He's trying to tell me something."

"What? That hell is hot?"

"What if his death is somehow connected to that man in the shed and Abner Simon?"

"Then all you have to do is find a traitor and you've found your killer."

Tonneman let loose a hollow laugh. "Thank you. Why didn't I think of that? There's also Nick and Geertie De Sille."

"What about them?" asked Antje.

"I don't know, but Nick's involved in this some way. Right up to his lavender-greased head."

"The English are going to win," Ten Eyck said abruptly. He thudded his mug on the table.

"Tell Stuyvesant that," Tonneman said.

"What do you think things will be like under the English?"

"To be honest, not much different, except I'll be out of a job."

"How close are they?"

"By water?" Tonneman shrugged. "Piss toward Breukelen and you'll hit them."

"Come on, little one. A walk to the pier and a smoke and off to bed with you." Ten Eyck tried to tickle the little boy, who backed away and laughed. "You coming, Tonneman?"

"No, I think I'll talk to Antje a bit."

Father and son went outside. Antje wiped the table with her cloth and sat down heavily, resting her hand on her swollen belly. "He's going to see if the English are nigh."

"I know."

"He's not as calm as he pretends. Nor is he as thickheaded as he pretends. About Smitt, I mean."

"I know." But did he? Ten Eyck seemed angry that Tonneman would question Smitt's suicide. This puzzled Tonneman.

"What about you?"

Tonneman blinked at Antje. What was she asking him? "What?"

"How do you feel? Are you calm?"

"Concerning the English? Calm enough. Concerning these murders? I'm pisspotting mad."

"And concerning the Jewess?"

He refilled his mug and drank, but did not respond.

"When you came in, I thought a little food would make you sober. You're more drunk now than before."

"That's true, but I'm calm."

"Is it because she's not one of us?"

He drank more beer and said nothing.

"I'm not going to talk to myself much longer."

"I have feelings for her."

"So?"

"So I'm bewildered."

"I don't doubt that. You're no boy with his first love. It's clear you care for her, you booby. Why don't you stop worrying about it and follow your heart? Ask her to marry you."

"What? I used to think you were a smart woman. Why should I want to get married? That's the most witless thing I ever heard. Moreover, her husband may be alive somewhere." He climbed to his feet and went outside.

"Solve all the problems of the world?" Ten Eyck asked.

"Yes, except how to keep your wife from talking." Tonneman started for the Strand.

Ten Eyck laughed. "I've been trying and failing at that for years. Can you get home all right?"

"Haven't I always?" Stumbling out onto the Strand intending to cross to his house, Tonneman remembered the paper. "Shit." He'd meant to ask Antje to translate it for him, but he'd had too much beer and too little sleep. "Tomorrow. I'll do it tomorrow."

He stopped to piss all over the two whitewashed stoops in front of the Boss's Great House, then he wobbled along Twiller's Road, singing the song Korbonski and the dwarf had been playing. He would have kept on going to the Fort, but he slipped on the cobblestones on Stone Street and came down laboriously. He lay there for a minute breathing hard and decided to go into the Wooden Horse Tavern instead and ease his thirst. Since it was not far from the Fort and had been started by one of their own, it was where most of the soldiers liked to drink.

As Tonneman got to his feet a man jostled him. "Why don't you watch where you're going?" Tonneman shouted.

But the man was gone, into the street and into the night.

The Wooden Horse was run by Philip Gerard's widow, Marie de Vos, who, short and plump, looked nothing at all like Tonneman's Maria. She was also old and gray, which Maria Tonneman would never be. Why else marry except to have someone to grow old and gray with? Tears flooded his eyes. How he missed his Maria. Racqel could never replace her.

Gerard had been a soldier for the Company while he ran this tavern. Way back in '42 he had been caught away from his guard post. The usual sentence was to ride the wooden horse, a long-legged carpenter's hurdle. The evildoer would be forced to lie across the horse with weights tied to his legs. But Gerard received extra punishment for his transgression. Just so everyone would get the point, he was also required to hold a sword in one hand and a pitcher of beer in the other.

Gerard did this, two hours every day for a week. Needless to say, following his punishment, the doughty Frenchman quit the Company and in an act of humor and defiance renamed his tavern the Wooden Horse. He had died nine years before.

The Wooden Horse, like the Pear Tree, was one chamber, although somewhat smaller. It was smoky, smelly, crowded, and noisy, which suited Tonneman just fine.

The first face he saw in the dimness was Pos's. "There you are, you old rascal."

"Here I am," Pos admitted, smiling broadly. "Buy me a drink."

"Can't," said Tonneman. "No money."

"Then I'll buy you one. Oho. I've no money, either. Two noggins of burnt wine, Marie. Mark it on my score."

"Two mugs of beer and I'll mark it in the water," the old woman said good-naturedly.

"All right, Pos, did you do what I asked?"

"Shit, I've been busier than a one-legged man at an arse-kicking contest."

"Some deputy you are. Anybody see Cutnose?"

"No. But I had a good time in the taverns asking."

"I believe that. What about on the ships? Did anyone know anything about the man with the spectacles? Did you learn anything?"

"No. I never got to it."

"What do you mean?"

"To tell the truth, after I had a few beers in the taverns asking about Cutnose, I forgot."

"I've been doing a bit of that, too, lately."

Pos moaned and sniffled. "My head feels as if the entire frolicking English army was in there."

"Have you had anything to eat?"

"Beer." He drew a large green nosecloth from his boot and blew his nose mightily.

"No food?"

"Beer is food." Suddenly the Rattle Watch captain started to cry.

"What's wrong with you?" asked Tonneman. His eyelids had grown heavy, his head drifted to his chest.

"Someone took my sword away."

"How's that?" Tonneman raised his head slightly.

"I was inspecting the Watch and my throat felt a little dry. You know how it is? I stopped in at the Blue Dove to ask the questions and to wet my whistle, and I got into a little altercation. Fellow hit me when I wasn't looking. Then the bastard had the gall to take my sword from me when I was down. I'm going back to get it. You coming?"

"I'll be along. Soon as I find my cudgel." Thus the two men, the Schout and his deputy, the defenders of the law of New Amsterdam, went out into the night on an important mission.

42

Thursday, 28 August. *Morning.*
De Sille spoke first. "Does Tonneman have the paper?"

"He did," said his partner. "But he doesn't have it anymore."

"Do you have it?"

"Yes," said the man.

"It's settled then. You and I will share in all enterprises."

"What about van Brugge? Or should I say *Bridge* now?"

De Sille laughed softly. "I'll take care of Mister Bridge."

"Agreed. Shall we seal it the way my father made the wool merchants do it in the north country?" De Sille's partner dropped a florin into a quart flagon and filled it with beer. "Drink."

"Are you saying if I don't finish with the coin in my teeth, we have no agreement?"

"That's what I'm saying."

"But that's ridiculous. After all we've been through, to have it determined by something so—"

"Drink."

When De Sille saw the expression in his partner's eyes, he put a smile on his face and, without stopping, drank the entire contents of the flagon, capturing the coin with his teeth. "There," he said, removing the coin with a flourish. "And the florin is mine, too."

"Of course," said his partner, smiling.

De Sille shivered. He was beginning to feel uneasy about his partner.

Tonneman was awakened by the sound of yowling cats. He knew from past experience there were no cats outside his window. The screaming beasts were inside his head and were his punishment for the night before, about which he could remember not a single thing. But it would come back to him. It always did.

Unexpectedly the cats stopped their caterwaul. The silence was like the silence on a ship at sea during a lull. Then came new wailing. Not of cats, but of a lost soul. A hand was clutching his throat. He could see it. A skeleton's hand. And the face behind the hand, Smitt's face. "No," Tonneman shrieked, coming awake, strangling on his own vomit. "No more. No more. Never again," he swore as he scrambled on the floor trying to find the chamber pot. He threw up bitter bile and wiped his watery eyes with the back of his hand. He must have drunk a lot, even for him. Maria, he thought, seeing her face shimmering before him, full of reproof. He lay back on his pallet and dozed, only to hear Katrina Root bustling about cooking his breakfast, which she would make whether he wanted it or not.

"Katrina. You don't have to make me breakfast," he called out weakly, and paid for the effort with a new explosion of pain in his head and cheekbones. His body felt as if he'd been kicked by a horse.

"No trouble, Heer Schout."

"It's not part of our bargain, just cleaning and evening meal."

"I won't charge you more. A man has to eat. Otherwise he can't work."

"No more," he muttered, too sick to argue. "I'm too old for this sort of behavior. It's time for me to accept Maria's death and go on with my life."

"Are you talking to me, Heer Schout?"

"No, Katrina." He picked up the water pitcher with shaky hands. There was a dead fly in the water. Just looking at it floating in a slow small circle made him dizzy. He plucked it from the water, cast it out the open window, and drank.

He heard Katrina leave and dozed again. In this half sleep he called out, "Maria," and woke himself. Katrina had left him a pewter plate piled high with samp. He pushed the cold, lump-filled Indian maize porridge aside and instead took halfhearted bites from a raw ear of corn and an onion from the wooden bin on the floor. Solid food and no drink. A new Tonneman.

Feeling a little more himself, he filled his pipe with his plain rough shag. He preferred the coarse tobacco, simple fare, not like the rosemary- and lavender-scented shit others smoked. Cloying lavender. Racqel used a lavender scent; Geertruyd, too. Nick slicked lavender pomade on his hair. Was Dinck smoking lavender tobacco? Tonneman's thoughts sped back to Racqel.

If he could prove her husband dead . . . but what of that? She was still a Jewess and he a Christian, God save him, even if he was not such a good one.

On a chair he found a neat pile of clean breeches and shirts where Katrina Root had left them. His head was a fog. Where had he been last night?

All at once he remembered too many things. The fight at the Pear Tree. No, it was at the Blue Dove. No, there had been two fights. At the Blue Dove he and Pos had gotten into it with almost everyone there. Tonneman examined his face and body. It was no wonder he ached so much. He was a mass of bumps and bruises. He recalled something about the Blue Dove. Pos's sword. A melee. Hands grasping him, searching for something. "Good God, you fool. The paper." He spun around, knocking over the chair, casting clean clothes every which way. Where was his jacket? He discovered it on a hook in the kitchen where Katrina had hung it. He searched the pockets, but found only the silver disk and the magnifying glass. The paper was gone. He'd lost the paper. But where? And when?

Then, like a bolt of lightning, it came to him that he was supposed to have gone back to the Fort at noon the day before. He got dressed. He couldn't find his cudgel. "Shit, I've lost that, too."

Knowing the ride would be good for both of them, he saddled Venus and raced to the Fort. He had all he could to do to stay mounted, so he barely noted the people, some standing still, others steadily moving along the East River. This was true all the way down to the tip of the island. Some were holding telescopes. Had Tonneman bothered, he would have noticed that they were looking and pointing toward the bay. All were curiously silent.

Numerous townspeople and, it seemed, the entire complement of soldiers in New Amsterdam were aimlessly milling around outside the Fort.

Inside the Fort it was more of the same, silent chaos. Those few soldiers on duty and the civilian workers were standing, waiting.

The Director-General was not in his office.

"Where's the Boss?" Tonneman bawled to Dirk Baalde, the blacksmith.

The giant redhead pointed to the shore side of the Fort. "He's yonder with the rest. I told you it would be over before it started."

Tonneman twitched the reins and guided Venus through the apprehensive crowd of soldiers and civilians to where P.S., van Der Werff, Johannes Megapolensis, van de Steen, Van Dillen, and most of the Council, including Nick De Sille, were standing. Stuyvesant had a glass to his eye. Each of the men, in his own peculiar battle dress, was looking out at the bay. Van de Steen was stroking his scar, Van Dillen was twisting his mustache. Around them, pressing anxiously closer to shore, were more citizens.

Venus shifted her weight just as Tonneman shifted his in order to dismount, and instead of dismounting as he'd done so many times during his life, drunk or sober, he fell off the horse and sprawled in front of the assembly. His hat rolled off to the side, ending up at Nick De Sille's shiny black boots. Councillor De Sille retrieved the dusty black hat and held it daintily between two fingers. "I think you dropped your hat."

The Director-General took the glass from his eye. "Have you been drinking?"

"They all do drink here," said De Sille grandly, as if he'd never taken a drink in his life. "From the moment they are able to lick a spoon."

"The book tells us wine is a mocker," Stuyvesant proclaimed.

"It also tells us to 'drink water no longer, but use a little wine for thy stomach's sake,'" Tonneman responded, unable to control his silly tongue or his wobbly legs as he tried to get up.

Stuyvesant's face grew purple. "Would you mock me, Schout? The devil take you. I don't care if we're in the middle of a war. If you can't handle your responsibilities, I will find someone who can."

"I'm all right," Tonneman insisted, righting himself, taking his hat from a sneering De Sille, and dusting it off on his breeches.

"I don't care if you grow wings and fly around like an angel, I don't believe you." Stuyvesant was enraged.

De Sille stepped forward. "I'd be happy to serve, Director-General. I know what's required. It's not as if I don't know the job."

"You'd love that, wouldn't you, Nickie?" Tonneman stood tall and with as much dignity as he could still muster. "Yes, sir, I'm here, a little late, but I'm here. What do you want me to do?"

"Best forget all that folly now," the colonel said sharply. "Look."

Four frigates, previously smudges on the horizon, each flying the English Union Jack, appeared in the bay in full view of the population. Nicolls's flagship *Guinea,* with her thirty-six guns, led the way, swaggering through the water, all her milky sails puffed and billowing. New Amsterdam was virtually sealed off.

43

THURSDAY, 28 AUGUST. *Morning.*

Stuyvesant growled like a cornered animal. "Colonel van de Steen. As of now your men are on twenty-four-hour alert. The same for the militia, Van Dillen. De Sille, I want you here with me. I need someone I can trust to help me defend the Fort."

Tonneman felt the sting of the rebuke. "And I, sir?"

"Go home and sober up. We have a war to fight, and you're not fit to fight it, Schout."

Chagrined and angry, Tonneman mounted Venus, and rode toward the Broad Way. The Blue Dove was just the other side of Lichtman's bakeshop. He urged the mare on in a frenzily twisted path around the people, industry having ceased as everyone gathered on the harbor front, watching.

When Tonneman found open ground, he dug his heels into the four-footer's flanks and galloped to the tavern.

He reined up abruptly at the Blue Dove, raising a cloud of dust, and immediately recalled further events of the night before. He and Pos and something about Pos's sword. The two of them had been falling down pisspot drunk. The image of himself in that condition made Tonneman cringe. "Sweet Jesus." Never again. He pulled on the reins and rode farther along the Broad Way, away from the tavern and its temptations.

Tall Matthew was squatting, both heels down, on a pier just inside the Wall on the North River. The African's customary ebon sheen was ash gray. He seemed haunted.

"You're on the wrong shore, Tall Matthew. All the excitement's down by the Fort. The English are here."

Tall Matthew didn't answer; he didn't even acknowledge Tonneman's presence.

Tall Matthew was what the whites called him. His true name he never spoke, tried not even to think, for fear the whites would learn it. They had captured his life. If they learned his true name, they would capture his essence, and that he could never chance.

The god of the river had come to him in the guise of a serpent the night before. It had emerged from the North River, complaining of the cold water. It said it had come these many miles to this disagreeable place to tell him what he had to do.

"And afterward?" he had asked the serpent.

"Afterward," the serpent had answered, "I will take you home."

"I need to talk to you about Abner," Tonneman said. "What did he tell you that night you came and fetched me?"

Tall Matthew didn't answer; he sat and stared at the North River. Tonneman prodded a bit more, but the African would not respond. Finally, seeing he was getting nowhere, Tonneman gave up and rode back to the Pear Tree to talk to Joost Zoelan about the missing paper and the man with the spectacles. But when he got there, he found the Pear Tree was closed up tight, and Joost was nowhere to be seen.

44

THURSDAY, 28 AUGUST. *Afternoon.*

Tonneman put Venus back in her stall in the shed and rubbed her down. Were they all somehow connected? Nick De Sille and the document? The man under the willow? The fire, Abner, and again the document? And Smitt.

Inside his house he stood blurry-eyed in front of the small looking glass, shaved with tepid water, and made himself more presentable. Somewhat refreshed, he walked down the Strand to his willow to have a good think. And he would do it without a bottle.

But as he reached the willow, Tonneman caught sight of an Indian in a canoe approaching shore. Cutnose? Tonneman ran toward the man. As he drew nearer he saw it was not Cutnose, but Foxman. Fine. He wanted to talk to Foxman, too. He wanted to talk to anyone who might give him answers. Tonneman arrived as Foxman was beaching the canoe. He was out of breath and striving not to let the Indian see it.

Neither spoke for a moment. Then Tonneman said, "The English are here."

Foxman grunted. He unloaded a bundle of pelts from the canoe. "I have been up-country."

"Did you run across Cutnose?"

"Cutnose is dead."

Tonneman grunted. He watched as Foxman pulled on buckskin breeches over his loincloth and a bright yellow homespun shirt.

"Knifed by his woman." The Mohawk fastened the bundle of pelts to his back with leather thongs and started toward the Strand.

Tonneman followed him. "Where are you bound?"

"Mendoza."

"Then you should have come down the North River. That would have put you right at the warehouse."

Why do you talk so much, white man, telling me what I don't want to know? I'm not listening. I give as much attention to you as I do to the blowing of the wind or the chattering of the birds. I listen only when I choose to listen.

"I like this river." The Indian stretched his thin lips over his teeth into what he considered an imitation of the white man's smile. "Perhaps I was coming to you to tell you about Cutnose."

"Cow flap."

Do you know how easy it would be for me to kill you, white man? I could snap your neck like a twig, then eat your flesh and watch your bones whiten in the sun.

"What do you know about the death of Abner Simon?"

"You ask a lot of questions," the Mohawk said.

"It's my job."

"Fuck your job," Foxman sneered. He quickened his pace, leaving the Schout behind. Tonneman, thumbs hooked in the waist of his breeches, watched the Indian proceed down the Strand.

"Shit." He wasn't getting anywhere with his investigation. He found himself standing smack in front of the Pear Tree. It was closed and locked as before. He pounded on the door. "Joost?" There was no answer.

He leaned back against the door and scratched under his hat where the cut at his hairline had formed a scab. Odd. Foxman carried only one bundle of pelts. Twenty-five to thirty at most. Not a bad haul for an ordinary Indian. But Foxman was no ordinary Indian. He wouldn't paddle down river just to sell twenty-five to thirty pelts. A canoeful, yes, but one bundle? Never. And certainly not when the English ships in the bay were visible to all. Unless he had a reason. And Foxman had gone *down* Pearl Street. He wasn't going to the warehouses on Staple Street. The more Tonneman thought about it, the more peculiar he thought it was. He decided it would be wise to see what mischief Foxman was up to.

Holding his sword so it wouldn't smack against his thigh, he ran quickly and as quietly as he could along the Ditch. He saw Foxman to his left, going in the direction of Jews Alley. When Tonneman got to Mill Street, Foxman was in front of the Mendozas's new house talking to David Mendoza.

With not much cover around, Tonneman couldn't get too close, but then the mill was not being used, so there was no noise. Through the slatted fence he saw the bundle of pelts on the ground between Foxman and Mendoza.

He heard David Mendoza saying, "Thirty-five pelts, I'll give you my note for five hundred florins."

"I don't want your note. I don't need money. I'll trade them for the woman who lives here."

"What?" Mendoza was amazed and furious. "You dare ask such a thing? It's bad enough when the gentiles want to marry our women. But a *heathen*—" He raised a fist to the sky. "Oh God in heaven, what have I done that you would punish me with such a prospect?" He looked at Foxman with disgust. "As the God of Jacob is my refuge, she is not for sale. Six hundred florins. Not a note. Wampum. Polished wampum of the first grade."

"No wampum. I want the woman."

"Seven hundred."

"No."

"Seven hundred. No note. No wampum. Florins. Cash money. My final offer."

"No. The woman. And I'll give you a fine horse, too."

"She's not for trade or sale," Mendoza spat. "You are out of your mind. She would never have anything to do with a savage like you."

"You talk much and say nothing. You know nothing. The

woman and I have desire for each other. I know this. I learned this when I took her to Breukelen."

"What? Get away from here." Mendoza's face was beet red, the veins threatening to burst from his throat.

Foxman turned his palms down as if he were holding his hands over a fire to warm them. His voice was soft and menacing. "I'll go, but I'll be back. I want the woman. When I come back with the horse, I'll take the woman with me," Foxman said. He turned abruptly and headed back toward the East River and his canoe.

"Take your pelts. Don't leave them here. We have no bargain."

But Foxman, with contemptuous disregard for the Jew, kept walking. David Mendoza was speechless at last.

Tonneman, bent low to the ground, moved quickly eastward. He wanted to get far enough away from Foxman and Mendoza. It was the first reason he had to laugh in a long time, and he wanted to enjoy it.

45

THURSDAY, 28 AUGUST. *Afternoon.*

To Racqel's eye the four frigates in the bay looked festive, almost gaudy. Colorful pennants fluttered from their tall masts, and above them, each ship flew the haughty Union Jack, a proud red, white, and blue blending of the crosses of St. George for England and St. Andrew for Scotland and St. Patrick for Ireland. White sails billowed and the full-rigged ships swayed gracefully.

The four ships seemed so immaculate, the water so clean. It all looked like a painting she had seen once. "Not very threatening," Racqel said out loud, shifting her burden of duffel cloth that she had carried from the warehouse.

"I wouldn't count on that, Vrouw Mendoza." The miller, John Woods, had joined the growing assembly of spectators. "A few blasts from their cannon and we'll be no more." He puffed on his pipe; an aromatic cloud surrounded him.

"Do you really think it will come to that?"

"Perchance . . . and then perchance not. If they blow up the City, they'll have no plunder."

"Plunder?" With that word and the realization of what it implied, she was suddenly frightened. One moment everything was as if in a painting, the next the reality of invasion was quite clear and quite horrifying. The Mendozas would be deprived of everything they'd achieved in New Amsterdam.

She bade the miller a good afternoon, walked along the western shore and then to Beaver Street where the sempstress Mathilde Rougemont and her daughter Zoë lived. As she approached she saw a small subdued party of soldiers; some were loading barrels into a wagon, others were looking seaward to the four ships. They stopped to stare at her in Rebecca Da Costa's too-short dress, elbowing each other and smirking. She lowered her eyes and quickened her steps.

Who would do the plundering? The English? Or men such as these staunch defenders of the Company? The village would surely be sacked by those within and those without.

The sempstress's door was painted a vivid blue. White anemones and bright almost golden buttercups grew abundantly in a box under the front window. The door was open, and sitting on a low stool attaching a sleeve to a calico dress was Zoë, the sempstress's daughter, a woman of twenty-some years, her crippled legs hidden by her skirts. A wooden crutch lay beside her.

"Good afternoon, Zoë. Is your mother . . . ?"

Hearing Racqel's voice, the widow Rougemont came to the sunlit threshold. She was a thin, wiry woman, swarthy, with dark shadowed eyes. Small tufts of gray hair showed from under her white cap. A faint mustache outlined her thin upper lip, which now spread in a smile. "Ah, madame." The sempstress appraised her critically, taking in the worn, ill-fitting dress.

"The fire. Everything is gone."

"Come in, come in." The woman wore an apron with vertical lines of straight pins, giving the garment the appearance of chain mail. She ushered Racqel into a sunny chamber with a broad hearth. To one side, a large bed; to the other, two sempstress's forms and the tools of her trade. Canvas patterns and bolts of cloth lay one on another in disarray. About the chamber were a low stool for fittings, hat forms, baskets of lace trimmings, and skeins of colored threads.

The clothes Racqel had lost in the fire were black and brown, as was the material she had brought with her. These were the accepted hues of the Dutch and Jewish community. Only Indians and wantons and Geertruyd De Sille, who saw herself as the most fashionable woman in New Amsterdam, wore bright things.

After taking Racqel's measurements, Vrouw Rougemont found a

score book on her cluttered worktable and wrote out the order. "Three dresses for Madame Mendoza." The Frenchwoman closed the book and looked up as Racqel was taking her leave. "No, no, madame. You cannot go from here in that garment." She darted to a large trunk, flung it open, and unfolded a dress in sapphire-hued calico with a white shawl trim around the neck and small pleats down the bodice. She held it up. "My daughter," she said, "was not born with those poor legs. She was tall and slim and straight as you, but she had a fever, the same as took my husband."

"It's very beautiful."

"Let it be my gift to you," the Frenchwoman said. So it was that Racqel reappeared on Beaver Street in a dress that might have been made explicitly for her. Over her arms she carried Rebecca Da Costa's dress. The shawl collar of the dress she wore was cut somewhat lower than her own garments, but it was such a splendid feeling to be dressed properly again, what did it matter?

The sun had begun its slow descent in the middle afternoon as Racqel returned to Jews Alley. Ahead she saw David pacing back and forth in front of their still-unfinished house. She could hear the sounds of the men working inside.

David Mendoza's mouth opened. No sound came from him, but his eyes bulged and his face grew red at the sight of her. "Come here," he shouted.

She stopped, unsure of what to do. His anger was so fierce. He was acting as if he were the Lord Jehovah himself. His continuous incivility was making life unbearable. Had some new terror happened? "What is it? Have the English landed? Is there fighting?"

He lifted his clenched fist and shook it at her. Even at a distance his anger was so potent that she flinched. Still she didn't move.

He came at her then. Grabbing her by the arm, he pulled her, protesting, to their house. His mad eyes flared at her like angry candles, sweat poured into his beard. She tried to pull away. He caught her free arm and jerked her closer. Rebecca Da Costa's dress fell to the ground. "You Jezebel, you harlot of Sodom. I know all about you now from that savage. Your sinful behavior is a curse on our family. It has gone further than I thought. Further than I could ever imagine."

He shook her as if she were a rag doll. The world began to spin around her. "You belong to me," he proclaimed. "The English are at our shore. After they have taken New Amsterdam, we will be married."

"I'd sooner wed Pieter Stuyvesant." The words made her laugh and then she couldn't stop.

Her laughter made him angrier still. He let go of her arms and she fell to her knees. Dazed, she stopped laughing and looked up. He slapped her across the face, once, lightly. It was almost a caress. Then he slapped her again, this time with such force that she fell face down into the dirt.

"No one else will have you. No decent man. No Jewish man. No white man. You have nothing. No dowry. What you brought with you in marriage to my brother from your father's house belongs to the Mendozas now. Without our charity, you are a beggar."

She lay in the dirt, stunned by his violence. He was right. Without the Mendozas she was lost. "I have a husband," she said, sitting up, touching the burning spot on her face where his hand had left its mark. A welt had formed there and her right eye pained her terribly. She could feel the swelling start.

"My brother is dead. He died without children. According to Halakhah, the surviving brother must marry his sister-in-law to perpetuate the family." He stared down at Racqel, then lifted her gently to her feet. "You make me do this. Don't you understand, I love you. I have always loved you." He touched her face where he'd hurt her and she pulled back. "Our fathers decided Benjamin should have you and I accepted that, but now Benjamin is dead and by law we must marry. And we will."

"Never!" she cried, picking up the soiled dress.

"You will have no choice."

46

FRIDAY, 29 AUGUST. *Afternoon.*
Tonneman found a place just off the Strand out of the wind. He leaned his back against the gnarled trunk of a chestnut tree and lit his pipe. The pleasure of the tobacco wrapped about him almost sensually.

From where he stood he had a clear view of the English frigates. They looked like colorful children's toys bobbing in the water. He made a snorting noise. Children's toys with big cannon, able to blast all of New Amsterdam to kingdom come. That alone was enough to make a drunkard sober.

Overhead the sky looked menacing; dark-edged clouds hovered, seemingly ready to pounce. Like the frigates, waiting.

David Mendoza. The man had a violent temper. At first Tonneman had thought what had happened yesterday between the Jew and the Indian was truly comical, but what of the woman? Was she in danger? It was enough to make the laughter die in his throat. And if Mendoza took his temper out on Racqel, what could he do about it? True, he was Schout, but she was a Jew and belonged to them.

Tonneman brushed his hand over his eyes. He wanted to hold her, protect her, kiss the place in her throat where he'd seen her pulse flutter, fill her life with children. Merciful God. Such thoughts and desires were better left asleep. To stir them up would only betray him.

He felt bruised and beaten. Antje and the Boss were right. He'd been more drunk than sober since Maria died.

A fine rain began to fall. Tonneman tore himself from his reflections and moved away from the tree toward the Fort. Citizens looked at him hopefully, as if he could be the bearer of good news, but he had none. Neither about the English nor about the murders. And as he understood their law, Racqel would stay married to a dead man unless someone found his body.

And what if the body were found? What chance did he have? He was a Christian, for better or worse. Just a Schout, no more. Not even that, with the English coming. The brother-in-law wanted her. That was that. Same family, same people.

Still, this was a New World. People made their own decisions about marriage. Even women.

A misty fog rose from the water, almost obscuring the frigates.

That piece of paper and the man with the spectacles were the key to everything. Since the paper was lost to him, he needed to know about the man. Yesterday he'd gone to the ships anchored in both rivers to ask after Spectacles, but the captains and crews were too concerned about the English and wanted to talk only about them. Tall Matthew was nowhere to be found. And when he tried the Pear Tree again, it was still locked tight.

Where the hell was Joost? He was a man who liked the feel of guilders in his hands; he had never before closed down the Pear Tree, not even when Smitt, his own partner, died.

Then again, with the ordinance against grain, Joost may have run low on beer and gone off in search of a barrel or two of contraband. Sweet Jesus, he was giving himself a thirst with all these thoughts of beer. "Arsehole." He laughed.

His laughter led him back to the absurd humor of Foxman's

clash with David Mendoza. It had refreshed Tonneman in some odd way. His thinking was clearer, about the killings, Racqel Mendoza, New Amsterdam. And the Boss. This war was lost, but his duty was with Stuyvesant until the end. Most important, he was cold sober.

Stuyvesant was again on the shore, watching. There were citizens around but none of the Council and not Colonel van de Steen or Captain Van Dillen. The Director-General hailed him heartily. "Tonneman! That's more like it. Are you ready for the English?"

"I'm as straight as a die and ready to piss vinegar."

"Splendid." Stuyvesant clapped him on the back. "City business first. It is my understanding that there is a Jezebel roaming about. A creature known only as Sweet Lips. An Englishwoman, to make matters worse. Not only is she a whore, she is probably an English spy. Is it not enough that I am plagued by the vile English ships? Do I have to suffer their harlots? I want this woman banned from New Amsterdam."

"Yes, sir."

"My understanding is that she is pandered about by a Jew, Korbonski by name. Curse these Hebrew blasphemers, they're like a plague of locusts in my hair wherever I turn."

"I'll look into it."

"You do that."

"Yes, sir."

" 'Yes, sir' is not enough," Stuyvesant screamed. "I want it done."

"Yes, sir."

"It's your duty. Each of us must do his duty. Shirking duty is a design of the devil." Quietly. "No more to be said, then."

"Yes, sir." The rain was getting heavier. Tonneman wiped some from his face. "Where's your new right arm, De Sille?"

"Envy does not become you, Tonneman. You should avoid it. It is another of Lucifer's tricks."

"Yes, sir."

"De Sille is with Van Dillen inside the Fort. We're in for a rough fight. A terrible fight. But with faith in the Lord, we shall stand steadfast. We are only on this earth a short time. Our test is how well we serve the Lord while we are here."

"Yes, sir. What's our situation?"

"I estimate that the English have seventeen hundred to two thousand men. Come with me. I mean to send a letter to that scoundrel Nicolls."

Stuyvesant marched into the Fort with Tonneman behind him. "Avercamp," the Director-General bellowed.

His clerk came rushing out. "Yes, Heer Director-General."

"A letter. Back inside." He threw open his door; Tonneman and Avercamp followed.

"To that English blackguard out there. 'Sir. Will you tell me the intent and meaning of the warships' approach without giving any notice to us.' "

"Is that it?" Avercamp asked, quill ready to continue.

"Isn't that enough?" The Director-General picked up his pipe and started packing it with his rosemary-scented tobacco. "Also, I want messengers on fast horses dispatched immediately to all our outlying towns. They must come to our aid."

Avercamp rushed from the chamber; Stuyvesant turned his attention to Tonneman. "You know what you have to do, Schout?"

"I do." Tonneman left Stuyvesant blowing air through his lips, about to light his pipe.

Nothing had changed in the body of the Fort except for an air of swelling agitation that seemed to infect everyone and everything, including the animals.

Nick De Sille and Van Dillen came out of the church and stood together, talking.

Tonneman moved quickly, cornering De Sille just as Van Dillen took his leave. "I think you have something to tell me about Abner Simon, Nick."

"Hold, Van Dillen," De Sille said to the departing man, ignoring Tonneman completely.

Tonneman seized De Sille's lace-covered wrists. "No, you hold, Nick."

The rain poured down on both of them.

"Let me be, Tonneman." He tried to shake Tonneman off but didn't succeed; Tonneman held him tightly.

There came a sharp tapping on glass. They both looked to see Pieter Stuyvesant at his rain-spattered window, puffing furiously on his pipe and beckoning to De Sille.

De Sille glanced at Tonneman's clutching hands and arched his left eyebrow. Tonneman released his grip. De Sille raised his right hand to Stuyvesant and started for the office. Midstride he stopped and turned to Tonneman. "This is your lucky day, Schout. You nearly got another thump on that thick head of yours."

47

Friday, 29 August. *Afternoon.*
Her father had taught Racqel to love the rain. When she was a child, he would take her walking in it. As she walked up the Strand luxuriating in the touch of soft rain on her face, she forgot about the English and Benjamin and David and her swollen right eye and thought only of her father and when she was young.

Racqel arrived at Tonneman's door, lifted the horseshoe that served as a knocker, and let it fall. She waited, listening for footsteps or any sounds of the living, then knocked again. The door yielded to her touch, so she pushed it open further. Tentatively, she walked in a few steps and peered into the great chamber. "Heer Tonneman."

Inside, she saw a pleasant and neat arrangement of furniture that did not seem like Tonneman. She hadn't expected him to be living in a barn, but neither had she expected this neat, unlived-in place either. Why did she feel surprised? He was a widower. He had lived long years here with his wife and daughter.

There was a corn-shuck mattress on the floor. Was this where he and his wife had slept? Puzzled, Racqel backed away and out of the house, closing the door firmly.

Sadness knifed through her and she began to cry. David was right. The rain was falling harder and mixed with her tears. What she felt for the Dutchman was like nothing she had ever felt before. A wild yearning that Benjamin had never evoked in her.

Racqel tipped her face up to the heavens and let the clean rain purify her and perhaps wash her terrifying thoughts away. Taking a deep breath, she crossed the short distance to the City Hall. She should have looked for the Schout there in the first place, she told herself.

Nicasius De Sille and three other members of the Council were coming out of the Hall. The three men paused and nodded, mumbling words she could not hear. With a deep courtly bow, Nick De Sille smiled and held the door wide. "Please, gracious vrouw." His bow wasn't as ornate as that of Subaltern John Brick-Hill of the King's Musketeers; still, it reminded her of the Englishman.

"Thank you," she said. Had he been mocking her? she wondered, touching her bruised cheek.

A young soldier with a harelip was leaning against a wall inside the Hall, gnawing on his fingernails. Racqel stopped before him, shielding her eyes against the rain.

"Do you know where the Schout is?"

He scratched his head and stared at her without expression. The rain dripped down his plain face. Light and noise came from the cellar.

"What about down there?"

The soldier shrugged and went at his fingers again.

There was no railing; Racqel went down the steep, confined staircase with caution. The steps were slick with wet and filth. She had never seen such dirt inside a building in New Amsterdam before. She heard a slight, sharp clicking noise and stopped. Again, the sound of claws on the wood stairs. Rats. She wanted desperately to leave this place. No, she must find Tonneman. With a shallow inhalation of dank air, she held the skirts of her new blue calico dress out of the slime and continued down the staircase. The idea of falling in such a foul setting made her skin prickle. It was damper and colder than even a cellar had a right to be.

"Who's there?"

The bearded face before her, illumined by the shadowy flickering light of a Better lamp, was marked horribly with small wounds, lacerations, and bruises. "Oh. Oh. Captain Pos." She covered the injured side of her own face with her hand. They all looked as if they had gone through a war and the English hadn't even landed.

"Vrouw Mendoza, what are you doing here?"

"Is . . . ?" She looked beyond Pos but saw only darkness.

"I didn't mean to startle you." Tonneman's deputy lifted the lamp higher. The shadows bounced grotesquely from his wounded face to the dark wet wall. With the lamp high she could now see beyond him. In small cells behind treen-barred doors was an awful aggregation of evil-looking men. The clammy air was rank with vomit, urine, and unwashed bodies. "I'm looking for Heer Tonneman," she said firmly.

"Have you tried his house?"

"Yes."

One of the incarcerated men called out in a high-pitched voice, "Chicken, chicken, be my bird and I will pluck your egg," then made noises like a demented rooster. Racqel didn't understand what the words meant, but still her cheeks grew hot with shame.

Pos flapped a menacing hand to the offender, but without much energy. "Shut it, animal, or I'll cut your stones off." He half smiled an apology to Racqel. "He could be at the Fort or the Pear Tree or his willow. You know where that is?"

"Yes," she said, "I remember." She turned to begin her climb. Again the sharp clicking sound. Racqel looked about for the telltale small bright eyes of the rat.

Pos followed her, limping. Shrill catcalls and other lewd noises came from the cells. "Or he could be at the Ten Eycks'."

"I know where that is. Thank you."

"My pleasure, Vrouw Mendoza."

She raced up the stairs past the harelipped soldier and burst into the open on the Strand. The rain had stopped as suddenly as it had begun. A gull swooped down, making a wide arc, and then flew away.

That morning she had baked the Sabbath bread in her new oven and prepared their evening meal as if nothing had happened. It was a waste of time to worry about what she couldn't change, she must deal with the things she could change. For two days now she had fretted about not being honest with Tonneman. The incident of the day before with her brother-in-law had at last convinced her that the only thing to do was to tell Tonneman she could read English, that she knew the contents of the document, and that she recognized the piece of silver with the lion emblem as her husband's. She had to know why Tonneman carried it.

The English ships were still in the bay. An old woman with a filched New Amsterdam fire bucket dug for clams on the shore, oblivious of ships and soldiers.

As before, Racqel found Antje Ten Eyck and young Conraet in the backyard. Antje was in her garden, awkwardly gathering green beans into her apron over her protruding belly. The boy was playing in the mud with little wooden soldiers, his bright head bent over a mock battle.

Antje looked up from her bent position. "I haven't seen him," she said in answer to Racqel's question. "He's most likely at the Fort. Ten Eyck has gone there also." She straightened, breathing heavily, holding the ends of the full apron. "I'm pickling. Come in and have some beer or a cup of tea." She stared at Racqel's face, too polite to comment on her injuries.

"No, thank you. The Sabbath is almost here and I must be home."

"Another time, then."

The little boy waved to her, then ran to his mother to steal some green beans. Antje kissed his dirty face. Racqel waved back sadly and started home. She walked slowly, finding pleasure in her walk even though it brought her closer to David and whatever new torment he had in store for her. But he wouldn't dare disrupt the Sabbath.

She was sorry she hadn't found Tonneman. She had wanted to unburden herself. And she had wanted to be near him.

If only she knew the truth about Benjamin. If only she knew what was going to happen to her. If only she had been able to talk with Abner Simon. If only the English weren't threatening their lives. If only Tonneman . . .

She stopped and watched the English ships in the bay. Soon enough their lives would change. She hurried homeward. God would provide.

48

SATURDAY, 30 AUGUST. *Morning.*
An expectant air, perhaps of false hope, floated over the village. The sky was clear, the weather mild in spite of a cloudless late-summer sky.

Everyone, including Tonneman, had been watching the English warships for two days, waiting for Nicolls's response. The people were provoked by the precariousness of their situation; there were to be no secrets now.

Tonneman collected Pos at City Hall and together they headed for the Fort. "You don't look too good, Pos. What have you been up to? Perhaps it was something you drank?"

"Very amusing." Pos groaned gloomily as he canted his head with an unnatural stiffness. The bruises from their scuffle at the Blue Dove had turned magnificent purple. "You're not the prettiest thing about either, oh great and noble Mijnheer Schout," he said, regarding his friend with his good right eye. The other was swollen tight.

Tonneman smiled and flinched when a spasm of pain hit his

head. He felt as debilitated as if he'd been on a roaring drunk. Maybe it didn't pay to be sober.

"Whatever the news is, Tonneman, it will be bad. It'll sound a lot better after beer. Let's hoist a few before we go to the Fort."

"Not for me."

"Getting soft and droopy of cock in your old age." Pos's good eye glinted with mischief.

"Mind your manners, deputy," Tonneman said, smiling. "I never droop, not even when asleep. At my peak I am more wondrous to behold than the whale at Beverwijk."

"I'll take your word for it."

Tonneman clapped Pos on the back and they moved forward.

"The Jewess was at the jail yesterday. She looked as if she'd been at the Blue Dove with us."

"What?"

"Vrouw Mendoza. She had a eye like mine. So I said she looked like she'd been at the Blue—"

Tonneman grabbed him by his shirtfront. "I said mind your manners, deputy." This time he wasn't smiling.

"I was only gleeking, Tonneman, a little jest. Don't take it out on me. *I* didn't hit her."

Tonneman released his hold on Pos's shirt. "No, of course you didn't," he said softly. "I'll kill him," he said just as softly. Pos stared at Tonneman, who was walking around and around Pos in mad circles. "I'll kill him," Tonneman repeated. Finally he took his bearings and started for Jews Alley.

"Wait, Tonneman, wait." Pos hobbled after him. "Kill who?"

"David Mendoza!"

"Why?"

Tonneman stopped in his tracks. Why indeed? Did he know for a fact it was Mendoza who had struck her? And if so, what concern was it of his? Even as Schout, it was outside his office. He hadn't seen it. She hadn't complained. It was a family matter. He had no right.

Pos, breathing hard, caught up with him. "What's wrong with you, man? Get a grip on yourself."

"When did you see her?"

"Yesterday. She came looking for you. It's a good thing for Mendoza, and you, that she didn't find you."

Their attention was distracted by a man on a wheezing horse, galloping from the waterfront toward the Fort.

"What news, Ter Meer?" Pos called, recognizing the young soldier on the sad brown gelding. The rider didn't answer. Both Pos and Tonneman hurried after him.

Tonneman arrived at the Fort well ahead of his friend. Ter Meer, now wheezing, too, had tethered his animal next to Bucephalus, the Boss's spirited bay stallion, which was pulling at its reins, agitated by the sounds both the boy and his gelding were making. "Dirk, isn't it? What news?"

The young soldier nodded. Sweat dripped from the sparse blond hair of his mustache and rolled down his pimple-blotched chin. "Office," he wheezed, completely spent.

P.S. was planted in front of his clerk, legs apart, arms waving when Tonneman walked in. "Read it again, Avercamp."

"Sir, there's a delegation at City—"

"Read the letter."

"Yes, sir." Avercamp chewed his fat red lips nervously. He cleared his throat.

"Get on with it," the Director-General howled. "This is from Colonel Nicolls," he told Tonneman, snatching the letter from his clerk's trembling hands. Fury darkened his beetle brow. "He demands we surrender or he will bring 'the miseries of war upon us.' "

"Is that all he says?" Tonneman felt that everything was getting away from him. "No terms of surrender?"

"What, are you willing to surrender? Are you against me, too?"

"Sir." Avercamp tried again as Pos stumbled into the office. "There's a delegation at City—"

"What is it?" Pos demanded. "What are the surrender terms?"

Stuyvesant roared. "Another one? You're all pusillanimous weaklings. Traitors. We are at the brink of Armageddon and you two talk of surrender."

"Boss," Tonneman said as calmly as he could, "we'll have to let the people know what Nicolls said."

Stuyvesant thrust the letter at Tonneman as if it were a sword. It was in English. In form it looked very much like the document he'd taken from Abner's eye socket.

Too impatient to wait, the Director-General tore the letter from Tonneman's hands and gave it back to his clerk. "Tell them, Willem. Tell them what that devil wants."

"He says he will let every man keep his life and liberty, and his home and possessions, if we surrender."

"Then what's the problem?" Pos asked, incredulous.

"Sir?" Avercamp shifted miserably from one foot to the other.

Stuyvesant whirled toward his clerk, pouring his fury with Tonneman and Pos onto the frightened young man. "What is it?"

"Another messenger . . ."

"Speak. Good God in heaven, get it out!"

"Another messenger rode in just before you got here. We've received word from Flatbush and Rensselaerswyck."

"Yes? Yes?"

"Both refuse to come to our aid."

"Just like those cravens at Esopus—"

"Rensselaerswyck says they are in imminent danger from savages."

"Liars!" Stuyvesant bellowed. "I am surrounded by enemies!" He gave Tonneman and Pos a hard look. "We all are. I have intelligence that in addition to the volunteers from New England and Long Island, savages and privateers have offered their services against us. There are six hundred Indians ready to take the English shilling and one hundred and fifty French privateers who now have an English commission."

"If they seize our ships, there's no hope for more ammunition," said Tonneman.

"Or beer," said Pos sorrowfully.

"You'll be thinking about your thirst on Judgment Day," said Tonneman.

Stuyvesant gave them a blistering look. "Write this down, Avercamp. People of New Amsterdam. It is my command . . . no strike that. It is *God's* command that we defend this island—"

"To what avail, sir? They won't listen. Even if you don't tell the people about Nicolls's offer, the English have had broadsides posted on Long Island with their surrender demand, and travelers have brought them into Manhattan. Some English citizens here in town have gone so far as to announce that they won't take up arms against their own countrymen."

Stuyvesant grunted and sat heavily in his chair. "Anything else?"

"Yes, sir," said Avercamp. "Most important. The delegation at City Hall . . ."

"Delegations, delegations, there are always delegations these days. Everybody wants a piece of me. Who is it this time?"

"Colonel van de Steen has sent word that there is a delegation from New England under a flag of truce."

Stuyvesant leaped up and stamped his silver-decorated peg on the floor. "Why didn't you tell me that in the first place?"

"I tried to, sir."

"Excuses. Always excuses. Why doesn't he bring them here? I've got more to do than run hither and yon after people."

"I'm sure the colonel doesn't want them to see our defenses here at the Fort."

"Or lack of them," Pos muttered.

"Get on about your duties, Captain. You have the look and smell of a sot. Have you no pride, man? Take your clever words and be gone. I have enough trouble with Tonneman when he forgets who he is. Tonneman, come with me. Who knows? Perhaps those contemptible English rascals have changed their minds and have sent the Johnnies to surrender."

"I don't think so, sir." Tonneman smiled. He was always surprised when Stuyvesant showed a rare flash of humor.

"Agreed. Let's get this over with. You too, Avercamp. Get your horse. I need you to translate. How anybody can abide that awful language, I'll never know. And Avercamp—"

"Yes, sir?"

"Monday is the eighth day of the brewer's ban against making beer. It must be renewed. Remind me."

"Yes, sir."

"And Market Field day is canceled until further notice."

"Yes, sir."

Outside, Pos nodded to Tonneman with a grin and started his trudge toward City Hall. Young Ter Meer and his horse were still resting but no longer wheezing.

"I don't have an animal," said Tonneman as P.S. mounted Bucephalus and Avercamp went around back to get his horse.

"Take that one." Stuyvesant pointed to Ter Meer's sorry gelding.

"But—" Tonneman began.

"No time for buts," Stuyvesant countered. "We've got a war to win." Bucephalus reared and neighed. Stuyvesant steadied him and shouted, "Avercamp!"

"Coming, sir." Avercamp appeared on a stunning black mare. On horseback the little clerk was a changed man. He sat the steed like a calvary officer. He leaned over the mare's neck, patted it, and cooed, lovingly, into her ear, "Easy, Violet."

"Let's ride," P.S. ordered. "Avercamp, work on the fortifications must be increased. More men. More hours."

"Yes, sir."

Ter Meer's gelding immediately started wheezing. Pos, who was hobbling ahead of them, stepped off the road. As they rode past him Tonneman was certain he heard a derisive wheeze from his deputy. When he turned around to look, Pos was holding his right hand up, his middle finger to the sky.

"Tonneman, what about that whore?"

"It's being taken care of."

"It had better be." The Director-General fell silent. Avercamp rolled his eyes at Tonneman, who shrugged.

It was a short ride. Stuyvesant snorted when he saw the crowd of citizens gathered in front of City Hall. "Tonneman, get rid of them at once."

"All right, everybody," Tonneman yelled. "This is not a show at the Market Field. Disperse, please. Let the Director-General through."

"What's going on?"

"Is this the invasion?"

"Are they at the Wall?"

"When can we have more beer?"

"Give them hell, Silver Leg."

The three men tethered their horses. Stuyvesant's face wore a dark scowl.

"Don't you have anything to say to us?"

Stuyvesant and Tonneman went inside the two-story building without responding to any of the remarks. The hapless Avercamp found himself encircled by the crowd.

"Avercamp!" the Director-General roared from inside the Hall.

The crowd picked it up. "Avercamp. Avercamp. Avercamp. You tell us."

"Come, it's your arse, too."

The clerk pushed his way to the door.

"Show your stones, you sorry little mite."

Avercamp stopped and faced the throng. His voice quivering, he shouted, "You ingrates, the Boss is doing the best he can!"

49

SATURDAY, 30 AUGUST. *Late Morning.*
Inside the hall, members of the Council clustered, talking in low voices. Nick De Sille was not among them. Tonneman wondered where he was and what he was up to.

Waiting impatiently were former Burgomaster Oloff Stevensen van Cortlandt, the two Burgomasters, Van der Grist and Steenwyck, and Willem Beekman and Colonel van de Steen. The colonel stroked his cheek scar with elegant display and led the Director-General to a chamber and the English delegation.

The two English representatives wore velvet coats and lace at their throats and wrists, reminding Tonneman again of the dead man in the shed.

"That ugly Johnny," someone said, pointing to a tall, lanky fellow in a claret coat with a pinched Johnny face. "That one is a commissioner from the Massachusetts colony."

The other, a small, tense man in blue velvet, Tonneman recognized. John Winthrop, the greedy Governor of Connecticut, who fancied New Amsterdam, Long Island, and all else the industrious Dutch had created.

He had seen Winthrop in New Amsterdam back in September of '61. Tonneman had been Schout for over a year at that time, and the governor was visiting with another delegation, on his way to London and an audience with the king. Stuyvesant had offered the English his hospitality. Now, three years later, no one talked of hospitality.

Without any preambles the New Englanders, speaking in English, asked Stuyvesant to surrender peacefully to save bloodshed. Avercamp translated. Governor John Winthrop of Connecticut nodded to the Director-General and to Tonneman and handed Stuyvesant a sealed letter.

"Avercamp." Stuyvesant handed the sealed letter to his clerk. "What does he want?"

Avercamp's hands shook. He ran his fingers fitfully through his thin hair and broke the seal, then read aloud at a rapid pace: " 'To his excellency, the Director-General—' "

"Never mind the cream. What does he want?"

" 'This is the Governor's private request for you to surrender. He personally extends a promise of a generous peace.' "

Stuyvesant, glowering, nodded curtly at the Connecticut governor and thumped out of the chamber. "He'll think about it," Avercamp said hastily, and ran after the Director-General. Tonneman followed.

"What's going on, Petrus?" Willem Beekman called out.

"When I know you'll know, Willi," Stuyvesant called back over his shoulder as he and Avercamp and Tonneman emerged from City Hall.

"Is it over?"

"Tell us what happened!"

"We have a right to know!"

Stuyvesant mounted Bucephalus easily. He was quite agile for an old man with a wooden leg. "Go home, all of you. Tonneman, send these people home. Better yet, put them to work on the defenses. Idle hands are the devil's own tools."

"Yes, sir. Do you need me at the Fort?"

"No. You have other duties. Attend to them."

Tonneman reentered City Hall as the English delegation was leaving. Winthrop brushed past him, turned, and looked strangely at the Schout for a moment, then went his way. "What was that about?" Tonneman muttered under his breath.

He started for the stairs to the jail but was stopped by van Cortlandt and some Council members. "What's old Silver Foot got on his mind, Schout?"

"If I knew that, Heer van Cortlandt, I might be a rich man. But I don't and I'm not." He raised his hat. "By your leave." He proceeded down the stairs, past the bags of salt, to the dank jail. The Hall was also a salt warehouse. Though why the salt was kept down here, Tonneman never knew.

The two sailors Tonneman had locked up for fighting and the three other prisoners were being fed by Vrouw Root. The doors to the cells were open and the kindly woman was going from cell to cell doling out great portions of hearty pea soup into vast treen bowls.

"Some soup, Heer Tonneman?"

He nodded, unable to resist smiling at her cheerful face.

"No beer again, Vrouw Root?" one of the prisoners complained.

"They don't make, I don't have. Not like some people in the taverns." She cast a knowing look at the Schout.

As Tonneman ate his soup Nick De Sille came into his mind again. More and more he was thinking that Nick had killed Abner Simon and most likely the man with the spectacles. And if he had killed Spectacles, it would be just like Nick with his distorted drollery to plant Tonneman's knife in the body. On the other hand, he was certain it was not Nick's voice he'd heard talking to Spectacles only four nights ago on the riverbank.

But why would Nick kill Hendrik? That was the question for all these deaths. Why? What was the motive? The most obvious was the missing document, which had to be the connection between Spectacles and Abner Simon. But what did Hendrik have to do with it?

"Ho, Tonneman." Pos hopped down the steep stairs on his good leg.

"What are those two still doing here?" Tonneman asked, jerking his thumb at the two German sailors.

"You never told me to let them go."

"I didn't tell you to piss this morning, but I'll wager you did. Is their ship still in port?"

"I don't know."

"God help me. Let them go. Let them all go. We don't have food for them. They're eating better than some of our citizens."

"All right, you don't have to bite my head off. Between you and the Boss, I'd be better off with the English. I don't think that man likes me."

The two German sailors were happy to get out and unhappy with each other. They were very vocal about it in loud German. "That's the last time I go anywhere with you," the big one with the thick black mustache said to his companion.

"Shut your mouth, just shut it," the moon-faced sailor responded.

"The two of you shut it," Tonneman shouted over their voices. The bickering ceased.

The other three prisoners, French trappers who had drunk their fur money away and were unhappy to be tossed back on the street, grumbled in thick-accented Dutch about it. They had found a home. "Do we have to go now?" one asked plaintively. "Vrouw Root is making a venison hutsepot tonight."

"And cherry soup," said a second.

"Can we leave tomorrow?" begged the third.

Tonneman pointed up the dark stairs. "Get out. And you two, don't ever let me see you here again. Next time I'll throw you into the bay."

"Next time," the larger sailor said softly in clear Dutch, "it won't be your bay to throw us in." His friend tittered nervously.

Tonneman waved Pos away, and the deputy escorted the five out. The Schout could hear the sailors laughing and the three trappers complaining in French about having to leave as they all lumbered up the stairs. When Pos returned, he was limping badly.

"You walk like a bear with a broken leg," said Tonneman, finishing the last of his soup.

"I *am* a bear with a broken leg."

"What did the Mendoza woman want here yesterday?"

"I told you. She was looking for you."

The idea that Racqel had come looking for him pleased Tonneman.

"She was wearing this blue dress. Not like what she usually wears." Pos pitched his voice high in imitation of a woman. "You're a devil with the women, Heer Schout."

"If *you* don't shut up, I'll throw *you* into the bay."

Silence, then Pos made a noise in his throat. "With no prisoners, I have no reason to stay here."

"No."

"A beer would be nice."

"Yes. I think one beer would be good."

"One? That doesn't sound right. Maybe two or three. All right?"

"Maybe."

They climbed the stairs slowly, like old men. Outside they discovered that the Pear Tree was still not open for business.

"The White Horse or the Blue Dove?" asked Pos.

"I should think you'd have had enough of the Blue Dove."

"The White Horse it is, then."

At the White Horse, Tonneman drank his beer in two long joyous swallows. For a moment he savored the taste still on his tongue and the scent of flowers still lingering in his mug.

"Two more," Pos called to Marie de Vos.

"Not for me," said Tonneman.

"I don't believe you," Pos exclaimed.

"You don't have to believe me," said Tonneman. "I believe me and that's all that matters. One more beer for you, and then I want you talking again to everyone in town. Foxman says Cutnose is dead. Be that as it may, find out if anyone saw Cutnose after last Tuesday night, or knows anything about our man with the spectacles. And this time do it right."

Pos didn't say anything. He just lifted his fresh mug of beer and drank.

Tonneman left the tavern feeling righteous and pleased with himself. As he stepped into the street a wagon pulled by one white and one black horse went rattling by, nearly knocking him down. "Hey," he yelled at the two men in the wagon. "You two, stop. Slow down. You're going too fast. Don't you know you're supposed to lead your horses in town?" He ran after the wagon, feeling every bone in his body creak. The wagon turned a corner and was lost to him, but not before he recognized the man handling the reins. Nick De Sille.

The man next to De Sille had been crouched low, his hat pulled down, but Tonneman knew him, too. John Winthrop, Governor of Connecticut.

50

SUNDAY, 31 AUGUST. *Morning.*

The church bells woke him. For a moment Tonneman thought Kruseman Wolters, the church sexton, was warning the village that the English had landed. No, it was Sunday.

He and Maria had always gotten up early on Sunday. She because she wanted to, he because she wanted him to. Dressing herself and little Anna in their best and going to church was one of the great joys in Maria's life.

Once up, he always found excuses. Maria would berate him, and he would put on the clean clothes she'd laid out for him, complaining all the while. Still, he would follow his little family to church. Even then, he never stayed. He would sneak off and she would find him under his willow tree, fishing and dozing. "I'm talking to God right here," he'd tell her when she found him.

And she would say, "God will never hear you when your tongue is thick with brandywine." She would smile at him because she knew his drinking was moderate. That was then. She would not have smiled if she could have seen what he'd become in his loneliness.

But all that was changed now because of Racqel Mendoza. He was certain her husband was dead. He had to be dead. Tonneman wanted him dead. Amazed at the ferocity of his thoughts, Tonneman knew he would not let David Mendoza have her.

She was not a compliant woman. Tonneman laughed out loud. He would speak for himself, and with God's mercy, they would find a path between her people and his. He had already seen many times how short this life could be.

His belly turned and knotted when in his mind he saw Racqel's bruised face and thought of her brother-in-law's temper and her helplessness. Then he smiled. Racqel was not so helpless, and he knew she felt something for him. Of that he was certain, now that his mind was clear of drink.

He pressed his hands to his temples. Pain only where the bruises were, no aching head from too much burnt wine. He stretched his long body on the corn shuck mattress and thought more about Maria, how happy she'd been about the little things in life.

After a time he rose and put on the clean breeches and shirt Vrouw Root had left. He would go to church, not for God, or for the sake of his soul, which was probably lost, but in order to remember Maria. And to see what more he could discover about the deaths of the foreigner and Abner Simon. New Amsterdamers were gleeful gossips.

But first he would allow himself some time under his willow tree to have a smoke and think over what he knew or thought he knew.

After seeing Nick De Sille and Governor Winthrop together in that wagon the day before, Tonneman had spent the rest of the day trying to find the two men again, but with no luck. It was obvious that De Sille was his man. That he was a spy was clear enough, too. Why else would he be with Winthrop? The scent of De Sille's lavender pomade put him at the scene when both Spectacles and Abner were killed.

Tonneman gave Venus her feed and made his way up the Strand, managing to deflect eager conversation. Everyone—men, women and children—was going to church this morning. Tonneman knew it was as much for information as for prayer.

Only the soldiers and militia remained at their posts, the soldiers making lewd jokes and the militia countering with lewder ones.

Behind the Peysers' fence their spaniel barked anxiously and threw itself at the latched gate. Tonneman reached over the fence and patted the dog's silky brown head, then continued on his way to the water and his tree.

As he idly watched the smoke drift up and mingle with the narrow spear-shaped leaves and the dense catkin spikes of small flowers of the droopy willow, Tonneman thought back to Wednesday night and the lavender pipe tobacco he'd smelled just outside the Pear Tree. He'd been too drunk to pay attention to the implications. Keyser or Joost? Or Dinck, for that matter, and what about the scratches on Dinck's face? Fell in a hole indeed. Oyster shells indeed. Dinck had been in some sort of a fight. It fretted Tonneman that Dinck's fight could have been with Abner Simon. He hadn't wanted to think it, but now he had to.

The church bells tolled again, like a summons.

"Christ's bloody hands," Tonneman said, getting to his feet. None of this made any real sense. It was all distraction, leading him away from the truth. De Sille was his man and that was that.

Tonneman parted the curtain of leaves and walked slowly to the Fort, following other stragglers to the Stone Church.

Kruseman Wolters was ringing the church bells again and making rebuking faces at those like Tonneman who were late.

Dinck stood just inside the church in his role as church greeter. He hailed Tonneman with a bit too much heartiness, or so Tonneman thought. "Good to see you on the Lord's day, Tonneman."

"Always good to see you, Dinck. This is quite a gathering. Are they all here because they love Jesus?"

Dinck's scraped jowls shook with mirth. "Would that it were true. I think they're all here because they love their collective arses and want to protect them."

In fact, so many people were in the church that day that the ushers were running out of places to put them. Tonneman stepped aside to let Jan Keyser, his wife, children, and the tanner's apprentices enter.

Reverend Johannes Megapolensis was waiting patiently at the altar for the crowd to settle, as was his son Reverend Samuel Megapolensis. Pieter Stuyvesant was sitting in the front row with his wife, Judith, a pretty little woman, and their sons, Balthazar Lazarus and Nicholas William. Like his older brother, sixteen-year-old-Nicholas had his father's strong nose and full lips.

Hat in hand, Tonneman found a bit of stone wall to lean against. He saw Stuyvesant's sister Anna Varleth and her second husband, the merchant, Nicholas Varleth, and their children sitting along side the Stuyvesants in the first row. All the Schepens and Burgomasters were in church, as were Avercamp and the blacksmith and the millers and all the bakers. For the first time in his memory, everyone was at church.

Many, like him, were standing; some not content to be still were wandering the church; almost all were gossiping, talking thirteen to the dozen. It was as noisy as a tavern. The elder Reverend Megapolensis cleared his throat. "Let us worship God," he droned, his stern eyes on his congregation, his huge mustache drooping.

The babbling continued.

"Let us worship God," the younger Megapolensis shouted. If his father was a giant, young Samuel was a bigger giant, with more ample shoulders, unrulier hair, thicker eyebrows, and a larger mustache. And where his father's hair was gray, young Samuel Megapolensis's hair was as yellow as corn.

Members of the congregation broke off their conversations and hurried to their places.

"In the name of the Father and the Son and the Holy Spirit. Amen," began the elder Megapolensis. His son stood to the side, nodding and saying amen.

"Amen," said the congregation.

"Oh come, let us worship and bow down," the elder Megapolensis continued. "Let us kneel before the Lord, our Maker. For He is our God and we are the people of His pasture and the sheep of His hand. Grace to you and peace from God our Father and the Lord Jesus Christ. Let us now sing a hymn of praise. Samuel."

Tonneman's eyes scanned the church, and as they rested upon each citizen he weighed and measured each as a possible murderer. For despite his own protests, Tonneman was a religious man, and he believed evil had to be punished. After all, wasn't evil the denial of goodness? And without goodness, life wasn't worth living.

The congregation was singing the *gloria patri.* "Glory be to the Father, and to the Son, and to the Holy Spirit. As it was in the beginning, is now, and ever shall be, world without end. Amen."

"Amen, said Tonneman. His gaze went back to Nick De Sille, his prime suspect. De Sille must hold all the answers to this puzzle. The trick was to get him to divulge them.

"Praise God from whom all blessings flow," droned Reverend Johannes Megapolensis. He regarded his assembly for a moment. "Matthew tells us, 'Blessed are the peacemakers: for they shall be called the children of God.' "

"Amen," said young Megapolensis.

"Amen," rumbled some members of the congregation.

Tonneman wondered if his ears were failing him. Had he heard true? He had assumed the predicant would want to fight the English till the day of doom.

"And James admonishes us to 'Be swift to hear, slow to speak and slow to wrath.' But when Moses faced the chariots of Pharaoh, he sang 'the Lord is my strength. The Lord is a man of war.' And Pharaoh's chariots and his host were swallowed up in the Red Sea."

"Amen," said young Samuel.

"Amen," said Pieter Stuyvesant, speaking for the whole of the Island of Manhattan.

"Amen," said other members of the congregation.

Tonneman pulled on his nose. No peacemaker here. This was fighting talk. He set his eyes roaming again. Nick De Sille was sitting directly behind the Director-General, but without Geertruyd. She and her pug bitch were probably at home lapping up brandywine and milk possets.

"Still," said the minister, his son nodding in agreement at every word, "Luke said, 'Glory to God in the highest, and on earth peace, goodwill toward men.' "

"Amen," said young Samuel.

"Amen," said some members of the congregation.

"We should not forget these words of Isaiah: 'They shall beat their swords into plowshares, and their spears into pruning hooks.' And Matthew, 'All they that take the sword shall perish with the sword.' "

"Amen. Amen," said young Samuel.

"Amen," said some members of the congregation.

Stuyvesant's voice was not heard.

Tonneman shook his head. That sly, cunning, old fox Megapolensis. He's straddling the fence. First the Boss's way, then the other way, though it seemed he had fallen finally on the peace side of the fence.

"However," the minister said, his big voice hot with passion, his right fist thrust into the air, "let us not forget the brave flag that flies o'er the steeple of this church. On that flag is a powerful strong heavenly arm wielding a terrible sword of a vengeful God, poised to strike down the wicked enemies of our Fatherland and our Church."

"Amen!" said young Samuel.

"Amen. Amen. Amen." The Director-General's voice was stronger than all the rest. He turned around, fiercely scanning the assembly, encouraging the more bellicose members of the congregation.

Tonneman nodded glumly. Old man Megapolensis had finally come down on the other side of the fence, with the Boss right alongside him. So much for peace.

But then, proving Dinck correct, the service was interrupted by worshipers who got to their feet and spoke about the feared invasion.

"When are they coming?"

"They're here, aren't they?"

"They're in Breukelen. They're going to slaughter us all."

"Twenty years I've put into this land. Twenty years of sweat and blood."

"Why are we being stupid? We're not soldiers. Didn't you read the broadside from Colonel Nicolls?"

"He said that we would be left in peace. The English wish us no harm, they only desire to live beside us in peace and harmony."

"Enough," Stuyvesant bellowed. "Sit down and be quiet, all of you. This is seditious talk. This is treason."

"We live here, we have a right. The people should have their say. And you should listen. You . . . you . . . you *peacock*."

"Yes. You're not really a Muscovy Duke, you know. You're just Director-General for the Company. And where is the Company now? They've abandoned us."

"Yes. Sit down, old Silver Foot. The people have spoken."

"The people? Bah the people," Stuyvesant replied. "We derive our authority from God and the West India Company, not from the pleasure of a few ignorant subjects." With that, Stuyvesant, ignoring the fact that divine services were far from over, thumped out of the church. His wife hurried after him.

Johannes Megapolensis shook his head and quickly spoke the benediction: "The Lord bless you and keep you."

Nobody was listening; everyone was watching the Stuyvesant family. The Director-General's sons sat motionless in their seats. Judith Stuyvesant stopped at the door, turned, and looked at them sadly.

The elder Megapolensis persevered. "The Lord make his face to shine upon you, and be gracious to you; the Lord lift up his countenance upon you and give you peace. Amen."

"Amen," said Samuel Megapolensis.

"Amen," said some members of the congregation, those who were still paying attention.

At last Balthazar nodded his head and went to his mother, his younger brother directly behind him.

Tonneman eased out of the church and watched as the family climbed into the plain open carriage, driven by a fat African and pulled by a matched set of black mares. The Varleth family followed in their carriage.

Amidst the shouting and argument, Nick De Sille had slipped away.

51

SUNDAY, 31 AUGUST. *Morning.*

On Sunday all the shops were closed. Very few people leaving church rode away in wagons or on horseback as the Stuyvesants had; most either strolled on the Strand or along the Broad Way, greeting each other before going home to eat.

Within minutes Tonneman spied Nick approaching the De Sille estate. But Nick went on past and continued along the Broad Way.

Tonneman stayed well behind. He didn't want De Sille hearing people greet him by name as they were wont to do.

The North River front was usually the busiest site in New Amsterdam. Vessels arrived from the Atlantic with European goods while others were heading home with fur or lumber from Pavonia or the north country.

Goods for the city were unloaded and transported by boat to slips along Staple Street, thence to the warehouses or the markets. The usual quota of ships from all nations dotted the North River today, anchored but rigged for sailing at a moment's notice. As if that would help if shooting broke out.

Tonneman followed De Sille through the Broad Way gate, closing up the space between them. It appeared that Nick was going toward the warehouses on Staple Street.

Beyond Staple Street, behind the warehouses, Korbonski and Sweet Lips had set up their large red pleasure pavilion on one of the wharves. The boisterous noise of the place could be heard fifteen yards away. Tonneman sighed. He'd have to do something about Sweet Lips, English invasion or no English invasion.

Right now he was more concerned with Nick De Sille, who had just disappeared into Sweet Lips's red comfort tent. "My, my, and on Sunday, no less," Tonneman said quietly. He waited a moment, then approached the red canvas and lifted the flap.

Inside the red pavilion, where it was darker and smokier than any tavern in New Amsterdam, were four small canvas nooks, barely big enough for two to lie in. Each was marked with a large whitewashed number.

"Your cunt attract flies as well as other stuff," a gaunt African woman screaked at a small blond woman with enormous breasts as both pushed each other coming out of tent number one. "I'll never work double with you again, biter bitch!" Each of the bawds was clad only in a long flowing red gown open down the front and held scarcely closed by a sash. Underneath they were bare-arsed as babes.

"I shit on you, Black Suzie. I piss on you. And I stick my arse on your head," said the blond woman, who would have to be the one Sweet Lips had told him about.

A beaming sailor, carrying a half-filled bottle of brandywine, came out of tent number one adjusting his breeches.

"Where are you going, lover?" the blond asked.

"To get some oysters. Then I'm coming back."

"Remember," she said, tickling him under the chin, "oysters are usually closed, but not mine, mine is forever open."

The sailor laughed, bowed to the two bawds, and left.

When they saw Tonneman, the harlots immediately forgot about their squabble and descended on him. The blond got to him first, but just barely. Their hands were all over him. "Whatever you want, darling, Frederika can give it to you."

"Don't listen to her, my little whore hunter," Black Suzie murmured softly, her gold tooth flashing. "She stinks all over. If you want to plug, I'm the one for you. I can do things to you you never dreamed of."

"I stink?" Frederika howled. With one vicious kick, she knocked Black Suzie's legs out from under her. The African fell hard on the wooden pier. "How do I smell from down there?"

Tonneman looked around the smoky gloom. Strangely, the place smelled more of the water than of the women or the smoke. Despite all the noise there were only about eight sailors visible, but there was no sign of De Sille. Two of the sailors were sitting on the floor, piss-potted, singing lustily into each other's faces. They were Norwegian, still it sounded like an English tune, something about tobacco. But what of it? They'd probably all be singing English tunes soon enough.

Tonneman edged over to tent number two and looked in. A small rail of a man was bouncing on a naked Indian woman, who was all the while picking lice from her head and crushing them. She looked over the man's shoulder at Tonneman. "Don't go away, sweetheart," she said, waving, "you're next to frolic." With that, she grabbed the thin man's rump with both hands and bounced him on her till he moaned and said something weakly in a language Tonneman didn't know.

Tonneman smiled and tipped his hat to her. "Not this time, sweetheart."

"Ask for Sparrow," he heard her call as he left.

Two new customers had entered the pavilion; Black Suzie and Frederika were at them, like beasts of prey. The newcomers were speaking Dutch, but they were Swedes.

"Meet me later," the younger of the Swedish sailors was saying to Frederika. Apparently he was in love.

"Of course, my dearest darling," Frederika said. "But first give me money and we'll do it here."

"Then you'll meet me later? At the Blue Dove. It's on the Broad Way. Do you know the Broad Way?"

"We can do it any way you like, you darling ninny," the whore answered, undoing his breeches. "Look at him, standing like an oak. Now, if he only has a few florins, we're in business." She towed him into tent number one.

Black Suzie took her customer into tent three.

Tonneman, seeking De Sille, moved toward tent number four but was stopped by Sweet Lips coming out of it. "Here to get your tiny frog thing wet, dear heart?"

Tonneman didn't waste time responding. His eyes were drawn to the interior of the fourth tent. Lines of sunlight thrust through the spaces in the planking. There was enough intermittent illumination for him to see the trapdoor under the canvas pallet on the floor. He shouldered past Sweet Lips and threw aside the pallet.

"Here, here, what seems to be the problem?" he heard Korbonski cry behind him.

Quickly Tonneman pulled open the trapdoor. A blaze of daylight flooded the small tent, revealing a ladder. Ignoring the whoremaster's protests, he descended. Below, under the wharf, were two rowboats. The water was not calm. It was swirling about. A third boat was disappearing into the shadows of the dock above. Again, curse it, just like yesterday with the wagon. "Stop," Tonneman called. "In the name of the law."

But the boat was gone, leaving only the rough splashing of the water against the other boats and the pier.

As he climbed back up the ladder his hand brushed against something on the wooden floor. It shone brightly in the sharp light of day.

He snatched it up, more angry with himself than anyone else.

"Find what you were looking for, love?" Sweet Lips asked, looking worried under her ready-to-please expression.

"Nice of you to pay us a visit, Heer Schout," Korbonski said, a slyness in his voice that Tonneman heard very clearly.

"Get out of my way," Tonneman yelled, pushing past them.

"Don't go away mad with us," Black Suzie called after him.

"Come back anytime," said Frederika.

The two Norwegian sailors were still on the floor, singing away. "Sing praise to tobacco. For tobacco is like love . . ."

Tonneman burst out into the open and ran to the end of the pier.

Around all the ships were many little boats. But he was too far away to tell if De Sille was in any of them.

Tonneman was certain Nick De Sille had been in that rowboat. And who else? He looked in his hand at the object he'd picked up inside tent number four. Another piece of silver.

52

SUNDAY, 31 AUGUST. *Morning.*
Spread before her in the scullery on a drying rack were the medicinal herbs, barks, and plants Racqel had gathered to replenish her store.

First, the hairy borage for fever. Next was the coarse white comfrey, a cousin to the borage. Her father had brought cuttings of both across the sea and planted them in their first garden; they were still good despite the fire. He had taught her that the comfrey root was good for loose bowels, and the leaves steeped in a tea would moderate coughing and sneezing or used in a poultice would ease a sprain.

Now the willow bark for pain, angelica for toothache and rheumatism, soothing red raspberry leaves for a woman's time of the month or nausea, purplish green basil for bee stings, white oak for woman's troubles or sores and wounds, bloodroot for cough.

Chickweed infusion was for bathing burns. The elder shrub was for salve. She had used both the chickweed and the elder after the fire and they had worked very well indeed.

The leaves and stems of the aromatic marjoram would be infused for sore-throat gargle and the powder from the dry leaves would be just the thing for nerves and headaches. The pale bluish-purple flowers of the lavender were for nerves, dead nettle to stop bleeding.

She found a joy in the orderly drying of herbs that took her out of her present troubles back to the time with her father. The Indians had taught him much about native herbs and remedies. Her thoughts floated to a better, peaceful time with Benjamin. And then from Benjamin to Tonneman. So involved was she in the sorting and trimming and dreaming that she did not hear the knock on her backdoor.

It was only when Rebecca Da Costa said her name that she came out of her reverie.

"Rebecca." She raised her hand to hide her eye and the bruise on her cheek.

There was an angry frown on Rebecca's usually gentle face, her voice was full of scorn. "Do not try to hide your sin, Racqel."

"My sin?"

"Yes. I know all about it. There are no secrets among us. We all know what you have become."

"What wrong have I done? To whom? And what do you think I have become?"

"I demand that you release David Mendoza from your wicked spell. Set him free so he can marry my Mariana."

Racqel laughed bitterly. "You forget that I am already married."

"And if Benjamin is found to be dead?"

"You can have David with my blessing."

Rebecca Da Costa bristled with resentment. Clearly she had come to have her say; accusations came tumbling out. "Your speech is virtuous but what you do is immoral. You are not the good and faithful wife you pretend to be. You flirt with all the men in New Amsterdam, Jew and Christian alike. Everyone has seen you with the Schout. And lately you've been traipsing everywhere. You have no shame. The way you act, is it any wonder that you drove your husband away?"

The bitter fury of this sudden attack wounded Racqel more deeply than any of David's blows. "Rebecca, I thought I was your friend."

"You're not my friend. You're a fallen wanton."

"Why should you of all people think such evil of me? You know better. I tell you here and now and anywhere you please for all of New Amsterdam to hear, I have no interest in David Mendoza. Your daughter—or the devil's daughter, for that matter—can have him. And to the bottomless pit with both of them."

But, she thought with guilt, I do want the Dutchman, God help me.

The two women stared angrily at each other in silence, then Racqel burst out crying. Sobs racked her slender body.

Rebecca Da Costa, shocked by the violence of her own words, started crying, too. "I'm so sorry, Racqel. I didn't mean what I said. It's just that I am a mother. I worry about my child."

"Please leave."

"Do you accept my apology?"

"Of course. Please go."

"You must accept my apology."

"I do. These are frightening times. We all say things we don't mean."

"If you want, I'll walk with you tomorrow to Maiden Lane. We'll do our wash together."

"All right," said Racqel, ducking her head.

Rebecca stood in front of her, trying to think of something else to say. At last she left.

Racqel looked at her medicines, not seeing them. Although Rebecca had apologized, Racqel knew that now there was a rift between them, and between Racqel and all the Jewish women. She had never felt so alone.

Setting the plants aside to dry, Racqel went into the kitchen to put the kettle of soup high over the fire so it wouldn't cook too fast. Guilt about her empty marriage to Benjamin and her yearning for the Dutchman choked her.

Was he playing a game with her? Did he know where Benjamin was? Dizzy with uncertainty, she poured water in a washbowl, washed her face, and patted her bruised skin dry.

Tonneman had to tell her how he'd come by the silver disk. And she would tell him about the English document. The decision made, she emptied her wash water on the charred grass behind the new house, stirred the soup, and hurried to the Dutchman's house.

He was in the shed grooming his horse. Faintly, she cleared her throat.

When he looked up, his blue eyes stared at her with such exposed longing that she had to turn away. She was shaken and didn't know what to do. He recovered first. "Good day, Vrouw Mendoza." Her eyes met his again, but the sweet longing was gone; he had retreated into his official capacity as Schout. Like Captain Pos's, his face was abundant with cuts and bruises.

"Heer Tonneman . . ." She was unsure how to proceed. He did not come to her aid, but continued brushing and stroking the long flank of his horse.

She closed her eyes. "I must confess something to you," she said haltingly.

"Yes?"

"The document, the one you took from Abner's . . ."

"Good girl."

Surprised, she opened her eyes and found he was talking to the horse.

"I read it, Heer Tonneman."

He stopped grooming his horse. "I should have known you'd be able to read English," he said.

"You can't?"

"No. I don't even have the paper anymore. It was stolen."

"Oh. Who . . . ?"

"You should have told me you read it. That would have saved
me a lot of trouble."

"I was afraid."

"What did it say?"

"It's an agreement between the bearer of the document and Governor Winthrop of Connecticut to benefit the bearer if he helps the
English conquer New Amsterdam."

De Sille. That's who the bearer of the document had to be.
Whenever he turned around, there were De Sille and Winthrop staring him in the face.

Abner Simon had claimed that the document was his. But what if
it was really De Sille's? If that were so, and Abner had stolen it from
De Sille, then De Sille might kill to get it back. But who was Spectacles? Was he Winthrop's man?

Tonneman got an apple from a basket hanging on a wall and fed
it to Venus.

Racqel waited impatiently for him to speak. He didn't and this
enraged her. "I thought it best to tell you." She kicked the hay on the
dirt floor of the barn.

"And you were correct," he answered, watching her furious face
with bafflement. Why was she so angry?

"Then farewell."

He nodded thoughtfully and rubbed Venus's soft nose. De Sille
and Winthrop. Where were they now and what were they doing? And
what part did the Mendoza family play in all this? And why had
Racqel Mendoza told him about the document? Was she honest? Or
was it a trick?

Although she'd said farewell, Racqel seemed to be waiting for
him to say something. He walked to where she stood. Her cheek was
bruised red and blue, and the tender skin around her right eye was
swollen. He lifted his hand and gently touched her face.

She shuddered.

He felt it through his fingertips, saw his hand tremble. He
wanted to tell her that no one would ever harm her again, that he
would kill the man who had hurt her.

"Racqel." His voice was so low at first, he didn't realize he'd
spoken aloud.

"Dear God," she said, and took a step backward. The spell was
broken. "Where did you get the piece of silver that was in your coat?"

"I found it under my willow tree. Why do you ask?"

"It's part of the belt my husband was wearing the last time I saw
him."

His blue eyes narrowed. "Describe it, please."

"It was made up of many silver links, each exactly like the one you found, held together by smaller silver loops."

Tonneman was torn by his feelings; he cared for this woman, but at the same time he suspected that she and her family might be part of an English plot. "Do you want to tell me anything further about this document?"

"I know only what I've told you. Do you think something terrible happened to Benjamin near the willow tree?"

"There or nearby." Tonneman was still holding the grooming brush. He put it down on the stall rail and took hold of her wrists. "What do you know of Abner's death?" His voice was harsh to his own ears.

"As much as you. Less, probably."

"And the man in your shed?"

"Nothing." She didn't pull away.

He looked down at his big hands clamped around her slim wrists. "I'm sorry." He released her. "He was an English spy, wasn't he?"

"I don't know."

He stepped closer. She could smell his breath. And it was sweet, with no liquor on it.

"Wasn't he?" Tonneman asked, his voice louder than before.

He was so close; all she could see was his face. His angry blue eyes fascinated and frightened her. "I don't . . ."

"And your husband and he were working together," he said sternly.

"I . . ." Her voice faltered. She didn't know what to say. She didn't want to lie to this man, but how could she betray the Mendoza family? This had to be the shame Abraham was referring to, what David called Benjamin's intrigue with the English. If she told Tonneman what she knew, that would only reinforce what he thought: that Benjamin was a traitor.

"Speak, woman. Tell me the truth, for Christ's sake." Tonneman was confused. He wanted to seize her and shake the truth out of her. At the same time he knew if he touched her again, he wouldn't shake her; he would press her to him, kiss the poor bruised eye. Hold her. Possess her forever. That's what he yearned to do with all his heart. Instead he found himself shouting. "I'm right, aren't I? Benjamin and the man in the shed were in this together. Who else is involved?"

"No." She stood her ground. "I don't know."

"It's obvious that Abner and perhaps all of you Jews have made a separate peace with the English. That was why we were released by the English officer Brick-Hill." He locked his hands behind his back to keep from touching her again.

"That's not true! If you suspected one Christian, would you blame all Christians? You think one Jew is guilty, then of course all Jews are guilty." Racqel backed away from him, her face tight with anger. "You're as bad as Pieter Stuyvesant. Worse. At least he owns to what he is."

They glared at each other.

Then she spun around and ran from him, and he, the helpless fool, with his feet locked into the earth, watched her go.

53

MONDAY, 1 SEPTEMBER. *Morning.*
Tonneman had spent a restless night. He'd gotten up several times, passed water, and looked outside. Except for the Rattle Watch calling the hours, it had been unusually quiet. But he wasn't thinking about the English or the killings. All he could think about was Racqel and the things he had said to her. He wanted to take the words back.

So engrossed was he by Racqel that he ate Vrouw Root's samp without even thinking about it, washing the porridge down with water. Then he sat on his back stoop with his first pipe of the day, contemplating the piece of silver he'd found in Sweet Lips's pleasure tent the day before.

This piece of silver wasn't like the other. This wasn't part of Benjamin Mendoza's silver belt. There was a lion on it, but not the Lion of Judah. This lion, in the upper right-hand quadrant, was much smaller, and it was an English lion that he'd often seen before. On the obverse side was the profile of King Charles II. This time the piece of silver was an English shilling.

He was still sitting there smoking, turning the coin over and over in his hand, when Pos peered around the back of the house. "There you are."

"Well, deputy?" Tonneman dropped the shilling into his jacket pocket.

"If those Jews don't take all."

"Meaning?"

"I was at the end of the Rattle Watch. There they were all at Asser Levy's house having a meeting. Old Abraham Mendoza, he comes out to me and begs me to inform the authorities . . . that would be you, I think."

"I think."

"He begs me to inform the authorities that the men of the Hebrew nation are armed and ready to fight for New Amsterdam, if they are asked. Impressive, don't you think?"

"Yes, I do."

"Something must have gotten them worked up."

"You may be right."

"I wonder what it was?"

Tonneman wondered the same thing. Could it have been his talk with Racqel?

"Those Jews seem to be as loyal, if not more than, any other citizen. I wouldn't mind standing next to one of them in a fight, I'll tell you that. Better than some of the fainthearted Christians I've seen around here."

"Better not let the Boss hear you, or you'll be damned for eternity."

Pos laughed and shook his head. "Christ, I'm damned anyway. Do you need me for anything?"

"No."

"Then I'll be down in the jail getting some sleep."

Tonneman nodded but he wasn't listening. He was thinking about what Racquel had told him the document said. So many little facts and no firm answers. And ever-changing, paradoxical conclusions. Today's conclusion challenged yesterday's conclusion, that the bearer mentioned in the document was De Sille.

Perhaps it was Abner and Nick together. Or the two of them and Benjamin Mendoza. Then, of course, there was the man in the shed.

Abner was dead, Benjamin missing, and except for his back he hadn't seen Nick lately. Or Joost, for that matter. What if it was Abner and Keyser? Or Abner and Joost? The last notion gnawed at him. He could confront Keyser. And Joost, if Joost ever opened the Pear Tree again. But until he knew more, he wasn't ready to do any confronting yet.

He had to talk to Tall Matthew again. "And this time that African must talk to me," he muttered, knocking his pipe against his boot to get the dot of ash out. The clay pipe broke. "Shit," he said, throwing the shards into the water.

The four English ships remained ominously in the Narrows. He accepted them as part of the horizon now. The ships were something he couldn't do anything about. Perhaps, if he put his mind to it, he could do something about finding a killer.

The Broad Way was busy with townspeople and sailors and patrolling soldiers; militiamen studded each crossing. All the conversation he heard along the thoroughfare was cut from the same discontented cloth. Strongest were the complaints about the Director-General's desire for blood. The soldiers were dispirited because the citizens of New Amsterdam had no desire to fight the English. So the soldiers were against the citizens and the citizens were against the soldiers.

Vrouw Martha van Ruyven, a small woman with dainty feet and a cheerful smile and a soft sweet voice, who was usually so demure, was on the Broad Way talking angrily about the soldiers to all who would listen: "The lousy dogs want to fight because they have nothing to lose, whereas we have our property here, which we should have to give up."

Even worse were some of the utterances made by the soldiers who seemed ready to turn against the New Amsterdamers. A gnarled old soldier stood, watching the clusters of people. "Now," he muttered, "we hope to pepper those devilish traders who have so long assaulted us; we know where booty is to be found, and where the young women live who wear gold chains."

Tonneman seized the soldier by his collar. "You talk too much, old man."

The old man struggled, his hand moved to the knife on his belt. Tonneman tightened his grip and the soldier went still, waiting to see what Tonneman was going to do next. He didn't say a word.

"Hey," said a plump young ninny, who was part of the old soldier's group.

"Stay out of this," Tonneman ordered, "or I'll finish you before the English even have a chance to start."

The young soldier wiped his sweaty face and backed away.

Tonneman was tempted to arrest the old bastard then and there, but there were so many like him. He couldn't arrest them all. One thing was certain, he had to bring this to Stuyvesant's attention and determine what to do about it. Disgusted, Tonneman released the old soldier and walked on. He could feel the young soldier's eyes on his back.

He found Tall Matthew where he'd seen him last, sitting on a pier on the North River. The African was working on a long branch with his knife, cutting one end into a sharp point. "That's quite a spear. Getting ready for the English?"

Tall Matthew did not respond.

"You've got to help me, Tall Matthew. You're the only one who can. Why would somebody want to kill Abner?"

Silence, except for the sound of knife cutting wood.

"Was he involved in anything that would make someone want to kill him?"

Again silence.

"Did he have something that someone else might want? Enough to kill him for? Like a piece of paper?"

The black man stopped carving. "Abner was my friend. Do you know what it means for an African to say that about a white man? Whatever he asked of me, I did. If he told me to get you in the middle of the night, I went and got you. If he told me to take a purse of gold coins to a man waiting for me at Coenties Slip, I did it without asking why."

"Tell me more about this man."

"I would know him by his red hat with a blue feather and his spectacles."

"Did the man with the spectacles give you anything in return?"

"Something in an elkskin pouch."

"A document?"

"I didn't look inside." He ran his callused hand lovingly over the smooth branch, almost as if he was stroking the limb of a naked woman.

"Where did Spectacles get the pouch?"

"I don't know."

"Would you have killed, if Abner had asked you to?"

Tall Matthew looked directly at Tonneman. His black eyes showed no emotion. "I would have, but he never did."

"Is there anything else you can tell me?"

The African didn't respond. He hefted the spear and peered out over the water as if seeking a target.

"And afterward?" he had asked the serpent.

"Afterward," the serpent had answered, "I will take you home."

54

TUESDAY, 2 SEPTEMBER. *Morning.*
People were crowding into the Fort, demanding to see the Director-General. They called to Tonneman repeatedly as he strode to the door of Stuyvesant's office where a five-man detail stood guard.

"Six days," people shouted. "Six piss-potting days the English sit out there at our throats. Tell him we want answers, Tonneman." A sudden breeze enlivened the drooping Netherlands flag in its bracket just outside the door, and it flapped robustly.

One of the guards was Dirk Ter Meer. "Good morning, youngster," Tonneman said. "Get your horse back all right?"

"Yes, Schout."

"How's he doing?"

"Wheezing along, sir."

Tonneman chuckled and went into the building.

"There you are," cried Stuyvesant, catching sight of him. He stamped about the chamber. "What have I done to deserve such torment? The devil take Winthrop and all the English to the fiery pit."

"The people are in no mood to fight the English," Tonneman told him. "But they're ready to fight you. They're out there. Can't you hear them?"

Stuyvesant stopped and stood at the window. Shouts and catcalls came from outside. "They'll be all right. When the time comes, the people will acquit themselves well."

"They're worried about giving up all they've worked for so long."

Stuyvesant made a noise in his throat but said nothing.

"They fear a bloodbath," said Tonneman.

"They're a chickenhearted lot," P.S. said, completely reversing his previous sentiment. He thumped back and forth across the chamber. "Not a man among them. At least the soldiers are loyal."

"I don't know about that. I've been listening to them. They sound ready to attack us all and loot the city."

"Let them try. As long as I have blood in my veins and power in my right arm and can stand on wood and flesh . . ."

Tonneman was in no mood for one of the Director-General's sermons. Surprisingly, Stuyvesant stopped talking. "It's not all bad news. The Jews are ready and willing to fight."

"Bah. I'd rather go to my death alone than live with them as allies. Judases, every one. They are Jews, and they are Portuguese, and all Portuguese, like all Spaniards, are the Antichrist. So they are twice despised."

Tonneman contained his smile; he'd gotten his sermon after all.

The noise of the discontented populace grew louder.

"We will put a stop to this treasonous behavior at once." Stuyvesant stormed outside. Tonneman followed. The five soldiers came to attention, then lined up, three and two, on either side of the Director-General.

"Is Keyser's tannery already in English hands?" a voice demanded from the crowd.

"Good if it is," another voice answered the first. "Then we'll be able to smell them coming."

A soldier dropped an empty water barrel; it made a large booming noise like a cannon and everyone jumped; a woman screamed, babies began crying. "Is that enemy artillery?" an elderly man asked anxiously.

"Hallo," someone yelled, "I think I smell them now."

"No," another replied, "that was just the great Muscovy Duke farting."

"I heard that," Stuyvesant bellowed.

"Tell us what's happening."

"Is it true they captured a boat on the bay with some of our African slaves?"

"What about the two Dutchmen who were taken prisoner on their way from Breukelen?"

"I heard it was *four* Dutchmen."

"I heard ten."

"We can't live like this."

The crowd pushed forward. "We need to know what's going on."

The soldiers pushed them back.

"All right!" Stuyvesant shouted. "Avercamp!" The clerk appeared, charily measuring the tone of the crowd. "What I am about to say is for the English villain out there."

"Yes, sir."

"I refuse to surrender. Did you get that?"

"Yes, sir."

"In English?"

"Yes, sir."

"Send it."

"Yes, sir."

"I'll take it," said Tonneman.

P.S. looked at him, shrugged. "All right."

"I'll need someone to row. Dirk, would you like a closer look at the English?"

The young soldier's face lit up. "Yes, Schout."

"You're it, then."

A short time later Tonneman and Ter Meer were in a boat on the bay, rowing out to the *Guinea*. The bright sun reflected shiny ridges on the water as it lapped softly at the English ship. The frigate with its milky-white sails was a peaceful sight, denying the force and power of the vessel's thirty-six guns and the men on board ready to use that power and more.

"Hoy, you in the boat," an English sailor called. "State your business."

"I have a message from Director-General Pieter Stuyvesant for Colonel Richard Nicolls," Tonneman answered in English. He heard movement and voices aboard the ship.

As the same sailor, a ratlike runt, descended the rope ladder that hung down the side of the vessel, a black-mustached man in bright yellow appeared on deck. His wide fleshy nose protruded from a narrow face. He peered over the side and his shoulder-length curly black wig tipped forward. Straightening the wig, he looked Tonneman over thoroughly, as if trying to memorize his face.

Without a word, the sailor leaned from the ladder and held out his hand. Tonneman gave him Stuyvesant's reply and the sailor scrambled back up with it. The yellow-clad figure read the brief letter in seconds. "You, Dutchman," he called.

"Yes," Tonneman answered.

"I am Colonel Richard Nicolls, representing his Sovereign Majesty, King Charles II of England, Defender of the Faith. Tell the man with the wooden leg he has forty-eight hours."

55

WEDNESDAY, 3 SEPTEMBER. *Morning.*
Racqel couldn't breathe. Smoke swirled around her.

Thrashing, she cried out and Caleb licked her hand anxiously. She woke with such a start that the sewing basket slipped from her lap and the darning ball fell with a clatter. Bathsheba pounced on the wooden ball in triumph. Racqel rose to splash water on her face.

The floors had been swept, two loaves of Indian-meal bread had been baked. The wash she had done earlier in the brook on Maiden Lane now hung over her new fence and would dry in no time.

In spite of her promise, Rebecca had not come on Monday or Tuesday. Nor would she come today. Racqel was disappointed but not surprised. She was very much alone now. Very well. She would make her own way.

The link of silver from Benjamin's belt had troubled her sleep. Tonneman said he'd found it under his willow tree. Perhaps if she looked there, she would find some indication of what had happened to Benjamin. A breath of dread, like a ghostly figure, trembled through her body. What if Benjamin were dead and buried under Tonneman's willow tree?

Quickly she hurried outside to escape her thoughts. The bright sun did not warm her. Summer was over. She went back in and got a shawl. Bathsheba, still worrying the darning ball, ignored her, but Caleb set up such a racket she let him out to play in the yard.

She could see crowds of people on Twiller's Road. All seemed to be surging toward the Fort. Perhaps there was some news about the English. In spite of her previous mood she was swept up in the excitement, and her feet took her to Twiller's Road. She was torn between going along with the crowd or going to the willow tree.

A familiar voice hailed her. "Good morning, Vrouw Mendoza." It was Lodowyck Pos.

"Good morning, Captain. What's the ado this time?"

"It's about the survey."

"What survey?"

"Our Burgomasters and Schepens spoke to the ten bakers in town. There are only about seven hundred and fifty bushels of grain left in New Amsterdam. Some bakers have nothing left. Without bread or, worse, without beer, we will be on our knees quick as a dying cow."

Racqel had to smile. "There are worse things in the world, Captain Pos, than to be without beer."

"Ah, gracious vrouw, you mock me. It's like listening to Tonneman all over again." Pos grinned at her and watched her dark skin flush to a darker hue.

This would never do. The merest mention of the Schout's name had unsettled her. "Why is everyone going to the Fort?"

"The Burgomasters and Schepens have marched from City Hall to the Fort to have it out with Heer Stuyvesant. I am on my way there myself."

"How soon do you think the invasion will come?"

"Soon. Right now what's happening at the Fort should be of more interest. Come, allow me to escort you. We'll hear the latest news when we get there."

She hesitated, but only for an instant. "Thank you."

When they arrived at the Fort, a mass of people was already crowding around the Director-General's office. The door opened and people surged in. As many as could fit, and then some. The five soldiers stationed at the door watched, making no attempt to intervene.

Racqel saw Oloff van Cortlandt and the new young minister, Samuel Megapolensis, just inside the office, and heard their voices raised in anger, but she couldn't make out what they were saying. The door slammed shut.

The grumbling sound of the discontented group outside was like thunder before a fierce storm. Each comment led to another, louder and more outraged than the last.

"We know what Nicolls promised."

"What did Winthrop write?"

"Yes, what did Winthrop say?"

"Let us see Winthrop's letter."

"We demand to see Winthrop's letter."

"Winthrop's letter. Winthrop's letter."

Then, as one, the crowd began to repeat the phrase over and over. "Winthrop's letter. Winthrop's letter. Winthrop's letter." Those like Racqel and Pos, who didn't raise their voices, were glared at by those who did.

A resounding roar issued from Stuyvesant's quarters. The door crashed open, driving back the people who had been close on it. Out stormed an angry Director-General, a parchment document clutched in his hand. He was followed by the equally angry Burgomasters and Schepens, his confused Council, and a group of others who had somehow gained entry to his office.

"You want the letter?" Stuyvesant shouted. "Here." He then tore the document to bits and pieces, strew the fragments at the crowd, and stormed back into his office.

The members of the Council stood nonplussed, not knowing what to do. The Burgomasters and Schepens strode out of the Fort toward City Hall, united in a fierce rage. The furious crowd trailed after them.

What now? Racqel wondered.

She heard someone in the crowd ask almost the same question. "What are we going to do now?"

"We demand action!" another voice yelled, and the throng caught up the impatient words.

As the Fort emptied of New Amsterdamers and their griping sounds diminished, only the soldiers and Racqel and Pos remained in front of the Director-General's quarters. Avercamp came out just as a breeze stirred; a small whirlwind of dust and paper followed. When the little clerk saw the first scrap of paper fly up into the air, he quickly seized it, gathered up as many of the other pieces as he could find, and placed them inside his black hat.

"Avercamp!"

"Yes, sir," the clerk said, clamping his hat to his head and racing back inside.

Bursts of bitter chatter carried back by the wind could be heard from the indignant citizens.

"Come," said Captain Pos to Racqel. "There's nothing more for us to see here. The show will be resumed at City Hall. Will you come with me?"

"Yes," said Racqel eagerly. As they chased after the throng her body tingled with excitement. In her heart Racqel knew her future life would be decided by the events she had witnessed and what was yet to come in the next few days. Frightened as she was of what might happen in New Amsterdam with the English at their throats, there was also a newfound joy that she couldn't explain. "Yes. Oh, yes."

The crowd was gathered in front of City Hall, inflamed and expectant. She saw Tonneman off to one side and nodded curtly to him. He nodded just as curtly to her and joined them.

"Did you hear?" Pos asked. "The Boss tore up the letter from Winthrop."

"I heard. Many times. I hear something else. Listen."

After a moment Pos asked, "What?"

"Listen."

"I hear nothing but the people complaining."

"That's right. No sounds of shovels or picks. The work on the walls has ceased."

Racqel no longer felt part of the event. They had closed her out, as men always did. As the Mendozas did.

Tonneman's presence had brought back all her uncertainty.

She drifted away from the others. As she walked along the Strand the crowd lessened. The wind rustled in the trees, raining leaves, which spun and floated to the ground. So peaceful. And so deceptive. For who knew what tomorrow would bring? War? Bloodshed? Would she be killed? Would Tonneman?

She turned on the waterfront and did what she had decided to do earlier. At Tonneman's willow tree she searched the ground, looking for more evidence of her husband. Again the possibility of Benjamin being buried here crossed her mind.

The thought tortured her; she sat under the tree, within the willow curtain, in the worn spot where Tonneman always sat.

She was tired. It was cool and quiet here, protected by the tree. She closed her eyes. Ever since Benjamin had left her, her life had been disordered. Even before he left, there had not been much happiness, only duty. Duty made her tired. David Mendoza made her tired. The English made her tired. Dear God in heaven, were it not for the Dutchman, she would be weary of life.

She lay back against the smooth trunk of the willow tree and wept.

56

THURSDAY, 4 SEPTEMBER. *Morning.*

"Yesterday I saw Pieter Stuyvesant tear up a letter from Governor Winthrop of Connecticut," Racqel said. She ladled porridge into orange-and-blue majolica bowls for Abraham and David. "No one knows what the letter said but—"

"Obvious," said David, brushing her comments aside. "A peace proposal. Stuyvesant's a fool."

"Our Director-General is worse than a fool," said her father-in-law. "The man is a hothead. He would have us fight the English, and if he does, Nicolls will show no mercy. Come, David, we have work to do."

They left her to go to the warehouse. "And what do I have to do?" she asked Caleb and Bathsheba. She wondered if Abraham and David were hiding the stores and the pelts. And where?

She scattered a large pinch of the green tea leaves on the bottom of the china pot, then doused the leaves with hot water, letting the brew steep briefly, continuing all the while her conversation with the dog and the cat. "And what of me? What of the other women? And the children?" Winter was coming. What would happen to all of them if the English destroyed their stores?

Work had finally ceased on the house. Not that it was completed; there were no workers to do it. They had all gone their merry way, supposedly to perform invasion duty.

The day before, on her way home from the willow tree, she had seen David and Goliath driving a cart of barrels to the North River. Invasion duty? Or were they still working for the Mendozas, emptying the warehouse on Staple Street and putting everything on a ship to return to Amsterdam?

And even if there were men able to work on the house, why build it if the English were going to blow it away with one cannon blast?

Racqel opened her front door. Another wondrously fair morning. At once Caleb started barking. Then she heard it, too, a drone like a great swarm of bees. All those in Jews Alley who weren't already a part of it came out on their stoops to see. Racqel took her shawl and hurried toward the sound, leaving her four-footers to fend for themselves. Had the war begun?

Once again, she joined the crowd pushing along Twiller's Road toward the Fort. Everyone was there, Jews and Christians, even the Africans. They were saying the same thing over and over. "What was in Winthrop's letter?"

Children chased each other in and around adults as if it were a festival. The much-trampled road had become hard and dusty under so much activity.

As she stepped inside the Fort, Racqel saw Tonneman and Pos just ahead of her and to her right, along with Antje Ten Eyck, her husband, and their boy. She hesitated for a moment, then made her way to the Ten Eyck family.

Antje waved and beckoned to Racqel. "Good day, Vrouw Mendoza, it's a lovely day for an invasion, is it not?"

Racqel smiled, unsure. Was that a jest? With Antje Ten Eyck one never knew. "Is it the invasion?"

Conraet Ten Eyck shook his head. To his wife he said, "Ah, woman, you have no respect for danger."

She laughed, holding the sides of her huge belly. "Oh my, oh my," she gasped. She pointed first to Ten Eyck then to her belly. "He did this."

Racqel, smiling, turned crimson. She glanced at Tonneman. He seemed very busy watching Stuyvesant's office door.

The bee buzz of the crowd, which had simmered down, rose again. All were demanding to know the contents of the Connecticut governor's letter.

At that moment Stuyvesant stepped out of his office into the sunlight.

"What was in Winthrop's letter? What was in Winthrop's letter?" came louder and faster. This was overridden by jeers and taunts and fleering laughter.

"Vrouw Mendoza, you are here just in time," Ten Eyck said pleasantly over the commotion. "The Director-General has deigned to come out of his sanctum sanctorum to speak to the people. He has ignored our demand to surrender to the English and has counterdemanded that work begin on the walls again. But no one is listening to him."

"We want answers first!" Pos shouted. "The forty-eight hours Nicolls gave us are up." He turned to Racqel. "A petition has been prepared demanding that Stuyvesant surrender to the English."

The jeers and taunts stopped; now there was fear and anguish in what the people said.

"We are doomed." one citizen called out.

"What was in Winthrop's letter?"

"Surrender."

"We cannot hold out against the English."

"Winthrop's letter."

"Read our petition."

"We must surrender to save our lives."

"And our property."

"What was in Winthrop's letter?"

"We have almost no black powder. In a week we will have no bread."

"Or beer."

"It will be the pits of hell with nothing to put out the flames but our own piss."

"And without beer to drink we will have precious little of that!"

Laughter rippled through the crowd. Only Stuyvesant didn't seem to think that was amusing. He grew more furious by the minute. Pos called, "Hear! Hear! Men after my own heart."

"Belly, you mean," said Tonneman, speaking for the first time since Racqel had arrived.

The crowd would not let up. Someone started the chant again. "Winthrop's letter. Winthrop's letter. Winthrop's letter."

Another group had a chant of their own. "Surrender. Surrender. Surrender."

Stuyvesant called for silence. The chants continued. He reached out and touched the red, white, and blue flag mounted in the bracket outside his door. "Surrender what?" he bellowed. "This? Our nation? Our honor?"

"Spare us the patriotic speech, oh great silver-legged Muscovy Duke," someone cried mockingly. "Just give us Winthrop's letter."

"Avercamp," Stuyvesant yelled, his face full of wrath. The clerk stepped out of the office. "The letter."

Avercamp licked his lips nervously. From inside his hat he produced a section of cloth upon which the Winthrop letter had been reassembled and glued. Blinking, he held it before him, and looked to Stuyvesant for instructions.

"Read it and be done with it."

The crowd became quiet.

" 'To his Excellency . . .' "

"Get to it, Avercamp," Stuyvesant said sullenly. "We don't need all of that blackguard's fancy talk. Just the meat."

"Yes, sir. Uh . . . uh . . . uh . . ."

"Now. Today."

"Yes, sir. He suggests that we be quick in accepting King Charles's gracious offer. That we immediately, as new subjects, declare our loyalty and avoid spilling of blood."

"Amen," said Antje Ten Eyck, reaching for her son's hand.

"Amen," said Racqel Mendoza.

The two women looked at each other with sad understanding.

57

THURSDAY, 4 SEPTEMBER. *Mid Morning.*

Pieter Stuyvesant glowered at the people and retreated to his office. Avercamp smiled woefully and hurried after his master.

"Talk to him, Tonneman," a woman's voice called out. "You're an intelligent man, a decent man. You have some influence with the old fart."

Tonneman looked out over the assembly to see who had spoken. It was Widow Wilbruch, the midwife, who ran the soldiers' hospital outside the Fort.

Next to her was Korbonski. "Good idea, Heer Schout." The whoremaster tipped his hat, grinning insolently.

"Go on," Pos said, elbowing Tonneman. "Give it a try."

Tonneman nodded to Widow Wilbruch and went inside; the shouting and chanting began anew. Tonneman couldn't help but wonder whose idea it was for the widow to say that to him. Hers or Korbonski's? That would mean Korbonski wanted to surrender to the English, but then again, so did anybody else with any sense.

Avercamp was standing in front of Stuyvesant's desk while the Director-General filled his pipe with rosemary tobacco. Stuyvesant's hand shook with anger as he put flint to steel and attempted to light his pipe. Colonel van de Steen reached over and did it for him, burning his own hand in the process.

De Sille and van Dincklagen were in a corner talking quietly, covertly. Dinck was whispering something into Nick's ear. Now what was that all about? A fine pair, those two. What sort of game was Nick playing? Or Dinck for that matter?

Both men looked up and saw Tonneman watching.

Dinck grinned affably; the scratches on his face had become scabious. "Good day to you, Tonneman."

"Ah, Heer Schout has arrived," De Sille said. "Just the man for the occasion."

Tonneman's blood boiled. What a pleasure it would finally be to put his fist in Nick's face. But that would have to wait.

The chamber had filled with the scent of rosemary. "What have you decided to do?" asked van de Steen, blowing on his burnt fingers.

"Do? Do? I'm going to fight. What other course is there for a man of honor?"

The scar on the colonel's cheek was pale against his sun-browned skin. "We can't win."

"You too?" Stuyvesant declared.

The shouting from outside grew louder.

"Outside, Avercamp. Tell that ruck they're giving me a headache."

"You'll have to talk to them," counseled the colonel as the clerk left the office.

"I just did," said Stuyvesant. "Why don't you talk to them, De Sille?"

Nick smiled. "I think it would be best if you did. Barring that, Tonneman would be better."

"Very well, Tonneman, then. Somebody."

"What would I say?" asked Tonneman.

The door to the office burst open. Stuyvesant leaped to his feet; Colonel van de Steen's hand went to his sword.

"What's the meaning—" Stuyvesant started.

"A thousand pardons, Director-General," an anxious soldier said as he was pushed into the chamber by a group of Africans. Three more soldiers pressed in behind them.

"What is this?" Stuyvesant demanded.

A small but powerfully built African, his black Dutch hat in his hand, stepped forward. "I am called Claes, Heer—"

"What is it?"

"With all respect, Boss, we ask for our freedom."

The other seven black men waited tentatively, their hats also in their hands.

The speaker went on. "If there is war and we fight, we want to fight as free men. If there is no war and the English—"

"Enough!" Stuyvesant snapped. "Done. The . . . eight of you are free men as of this day. Avercamp, make a note. Now leave me be, you free citizens of New Amsterdam."

The spokesman bowed deeply. "Our gratitude and our loyalty are yours, sir. And if need be, our lives. Thank you."

"Thank you, thank you," the seven others echoed. They hastened from the chamber, followed by the soldiers.

The anxious soldier said, "I hope the Director-General—"

"Out!"

At that moment a shrill furor rose from outside, worse than before, a noise filled with fear and panic.

"What now?" Stuyvesant clenched his fists and raised his eyes to the heavens.

Avercamp pushed through the departing Africans and the soldiers into the room. He was followed by the ministers, father and son Megapolensis.

"Tell that rabble to be still. I'll look at their preposterous petition in a moment."

"Sir, it's not the petition. The four English ships have begun to move into the upper bay."

P.S. thumped and thudded out the door. The rest hurried after him, all eyes focused on the bay. Tonneman had expected something like this. Still, he was stunned by the sight.

Four heavily armed frigates were poised, ready to strike, their chalky sails and red, white, and blue Union Jacks vivid and menacing in the wind. Nicolls had anchored the thirty-six-gunned *Guinea* and the eighteen-gunned *Martin* at Nutten Island, thereby containing Manhattan and Breukelen equally. He'd sent the *Elias* with her thirty guns and the ten-gunned *William and Nicholas* to position themselves above New Amsterdam.

An infuriated Pieter Stuyvesant seized the flag of the Netherlands from its mount at the entrance to his office and clumped to the nearest of the cannons facing the bay. Tonneman, Colonel van de Steen, Dinck and Nick, and Johannes and Samuel Megapolensis followed close behind him.

Two full-rigged frigates sailed by, training their guns at the shore with all the people of New Amsterdam watching, terrified. The people fell silent, except for those few who began to pray. A baby cried. Overhead the sun was approaching its midway point in the sky.

Stuyvesant shook his flag at the frigates. "This is the first time in seventeen years that any ship has dared to come into my harbor without my permission."

A gunner, standing ready at the cannon, held a lighted fuse. The Director-General raised the flag high over his head. He was the standard bearer. Then a sound came out of him, from the depths of his soul, like that of a wounded animal. It started low and guttural and grew into a piercing scream. "All I have to do is give the order. The gun will fire and the battle will begin. There would be no turning back." He waved the flag vigorously; it flapped and fluttered almost drowning out his words. "Then this gutless rabble would have to fight."

Tonneman, Lubbertus van Dincklagen, and the two predicants

exchanged quick looks and came swiftly to Stuyvesant's side. Pos separated himself from the crowd and ran toward them.

"No!" Dinck shouted. "Don't you remember the destruction of battle? The awful sight and stench of blood. We're not soldiers. We're families. Women and children. For the love of God, think of the humanity that will be destroyed, killed, or worse, mangled."

Stuyvesant glared at van Dincklagen with disdain. "Mangled? You fat fool, how in God's name do you think I lost this?" he said, pointing his wooden leg at him. "Twenty years ago, and I remember it as if it were yesterday." He edged closer to the soldier with the lighted fuse. The soldier, a boy really, looked at him, terror mixing with excitement on his child's face. "Before the fight they drenched the decks with water in case of fire. After that the sand so you don't slip in the blood." He was now almost within arm's length of the gunner with the fuse.

Pos and Dinck positioned themselves between Stuyvesant and the gunner. Stuyvesant smiled as if he hadn't noticed and circled around the other way. Tonneman watched him carefully.

"Cannon shot is an extraordinary thing," said Stuyvesant. "One piece of metal. Many pieces of metal. They get larger and larger as they approach, and they always look as if they're coming straight at you, only you." He stared out into the bay at the four juggernauts of destruction; their snapping banners seemed to taunt him. "Don't preach to me about the horrors of war, van Dincklagen, you puffed-up simpleton." He made a rush toward the gunner and the lighted fuse.

But Tonneman nimbly blocked his way. "Let's go, Boss," Tonneman said firmly. "You don't want to do that."

"Heer Stuyvesant, if you love the Lord Jesus, desist," said Johannes Megapolensis. With great kindness, the minister and his son grasped Stuyvesant's arms and led him away from the cannons. Tonneman and Dinck followed.

The peril in the bay had won this round.

"No!" the Director-General raged. "No, I will not allow this!" His flag dragged in the dust. Colonel van de Steen came forward to take the banner, but Stuyvesant jerked it away.

"Please, sir," said Dinck. "Forbear. Can't you see all those mighty guns trained on us? If this terrible fight is allowed to begin, they will give a full broadside on this open place, then take it by assault and make a scene of pillage and bloodshed."

"You mealymouth, pettifogging chickenhearts," Stuyvesant snarled.

As he spoke the four white-mantled English machines of war glided by Fort Amsterdam, past the silent people on the shore.

Stuyvesant broke free of his guardians and brandished the flagpole at them like a quarterstaff. "Shame. Shame. Shame. You've stopped me from sinking those devil ships, but there's more than one way to skin an English cat." He planted his two feet, one flesh and blood, the other wood and silver, firmly on the ground. Flag raised high again, he bellowed, "De Sille, take command of the first five squads and hold the Fort! Get these women and children out of here! Colonel, the rest of you, rally on me."

Colonel Caspar van de Steen caressed the scar on his cheek, then swiftly drew his sword, saluting the Director-General with it. "You lead, sir, and I follow."

"You can rely on me, sir," De Sille called. "I'll hold till doomsday!"

The billowing red, white, and blue colors of the Netherlands held aloft, Stuyvesant charged out of the Fort, leading his loyal troops, his peg leg thumping over the hard-packed streets, his proud beak of a nose taking the point and directing the way to where he would rally his small army for the attack. "Follow me," he cried. "As sure as Christ will come again we will win. Victory and salvation!"

"The old fool," Tonneman muttered, moving to stop Stuyvesant.

Dinck put a hand on his arm. "Let him be. The situation is hopeless, but let him be."

Willem Avercamp, steadfast throughout, went hurrying after the defenders of New Amsterdam, such as they were.

Widow Wilbruch separated herself from the crowd, and she, too, followed, carrying a large canvas pack on her wide back, waddling staunchly toward town. With her, surprisingly, was Luis da Silva, the Jewish physician.

And slowly, reluctantly, the two ministers followed Stuyvesant's pathetic little army, too.

The citizens, angry and confused, wandered about rudderless. Some trailed after Stuyvesant with little heart; others remained to grumble around the Fort.

Pos shrugged at Tonneman and smiled dolefully.

Tonneman beckoned Pos to him and said to Dinck, "Do we stay or follow the old fool?"

The fat lawyer mopped his brow. "Either way, the English will come, and you know me. With my girth it's my nature always to stay when I have the choice."

"Yes, I do know you. That's the trouble. You're an old friend,

Dinck, but I must do my duty. Tell me the truth, how did you come by those scratches on your face?"

"I told you. I fell in a hole."

"You were in Breukelen last Wednesday, weren't you?"

"I haven't been to Breukelen in over a year. What's ailing you, Tonneman?"

"What were you and Abner Simon cooking up?"

"My friend, I think you need a drink. Whatever the Great Muscovy Duke has is contagious, and you've caught it. You're both crazy." He stalked off.

Dinck's heated response didn't completely eliminate him from Tonneman's list of suspects, but it was enough to give Tonneman doubts. Abner Simon marked his killer. "If not Dinck, who?"

"Not me," said Pos.

Tonneman returned to the matter at hand. "These civilians could get hurt here."

Pos nodded. "Those of you who want to fight," he announced loudly, "join Heer De Sille or follow the Director-General and the colonel. The rest of you go home."

In the crowd, Tonneman found the Ten Eycks. "Go home. It's the safest place."

"What are we going to do about Stuyvesant?" asked Ten Eyck.

"I need to think it through," Tonneman told him. "I don't know."

"I do," said Ten Eyck. "We have to go after the old bastard and tell him we don't want anyone to die. He'll probably be at the City Hall. I'll see you there after I get Antje and Conraet home."

"I can find my own way home," said Antje.

"I know that," Ten Eyck said firmly. "Still, I'm taking you home."

Racqel stood several paces off, feeling an outsider.

"Can't I watch the fighting?" asked young Conraet.

"Home, you bloodthirsty little beast," his mother said.

"Would you see that Vrouw Mendoza gets home?" Tonneman asked in a low voice to Ten Eyck.

The silversmith grinned at him. "Why don't *you?*"

"I'm still the Schout. I have to stay here," he answered.

"Of course you do," Antje said with sarcasm. "Husband, do what you have to do. Tonneman never does." To Racqel she said, "Come, Vrouw Mendoza. We'll go home together, all of us."

Ten Eyck looked anxiously in the direction Pieter Stuyvesant had taken, then to Tonneman. "Are you coming with me?"

Tonneman thought long and hard about Ten Eyck's question. Why fight for the West India Company and their property? No, no property was worth a man's blood, let alone his life. It was clear. To fight would be stupid. Even evil. His duty was no longer to Stuyvesant. His duty now was to New Amsterdam, and himself. "I'll be right behind you." He looked at Racqel, but he didn't move.

Ten Eyck shook his head. "Arsehole."

Only a few stragglers now remained at the Fort with De Sille's small band of soldiers. The English ships lay out there, waiting.

"Go on, Ten Eyck," Antje said, looking at her husband's worried face. "We can manage without you, can't we, Vrouw Mendoza?" A spasm struck her, but she dissembled with a small smile.

"Conraet, take care of the women," Ten Eyck said. His eyes were looking everywhere. "Antje, I'm going to City Hall. We've got to stop Stuyvesant before he goes too far." He left them, on the run.

The women walked slowly, young Conraet dancing in front of them, picking up stones and throwing them at the trees, gleeful when they brought down leaves and acorns. "Take that, you English dogs."

"Men can be such fools," Antje Ten Eyck said.

They were almost to Jews Alley. Racqel turned to offer her thanks to Vrouw Ten Eyck and saw the pain in the woman's eyes. "Are you all right? Perhaps you should come in and rest."

Antje pressed her protruding belly with her hands. "Please," she said, "take me home."

58

THURSDAY, 4 SEPTEMBER. *Mid Morning.*

Tonneman was watching the activity at the Fort, listening to De Sille barking orders, but he was thinking more about Racqel Mendoza than De Sille or the English. What had her role been in all this? Until he knew that, he couldn't act.

One way or another, this war—if they could call it that—with the English would be over soon, and he'd be out of a job. Still he knew, Schout or not, he'd have to see for himself who bore Abner Simon's mark. Nick De Sille was the most obvious suspect, the man

Abner was afraid of, the man who killed him. But it could be anyone. Dinck, with those scratches. Even Keyser, the hothead. Then there was the strange disappearance of Joost. . . .

The man in the shed was scalped and Abner was killed with a tomahawk. Cutnose could have done it, but he carried the wrong kind of tomahawk. It could have been Foxman. Or some cursed Indian he'd never even seen. Devil take it, there were too many things to think about. As soon as this foolish war was out of the way . . . Pos came to stand beside him.

"We've got to help Ten Eyck stop that madman."

Pos shoved his hat back. "I was only waiting for you to say the word."

They found Ten Eyck along with the ministers and about a hundred others including Stuyvesant's son Balthazar, van Cortlandt, and Goovert Lookermans, marching up the Strand.

"We have a remonstrance for old Silver Foot," Ten Eyck told them. "Are you with us?"

"Does a Dutchman like beer?" asked Pos. "Bring me ink and a quill," he yelled. "I'll sign. Or shall I use my own blood?"

"You and Tonneman can sign later," said Ten Eyck as the petitioners moved doggedly onward. "The important thing is to find Stuyvesant before he speeds us to kingdom come."

"Then why are we wasting time talking?" said Tonneman, pushing Pos. The two fell in with Ten Eyck and the rest.

"If I only had a beer," Pos moaned.

P.S. was in front of City Hall bellowing orders. Willem Avercamp stood loyally beside him. Most of his Council was with him, too, standing on or near the City Hall stoop.

It gave Tonneman pause to see that weasel Korbonski and Vrouw Wilbruch again. There they were in front of the Pear Tree, talking. The midwife was nodding and smiling affably. Suspicions galloped through Tonneman's mind. When did those two get so friendly? Of course, it could be that one of the whores was with child. Then again, it could be something else.

What was Korbonski doing here anyway? This was not his fight. Or was it? The Pear Tree appeared deserted. Where was Joost? Tonneman had seen neither hide nor hair of the tavern keeper in days.

Soldiers, in complete disarray, were dashing this way and that, impeded by anxious and incensed men and women and the excited and confused children of the City, all of whom were trying to get the Director-General's attention. The children were boisterous and infants were crying stridently.

The Reverend Johannes Megapolensis approached Stuyvesant, a

roll of paper in his hand. Stuyvesant eyed him with fury, pawing at the ground with his wooden leg like a wild stallion. "What have you there?" he demanded.

The minister unrolled the paper. The petition had been composed in haste and was difficult to read.

" 'Remonstrance to the Director-General and Council . . .' "

"Avercamp, my pipe. This will be long-winded, I'm sure." The clerk ran inside the hall.

Tonneman edged toward the Pear Tree, slurring his feet as he used to when he was a drunkard and assuming the vacant, sotted expression that went with it.

Megapolensis, undaunted by Stuyvesant's sarcasm, continued. " 'Right Honorable. We, your sorrowful commonalty and subjects, beg to represent, with all humility . . .' "

Korbonski's voice became clearer as Tonneman drew closer to him. ". . . the circumstances are difficult, good vrouw. It is the nature of man. . . ."

"Have no fear, Heer Korbonski. When Hilletjie Wilbruch gives her word, it is solid as a rock and as good as gold."

Reverend Megapolensis's voice was growing hoarse with emotion. " '. . . misery, sorrow, conflagration, the dishonor of women, murder of children in their cradles, and, in a word, the absolute ruin and destruction of about fifteen hundred innocent souls, only two hundred and fifty of whom are capable of bearing arms.' "

"Please, Heer Stuyvesant," cried a woman, "you're killing us."

"Get these people out of the way," Stuyvesant ordered.

"Back, everybody," Avercamp shouted as he came out of City Hall with a pipe and a lit candle. "When the fighting starts, you'll only get hurt."

"Ha, and what will we be if this lunatic has his way?" a man from the crowd shouted back.

Avercamp placed the packed pipe in Stuyvesant's mouth and offered the candle for a light. Now many of the women and some of the men were crying, too. "Submit," a weeping woman begged. "You must submit for all our sakes."

"Submit?" Stuyvesant yelled between draws on his pipe. "I had rather be carried a corpse to my grave." The odor of rosemary floated over the crowd.

Through the hubbub, Tonneman strained his ears to hear Korbonski and the widow. "You foresee no problems, then?" asked the Jew.

"None whatsoever," the widow answered.

"Good. Tomorrow . . ."

The rest was drowned out by the cry of a young woman from the crowd. "Submit. Please. We don't want to die."

"I am not afraid," said Pieter Stuyvesant.

"Well, we are," said Ten Eyck.

Korbonski was close up to the widow, his lips almost to her ear. Tonneman moved as near as he dared; he could scarcely hear what the pimp was saying. ". . . a matter of life and death . . ."

Vrouw Wilbruch waved her meaty hands as if she were shooing geese away. "I assure you that everything you wish will be done, and with great care. . . ."

Just then the predicant raised his voice to make a point. " '. . . should we prove, obstinate and headstrong, we must expect all the aforesaid miseries and misfortunes.' "

"How generous," Stuyvesant said dryly.

"More than generous," young Samuel Megapolensis replied.

"Good then," said Korbonski. "Tomorrow at dawn." Tonneman heard coins clink, but the Jew had his back to him, and he couldn't see the man's hands.

" 'On all sides,' " said the elder Megapolensis, " 'are we encompassed and hemmed in by our enemies.' "

The midwife chuckled. "I've heard you were a generous man, but I never knew how generous. Have no fear, I will give value. You shall not find my services wanting."

"That Fort couldn't keep out the hogs and the cows," someone called out. "How can it keep out the English?"

Korbonski turned. He was looking right at Tonneman. Tonneman wobbled past them toward the Pear Tree. He fell on the door and shook the knob. "Joost, where the blazes are you? I need a drink!"

"Easy, Heer Schout," Korbonski called to him. "We're going to need you in the fray." He laughed, then lowered his voice to Vrouw Wilbruch. "Is there anything else?"

Johannes Megapolensis held his hand over the crowd of people. " '. . . we humbly, and in bitterness of heart, implore Your Honors not to reject the conditions of so generous a foe, but to be pleased to meet him in the speediest, best, and most reputable manner.' "

"Joost? Joost, are you in there?" Tonneman lifted his head slightly. The widow and Korbonski had parted.

The minister's voice soared now. " 'Inasmuch as the aforesaid English colonel hath stated and threatened that he shall not wait longer than this day . . .' "

"Is there much more, Reverend?" the Director-General demanded. "I have a war to fight."

"No. No fighting," an old woman cried.

"Good morning, Tonneman."

Tonneman abandoned his inebriated pose. "Good morning, Hilletjie. You should be more careful who you talk to."

"Fiddle-faddle." The midwife laughed. "I'm talking to you, aren't I?"

"What's your business with Korbonski?"

"Submit," a woman cried.

"In God's name," called another.

"Yes, in God's name," said the minister.

"It's not really any of your business to know my business, Schout, but one of his chickens is getting a big belly. And since that would be bad for *his* business, he asked me to do *my* business."

Tonneman watched Hilletjie Wilbruch wend her way through the crowd and turn right at the Ditch. He wasn't listening as Reverend Megapolensis brought his remonstrance to a close. He was thinking he'd known the midwife for a long time, and if there was one thing about her he knew for certain, it was that she was a skilled liar.

The elder Megapolensis had raised his voice to lofty heights. " '. . . and conclude, with God's help, an honorable and reasonable capitulation, which may the Lord our God in his great mercy be pleased to grant us. Amen.' "

"Submit. Submit. Submit."

By late afternoon, when Colonel Richard Nicolls had New Amsterdam in the range of his guns, Pieter Stuyvesant, conceding at last that his cause was lost, followed the will of the people and sent a message to the colonel requesting a meeting.

The battle of New Amsterdam was over.

59

Friday, 5 September. *Noon.*

With the abrupt end of war, the disquiet in the village began to ease. Soon there would be grain once more for bread and beer. The air was celebratory; the autumn sunshine, radiant.

On the Strand Tonneman was hailed by one and all. "Good day, Heer Schout. Wonderful weather, Heer Schout." Their mood was clear: they were congratulating themselves on their bravery and perseverance.

Throughout the surge of events Tonneman had accepted the fact that shortly he would no longer be Heer Schout. Still, he had two tasks to complete before that moment: find a murderer and locate the remains of Benjamin Mendoza.

Tall Matthew had provided the link between Abner Simon and Spectacles. Tonneman had come to believe that these deaths were not random, that they were indeed connected to the English document and done by the same hand. Benjamin Mendoza had business with Abner. Another connection. What still didn't connect was Smitt.

From the water's edge he watched the merchant ships on the East River. Things would continue as they had been, under the English. New Amsterdam would grow and prosper.

He thought how fine it would be to marry again, make a new life, do a little farming and have plump, laughing children to dandle on his knee, and carry a happy heart into his old age.

Anna! Her baby wasn't due for another month yet; still, one never knew. He would have to get up to New Haarlem soon.

So lost in thought was he that he stubbed his toe on the closed lower door to the Ten Eyck house. His friends were in the great chamber at their midday meal.

"Ho, Antje, see who's favoring us with a visit. Sit down, Tonneman. You're just in time."

Antje had laid out a table of bread, cold ham, and a pitcher of beer. "I saved the last bit of flour for a celebration." She was enormous, breathing heavily, sweating, rubbing her aching back. She had felt for certain the day before that her time had come, but it had only been a false alarm.

Young Conraet sat on the floor near the table, working on a yellow kite. The sturdy boy was disappointed at missing all the joy of the day before and was full of questions. He tugged at Tonneman's boot. "Tell me about the battle."

"There was no battle."

"That's what my father said."

Ten Eyck laughed.

The boy wrinkled his nose. "Does that mean Heer Stuyvesant lost his honor?"

"No," Tonneman replied. "What Heer Stuyvesant did was good for all of us. A very honorable thing to do. He sent a message to the English colonel asking for a meeting so they could fashion a peace."

"Did anything else happen?"

"You're a greedy lad. Four English ships menaced our shore. What more do you want?"

"Excitement. Things never happen when I'm about." The boy jumped to his feet, kite in hand. "Come out with me, Tonneman. There's a good wind blowing."

Antje smiled through a groan, her hand at her back.

"Go on, Tonneman." Ten Eyck's mouth was full of bread.

Tonneman followed the boy into the yard; there wasn't a cloud in the sky. "Little one, did I ever tell you about the whale?"

The boy's blue eyes showed amusement. He knew what was coming. "No." This was not so. Their back-and-forth was part of the game. Tonneman had told him the story before, many times, and with many variations.

"My grandfather swore this was true. And we don't want to call my grandfather a liar, do we?" They left the yard, the boy on the run, holding the string, trailing the kite behind him. The kite caught the wind, lifted, and rose, its sails bursting.

"No." A small giggle as the boy routed the kite away from a tall oak.

"It happened in 1598, in the old country. A whale came up on the beach. It was a hundred feet long."

"No, it wasn't," said the boy happily. "It was fifty feet."

"And it lay on the beach for twenty years."

The boy laughed, but his attention was really on the kite. "Four days," he shouted, running with the kite. And when he came back toward Tonneman: "Four days it was there."

"Whatever. My grandfather saw it, touched it. Then it died. And did it stink." Tonneman had to shout so the boy could hear him. "It stank so much the Indians here in this New World could smell it."

"No, they couldn't," the boy shouted back.

"Yes, they could. It had two hundred big white teeth."

"No, it didn't. It had forty teeth."

"So it did. You're getting too smart for me." The kite was a beautiful yellow creature, and it soared like a bird with its pretty many-colored tail. A shiny device at the end of the tail caught in the sunlight and dazzled.

"What's that on the tail of your kite?"

The boy didn't hear; the joy of the yellow creature kept tugging at him, and all he could think of was guiding his kite into the wind.

"Conraet!"

Surprised at Tonneman's stern tone, the boy slowed his running and looked at him.

"Would you pull your kite in for me?"

With good cheer the boy pulled the soaring kite in. Attached to the tail was a small silver disk.

"Did you get this from your father? Something he was working on?"

"No. I found it by the water." Young Conraet pointed to the East River.

Tonneman dug in his coat pockets. "Here we are," he said, bringing forth the magnifying glass. He examined the piece of silver more closely. No English shilling *this* time. He was holding another piece of Benjamin Mendoza's silver belt. "Not as clear as the other but it's there. What do you think? What do you see?"

The boy looked at the dim impression, through the glass. "It's a lion." His face puckered with delight. "A magic glass."

"How do you know it's a lion?"

The boy made a face at him. "There's a picture of a lion in our house. Daniel in the lions' den."

"Is that so?" Tonneman was no longer listening.

The boy threw himself to the ground and began using the glass to examine the grass, insects, everything.

Tonneman scratched his head. Something was badgering him. He closed his eyes and like a burst of flame he remembered the death's-head vision he had when he was thrown into the water, the night he had found Spectacles' body the first time.

"Look," cried the boy. "See how this ant gets bigger in the glass."

But Tonneman wasn't there to hear. He was racing toward the river. Thrilled, the boy abandoned his kite and followed after Tonneman.

At the water Tonneman pulled off his boots and his clothes till he was down to his breeches.

"Where did you get those scars?" the boy asked. "Were you in a fight? Was it the English? Was it Indians? What are you going to do? Are you going to have a swim? May I come along?"

"No. You stay here."

"I never get to do anything." The boy plumped down heavily on the grass and immediately found a spotted red beetle to examine through the magnifying glass.

Tonneman walked into the river, dived, came up for a breath, went down again into the cold waters. Nothing. He took another breath and swam against the current, alongside the grassy bank toward his willow tree. Still nothing. Tired now, he dived again, allowing the current to take him back toward the pier, all the time searching for what he was certain was there.

And then he saw it: a skeleton in shredded garments at the base of the pier, caught on a nail, the skull gaping at him. He felt a rush of triumph. The back of the skull was shattered. The left foot and some fingers on both hands were missing.

He was so occupied with relishing his triumph that only the pain reminded him that his lungs were bursting. He brought the skeleton to the surface, losing the other foot and some small bones along the way.

"Oh, oh, oh." The boy ran toward him, screaming ecstatically.

"How's this for excitement?" Tonneman asked. "And you said things never happen when you were about?"

"Mother, Father," Conraet called. "Come quick. See what Tonneman found. It's better than a whale." The boy knelt beside the bones and peered at them through the glass. "Look, Tonneman. A little fish."

Antje came out and watched while Tonneman took the glass from the boy and examined the skeleton and its clothes, which were more strips of rags than clothes. Next, Tonneman gave his attention to the most prominent thing: caught in the ribs was the rest of the silver belt. The pieces of silver hung down by a fragile link. Only a miracle had brought him here. A few more days, a few more ebbs and flows of the salt river, and there might have been nothing to verify the identity of these bones. God was with him. "Lions," he said. "A pack of lions."

"A pride of lions," said Antje, looking over Tonneman's shoulder.

"What's going on?" Ten Eyck called as he approached. "Oh, shit, not another dead man?"

"You bet your arse, what's left of one. Conraet, go find Pos. In all likelihood he's in the jail snoring. Tell him to get David Mendoza and to bring him here, and a wagon, they'll need a wagon. Can you remember that?"

The boy, glad at being asked to perform a grown-up task, ran toward City Hall.

Ten Eyck peered at the white pile that had once been human. "So, have these bones given you some answers?"

"No, only more questions." Tonneman got to his feet. "If this is Benjamin Mendoza, and I think it is."

"Do you know who killed him?"

"Antje, if I knew that, I could sit under my willow all day and count the blades of grass. Instead I have more work to do. Benjamin Mendoza disappeared in December about the time Hendrik started getting so troubled. Remember? He was drinking too much, always in a foul temper. But Hendrik didn't die until July. What happened in December? Did Smitt kill Benjamin Mendoza and drop him into the East River?"

"Hendrik was no killer," Ten Eyck said.

"I agree."

It wasn't long before young Conraet returned with Pos, followed by Abraham and David Mendoza leading a horse and cart.

The old man stood to the side, swaying forward and back, chanting.

David knelt and fingered the silver belt. "This was my brother's belt. This was Benjamin Mendoza." He pulled at the right side of his coat, but the stubborn material wouldn't yield. Maddened, tears welling in his eyes, he pulled again until finally the required rent was made.

"I knew it, I knew it," Abraham cried. "Benjamin, my son." He ripped at his clothing, too. Now both chanted Kaddish, the prayer for the dead.

Little Conraet stared openly at the strange Hebrews. Antje took the boy by the hand and the Ten Eyck family withdrew.

Tonneman dried himself with his shirt while he waited with Pos, who was silent, for once. His eyes went to the Strand. A woman, a black shawl covering her head, watched. She turned and walked quickly away down the Strand. Racqel Mendoza, he thought. He was sure of it. The Widow Mendoza. His blood was a torrent in his veins. He wanted to shout it: *Widow Mendoza.*

"How could he fall in the water?" asked Abraham. The old man's face was gray with grief.

"He didn't fall in," said David. "He was hit over the head, can't you see?"

"I fear your son is right, Heer Mendoza."

"Then who did this? Who killed Benjamin?"

Tonneman shrugged.

David Mendoza cautiously fingered the tatters clinging to the skeleton.

Abraham sobbed. "My son, my son."

David's dark eyes were dead with sorrow. "We will take my brother now, Heer Schout."

Tears streamed down Abraham's wrinkled face into his gray beard. "If Benjamin has been murdered, we won't even be able to shroud him in cerements."

"He has to be buried in these corrupt garments," David Mendoza explained to Tonneman and Pos. "The blood of the slain cries out to God for vengeance and must not be hidden when the dead man appears before Him."

"We must hurry," the old man said, more restrained now. "Burial must be immediate. Before the Sabbath begins."

"I'll help you carry him to the wagon," said Tonneman.

"I'll do it," said David. "Thank you for your kindness." As David knelt to wrap Benjamin's remains in a white linen sheet Abraham attempted to help. "No, Father, I can do it. There's no reason for you to touch him. Let it be just me."

The old man stood back as David gathered the bones in his arms and carried them to the wagon.

Tonneman put on his shirt and thrust his feet into his boots. Antje and Ten Eyck came out to him. "How sad for them," said Antje. "Well, now you know for sure that it's Benjamin Mendoza."

"That was the simple part." Tonneman chewed his lip.

"Come," said Antje, "you deserve a mug of beer for your work this day."

Tonneman was with his own thoughts. "What," he asked pensively, "if Hendrik saw someone murder Benjamin Mendoza?"

"Yes," said Antje. "Yes. And what if, to keep him from telling, the murderer killed Hendrik and made it look like suicide?"

"That makes sense, terrible sense," Ten Eyck offered.

"But why in July?" asked Tonneman. "Why not in January? Too much time went by . . . unless the man Hendrik saw murder Mendoza was someone he knew well, a friend. And the friend thought he could trust Hendrik not to tell."

Antje shook her head. "But Hendrik was a good man. He couldn't keep such an evil secret."

"Which was why he started drinking too much," said Ten Eyck.

Tonneman nodded. "And in July the friend decided he couldn't trust Hendrik any longer."

60

Friday, 5 September. *Middle Afternoon.*

Racqel felt her horrible nightmare was close to an end. She walked behind Benjamin's coffin as a widow must, with a black shawl covering her head.

Abraham had declared that today, the day his bones were found, was Benjamin's day of death. And even though there was nothing left of Benjamin but bones, Abraham had insisted on observing all the rites. She had heard him tell David to have the bones washed in warm water and scented with spices.

Benjamin was then dressed again in the rags in which he was found. A prayer shawl was draped about his neck, and he was placed in his coffin. Then they had gone seven times around the coffin chanting the Song Against Plagues. She had contemplated the vacant eye sockets of the skull, searching for any sign of the husband she had known. Naught, yet she knew in her heart it was he.

As the mourners walked the winding route up and down the streets in order that as many people as possible could join the procession, Sara Cardoza, the wailing woman, moaned and sobbed and proclaimed what a good man Benjamin had been.

For lack of others, Asser Levy, as leader of the Jewish community, had hired Isadore Korbonski and the little African to play the flutes and walk with the wailing woman as was the custom.

David did not like using the two base rogues. In his view, Korbonski was not a Jew, and as for the little black barbarian, that went without saying, but he did not dispute Asser Levy's decision. Though Abraham had called for every observance, it had to be done in haste, before the sun set and the Sabbath was upon them. By Jewish law, no burial could take place on this holy day.

Her head was bowed, but Racqel noticed certain people: Lubbertus van Dincklagen, Joost Zoelan, Jan Keyser, Nicasius and Geertruyd De Sille. Only Heer van Dincklagen raised his hat in respect.

Finally they passed through the Water Gate and arrived at the small Jewish cemetery, which had been established, following much strife, at the beginning of '56, a little more than a year after the Twenty-three had arrived.

Water was brought, hands were washed, and they went inside.

Abraham cried out his anguish and tore a new mourning rent the breadth of a hand in the right side of his clothes, as did David.

The wailing woman wailed.

Tears spilled from Racqel's eyes, and she tore a mourning rent in her clothes, too, at her right breast.

"May he come to his place in peace," Abraham said as the coffin was lowered.

"May he come to his place in peace," Racqel and the others repeated. Each in turn, Abraham, David, Racqel, scattered three handfuls of earth upon the coffin. And then the others did the same.

Abraham and David said the special Kaddish.

Water was brought again and hands were washed again. "Our hands have not shed this blood, neither have our eyes seen it," each mourner said.

Abraham and David put their hands over their eyes. "He will destroy Death forever," said Abraham, his voice breaking.

"Yea," said David. "The Lord God will wipe away the tear from off every face."

Not my face, thought Racqel. What is my life now? Until I know that, I will have many tears on my face. As they left the cemetery she threw some dirt over her shoulder. "He remembers that we are dust."

61

SATURDAY, 6 SEPTEMBER. *Early Morning.*
Dawn on this day, when there could have been catastrophe, came up in a pink hazy hue, sweet, and with just a touch of coolness.

A rooster crowed, and then another.

Tonneman sat on his stoop, smoking, listening to the morning sounds, the roosters, Venus neighing softly in her stall, a dog barking, gulls chattering, the renewed voices of the people and the mills grinding. Now, those were sounds worth getting up early for. What he didn't hear was important, too. No sounds of preparations for war. No feeling of being embattled.

It was a renewed town.

And he was a renewed man with hope in his life; he had quite made up his mind that Racqel Mendoza would be his, no matter the obstacles. His pipe was out. He got up and set it inside his door and walked toward the North River.

The mellifluous music of grinding that he heard from the Old Mill told him that wheat was once more arriving from the north. Soon things would be back to normal. Well, not quite. There would be no more Heer Director-General Stuyvesant and no more Heer Schout Tonneman.

His destination this morning was the tip of the island below the Fort, but since he still hadn't had any breakfast, he headed first for the Broad Way. For the first time he was out before Vrouw Root arrived. Poor woman, she would be upset.

People were up and about on the Broad Way. Many shops were open for custom, including the Blue Dove and Lichtman's bakeshop. He went into the bakeshop. "Good morning, Lichtman."

"Good morning, Heer Schout. Have a stuiver roll."

"Thank you." He dug in his jacket pocket for his purse. "Devil take it, where'd I put . . . I'll have to pay you tomorrow. I left—"

"Makes nothing. From me to you. Good size, eh? Fresh wheat. Did you ever taste anything like it?"

"Very good," said Tonneman, savoring the wheat bread. "It's a good day, isn't it?"

"Not so bad," said Lichtman.

"Do you know how to make crumpetcake?"

"Get out," the baker said, laughing, and he moved to serve another customer.

Tonneman exchanged morning greetings with his fellow New Amsterdamers along the Broad Way. All were excited, curious, and just a bit apprehensive.

"What do you think is going to happen, Tonneman?"

"Your guess is as good as mine."

"Do you think they'll take us to England and lock us up?"

"I doubt that. Why don't we stop worrying and wait and see what happens next?"

"That sounds like a good idea. Everything will be all right, won't it?"

"The Good Lord willing," Tonneman answered. Listen to you, he thought with a smile. Maria would have loved to hear you say that.

At the shoreline Tonneman and the others joined a group on the beach, looking out on the bay. Two small boats from the *Guinea* were headed straight for them.

"Wouldn't it have been better to anchor off Staple Street?" someone asked.

"What are you, an idiot?" another challenged. "The English are taking no chances. This way Nicolls keeps his guns on the Fort and his eyes on both rivers."

"But it's over, isn't it? There's no more chance of war."

"It's not over till the man with the wooden leg says it's over," said still another.

"A question of tactics. It's plain you've never been in the army."

"And I don't intend to be, thank you."

"It's not so bad. The reason the *Guinea* won't go up to Staple Street is in case we change our minds and become belligerent. Nicolls doesn't want to be hemmed in by a lot of merchant ships."

In one boat Tonneman counted six English plus the two sailors who rowed. As they drew closer he saw that one of the six was John Winthrop.

In the second boat, rowed by one sailor, a lone man sat like a prince. Nicolls himself. By this time the English had disembarked from the first small boat. Nestled in Nicolls's arms was a small, black-and-tan spaniel about two and a half hands high.

"Who is that man?" someone in the crowd asked.

"That's Colonel Richard Nicolls, the new governor of this place," John Winthrop said, in fairly good Dutch.

Tonneman adjusted his hat. The bastard Winthrop could speak Dutch all the time.

Nicolls was dressed as Tonneman had seen him before, in yellow. He wore black shoes with silver buckles over white stockings. Silently, the crowd studied the colonel as he set his dog down, watched it piss, and strode back and forth on the beach with the six men following him. He talked softly and rapidly, with broad gestures. At one point he reached into the left pocket of his yellow coat, brought forth some snuff, sniffed it into his fleshy nose, and sneezed twice. The dog, as if in response, also sneezed twice. The crowd tittered uneasily. Nicolls picked up the floppy-eared beast, got into his boat, and was rowed back to his ship.

A murmur of disappointment rose from the people, but then the noise of hooves and a gale of dry road sand announced the arrival of the six Dutch Commissioners, followed by Avercamp on his black mare. The little clerk led a string of six fresh horses for the English guests.

People thronged around, making quiet caustic comments while the Dutch Commissioners, who had come to show the English the way to the Bouwerie for their eight o'clock meeting, dismounted.

Amidst the coughing and flapping of nosecloths, names were exchanged. The six Englishmen—Robert Carr, George Carteret, John Winthrop, Samuel Willys, John Pinchon, and Thomas Clark—met the six Dutchmen—John De Decker, Nicholas Varleth, Samuel Megapolensis, Cornelis Steenwyck, Jacques Cousseau, and Oloff Stevensen van Cortlandt.

Neither Nicolls nor Stuyvesant was to participate in the preliminary meeting.

The Englishmen bowed graciously to the townspeople.

Van Cortlandt, the only Dutch Commissioner who could speak English, spoke. "Shall we mount or do you require a chance to stretch your legs? It would give the people a treat if we walked for a bit and they could have a look at you."

"By all means," said Winthrop, "let's walk, at least so far as the Wall."

Tonneman's eyes narrowed. So far as the Wall, indeed. That Johnnie knew this town right enough, didn't he? The tricksome English bastard must have spent his time well here in '61.

With van Cortlandt leading, the English and Dutch representatives walked their horses along the Broad Way. The crowd closed in behind them, calling out to the Dutch Commissioners, shouting counsel and suggestions.

"Get us a good bargain, De Decker. We're counting on you."

"We trust in the Lord, preacher, and in you."

"Ho, van Cortlandt, if the English won't come to good terms, buy them out."

Even Sweet Lips and her chickens had taken up positions along the Broad Way. So had Korbonski and his fiddle and the bearded dwarf, Lizard, with his capuchin monkey. Its tail was wrapped around the dwarf's leg, and it tipped its red felt cap repeatedly as the people passed.

The tall man and his little companion were playing for all they were worth, but today, instead of the flageolet, the dwarf was playing a fife and beating his tabor. Sweet Lips and her chickens waved fans. Korbonski's old black hat lay on the ground waiting for bestowals.

"Good morning, Your Honors," Korbonski called to the passing notables while the monkey chattered. "We have just played a Dutch favorite, 'The Breda Small Beer.' Now for our distinguished guests, the visiting Commissioners, we will play an English favorite, 'Greensleeves.'"

"Next time you're here, just ask for the red tent," Sweet Lips called. "Everyone knows where it is."

As he passed her Tonneman wagged his finger at the procuress but did not stop to chastise her.

"What are you doing up so early, Sweet Lips?" someone called.

"Haven't been to bed yet," she answered.

"I doubt that," someone else said, and was encouraged by hoots and howls.

The twelve mounted at the Broad Way Gate and rode off, leaving most of the crowd behind them in their dust.

Some citizens followed the group beyond the Wall, toward Stuyvesant's Bouwerie, where the six Dutchmen and their English counterparts were to discuss surrender terms. This treaty would affect all their lives and was going to be something to tell the grandchildren about. Tonneman himself was not about to miss it, but he would not walk behind, eating the horsemen's dust. He would wait a short bit then ride out.

At last it's over, he thought, heading back toward the Strand to get Venus. Now there would be peace. Pearl Street was deserted. Everyone was on the Broad Way and at the Bouwerie, watching what the English would do next.

Everyone, that is, except Joost Zoelan. The Pear Tree was locked up tighter than a drum. Something about the deep silence surrounding it made Tonneman wonder if Joost was still among the living.

62

SATURDAY, 6 SEPTEMBER. *Morning.*

The boy Conraet ran out onto the Strand. His mother had told him that he was to find his father or Tonneman at City Hall and they were to tell the Widow Wilbruch that she must come at once.

But no one was at City Hall except two drunken soldiers sprawled asleep on the stoop. In fact, no one was to be seen anywhere, although he could hear shouting from the north.

He had to do something; his mother was mad with pain, and all he could do to help her was get her to the bed. What was he to do? He had to find help.

The boy ran along Pearl Street, hoping to see a familiar face. Nobody. Stopping at the gate to the Peyser house, he called, "Anybody home?" All he got for his trouble was a scolding from their dog. Unsure and frightened now, he turned and started running in the opposite direction.

As Conraet approached Twiller's Road, a familiar black-and-white four-footer threw itself at him, leaping, yipping, licking the boy's hands like an old friend. Caleb, Vrouw Mendoza's animal. Conraet hugged the dog and the dog slobbered all over his face. Vrouw Mendoza would help him. He lifted the scruffy mongrel's earflap. "Where's your mistress?"

As if he heard and understood, Caleb ran off barking, stopping short, looking for Conraet to follow, which the boy did, all the way to Jews Alley.

Racqel stood in the front door threshold of the newly painted red house, looking out. Her shawl over her hair, the young widow was wearing the same dark brown dress she had worn the day before for her husband's funeral. The morning was cool and clear. The soft dew smelled sweet. She heard the grinding and the squeaking as John Woods's horses trudged around and around over at the Old Mill. Through that came Caleb's shrill bark. Close by. Up to his old games, he had somehow escaped the yard to forage for food and mischief. She smiled. "Caleb."

"Come away from the door," David called from within. "That is not the way to sit *shibah*. You forget your duty."

She had a sharp answer ready on her tongue but was saved from speaking it by the sight of Caleb running back and forth, and behind him, the Ten Eyck boy, stumbling and crying.

Without a thought Racqel went to him.

"Please," Conraet cried when he saw Racqel. He ran to her, Caleb on his heels, still barking. The boy clutched Racqel's skirts. "Please, my mother . . ." His face was streaked with dirt and tears.

She knelt beside him. "The baby?"

He nodded vigorously, gulping back tears. "I can't find my father or Tonneman. My mother needs the Widow Wilbruch. I can't find her, either. My mother is very sick. She hurts a lot."

Racqel stood. "Stay here for a moment," she said, patting the boy's head.

"What are you about?" asked David as she passed the great chamber where the *shibah* was being observed.

No longer caring what he said or did, she did not respond. In the scullery a large table was laden with fruit and sweet cakes brought by their neighbors.

Yesterday when they arrived home, after making seven ritual stops along the way, Vrouw Levy had prepared a meal of hard-boiled eggs, lentils, and bread for them. And that was that. Benjamin was dead and buried, and now *shibah* had begun. And her life? Was this the end or the beginning?

This was no time for selfish thoughts. Under the table was her father's case. She reached for it.

"What are you doing?" David had followed her.

"Vrouw Ten Eyck is having her baby."

"What is it to do with you?"

"There is no one else."

"You are not going anywhere. It is the Sabbath. We are in mourning. Have you no feelings? The Lord God has punished once already. Would you give Him reason to punish us again?"

"Have *you* no feelings, brother? God will not punish us for helping someone in need. This is my choice, not yours." She had the case; she held it in front of her with two hands and attempted to leave.

"You dare make judgments for God? I demand that you stay. In God's name, for the honor of my brother."

"Let me go, David. I must go. The boy says she's in great pain."

"Then let him go to Widow Wilbruch's soldier hospital," he shouted.

"What is this?" Old Abraham came into the scullery. "How dare you raise your voices to each other at this time?"

"Father, she is going out to help the gentiles."

"Racqel?" The old man appeared shrunken and withered. The loss of his son had truly aged him. "Can this be?"

"Vrouw Ten Eyck is having her baby."

"Let her own people help her," said Abraham. "You belong here."

"There is no one else." She pushed by David, determined.

"If you go," said David, shaking a fist at her, "you will not again be welcome in this house!"

Racqel paused in the scullery doorway.

Abraham looked at Conraet, who was fighting tears. After a moment the old man spoke. "Go, daughter. In my grief I forgot God's command to do good. I was wrong." He smiled gently. "When you save one person, you save the world. Go. What you do is a blessing."

David's eyes rolled to the top of his head with frustration. "How can you say—"

"Silence, David. There will be no more anger in this house. I have spoken."

63

SATURDAY, 6 SEPTEMBER. *Morning.*

With young Conraet at her side and the dog close behind, Racqel made haste along the deserted Strand to Coenties Alley. The boy and the dog now ran ahead of her. "Hurry," Conraet shouted. Caleb danced fitfully and barked.

The front door stood open, and within at first all was quiet. Too quiet. Then a moan. The mongrel stopped at the sound and lay down on the stoop.

Conraet rushed inside to the bedchamber. "Mother, I've brought help."

Antje lay on her back in her bed, writhing in pain, soaked with sweat. "The baby's almost here. I've broken my sack. Water is on the fire in the big pot. . . ."

Racqel became at once who she always was, the physician's daughter. She set her case down on the side table, pushing aside the beautiful silver bowl and candlesticks. "Conraet, see if the water is ready. It must be boiling hot."

The boy looked at his mother for a moment, then without a word, went to do as Racqel had asked.

"Lie back, please," Racqel said gently. She bent over Antje and removed her voluminous dress. "Antje. I'll need cloth."

"In the . . ." Antje screamed. "Oh, the pain." She bit her lips. "The kas in the great chamber. I was going to make a . . ." She screamed again. Her face was beaded with sweat.

Racqel quickly tore the hem of her own pettiskirt and dipped the scrap of cloth into a pitcher of water on the table next to the bed and wiped Antje's brow. The woman was burning up. The bedchamber was close; there was no air. "I won't be long." She went to the great chamber. In the kas was some white muslin and nearby on a stool was a sewing box. She would need the thread and scissors. When she returned to Antje with the cloth and the sewing box, she found Conraet fanning flies away from his mother.

Antje's teeth were biting hard on her lips. Racqel could see she was in great pain and trying not to let the boy know. One look at Conraet, however, told her that he knew very well. He smiled manfully at her. "Will it be long now?"

"Not long," said Racqel, praying she was correct. She rolled the sleeves of her dress up over her elbows and opened her father's case to find some agent to relieve Antje's pain.

Abruptly Antje put her head to the side of the bed and threw up. "Oh, oh," she said desperately. "This one is going to take his time. I can tell. Just like Conraet." She turned to her son. "I love you, my little man, but you did cause me so much pain." She lay back in a swoon.

Racqel wiped Antje's face, then delved into the doctor's case. She came up with two small silk packets. Willow bark for the pain and red raspberry leaves for the vomiting. "Conraet, can you brew a tea?" She handed him the raspberry leaves.

The boy's face brightened. "Yes, I know how." He ran from the chamber.

"Make it strong," she called after him.

She spread the muslin at the foot of the bed and bathed Antje's face again. Antje opened her eyes. Her fists were clenched. "You're a good woman, Racqel. A good friend." Her body convulsed with pain.

Soon the boy brought a tray with a pewter pot, two cups, and two spoons. Racqel emptied the willow bark into one of the cups and poured a bit of the strong tea over it, then blew on it to cool it. "Drink this all down. It's for the pain."

With difficulty, Antje lifted her head and did as Racqel asked. "Oh, that's vile."

"All of it. That's the way." Racqel now poured more of the tea and held it so Antje could sip it.

Antje pushed it away, moaning. "Too hot."

"Drink. It's good for you. It will hurry the labor and stop the vomiting."

Antje drank, then fell back on the pillows as the pain eased.

"Where is everyone?" asked Racqel.

"With the English," Conraet told her.

Antje was silent. Racqel touched her forehead. She was cooler. She was sleeping.

"Tonneman's a good man," Antje whispered hoarsely.

"I thought you were asleep," said Racqel, wiping Antje's face with the wet cloth.

"You know that, don't you?"

"I know."

Antje groped for Racqel's hand and squeezed it. "He loves you, he would marry you."

"I'm a Jew."

"It makes nothing to him. Two people who are alone, who care about each other, should be able to build a life together. This is the New World."

"Oh Antje, I wish it could be that simple."

Antje smiled and tightened her grip as the pain returned. "Life is for the living," she gasped. "A gift from God."

"You have the gift from God," said Racqel. "I envy you."

"No, you don't," said Antje, smiling horribly. Then she groaned and screamed. "Oh my God, the pain, my baby."

Racqel kept wiping Antje's brow and speaking softly to her. It would soon be time. "Can you carry the pot of water?" she asked Conraet.

"Yes."

"Get it then, please." She continued wiping Anjte's face and concentrated on the memory she had of helping her father with other births. She had never done one by herself before.

Conraet, struggling, brought the large black kettle of steaming water into the chamber. The kettle, which was almost half the boy's size, obscured his legs and was barely off the floor. It shook as he carried it and some of the water spilled. "Be careful. Don't burn yourself."

"I won't. Will this be enough?"

"More than enough. Set it down on the floor next to the bed. Thank you. Now take Caleb and wait in the yard."

"Do I have to?"

"Yes. Go." When he was gone, she washed Antje thoroughly.

It was starting. "Antje, whenever the baby squeezes, I want you to bear down and push."

"I know, I know."

Racqel pressed gently on Antje's stomach. The contractions were coming closer together. Finally, there came a push and the child showed, but it was wrong. All wrong.

The infant was presenting itself incorrectly. The feet were showing, not the head. She would have to turn it. Racqel washed her hands in the hot water as her father had taught her. Then, while her left hand pushed and guided from the outside on the stomach, she reached in with her right hand to turn the child.

The baby slipped from her grasp. Sweat streamed from under Racqel's cap and down her face. She dried her right hand on a piece of muslin and tried again. Carefully, she took hold of the tiny body, firmly, so she wouldn't lose it again, but not so tight that she would do harm.

Gently, she turned the body around.

Now the head was crowning properly. Antje moaned once and fainted. "Don't leave me now, Antje. I need your help. Antje?"

Groaning, Antje came back to herself and pushed. Racqel could see almost five inches of the child's head. She placed her left palm over the baby's head and the curved fingers of her right hand between Antje's legs in order to feel the baby's chin, still inside Antje's body; thus she was able to control the infant's progress.

"Press hard," Racqel instructed. "Now stop. Press hard. . . ."

Antje gasped. "He's coming."

"It's all right now," Racqel said. When the head was delivered, she put gentle pressure on it. Then came the shoulders. She lifted the head slowly, and the rest of the body slid out without difficulty, followed by the afterbirth. "Praise God," Antje whispered, and fell back against the pillows.

"Praise God," said Racqel. She was crying as she tied the cord off with thread in two places the way her father had shown her, as close to the child's belly as possible.

When with trembling hands she dropped the iron scissors and they broke into pieces, Conraet was there quick as a wink with a knife. Racqel had not noticed that he'd come back into the chamber. Taking the knife, she smiled at the boy and, again as her father had shown her, snipped the cord between the two knots of thread.

"How has God blessed me?" Antje asked faintly.

"A healthy boy." Racqel placed the baby on the muslin and gently cleaned its nose, mouth, and throat of mucus. She gave him a little smack on his behind. An irritated cry came from the infant, and the two women grinned at each other.

Racqel then washed the baby of blood and afterbirth and bound him tightly in swaddling cloth to keep him from moving too freely and injuring himself. She placed the complaining bundle in Antje's ready arms. His tiny mouth found Antje's milk-swollen breast and was silent.

After Racqel bathed Antje's face, she cleaned herself and rolled the sleeves of her dress back into place. When she started to clean the floor, Conraet took the cloth from her hand. "I'll do it."

Grateful for his help, Racqel sank exhausted into a chair.

Antje was staring into the red-puckered face of her new son. "Not too bad, hey?"

"He's beautiful. I have to go soon."

"Thank you. For everything." Antje sighed. "Forgive a friend's meddling, but Tonneman needs you. And I think you need him."

The baby released Antje's breast, gurgled, and fell immediately asleep.

"Poor child," said Antje, stroking the fine blond hair on his head. "He's probably the first Dutchman on these shores born an English subject."

64

SATURDAY, 6 SEPTEMBER. *Morning.*

Water Gate Road became Bouwerie Road. The land was recovering from the long summer's heat, and the dry rustle of the leaves from the majestic oaks along both sides augured an early autumn. In a quarter of an hour at an easy gallop Tonneman reached the Stuyvesants' farm.

He reined Venus through the large wide-open gates to the rail fence that encircled the Bouwerie and rode into the vast farmyard amidst the screaking flock of chickens.

Most of the citizens had arrived before him and were gathered in front of the Director-General's stone farmhouse. Only the Jews were missing, this being their Sabbath.

The house was big, with many casement windows, a steep pitched, oak-shingled roof, and three chimneys. To the left a well, to the right a stand of birch trees.

Not far was a smaller house, also of stone. This was Pieter Stuyvesant's chapel. Three wooden barns of varying sizes were on the other side of the chapel.

Stuyvesant's land spread from the banks of the East River to the Broad Way and stretched for a little more than a half mile. He'd paid sixty-four hundred guilders to the Company in '51 for the land, a house, a barn, a pair of horses, six cows, and a pair of young Africans.

Two powerful, short-haired mastiffs, each almost eight hands high, were running around the verge of the crowd, their short, drooping ears flapping wildly, barking at all these rare visitors.

Tonneman dismounted, tied Venus to a low branch of one of Stuyvesant's shady elms, hurried to the front door, and knocked.

"Go away," called a shrill male voice. "Vrouw says everybody go away."

"Please," came the exasperated voice of Judith Stuyvesant. "You must wait outside. Orders of the Director-General."

"What Director-General?" someone in the crowd behind Tonneman shouted.

"Not for long," said another.

"The retired Director-General," offered still another.

There were some whistles at that and someone hooted like an owl.

"Vrouw Stuyvesant, it is I, Pieter Tonneman."

The door was opened by Tobias, the same fat African who always drove the Stuyvesant carriage. He was dressed in brown duffel, which color was almost that of his dour brown face above his wide white collar. Behind him, also in brown duffel, was the diminutive and usually amiable Judith Stuyvesant. "Quickly, Tonneman. The Commissioners are talking in the great chamber."

"And where is he?"

"In his chapel, waiting, praying."

The furnishings were simple and plain: a good solid kas, a brass chandelier, a great oak table covered with a woven rug to the side of the whitewashed hearth. Several looking glasses on the walls reflected the sunlight from the many windows.

Softly and quietly, Vrouw Stuyvesant opened the door to the chamber. Nick De Sille stood close inside. He put his fingers to his lips when he saw Tonneman and closed the door in his face.

Hot with fury, Tonneman applied firm pressure and pushed the door open.

Nick rubbed his hand that had held the doorknob. "A pity that with such strength and determination, you weren't with us at the end of the fighting."

"What fighting?" Tonneman was scornful. "It was all grown men playing little boys' games, playing soldier. What are you doing here?"

"I could ask you the same thing," said Nick. "Shh." His forefinger was once more to his lips. "Governor Winthrop is speaking."

That's how and why Nick was here. Winthrop.

". . . for now, all your laws and customs will stay." Fists hammered lightly on the table as the Commissioners sat around. "Mister Stuyvesant will step down, as will his Council. And Colonel Nicolls will be deputy governor to His Royal Highness, James, the Duke of York, brother of His Majesty, King Charles."

"Well done," said the English contingent repeatedly, pounding the table, whenever Winthrop said something new.

The Dutch for the most part pounded the table or clapped politely and briefly. De Sille's applause was loud and long.

"Our City Burgomasters and Schepens—or as they will now be called, Mayors and Aldermen—will stay, as will the City Sheriff."

Nick's pale eyes fell on Tonneman with displeasure. Winthrop's words had taken both of them by surprise. Tonneman had not once considered that he might continue as Schout. Well, that would be just fine with him.

"All your soldiers will give up their arms," said Winthrop. "Any who would stay as farmers will be given the gift of fifty acres of land. What do you think? Any beetle-crushers in your little army?" He laughed as if this was the greatest of jests. When no responding laughter was forthcoming, he cleared his throat and continued. "Those who do not choose to accept this gift will be granted the dignity of marching out of the Fort, bearing their arms, with flying colors, drums beating, and their bullets in their mouths."

"All this is very generous," van Cortlandt said in English. "We have one request, though, if I may."

"Yes?"

"The Johnnie soldiers from New England and Long Island. If they could be kept out of the town . . . our people dread most being plundered by them."

"Done. We don't want you thinking us bloody-minded. They will be kept in Breukelen. I pledge you my word, there will be no plunder and no damage to any citizen or his property."

Hearty table pounding came from the Dutch.

"All right," said Winthrop. "To work, then. We will start from the beginning. Articles of Capitulation. Article One . . ."

Before the afternoon had passed, it was done.

"Are we all agreed?"

"Agreed."

"Now, as I call your names, please come forward and sign."

Everyone seemed content, English and Dutch alike, that this unpleasantness was coming to an end.

When the six Dutchmen had finished signing, Winthrop sanded and shook the parchment. "Now I'll sign. John . . . Winthrop.

Now, Englishmen, if you please." The eager English jumped quickly to their task.

After again sanding and shaking, Winthrop smiled triumphantly. "I will present this document to Colonel Nicolls for his consenting signature."

The surrender was official.

Nicasius De Sille looked at home among the English in his blue silk breeches and coat. If one didn't know better, one might think he was the host, Tonneman thought. He watched De Sille press forward, greeting the Englishmen and then issuing an invitation to them and their officers, and by all means, to Colonel Nicolls, to a reception in their honor at his home on the lower Broad Way. His Dutch friends, of course, were also invited. "You too, Tonneman. I'm sure you and Colonel Nicolls have a lot to talk about. Such as a certain missing emissary killed by your knife."

65

SUNDAY, 7 SEPTEMBER. *Morning.*

The weather had turned cold. A dense fog hung over the island and a fine drizzle fell.

Church services were led by Reverend Johannes Megapolensis at the Stone Church, after which Reverend Samuel Megapolensis went to City Hall and, ignoring the weather, stood on the stoop and read the surrender terms to the population. Pieter Stuyvesant's sons were there, but neither their father nor mother was present.

Tonneman leaned against the tree in front of the Pear Tree, the one for which it was named. Smitt's death tree. He scratched the yellow hound's ears while the animal dug at the ground. The tavern was full to bursting. You could almost see its sides bulge. Tonneman was more than curious to know where Joost had been all this time, and when young Samuel was done talking, he was sure as the devil going to find out.

The yellow hound unearthed something and pushed the clammy thing at Tonneman. Tonneman brushed the four-footer away and concentrated on the preacher, who was now on Article Two.

" 'All public houses shall continue for the uses which they are for.' "

There was a great shout of joy from the men. "Well done, well done."

" 'Article Three. All people shall still continue free denizens, and shall enjoy their lands, houses, goods, wheresoever they are within this country, and dispose of them as they please.' "

The yellow dog made a small noise in its throat and bounded away.

" 'Article Four. If any inhabitant have a mind to remove himself, he shall have a year and six weeks from this day to remove himself, wife, children, servants, goods, and to dispose of his lands here.' "

"There you are, Keyser!" Pos shouted. "You've been complaining about the English coming. You've been threatening to go back to the Fatherland. Here's your chance!"

Keyser and Pos each had a tankard of beer in his hand, and each was swaying in the light rain. Behind them Dinck, Chief Fire Warden Claes van Der Werff, and Wouter Groenveld, the schoolmaster, watched and listened in amusement. "What about you?" Keyser shouted at Pos even though they were standing nose to nose.

"Not me. I like it here."

"With the English?"

"What difference will it make?"

Out on the bay the fog was so thick no ships could be seen, except when a light cut through.

" 'Article Six. It is consented to that any people may freely come from the Netherlands and plant in this colony, and that Dutch vessels may freely come hither, and any of the Dutch may freely return home, or send any sort of merchandise home, in vessels of their own country.' "

The people shouted in the wet air. The men waved their hats; some waved their tankards, sparging beer on the street. The women laughed and waved little nosecloths. The yellow hound dug a new hole and reburied its treasure.

" 'Article Seven. All ships from the Netherlands, or any other place, and goods therein, shall be received here, and sent hence, after the manner which formerly they were before our coming hither, for six months next ensuing.' "

"What happens after six months?" Keyser called.

"You go home, tanner, and complain to the States General."

" 'Article Eight. The Dutch shall enjoy the liberty of their consciences in divine worship and church discipline.' " The young predicant smiled. "Amen to that."

Fervent amens came back to him from all directions.

" 'Article Nine. No Dutchman here, or Dutch ship here, shall upon any occasion be pressed to serve in war against any nation whatsoever.' "

"And amen to that," said Pos.

There was a boisterous whoop from his friends.

" 'Article Ten. That the townsmen of Manhattans shall not have any soldiers quartered upon them. . . .' "

"Where have you been?"

"Oh, Ten Eyck."

"I have news."

"What?" said Tonneman. There was so much noise he couldn't hear either Ten Eyck or the preacher.

"I'm not going to tell you out here," said Ten Eyck. "You couldn't hear me anyway." The silversmith seized Tonneman by the arm and led him into the Pear Tree. "Two brandywines," he bellowed.

"Not for me. I'll stick to beer."

"After today. Two brandywines." Joost set the drinks in front of them.

"Ho, Joost," Tonneman shouted. "You old piss pot. Where have you been?"

"To sea." Joost, amused by his own words, laughed loudly.

"What's so amusing?" asked Tonneman.

"You'll find out," the tavern man replied. "Two florins for the brandy."

"That's steep, isn't it?" asked Ten Eyck.

"English prices."

"I was going to tell you to pour one for yourself but to hell with you."

"I'll pour it anyway. No charge."

"What's the occasion?" asked Tonneman.

"You are one complete arsehole," said Ten Eyck. "Drink up and congratulate yourself."

"Why? Because the war is over? Oh, I know. For keeping my job."

"Because you have a godson, you ninny. If Antje hadn't been feeling so poorly, we would have been to church this morning with him. He's a lusty little monster. Pieter Barent Ten Eyck."

"Pieter after our noble leader, I suppose," Tonneman said, smiling broadly.

"No, arsehole, after you, though I'm beginning to have my doubts about the wisdom of that."

"Drinks for everyone," Joost called. "On the house. Ten Eyck has a son."

The thirsty men pushed to the bar.

"How is Antje?" asked Tonneman, over the cheerful noise.

"All right, but it was difficult. Thank God, Vrouw Mendoza was with her. Conraet couldn't find Widow Wilbruch. I understand she was busy at the red tent on Staple Street. That Jewess is a saint. I will thank God for her for a long time coming." He gulped his brandy. "I've got to go. Come over and see the baby, Godfather."

"I will," Tonneman said, walking Ten Eyck out, "but not right now."

"Don't make it too late. Antje and little Pieter both need their sleep."

The younger Megapolensis was still going strong. " 'Article Sixteen. All inferior civil officers and magistrates shall continue as they are, if they please, till the customary time of new elections and then new ones to be chosen by themselves, provided that such new chosen magistrates shall take the oath of allegiance to His Majesty of England before they enter upon their office.' "

"Say, Tonneman," Keyser called. "What will you give me to vote for you?"

"I won't arrest you for trying to bribe an officer."

Hoots and whoops.

"Sheriff Tonneman—"

Tonneman turned to see Asser Levy, a large, pleasant man with thick features, black hair and beard, speckled with gray. On the crown of his head was a small black velvet cap.

"Heer Levy."

"Good news we're hearing."

"Yes."

"Excuse me, please. I am on my way to the Mendozas to sit *shibah* with them."

"Shibah?"

"The family must mourn for the seven days of *shibah,* the mourning period, surrounded by friends."

Tonneman had intended all along to stop by the Mendoza house. Troubled by Benjamin Mendoza's death, he needed to know more about what Benjamin had been involved in. Meeting Asser Levy was a stroke of luck, and now he took advantage of it. "If you don't mind waiting until the preacher is finished, I'll walk with you, pay my respects."

"I'll be pleased to wait."

" 'Article Eighteen. If it do appear that the West India Company of Amsterdam do really owe any sums of money to any persons here, it is agreed that recognition and other duties payable by ships going for the Netherlands be continued for six months longer.' "

"That's good news," said Tonneman, who was owed his last month's salary of sixty florins.

" 'Article Nineteen. The officers military, and soldiers, shall march out with their arms, drums beating, and colors flying and bullets in their mouths; and if any of them will plant, they shall have fifty acres of land set out for them. . . .' "

Like Keyser and many others, Pos was drinking his beer out on the street. Today Tonneman would do nothing about it. Tomorrow . . . That would be another story. "How many more articles, preacher?"

"Three."

"Get on with it, then," Keyser shouted.

The minister cleared his throat and talked faster, racing toward the end. " '. . . from Colonel Richard Nicolls, deputy governor under His Royal Highness . . .' "

"And which stinking Royal Highness is that?" roared Keyser.

"The Duke of York," said Tonneman, "King Charlie's brother, James. Finish, preacher."

" 'That the copies of the King's grant to His Royal Highness's Commission to Colonel Richard Nicolls, testified by two Commissioners more, and Mr. Winthrop, to be true copies, shall be delivered to the Honorable Mr. Stuyvesant, the present governor, on Monday, next, by eight of the clock in the morning, at the Old Mill.' "

"Do I get paid for that, Tonneman?" John Woods demanded.

"You know you do, Englishman," Keyser said nastily. "See, it's starting already. Favoring their own."

Tonneman showed Keyser his fist. "Shut up, Keyser."

" '. . . at the Old Mill, and these articles consented to, and signed by Colonel Richard Nicolls, deputy governor to His Royal Highness, and that within two hours after the Fort and town called New Amsterdam, upon the isle of Manhatoes, shall be delivered into the hands of the said Colonel Richard Nicolls, by the service of such as shall be by him thereunto deputed, by his hand and seal.' " Reverend Megapolensis dropped the document to his side. "That's it. Signed by the twelve Commissioners. All that is needed is Colonel Nicolls's approval and signature to be legal. I am assured he will."

The people cheered. Pos and Keyser and their friends adjourned to the Pear Tree to continue their revels. Others went with the predicant back to the church to say prayers of thanksgiving.

Asser Levy cleared his throat.

"Why are you wasting time out there, Tonneman?" Joost stood in the door sneering at Asser Levy. "Make sure you still have your purse."

Keyser, giggling, slobbering, showed his head between Joost's legs. "What's that stink out here? Smells like Jew."

Joost laughed roughly. "Coming from you, tanner, that's indeed an insult."

Keyser backed away on all fours, barking like a dog. The yellow hound answered him and ran around Joost into the street.

Joost rubbed the back of his neck vigorously. "A man's happier with his own kind, Tonneman."

Tonneman frowned. "What?"

"These Jews come here by our grace and make money from business that Christians should have by right."

Keyser was back between Joost's legs. "Come on in where it's nice and dry."

"You mean wet," said Pos, over Joost's shoulder. "Beer wet. Coming in, Schout?"

"By and by. Keep a level head."

All he got in response was loud unrestrained laughter as Joost and the drinkers tumbled back into the tavern.

"And that's that," said Tonneman.

"Yes, it is," agreed Asser Levy, his face impassive. "Shall we go now?"

"I beg pardon for my friend's words. He didn't mean them."

"Ah, but he did. Do not distress yourself over it. I am a Jew. I am used to it. We need not talk of it anymore. It is the way of the world."

They walked along in silence in the light rain until Asser Levy said, "Do you know what the Covenant is, Heer Tonneman?"

"No."

"The Covenant is a solemn agreement Jews must keep with God. It is our mission in life to keep the Covenant and the Torah alive. Do you know what the Torah is?"

Tonneman nodded.

"God promised the ancient Israelites to always protect them if they kept his law and were faithful to him. We were faithful, we are faithful, and once more he has protected us."

"Amen," said Tonneman.

"Amen," said Asser Levy. He pulled his beard and then he said, "We Jews have a covenant with each other, too. Do you understand what I'm saying, Heer Schout?"

"No."

"I think you don't want to understand."

"Perhaps."

No more was said on the subject until they reached the red house.

"Please remember what I said, Heer Tonneman. Also, please do not speak to the mourners before they speak to you. It is our law."

The door was open. Jewish neighbors had brought food for the mourners and news of the peace. Tonneman took a deep breath as he caught sight of Racqel seated on a low stool near the hearth, her shawl covering her hair, her head bowed. He looked at Asser Levy. The old Jew was watching him. This was not the time for Tonneman to speak the words to Racqel that had to be spoken. But they would be spoken no matter what Asser Levy or anyone else felt about it.

Over the low murmur of voices he could hear one man chanting, a soul-touching sound of deep sorrow.

Racqel flushed at the sight of the big Dutchman behind the butcher. "We are in God's hands."

"Amen." Levy bobbed his head. "The surrender is a fact. It's over."

"We heard," she said. "Peace at last."

Levy smiled sadly. "What a pity Benjamin didn't live to see it. Let me go and be with your father." He nodded at Tonneman. "The Sheriff is here to pay his respects."

"That and more," said Tonneman, feeling ill at ease. He watched Levy making his way across the chamber to Abraham Mendoza. With effort he looked at Racqel. "I need to talk to the family about Benjamin."

"That will have to wait." She rose. "This house is in mourning. But please." She beckoned to Tonneman and he entered, hat in hand. "My father-in-law and David are over there," Racqel said, pointing across the great chamber. "You may come in."

Thick-tongued, he fumbled for words. "I'm sorry for the death of your husband."

She nodded and bowed her head, returning to the low stool.

In the center of the chamber Tonneman saw a table, covered with a gold-embroidered blue velvet cloth on which stood one lone candle. People sat on wooden chairs; some sat on the floor. Abraham was in a corner on a low stool, his head moving up and down, his mournful voice rising and falling as if his heart would break. David sat next to him on another stool, not singing, but his head was bobbing along with his father's. His eyes met Tonneman's. A spasm of rage clouded them.

Tonneman looked away. The old man was in too much pain. It

was bad enough to hear; he didn't want to see it, too. He looked instead at the pieces of cloth draped over several sections of the wall. Asser Levy appeared at his side. "The mirrors are veiled," he said in a low voice.

Tonneman nodded. David was coming toward him. Tonneman put out his hand. "I'm sorry about your loss, Mendoza. I've come to tell you that I agree with your conclusion. The back of Benjamin's head was crushed. I think he was murdered." Belatedly Tonneman realized he had spoken first.

David ignored Tonneman's hand. "So? Why bother us? You are still Schout. Go find his murderer. That's your job. Leave us to mourn my brother in peace."

"Then help me."

"Leave us be."

" 'The blood of the slain cries out for vengeance.' You said that."

"You poor benighted fool," David said softly, placing his right hand on his head, sliding his black silk cap first back, then forward, till it returned to where it had been in the first place. "What else am I to expect from a gentile mind? Vengeance must come from God, not from man." He stared at Tonneman, then walked away from him.

There was nothing here for Tonneman. He was an intruder. As he was leaving he overheard two of the mourners talking. "Now David can marry Racqel," said one.

"And about time," said the other. "For them both."

Tonneman put on his hat and hurried out, heading straight for the Pear Tree.

At the tavern Tonneman ordered one beer and stared at it.

"Are you going to drink that beer or read it?" Joost asked in passing.

Tonneman's mind was confusion. Ten Eyck's news about the baby was wonderful, but all he could think of was Racqel. Bewildered, he pushed her from his mind. "Joost, give me a minute."

"That's exactly what I don't have," Zoelan shouted as he shoved more beers across the bar.

"Where have you been these last few days?"

Joost reached into his pocket, took out some snuff, sniffed it, and sneezed noisily. The yellow hound, under the bar, whined in his sleep. "Can't talk, Tonneman. No time. Much too busy. It's bad enough you've stopped drinking. Look at you standing there with one stale mug of beer in your hand. I can't make any money from you. And if I stop to talk to you, I'm not serving drinks; if I'm not serving drinks, there I am again, not making money."

The way people were pushing, Tonneman soon found himself

pushed back by the eager drinkers. Even Heer van Cortlandt was there.

"And no City official is to be replaced, including you, Heer Schout," van Cortlandt told him, smiling, as if he were the first to tell him the news. "What do you think of that?"

Heer Schout, the godfather, didn't say anything. Once more his thoughts were of Racqel Mendoza.

66

MONDAY, 8 SEPTEMBER. *Before Dawn.*
Racqel sat on the stoop wrapped in her shawl against the predawn chill. She had not been able to sleep. Whenever she put her head down, she felt as if she were drowning. Abraham and David were still abed and she was glad for the solitude.

A cool, damp ripple of a breeze came up from the East River, painting dew on her cheeks and shawl. She knew that Benjamin had been murdered and wondered whether it had been one of the Jew haters in the community. Or did his death have to do with what she'd overheard Abraham and David talking about? Some plot Benjamin had become involved in?

The big Dutchman would find out what had happened. . . .

Racqel buried her face in her hands.

Minutes passed. A cock called dawn and a cow mooed softly. Small sounds from within the house told her that her in-laws had risen and were at their devotions. She raised her head and saw the first pale pink streaks of dawn. Then, as if by magic, shadowed against the brightening sky, there appeared a shimmering figure on horseback slowly riding toward her. He was wearing the blue coat she'd last seen Benjamin wearing that fateful, December day. Was she dreaming?

Racqel stood up, dropping her shawl on Bathsheba, who made a game of fighting with it. Caleb opened his eyes and sat up, growling.

"Benjamin!" Racqel cried. He was not dead.

Caleb's small ears flattened and he started barking.

The four-footer's noise broke the spell. How could it be? Benjamin was dead.

Breath steamed from the horse's nostrils. Racqel lifted her hand to her forehead and squinted into the growing light. It was Foxman astride the prancing white animal, with three brown horses behind, all heavily loaded.

He was wearing Benjamin's blue coat.

The Indian, having spied her, prodded his steed and approached at a trot.

"Where did you get that coat?" She should have been afraid, but she was not.

"I have come for you," he said, scorning her question. "And look, I have brought not one horse, but three." Racqel heard the door open behind her but couldn't stop staring at the Indian in Benjamin's coat. Had Foxman murdered her husband?

"Your husband is dead."

"Indian, get off my land," David shouted. "Racqel, are you mad?"

"That blue coat," Racqel persisted. "Where did you get it?"

"Mendoza," Foxman said, looking past her. "I offer these three excellent mares and the choice beaver pelts they bear." He dropped the animals' reins and they wandered several feet to feed on the scattered tufts of grass. To Racqel he said, "You are my woman now." He leaned toward her.

"The coat. Tell me."

Foxman beckoned.

She stood as close to his prancing horse as she dared. "Tell me."

"My coat," he said, preening. "From Joost in a trade. During the last of the cold moons. A horse and many pelts. A good bargain." He wheeled his animal suddenly, reached down, and caught her by the waist, scooping her up.

Racqel screamed.

The arm that held her against the heaving flank of the animal was blue-clad. It was as if Benjamin was holding her. But Benjamin was dead. Struggling desperately, Racqel tore at the cloth of Benjamin's coat.

She heard David's shout, Abraham's cry. Her hair, unbound, flew wild. David chased after Foxman's stallion. "Foxman, you lunatic heathen. Put her down." But he was blinded by a cloud of dust.

There were other cries. Everyone was on the street now. But the Indian was carrying her away triumphantly like another bundle of pelts.

Foxman turned abruptly and ran David to the ground, calling,

"A good bargain for you, Jew-man, three horses and many pelts. A very good bargain." He threw the flailing Racqel across his horse and rode off, oblivious of the screaming populace, toward the Water Gate.

67

MONDAY, 8 SEPTEMBER. *Morning.*

The sky was already brightening as Tonneman stepped out his door. Cooler than yesterday. On this day the Dutch soldiers would march out and the English soldiers would march in.

He had slept badly, his thoughts coming back again and again to his two good friends, Hendrik Smitt and Joost Zoelan. If Hendrik hadn't hanged himself, and Tonneman was sure he hadn't, then he'd been murdered. The best reason for his being murdered was that he had witnessed Benjamin Mendoza's death.

All these years, no murders in New Amsterdam and then one, two, three. It stood to reason that whoever killed Mendoza and Hendrik had also killed Spectacles and Abner. It was surely the work of a man who had lost his reason, a madman who lived unknown among them.

The scent of lavender put the last two deaths in the same basket. More to the point, there had been blood under Abner's nails; his killer was sure to have Abner's mark on him.

Hendrik's death had left Joost with the Pear Tree all to himself.

Tonneman rubbed his finger on the side of his nose. He was looking at the obvious here, and he'd known it for some time now.

The sound of screams broke into his cogitation. Tonneman stepped out onto the Strand, peering toward the Great House.

A horse and rider were coming toward him agallop. David Mendoza, his hair and beard wild, was running behind and lagging with every step. "Stop him!" David Mendoza cried.

The horse, coming hard, was almost on Tonneman.

Foxman.

The Indian was going to run him down.

Tonneman held his ground. He seized the horse's bit and leaped to the side. The force almost tore his arm off, but the animal stopped short, whinnying angrily, and fell to its knees. Foxman righted it quickly. "What's wrong with you, Tonneman? This is my best horse."

Racqel, shaken, fought to right herself. Foxman held her fast.

"Going somewhere, Indian?"

"Get out of my way, Tonneman. I have no quarrel with you."

"But I have one with you. Release the woman."

"She wants to be with me."

"No," Racqel cried, pounding on the Indian's forearm.

Tonneman reached for her.

Foxman placed his hand on his knife. "She is mine. I traded fair for her."

David Mendoza ran to them, limping and panting for breath. "Thank God, Heer Schout. Thank God, for you."

Tonneman's eyes never left Foxman's hand. "Don't do it, Foxman."

Foxman drew his knife.

Tonneman drew his. "Kill me, you'll be dead, too. We just avoided one war. Are you looking for another?"

The Indian sneered at him. He had no fear. "What do I care? War is a good thing. This woman is mine."

"Not so. She's been promised to me. Just slide off the horse, Racqel."

"No!" Foxman shouted. Racqel's ears rang with it and her heart pounded with fear. Foxman placed the point of his knife at her throat. "Then she dies first."

"Why?" demanded Tonneman.

The Indian offered no reason. His white horse pawed the oyster-shell road, crackling, crackling, while people stood watching. No one made a sound.

Tonneman smiled. "Let's have the woman decide."

"Women don't choose, men choose. Women follow."

Tonneman took a deep breath. "I'll tell you what, we'll share her. Cut her in half."

Racqel gasped.

David gasped.

The crowd gasped.

Tonneman walked right up to the white horse. "Which do you want? Top or bottom?"

Foxman showed his teeth and with one hand raised Racqel to a sitting position. The knife never left her throat and his brittle eyes never left Tonneman.

"I'm tired of you, white man. Last chance, woman, this drunken old man or me."

"I choose Tonneman."

David groaned, anguish on his face.

"All women are crazy." The Indian shoved Racqel at Tonneman. Tonneman caught her, lost his balance, and carried them both to the ground.

Foxman clamped his knees to the stallion's flanks and thundered up Pearl Street as David helped Racqel to her feet. David then offered Tonneman his hand. With the smallest of smiles tugging his lips, he said, "Thank you, Solomon."

68

MONDAY, 8 SEPTEMBER. *Morning.*

Tonneman set off for the Old Mill, his mind roving far from Pieter Stuyvesant's final hour as Director-General.

Foxman had been wearing Benjamin Mendoza's blue coat, received in the cold moons from Joost for a horse and pelts. This Racqel had told him as David Mendoza stood by. She had then thanked him in a dignified manner and gone off with her brother-in-law. As if nothing had taken place between them.

Tonneman heaved an unhappy sigh. Foxman was right. Women were crazy. But the matter at hand was a spy and traitor. And a murderer.

At once, the sky opened up and rain came down steadily, giving everything and everyone a good soaking. Altogether fitting. The marching in and marching out would be a downright muddy affair.

At the mill he waited in the rain with Stuyvesant and the Council for the articles to arrive. When they did, delivered by a detachment of three English soldiers, the entire party removed to the Fort.

"Tonneman!"

The Boss was blustering like his old self. Tonneman left the Council members and caught up with Stuyvesant and the three soldiers as they entered the Fort. "Sir?"

"Not my finest moment, is it?" Stuyvesant, in battle dress, bore himself proudly. He looked around, endeavoring to preserve the scene to take with him to the Netherlands.

Tonneman felt pity for the man and a sweet melancholy for the old days. "I disagree, sir. You handled the entire affair with honor. And nobody died."

"Good of you to say so." He clasped Tonneman's hand warmly. "This may be our last chance to speak. God be with you, comrade."

They had never been comrades, but they had seen a Company town become a true city. "And God be with you," Tonneman said.

Quickly and with minimum ceremony, Stuyvesant formally turned over the Fort to the three English soldiers. The Dutch flags were lowered and the Union Jack was raised. Then, Colonel Caspar van de Steen just behind him, Stuyvesant led the Dutch soldiers out of the Fort, with the promised honors of war: flying colors, drums beating, and their bullets in their mouths. All was done with as much dignity as possible in the heavy pouring rain. Tonneman walked alongside them, respectfully; it was a sad day.

On the other side of the road Korbonski's little friend, Lizard, and his capuchin monkey also escorted the Dutch forces. While the monkey ran back and forth tipping his red cap to all and sundry, the dwarf played on his fife to the beat of the military drums.

The soldiers in their blue uniforms marched down Beaver Street to the waiting Netherlands-bound *Gideon* and boarded. Old enmities forgotten, the townspeople stood in the rain along the way, cheering and bidding them good-bye. It was a day of endings, Tonneman thought, but also of beginnings.

He watched as Colonel Nicolls's soldiers, one hundred and sixty-eight strong, came down the planks of the *Guinea* and the *Martin* onto the muddy streets of a rain-drenched New Amsterdam. Spread six columns wide, they were on the walks, brushing the buildings as they went past. In their wet scarlet uniforms they paraded through town while Sir George Cartwright and his men occupied the City gates and City Hall. Old fears, like old enmities, forgotten, the people along the way cheered and bade the newcomers welcome.

The English also had their drummers, and they, too, had Lizard and his monkey to accompany them. As he had played the Dutch out on his fife, so he now played the English in. It was an historic day, one of strangely mixed loyalties.

The Burgomasters—or as they now were to be called, Mayors—Van der Grist and Steenwyck, proclaimed Nicolls Governor. The colonel, who wore bright green today, handed his dog to a soldier, took some snuff from a small box in the pocket of his coat, and sneezed once, to which the spaniel responded with a single sneeze of its own. Amidst the laughter of the crowd, the colonel thanked the Mayors for their kindness and looked benignly at the group of citizens surrounding him.

"Long live Governor Richard Nicolls!"

"Nay, rather long live His Majesty King Charles, and His Highness the Duke of York. My Dutch is not proficient; I can only hope that over the time we will be spending together it will improve, as will your English. My apologies for the rain. Bloody English weather, you know."

The Mayors laughed. So did some in the crowd.

"Where is our Sheriff?"

Surprised, Tonneman lifted his hat and held it over his head. The cool rain drizzled down his face.

"Tonneman, isn't it? Good. I'll see you in City Hall in one half hour." He turned back to the populace. "Guilders and stuivers will still be accepted, but the official coin henceforth will be English pounds and shillings. Further, in honor of His Royal Highness, James, the Duke of York, Fort Amsterdam will henceforth be known as Fort James and this City will be known as New-York."

The new Governor and the Mayors went into City Hall as the people applauded roundly; what did a name matter if their lives and possessions were spared?

Clamping his hat back on his head, Tonneman blew out a stream of hot bitter breath. One half hour. That should give him enough time.

69

MONDAY, 8 SEPTEMBER. *Morning.*

Joost stood atop a ladder in front of the Pear Tree, working awkwardly with the sign as the rain fell. At the foot of the ladder, holding another sign, was Nicasius De Sille. The yellow hound, some object trailing from its mouth, danced in circles about the ladder, splashing mud.

"What are you doing?" Tonneman called as he approached.

"Changing the name of the place. See." Joost reached down to De Sille and they exchanged signs. Joost held up the new one for Tonneman to see. "The King Charles. What do you think?"

"You don't want to know. What were you two talking about?"

The yellow hound shoved his soggy plaything at De Sille. "Nothing of any consequence," Nick said, shooing the dog away with the old sign and wiping mud spatter from his bright buff breeches.

"Did you give the Governor an earful about my knife?"

"Everyone had a grand time at our reception," De Sille murmured. "Geertie was in her glory. Too bad you had to miss it."

"I was otherwise engaged."

De Sille pursed his lips in disdain. "I have business to attend at Fort James." He dropped the old sign into the mud. "Good day, to you both."

The hound butted Tonneman with his trophy. Tonneman waved the dog away.

"Hand me up my beer," Joost said, referring to the tankard on the ground. Tonneman held the tankard up to him and Joost drank deeply, then returned the tankard to Tonneman. "It was time for a change anyway. You want the old sign? Keep it, it's yours." Joost paused to light his pipe and Tonneman got a good whiff of Joost's lavender-scented tobacco.

Thinking of how Maria had worked on the tavern sign for their friends Hendrik and Joost, Tonneman recovered it from the mud. Hot coals of long-pent-up anger filled his chest. "Get down."

"What?" Zoelan stood on the ladder admiring his new sign.

"No games, Joost. Get down." Tonneman dropped the sign and tankard in the mud and shook the ladder.

Joost climbed down. "What sort of bug do you have up your arse?"

It was all Tonneman could do to keep from strangling him with his bare hands. "How long have you been smoking that lavender shit?"

"Not long. Ever try it? Very soothing."

"Take off your shirt, Joost."

"In this pour? Why?"

"I said, take off your shirt!" Tonneman's hands clenched into fists. The weight of the rain made his hat droop drunkenly.

Seeing that Tonneman meant business, Zoelan slipped out of his shirt. Rain fell on the sinewy man, matting his uncovered reddish-blond hair, but it couldn't wash away the deep red crusted scratch marks on his right arm. "How long do I stand here getting wet for you?"

"What's that?" asked Tonneman, pointing to the arm.

"What's what?"

"Those marks on your arm."

"A little trouble last night with . . . Cutnose. I had to throw him out again. That's all."

"Did you indeed? That would be a fine feat if you did."

"What's gotten into you, Tonneman?" Joost pulled his shirt back on angrily.

"When Hendrik died, you became sole owner of the Pear Tree. . . ."

"Yes." Joost edged away, as if Tonneman were crazed.

"He didn't kill himself, did he?"

"What are you talking about?" The yellow dog tried to give Joost his treasure. Joost kicked him away savagely.

"Murder. It wouldn't do till you were the biggest hog at the trough, would it? Was having the Pear Tree to yourself so important that you killed your best friend? *Our* best friend."

Joost shook his head vigorously. "I'm not that kind of animal."

"Really? What kind of animal are you? Admit it, you bastard, you killed him!"

"No, I didn't kill him. I thought you were my friend. How could you think that of me?"

"Because Foxman has a blue coat and I've finally found my wits." Tonneman moved quickly, grabbing Joost's shirt at his throat and slapping him across the face. Joost's face reddened with the blow, then whitened with anger as he struggled to wrench himself from Tonneman's grip, tearing the shirt.

"Go home, Tonneman," Joost croaked. "You're drunk. I told them that's all you are, a drunkard."

"Who did you tell, your English friends?" Tonneman lifted the struggling man off his feet and shook him. "Why? Why did you kill him? And the others? Was it for the letter from the king? So you could kiss English arse and get rich?"

Joost's eyes went soft and closed, his knees bent; he became deadweight. Tonneman relaxed his grip for just a second. Joost pulled free and grabbed the ladder. Using it as a weapon, Joost knocked Tonneman to the muddy ground.

Tonneman's hat flew off and the yellow dog pushed at it with his prize. Joost threw the ladder at Tonneman and ran for the tavern, kicking up mud. Dodging the ladder, Tonneman dived for Joost's legs, bringing him down, spattering more mud.

The dog stalked them, dragging its trophy, whimpering, running in mad circles around the two men. People ready to see yet another show gathered to watch Tonneman and Joost wrestling and rolling along the muddy Strand. Among the people was Tall Matthew with his spear. Joost drove Tonneman's back to the ground; each man had his hands around the other's throat. "Murderer," Tonneman growled.

Joost whipped his hands to the sides, breaking Tonneman's hold. He pulled a knife from his boot and stabbed at Tonneman's face. Tonneman jerked his head to the side and felt the knife take a bite of his left earlobe. He rolled away and jumped to his feet. Joost had lost the knife in the mud. Tonneman kicked at him. Joost, unable to retrieve the knife, grabbed Tonneman's leg, and they both went down in the muddy shell road again.

Tonneman got hold of Joost's right arm and pulled it behind his back. "You did it, you bastard. Say it or I'll break your arm."

"Did what?" Joost asked. "Let go. I didn't do anything." He turned to the curious crowd. "He's crazy drunk again."

Still holding Joost's arm captive, Tonneman raised him up. They had rolled up Pearl Street a good distance from where they had started. Both were bloody, covered with mud, and wet to the skin. Tonneman started force-walking his prisoner toward City Hall. The dog followed, as did the townspeople.

"Tonneman, what is this?" Jan Keyser asked, coming closer to them. "What did Joost do to deserve such treatment?"

"Go away, tanner."

"I counted on you staying drunk," Joost complained, unresisting and submissive. "It was Hendrik's bad fortune to be where he shouldn't."

"With the English coming, you expected to be rich. And you couldn't let anyone stand in the way of that. Not even a friend."

Keyser came after them. "What's going on?" he asked.

"Stay out of this, Keyser. This is Sheriff's business."

The little man made a face and went back to the anxious crowd, shrugging. The yellow hound followed Keyser, offering his prize; Keyser accepted, staring.

Tonneman dragged Joost past more curious people into City Hall and to the steep steps leading down to the jail. Cautiously, the yellow hound followed them.

"What does Nick have to do with all this?"

"You'll never get away with this. I have important friends!"

"Did you kill the man with the spectacles, too? Or was that Nick's doing?"

"Nick doesn't have the stones of a capon. Not once in his life has that poltroon ever put his arse where his mouth is."

"And Benjamin Mendoza?"

"The Jew went back on our bargain. He was going to tell Stuyvesant. What does one Jew more or less matter? Hendrik was a fool. We could have had the Mendoza Trading Company for our very own. But no, he couldn't see it my way."

"What about Cutnose? Did you kill him, too?"

"Oh, is he dead?"

"For several days now."

"So, that's how you knew. Well, someone else did it. Can't hang me for that one."

"We have plenty to hang you once and that's enough." Tonneman laughed harshly. "I thought we'd never use the Fort gallows. Shows you how wrong a man can be."

Now it was Joost's turn to laugh. "One hundred florins says you'll never hang me, Tonneman. I told you, I know the right people."

"Not even King Charlie himself can help you."

"It may just come to that." The tapster lowered his voice. "We could share, you know, there's plenty, more than enough."

It was all for greed, thought Tonneman. For wealth, for property. "To hell with you, Joost. And God bless absent friends."

"God bless absent friends," Joost repeated, grinning. He smelled like one of van Etting's hogs and his voice was low as if he were talking to a woman. "What do you say? Partners, you and me." With an obscene touch of joviality in his voice: "As for what really happened, no one will ever know."

"The people will know."

"The people. Ha. They don't know anything, not until you tell them. Tell them you caught me bringing in illegal grain. We don't have much time. Once you tell one person, there will be no turning back. Let me go now and no one will ever know."

"I would," said Tonneman. "I don't give a Englishman's damn about the others, but why did you have to kill Hendrik?"

The baffled yellow hound began barking softly, its tail down but wagging in short, uncertain strokes. "That's my good dog," said Joost, leaning forward as if to comfort the four-footer. It was the same tactic he'd used before, and Tonneman should have been ready for it, but he wasn't. When Tonneman relaxed his hold, Joost poked him in the stomach with an elbow, pulled free, and hit Tonneman again, this time in the throat.

As Tonneman fought for breath Joost ran out the front door.

70

MONDAY, 8 SEPTEMBER. *Morning.*
"What's going on up there?" Pos's sleepy voice called from below. "Can't a man get some rest?"

Tonneman shook off the effects of the Joost's blow and tottered to the door of City Hall. He saw Joost slipping and sliding up the Strand toward the Water Gate. Tonneman ran after him with the dog in pursuit. The animal, now thinking it was all a game, was barking joyfully.

Governor Nicolls and Nick De Sille came out on the stoop of City Hall. When the Governor saw what was going on, he raised his hand to beckon Subaltern Brick-Hill, who was standing nearby. Nick stopped him with, "Why don't you let it run its course? Then we'll see if Sheriff Tonneman is up to the job."

Many confused towners gave chase, not to help the Sheriff, but to see and savor. Some shouted encouragement to Tonneman, some to Joost.

Tonneman caught up with Joost and flung him headfirst into a tree. Joost screamed; his nose was broken, streaming blood. He crumpled like a felled ox.

"Let's go, you bastard," said Tonneman. "I'm going to deliver you to the English now before I kill you."

When Tonneman reached to bring Joost to his feet, Joost clasped his hands together and brought them up hard between Tonneman's legs. Tonneman staggered back, doubled over in agony. People were shouting, calling to him.

Now Joost was running back down the Strand. Painfully, stumbling, Tonneman pursued Joost once more.

The rain had stopped. Just west of City Hall on the Strand, Subaltern Brick-Hill stood with his sergeant. Pikemen stood behind them in formation. A drove of wandering hogs was ahead of Joost, snorting and grunting, nosing around and blocking his way, forcing him to change direction.

Behind Joost, Tonneman came on, slowly but surely. The hogs

had found a hollow in the road and were wallowing in the mud. As Tonneman passed the new King Charles Tavern he grabbed up the Pear Tree sign from the ground and threw it at the back of Joost's legs.

Joost staggered and fell, then climbed slowly to his feet. Tonneman was ready for him. Like all fights, the one who was left standing would win this one.

Exhausted and spattered with mud, they glared at one another. Tonneman took in a breath and with much effort punched Joost again, this time square in his already damaged nose. Once more Joost dropped to the ground.

Looking around blearily to see where he was, Tonneman heard the yellow dog barking. The people were crowding in on them. At their fore was Tall Matthew with his spear.

Tall Matthew stepped back several feet; it was almost a dance. The people, as if they were part of the dance, made room for the African. But Tonneman had no time for Tall Matthew. Joost was kicking at his feet.

Tonneman tumbled heavily to the ground and Joost leaped on him. The old Pear Tree sign lay in the mud beside him. Joost found it and hit Tonneman on the forehead, a glancing blow, but it was hard enough to cleave the sign in two and hard enough to hurt. Joost tossed away the smaller part of the sign and raised what was left to hit Tonneman again.

Tall Matthew drew back his powerful arm and let loose his spear. It went dead center into Joost's chest. Astonished, Joost made a single, quick puffing noise and pitched forward on top of Tonneman in a macabre embrace. The sign fell harmlessly just over Tonneman's head. He pushed Joost's bloody body aside and struggled to his feet.

An English soldier, his pike extended, as his sergeant had taught him, yelled and charged into Tall Matthew. He meant to stick the African in the chest, but the spike of the halberd went into his stomach instead. Tall Matthew uttered one short scream and then, by force of will, made no other sound.

"Damn niggers," Brick-Hill said angrily. "I don't know which are worse, them or the flaming heathen Indians."

Blood and life bubbled out of Tall Matthew's mouth as he sank to the muddy ground. He died only inches from the man who had murdered his friend, Abner Simon.

"And now?" Tall Matthew asked the serpent.

"Now," the serpent said, "I will take you home."

. . .

Tonneman gazed sadly first at Tall Matthew, then at Joost Zoelan in the mud. The two lay surrounded by clamorous hogs, their bodies probed and rooted at. The yellow dog, its tail sagging, came running to its fallen master and licked his face.

The hogs grunted and snorted louder, and the dog began to howl. The howl continued unabated, the sound so pathetic and eerie that people began to stream from City Hall and their homes to learn the cause. Pos appeared, shaking sleep from his head; his mouth hung open in incredulity.

"Biggest hog at the trough," Tonneman muttered hoarsely. *"Deadest* hog at the trough." Then slowly Tonneman picked up the broken pieces of the tavern sign, matched them together and stared at the cracked picture of the Pear Tree for a long time.

"Tonneman? Blast it all, Sheriff. What is this bloody cock-up?"

Wondering what the devil had happened to his hat, Tonneman looked up. It was Governor Nicolls.

Tonneman put the boards under his arm and walked briskly toward City Hall. "Coming, Boss."

71

TUESDAY, SEPTEMBER 9. *Morning.*

It was a badly bruised and battered Tonneman who sat with Pos at the Ten Eyck table, drinking beer. Ten Eyck himself and Antje were drinking green tea.

Near the hearth the new baby lay sleeping in the cherub-and-tulip-painted pine cradle, which Antje set in motion with her foot whenever she went by.

"Where are my crumpetcakes?" Tonneman called, beating his mug with a pewter spoon.

"Be quiet," Antje answered, smiling, "and drink your beer."

"He doesn't have to drink it," said Pos. "That way there's more for me."

Tonneman waved his hand over the table of food and drink.

With strong irony, he said, "The English have been our masters only a short time and look at this wonderful bounty."

"They're not *my* masters." Pos took an angry bite of bread.

"This food is no thanks to the English," said Ten Eyck, "but rather to Antje's husbandry."

"You mean she hoarded it," said Tonneman.

Antje rapped him on the top of his head with her knuckle. "Are you going to report me, Sheriff?"

"No, I'm not on duty. But tomorrow . . ."

She rapped him again.

"Ow." Then he laughed. "Have pity, woman. I'm a wounded man."

Ten Eyck examined Tonneman and Pos in turn. "Both of you look as if you've been through the war we never had. If my other son were here instead of at his lessons, do you know what he'd say?"

Tonneman and Antje answered together, "You look terrible."

Pos, not getting the jape, kept eating. Chewing vigorously, he muttered, "Joost a traitor," and shook his head.

"I don't know which is worse, traitor or murderer," Antje said. "I never thought of him as being such a bloodthirsty fellow."

"Greedy, you mean," corrected Ten Eyck. He applied the metal cutter to the whitish cone of sugar on the table and cut off three large pieces of sugar for his tea. "It was all about money. Everyone involved had a fortune to gain if the English took over New Amsterdam."

Antje set the plates of pancakes and fried coney and eggs all around. Tonneman, his bruised right eye half-closed, ate ravenously. He couldn't remember when he'd eaten last. "The whole thing was like a snowball rolling down a hill," he said, through a mouthful. "It kept getting bigger and bigger. Joost brought Abner in for the sole purpose of getting to Benjamin Mendoza." He chewed thoughtfully. "Takes a Jew to get a Jew and all that."

"And all that," Pos repeated.

The Ten Eycks nodded. Tonneman drained his mug of beer and held it out for Antje to fill again. "His plan was to get the English to give him the Mendoza trading business when they won, but Benjamin spoiled everything when he changed his mind and said he was going to tell Stuyvesant. Joost couldn't have that, so he killed him."

"That's clear enough," said Antje. "But some other things aren't."

"This is good rabbit," Pos said, spearing a piece of coney with his knife.

"Who was the man with the spectacles?" Ten Eyck asked.

"Thomas Atkins," Pos answered, grinning proudly at his knowledge. "He was Winthrop's man in New York, an agent of the English crown in New Amsterdam and Zoelan's go-between." Pos pounded the table, angrily, slopping beer all over it. "What a bastard Joost was." He turned to Tonneman "Correct?"

Tonneman was looking out the window at the *William and Nicholas,* the smallest of the English ships. The ten-gun frigate was now stationed in the East River. But he wasn't thinking of ships, he was thinking of Maria . . . and Racqel. They would have liked each other.

"Where are you, Tonneman?" Pos yelled.

"That's a good question," said Antje.

"I'm right here," said Tonneman. "I heard everything you said. Atkins was also Abner's thief. He stole the document from Joost and sold it to Abner."

"Why did Joost have to kill Hendrik?" asked Antje, wiping up Pos's beer spill with a rag. She bent over the cradle. "Such a pretty baby. Aren't you, little Pieter? Yes, you are."

"Because," said Tonneman, "Hendrik saw him kill Benjamin Mendoza. That's when the snowball started. Abner suspected that Joost had murdered Benjamin, and partly out of greed and partly to protect himself, he bribed Atkins to steal the letter from Joost."

Pos belched loudly. "The letter from Winthrop was good as gold to anyone who had it. It meant the bearer could present it to the English. Whoever he was, of service to the crown or not, he would be rich."

"Give the man another beer," said Tonneman. "Atkins stole the document from Joost, passed it on to Tall Matthew, who gave Atkins a purse of gold coins and delivered the document to Abner in Breukelen. I didn't know it at the time, but I heard Joost confront Atkins and demand return of the letter." He grinned at Antje. "I thought it was Hendrik talking, not Joost. I was half-asleep."

"Ha," she said. "More half-drunk."

"Joost found the gold on him. I heard that. I reckon that's when Atkins admitted he gave the letter to a black man. I didn't hear that."

"Tall Matthew," said Pos.

"Yes. Joost killed Atkins, took the purse of gold, and threw me into the river. It was getting easy now."

"Was he trying to kill you?" asked Ten Eyck.

Pos snorted. "What do you think?"

Antje looked grim. "Practice is the best of all instructors, they say."

"And the fire?" asked Ten Eyck.

"Joost," said Pos.

Tonneman nodded. "To cover up how and where Atkins died and cast blame on the Jews."

"And on you." Pos just about shook with indignation. "Joost stuck him with Tonneman's knife."

"Yes," said Tonneman. "Nick knew about the trick with the knife. Tweaked me with it. That's why I thought he was the killer."

"What was Nick and Geertie De Sille's role in all this evil business?" asked Antje.

"That's easy," said Pos. "Now that I think about it, every time I've seen Nick in the Pear Tree over the last few weeks he's been huddled with van Brugge. Heer Carel van Brugge, also known as Mister Charles Bridge, is English, in case you've forgotten. I'll venture they were in this with Joost."

"And Geertie would do anything for Nick . . . or money," said Tonneman. "Don't ask me which comes first, but what you said about Nick and van Brugge sounds good to me. I don't know if van Brugge had anything to do with spying. Nick is another story. He's managed to ally himself with the victors . . . for now. One thing is certain, they were all out to make a dishonest florin."

Ten Eyck knelt and tickled young Pieter under his chin. The infant made delighted gurglings.

Antje beamed at her husband and child and shook her head at Tonneman. "But now Nick De Sille is a dear friend of the English, and he'll realize a great deal of money because of that friendship. Perhaps he didn't commit murder, but I'm sure he did everything else. And he's going to get away with it. That's not right."

"But that's the way it is, my beloved." Ten Eyck rocked the cradle, then rose and kissed his wife on the cheek.

Antje touched her husband's lips with her fingertips. With a wink to him and Pos, she said, "What about the Mendozas? Are they also dear friends of the English?"

There was a silence. Tonneman was looking out the window again. When he came back to himself, his friends were smiling at him. "Uh . . . no. When the English came upon us in Breukelen, I thought so. I saw that Brick-Hill matched our names against a list of what I thought were people friendly to the English. I supposed we were released because the Mendozas were on that list. Yesterday I

learned that the list was of Dutch officials in New Amsterdam—Stuyvesant, myself, et cetera. Brick-Hill had orders that no changes were
to be made in the City government and that no City official was to be
detained. Fool that I was, we were released because of me. It wasn't
the Mendoza name he found on the list, it was mine."

Antje had taken the infant out of the cradle and was rocking him
in her arms. "I still don't understand why David Mendoza was in
Breukelen."

Tonneman lifted his shoulders. "To follow his sister-in-law? To
ask Abner not to tell her about Benjamin? I don't know. It doesn't
matter anymore."

Pos scratched his head. "I'm not so sure about De Sille not com-
mitting murder. Has anyone seen van Brugge lately?"

"Ah," said Antje softly, her nose pressed to the baby's neck.
"You're as bloodthirsty as Joost . . . but you're not, are you, precious?"

"It's something to consider," said Tonneman. "I was quite willing to believe Nick killed Abner. Given the opportunity, he might
have. He wanted that piece of paper. When I talked to him yesterday,
he said Joost told him that Abner had the paper and Joost was going
to deal with Abner himself in the morning. Then Joost, contrary to
what he told Nick, went to Breukelen that night and killed Abner, but
he couldn't find the paper."

"Nick's very cooperative, all of a sudden," said Pos. "Did he
happen to mention where van Brugge is?"

"No," said Tonneman. "Of course Nick is a blackguard, a traitor, and a plotting exploiter, but I don't think he's a murderer. I agree
with Joost there—he doesn't have the stones for it. Still, even if Nick
did aid Joost in any of the killings, I can't prove it, so Nick will be
very successful here in the English village of New-York. And as Ten
Eyck says, that's the way of the world. He's guilty as sin of a lot of
things, but with his friends in power there's nothing I can do about it,
and he knows that full well. The bastard went so far to say that he
was in Breukelen. He says he was unaware that Joost was ahead of
him, and that he found Abner's body and was searching for the document when I arrived. He was the one who hit me over the head."

Pos laughed. "He admitted that?"

"Proudly," said Tonneman. "He enjoys having bested me every
which way."

"I guess you've been stupid ever since you were hit," said Antje,
still nuzzling her son.

"What do you mean?"

"It's as simple as the nose on your face, you ninny," Ten Eyck said. "Why are you sitting here with us, swilling food and drink when you have more important things to do?"

Antje looked up from her baby and said, "The woman, you dumb Dutchman. Go find the woman."

72

TUESDAY, 9 SEPTEMBER. *Morning.*

On the Strand everything was as it had been before the threat of war, alive and in business again. The weather was cool, the sky gray and moist.

When he left the Ten Eycks' house, Tonneman stopped for a moment to enjoy the scene. He, too, felt at peace. His friends were right. It was time for him to face Racqel and declare himself.

"Tonneman." Keyser was running toward him, breathless. "I have something you might like to buy." The tanner held out a loop of dirty wet rope.

Tonneman took the rope and pulled at the loop. It wouldn't give. "Where did you get this?"

"Joost's hound shoved it into my hand yesterday."

Pos came out from Coenties Alley and saw them. "Tonneman, you still here? That woman won't wait forever, you know."

Tonneman smiled. "Keyser wants to sell me this rope. Do you know why?"

"Not for the life of me."

"Look." Tonneman showed Pos the thick knot and the nonslip loop. "It's the rope Hendrik Smitt died by. Only three people I know could have made that knot. Me. Nick. And Joost."

"Get away," said Pos. "That's a bowline. Any sailor could have tied that knot, and there are more sailors on this island than you can shake a stick at."

Tonneman nodded. "But it's tied different from most bowlines. The three of us learned to do it that way from the same boatswain when we sailed together on the *Princess of India.*"

"It's what you wanted, isn't it?" Keyser whined.

"Yes."

"So, how much do I get paid?"

"Go away, Keyser."

The little tanner started to say something else, but Pos turned him around and pushed. Keyser left, heading for the Broad Way, grumbling.

Tonneman smiled wryly. "Hmm. Had I paid attention to that yellow hound, I might have solved these crimes sooner."

"What you're saying is that Nick could have killed Hendrik."

"I suppose you're right," said Tonneman. Turning, Tonneman caught sight of Racqel hurrying up Pearl Street. It was a sign, an omen, her being there now.

He thrust the grimy piece of rope at Pos. The rope could wait. Everything could wait. "It could have been Nick," he called to the grinning Pos, "but I doubt it."

Tonneman ran after Racqel, rattling the wet shells of the Strand. By the time he reached her, she was approaching the Water Gate.

"Vrouw Mendoza . . . Vrouw Mendoza . . . please."

She clutched her shawl tighter about her chin. "It's not seemly for me to speak with you."

He walked at her side as they passed through the gate. "Seemly or not," said Tonneman, "I must talk with you. Are you promised to David Mendoza?"

She stopped, letting her shawl fall open; her fingers touched the mourning tear at her right breast. She gazed at him with her dark, solemn eyes. His heart reeled.

"I am promised to no one," she said, "but I have no means without the Mendozas." Her hand at her breast trembled.

"I want to marry you." He reached for her hand.

She stepped back. "I have no dowry." Her voice was so low he could barely hear her.

"What do I care? You are your own dowry."

She turned away from him and walked on. He followed. She stopped. "I am barren."

"I have had children. And that remains to be seen."

"I am a Jew. And you are a Christian."

"Heaven will have us both," he said. They were at the gate to the Jewish cemetery. He stood close beside her. "And God will love us both."

Her hand moved first to the horrible large bump on his forehead, then along his damaged left ear, and then toward his discolored and swollen right eye, without touching him. "Your poor face. Every time I see you you have a new hurt."

Now he lifted his hand to her face, to her right cheek. But he also did not touch. "You, too."

It was as if she stumbled. His hand made no move but her face did, and his hand was touching her cheek. They pulled apart.

"Under your eye is turning blue," she said.

"Under yours, too," he answered, a small smile on his lips. "It will pass. Everything does."

"Word reached us about Heer Zoelan. There is anger and bitterness in the Mendoza house."

He said nothing.

She lay a large handkerchief on the muddy earth at the fence near the entrance to the cemetery and knelt, careful to keep her skirts from the mud.

"Why don't you go inside?" Tonneman asked.

"I am here to see my father, not my husband. The law says I must not go anywhere near Benjamin's grave, and it is too small a place for me to avoid that if I go inside."

Tonneman removed his hat and stepped away to give her privacy.

Racqel plucked up a blade of grass. "May all who lie here rise up on the day of resurrection, as the grass grows from the earth." She bowed her head, then rested her forehead on the treen slat of the fence. "Father, I miss your presence here more than I can ever say."

Then she prayed.

After a while she got to her feet and went to Tonneman. "I am like Moses, a stranger in a strange land."

He allowed himself a smile. "Here, in this country, we are all strangers in a strange land."

"What is your name?"

"My Christian name?"

They both smiled.

"Pieter," he said.

"Pieter," said Racqel. "The same as . . ."

"Yes."

"I shall continue to call you Tonneman."

"Fine. If you are beside me to call my name, I'll be content."

"Before long it will be the first day of Tishri," she said. "The sacred ram's horn will sound for Rosh Hashanah. We will thank our God for a year of goodness, bounty, and peace, for absolution and mercy. On Yom Kippur we will look back, repent our sins, and then look forward to the New Year just beginning."

"I like that. It's something to build a life on. Looking forward." He touched her injured cheek again with his hand. This time she didn't pull away. "You and me, together."

She looked up at him and felt light-headed, as if she were a young girl again.

He took her hands in his.

"I prayed for a sign," she said.

"How does a Jew pray?"

"As a Christian does. To God. I said, 'Lord, I love this man, but he is a gentile. Without him I have no life, but with him I may have no life either. Tell me what to do. Give me a sign.'"

"And what was the answer?"

"I'm afraid there was none. It won't be easy for either of us, but if you'll wait for the period of mourning to be over, I will marry you."

For the first time since they had met they looked at each other without restriction. It was very quiet; from a distance the high free laughter of children at play rose over the city, breaking the silence. Then a hazy sun peeked through gray clouds, warming the air.

"Look, Tonneman, the sun." She lifted her face to the sky, radiant.

"It's not the burning bush," he said.

"I know. But it will have to do."

A FOOTNOTE

We have tried to be historically accurate. Hogs did run in the streets; Pearl Street was paved with oyster shells; most of the citizens of New Amsterdam were against fighting the English.

And Pieter Stuyvesant did free African slaves on their petition. Pavonia was the name for the land across the North River where New Jersey is today; Nutten Island is now called Governor's Island.

Asser Levy was the first kosher butcher, and Pieter Tonneman was Schout of New Amsterdam during this period. Van Dincklagen did exist, and the lawyer was in constant argument with the Dutch West India Company about his pension and his welfare.

But the reader should keep in mind that this is a work of fiction. We have taken some liberties for the sake of our story.

The map is a fiction based on fact, too. There was no such road as Twiller's Road. City Hall was actually opposite Coenties Slip, but we moved it slightly to make room for Tonneman's house and the Pear Tree.

Our intent from the beginning was to use words that were in use in 1664 or earlier. The only on-purpose exception to this is the reference to *Ashkenazic* and *Sephardic* Jews. The distinction is needed, and the words didn't come into use until the nineteenth century. Hanukkah wasn't in use in English at that time either. But then, our characters are speaking Dutch.

The most amazing thing we found was that New Amsterdam then, and New York City now, in terms of its people and what moves them, are strikingly similar.

M.M.
A.M.